TIGERS IN
RED WEATHER

Liza Klaussmann

TIGERS IN
RED WEATHER

PICADOR

First published 2012 by Picador

First published in paperback 2012 by Picador

This edition first published 2013 by Picador
an imprint of Pan Macmillan, a division of Macmillan Publishers Limited
Pan Macmillan, 20 New Wharf Road, London N1 9RR
Basingstoke and Oxford
Associated companies throughout the world
www.panmacmillan.com

ISBN 978-1-4472-1207-2

The publishers gratefully acknowledge Faber and Faber Ltd for
permission to reproduce lines from 'Disillusionment of Ten O'Clock' and
'Depression Before Spring' from Collected Poems by Wallace Stevens.

1 3 5 7 9 8 6 4 2

A CIP catalogue record for this book is available from the British Library.

Printed and bound by CPI Group (UK) Ltd, Croydon, CR0 4YY

Visit www.picador.com to read more about all our books
and to buy them. You will also find features, author interviews and
news of any author events, and you can sign up for e-newsletters
so that you're always first to hear about our new releases.

To my grandmother, for the bravery.

And to the rest of my family, for everything else.

NICK

1945: September

"I'm not sure if it's a blessing or a curse," Helena said.

"At least it's something different," Nick said. "No more goddamn ration books. No more taking the bus everywhere. Hughes said he's bought a Buick. Hallelujah."

"Lord knows where he got it," Helena said. "Probably from some cheat fixer."

"Who cares," said Nick, stretching her arms lazily toward the New England night sky.

They were sitting in the backyard of their house on Elm Street wearing their slips and drinking gin neat out of old jelly jars. It was the hottest Indian summer anyone in Cambridge could remember.

Nick eyed the record player sitting precariously in the window. The needle was skipping.

"It's too hot to do anything but drink," she said, laying her head back against the rusting garden chair. Louis Armstrong was stuck repeating that he had a right to sing the blues. "The first thing I'm going to do when I get to Florida is get Hughes to buy me a whole bushel of good needles."

"That man," Helena said, sighing.

"I know," Nick said. "He really is too beautiful. And a Buick and fine record needles. What more could a girl ask for?"

Helena giggled into her glass. She sat up. "I think I'm drunk."

Nick slammed her glass down on the arm of the chair, causing the metal to tremble. "We should dance."

The oak tree in the backyard cut pieces from the moon and the sky was already a deep midnight color despite the warmth of the air. The fragrance of summer lingered, as if no one had told the grass that the middle of September had rung in. Nick could hear the nocturnal musings of the woman in the triple-decker next door. Tasting the flavor of the week.

She looked at Helena as she waltzed her across the grass. Helena could have turned into that kind of woman, Nick thought, with her body like a polished cello and wartime beaux. But her cousin had managed to retain a freshness, all sandy curls and smooth skin. She hadn't gone ashen like the women who had gone to bed with one too many strangers blown up by mines or riddled by Schmeissers. Nick had seen those women wilting on the ration lines, or creeping out of the post office, threatening to fade away into nothingness.

But Helena was getting married again.

"You're getting married again," Nick exclaimed, a bit drunkenly, as if the thought had just crossed her mind.

"I know. Can you believe it?" Helena sighed, her hand warm against Nick's back. "Mrs. Avery Lewis. Do you think it sounds as good as Mrs. Charles Fenner?"

"It's lovely," Nick lied, spinning Helena out and away.

To her ear, the name Avery Lewis sounded exactly like what he was: some Hollywood wannabe selling insurance and pretending he had dated Lana Turner, or whoever it was he was always going on about. "Fen would probably have liked him, you know."

"Oh, no. Fen would have hated him. Fen was a boy. A sweet boy."

4

"Dear Fen."

"Dear Fen." Helena stopped dancing and walked back to the gin glass waiting for her on the chair. "But now I have Avery." She sipped from it. "And I get to move to Hollywood, and maybe have a baby. At least this way I won't turn into an old maid, mad as a hatter and warts on my nose. A third wheel at the fireside beside you and Hughes. Heaven forbid."

"No third wheel, no warts, and one Avery Lewis, to boot."

"Yes, now we'll both really have someone of our own. That's important," Helena said thoughtfully. "I just wonder . . ." She trailed off.

"Wonder what?"

"Well, if . . . if it'll be the same with Avery. You know, the way it was with Fen."

"You mean in bed?" Nick turned quickly to face her cousin. "Well, I'll be goddamned. Has the virginal Helena actually mentioned the act?"

"You're mean," Helena said.

"I know," Nick said.

"I am drunk," Helena said. "But I do wonder. Fen is the only boy I really loved, before Avery, I mean. But Avery is a man."

"Well, if you love him I'm sure it will be just grand."

"Of course, you're right." Helena finished off her gin. "Oh, Nick. I can't believe it's all changing. We've been so happy here, despite everything."

"Don't get weepy. We'll see each other, every summer. Unless your new husband is allergic to the East Coast."

"We'll go to the Island. Just like our mothers. Houses right next door."

Nick smiled, thinking about Tiger House, its airy rooms,

the expanse of green lawn that disappeared into the blue of the harbor. And the small, sweet cottage next door, which her father had built for Helena's mother as a gift.

"Houses, husbands, and midnight gin parties," Nick said. "Nothing's going to change. Not in any way that really matters. It will be like always."

Nick's train from Boston was delayed and she had to fight her way through the crowds at Penn Station, all rushing off to be somewhere in a muddle of luggage and hats and kisses and lost tickets. Helena must be halfway across the county by now, she thought. Nick had closed up the apartment herself and given the final instructions to the landlady as to where everything was to be sent; boxes of novels and poetry to Florida, suitcases full of corsets to Hollywood.

The train, when she finally got on it, smelled like bleach and excitement. The Havana Special, which ran all the way from New York to Miami, would be the first overnight journey she had ever taken alone. She kept pressing her nose to the inside of her wrist, inhaling her lily-of-the-valley perfume like a smelling salt. In the dizziness of it all, she almost forgot to tip the porter.

Inside her roomette, Nick set her leather case on the rack and clicked it open, checking the contents again to make sure she hadn't forgotten anything. One nightgown for the train (white), and one for Hughes (green, with matching dressing gown). Two ivory silk slips, three matching pairs of ivory silk underpants and brassieres (she could wash them every other day until the rest of her things arrived in St. Augustine), her ditty kit (travel vial of perfume; one lipstick, red; the precious Floris hand cream Hughes had brought her from London; one toothbrush and paste; one washcloth; and one cake of Ivory soap), two cotton dresses, two cotton blouses, one pair of gabardine trousers (her Katharine Hepburn trousers), two cotton skirts, and one good summer-weight wool suit (cream). She also counted out three pairs of cotton gloves (two white, one cream), and her mother's pink-and-green silk scarf.

Her mother had loved that scarf; she always wore it when she was traveling to Europe. Now it belonged to Nick. And although she wasn't going as far as Paris just yet, going to meet Hughes after so long seemed more like going to China.

"Beyond here be dragons," she said to the suitcase.

Nick heard the whistle blow and quickly snapped the lid shut and sat down. Now that the war was over, the scene outside the window, women waving handkerchiefs and red-eyed children, was less affecting. No one was going off to die, they were just going to an old aunt's house, or some boring work appointment. For her, though, it felt exciting; the world was new. She was going to see Hughes. Hughes. She whispered his name like a talisman. Now that she was only a day away from him, she thought she might go crazy with the waiting. Funny, how that was. Six months, but the last few hours were unbearable.

The last time they had seen each other was spring, when his escort ship had docked in New York for repairs and he had gotten liberty. They had stayed on board the *U.S.S. Jacob Jones*, in one of the rooms for married officers. There were fleas, and just when Hughes had his hand down her skirt, her ankles began to burn. She had tried to concentrate on the tip of his fingers searching her out. His lips on the pulse in her neck. But couldn't help crying out.

"Hughes, there's something in the bed."

"I know, Jesus."

. They had both rushed to the shower to find their legs covered in red bites and the water in the drain a pool of pepper. Hughes cursed the ship, cursed the war. Nick wondered if he'd notice her naked body. Instead, he turned his back and began soaping himself.

But he had taken her to the 21 Club. And it had been one of those moments when it seemed that the whole world was conspiring for their happiness. Hughes, who would never take money from his parents and wouldn't let Nick spend her own, didn't earn enough on his lieutenant junior's salary for a meal there. But he knew how much she loved the stories of the sharkskin-suited gangsters and their glamorous molls who had kicked up their heels there during Prohibition.

"We can only have two martinis and a bowl of olives and celery," he said.

"We don't have to go there at all, if we can't afford it," Nick said, looking at her husband's face. It was sad; sad and something else she couldn't put her finger on.

"No," he said. "We can afford just this. But then we have to leave."

They arrived in the dark-paneled Bar Room, with its crush of toys and sporting artifacts hanging from the ceiling, and Nick instantly felt the impact of her own youth and beauty. She could feel the eyes of the men and women at small tables pass over her red shantung dress and glance off her short, thick black hair. One of the things she loved about Hughes was that he had never wanted her to resemble the celluloid blonds tacked up in every boy's room across the country. And she didn't. She was a little too severe-looking, her lines a little too crisp, to be considered pretty. Sometimes it felt like a never-ending battle to prove to the world that, in her difference, she was special, discrete. But there, at the urbane 21 Club, she felt her own rightness. It was a place full of streamlined women, with intelligent eyes, like bullet trains. And there was Hughes, so honey blond, with his elegant hands and long legs and Service Dress Blues.

The waiter seated them at table 29. There was a couple to their right. The woman was smoking and pointing out lines from a slender book.

"In that line, I really see the whole film," the woman said.

"Yes," the man said, with just a touch of uncertainty.

"And in some ways, it is so Bogart."

"It does seem like he could have been the only logical choice."

Nick looked at Hughes. She wanted to communicate to him how much she loved him for taking her here, for spending too much money just to have a cocktail, for letting her be herself. She tried to radiate all these things in her smile. She didn't want to talk just yet.

"Do you know what?" the woman said, her pitch rising suddenly. "We're at their table. Do you realize we're at their table and we're talking about them?"

"Are we really?" The man took another sip from his Scotch.

"Oh, that is so 21," the woman said, laughing.

Nick leaned in. "Whose table, do you think?" she whispered to Hughes behind her gloved hand.

"I'm sorry?" Hughes said distractedly.

"They said they're at someone's table. Whose table?"

Nick realized that the woman was now eyeing them. She had heard her, seen her try to hide her curiosity behind her hand. Nick flushed and looked down at the red-and-white-checked tablecloth.

"Why, it's Humphrey Bogart and Lauren Bacall's table,

dear," the woman said. She said it kindly. "They went on their first date at this table. It's one of the things they brag about here."

"Oh, really?" Nick tried to hit a note somewhere between polite and nonchalant. She smoothed her styled hair with her palms, feeling the softness of the suede loosening the hairspray.

"Oh, Dick, let's give them the table." The woman was laughing again. "Are you two lovers?"

"Yes," said Nick, feeling bold, sophisticated. "But we're also married."

"That's a rarity," the man chuckled.

"Yes, indeed, it is," the woman said. "And that deserves Bogart and Bacall's table."

"Oh, please don't let us disturb you," Nick said.

"Nonsense," the man said, picking up his Scotch and the woman's champagne cocktail.

"Oh, really, you've been bedeviled by my wife," Hughes said. "Nick . . ."

"Oh, we'd love it," the woman said. "And she is especially bedeviling."

Nick looked at Hughes, who smiled at her.

"Yes, she is," he said. "Come on then, darling. We're all on the move for you."

The martini that arrived reminded Nick of the sea and their house on the island: clean, briny and utterly familiar.

"Hughes. This may be the best supper I've ever had. From now on, I only want martinis, olives, and celery."

Hughes put his hand to her face. "I'm sorry about all of this."

"How can you say that? Look where we are."

"We should get the bill," he said, motioning to the waiter.

"Is everything all right, sir?"

"It's fine. May we have the bill, please?" Hughes was looking at the door. Not at Nick, not at her red dress, or her shiny black hair that she'd had to keep in a net on the train all the way from Cambridge to Penn Station.

The waiter glided away.

Nick fiddled with her handbag because she didn't want to look at Hughes. The couple who had switched seats with them had left, although the woman had squeezed her shoulder and winked at Nick when she'd risen. She tried to stop herself wondering what Hughes might be thinking about. There was so much that she didn't know about him, not really, and although she always wanted to confront, to slice him open in one deft movement and peer inside, something animal in her told her it was the wrong way to proceed with him.

"Sir, madam." Nick looked up. A man with the air of a walrus had appeared at their table. "I'm the manager. Is anything wrong?"

"No," Hughes said, glancing around, presumably for the waiter. "I'd only asked for the bill . . ."

"I see," the Walrus said. "Well, it's entirely possible that you weren't aware, sir, but dinner," and here he paused, letting his handle-bar mustache take full effect, "dinner is on the house for the navy tonight."

"I'm sorry?" Hughes said.

"Son," the Walrus smiled. "What can I bring you?"

Nick laughed. "A steak, oh please a steak," she said, and everything else vanished.

"A steak for the lady," the Walrus said, still looking at Hughes.

Hughes grinned, and suddenly Nick saw the boy she'd married revealed in the untouchable man who'd come back to her. A boy in a stiff cardboard collar and a very pressed blue uniform. And their predicament, which was just like everyone else's.

"A steak, if you can find one in this city. Or this country for that matter," Hughes said. "I wasn't sure they still existed."

"They still exist at the 21 Club, sir, such as they are." The Walrus snapped his fingers at the waiter. "Two more martinis for the navy man."

Later, it was the fleas, again. And Hughes was tired, he said, from the steak. Nick folded her red dress and put on the black nightgown, which he wouldn't see in the dark. She lay on the bed listening to the noise of the fixers, working on the ship in the dock. The empty hammering of the steel.

Just outside of Newark, Nick decided to go to the lounge. She had packed three hard-boiled eggs and a ham sandwich for dinner so she wouldn't have to spend the three dollars in the dining car. But she couldn't resist the lure of the bar. It had been advertised as serving all the "new drinks," and she had put aside fifty cents for extras.

The Havana Special. No husband, no mother, no cousin: she could be anyone. She smoothed her gray skirt and applied her lipstick. She inspected herself in the mirror; one dark lock fell over her left eye. She was about to step into the corridor when she remembered her gloves. As she slipped them on, she smelled her wrist once more before closing the door sharply behind her.

Entering the lounge car, with its curved wooden bar and low-slung burgundy seats, Nick felt a trickle of sweat begin to pool between her breasts. She ran her gloved hand over her upper lip and instantly regretted the gesture. A waiter approached and showed her to an empty table. She ordered a martini with extra olives, wondering if they would charge her more for them. She pushed back the felt curtain and stared out into the night. Her own reflection stared back. Behind her head she could see a man in a navy blazer looking at her. She tried to make out if he was handsome, but a passing train obliterated his image.

She leaned away from the window and crossed her legs, feeling the shift of her nylons between her thighs. The waiter brought her drink and when Nick offered up her cigarette to be lit he fumbled to locate his lighter. The man across the way stepped in, flicking a silver Zippo. All the young men back from the war carried Zippos, as if they were issued along with the uniform.

"Thank you," Nick said, keeping her eyes on her cigarette.

"You're welcome."

The waiter disappeared behind a partition of frosted glass.

"May I join you?" the man asked. There was nothing hesitant in his request.

Nick motioned to the seat, without looking up. "I'm not staying long," she said.

"Where are you headed?"

"St. Augustine."

He had dark hair, slicked back with pomade. He was handsome, she supposed, in a Palm Springs sort of way. Perhaps a little too much cologne.

"I'm going to Miami," he said. "I'm going to see my parents in Miami."

"How nice for you," Nick said.

"Yes, it is." He smiled at her. "What about you? Why St. Augustine?"

"I have a brother there," Nick said. "He's decommissioning his ship. I'm going to see him."

"How nice for him," the man said.

"Yes, it is." This time, Nick smiled back.

"I'm Dennis," the man said, extending his hand.

"Helena," said Nick.

"Like the mountain."

"Like the mountain. How original."

"I'm an original guy. You just don't know me very well, yet."

"If I knew you better, I would feel differently?"

"Who can say?" Dennis finished his drink. "I'm having another drink. Would you like another drink, Helena?"

"I don't think so," Nick said.

"I see. Drinking alone. How sad for me."

"Who knows, if you hang around long enough, maybe you'll find a companion." The martini was making her feel brave.

"I don't want another companion," Dennis said. He sighed. "Trains make me lonely."

Nick was aware of the night rushing by, the whine of steel hitting steel.

"Yes," she said. "They are lonely." She pulled out a cigarette. "I suppose I will have that drink."

Dennis signaled to the waiter. This time Nick's martini had only one olive. For some reason, it made her ashamed.

"What's your brother like?"

"He's lovely," she said. "And very blond."

"So you don't look alike."

"No, we don't."

"Well, he's one lucky guy to have a sister like you."

"Do you think so? I don't know how lucky he should feel, really."

"I'd like a sister like you." He grinned at her.

Nick didn't like the way he said it, or the way he grinned, as if there was a complicity between them. Now that he was too close to her, she could see that he had brown hairs protruding from his nostrils.

"I have to go now," she said, trying to keep her balance as she rose to her feet.

"Oh, come on."

"Don't bother getting up."

"Don't get all huffy. I was only kidding."

Nick walked out of the lounge. He could pay for both her damn drinks.

"Any time you want some brotherly love," she heard him call after her, laughing, before the compartment door cut him off.

Back in her roomette, she practically ripped her blouse trying to get it off. Her head was pounding. She pulled off her skirt, and standing in only her brassiere and underpants, she bent over the small sink and splashed water over her breasts and around her neck. She switched off the overhead light and pushed the window down to let in some fresh air. The porter had turned down her bed while she had been in the lounge. She sat on it and lit a cigarette. When she was finished with that one, she lit another and pressed her head against the pane. The darkness went by. After a while, she lay down, the smell of the smoke lingering around her.

It was five o'clock in the morning when they pulled into Richmond. The sound of people moving in and out of the train had woken her up. She hadn't closed the curtains and the window was still open.

"Goddamn it," Nick said. She tried to inch herself up the bed, aware that she was still wearing only her brassiere and underpants, for all the boarding passengers to see. The far curtain was just out of reach, so she tugged at the one nearest and got behind it. Standing there, covered only in green felt, she peered out. Nick thought she could detect the earthy traces of the James River. The air was more gentle here in the South. Not like at Tiger House, where the sea took it by force. There was also the smell of pine, cleaning away the last vestiges of her martini. She pulled the other curtain shut, tied the sash of her robe around her waist, opened the door, and called to the porter for coffee.

She would be in St. Augustine by eleven tonight. And with Hughes. Had she dreamt of him? She tried to remember. The porter came with the steaming coffee. She drank it, watching the sleepy passengers boarding for Florida. Helena would be arriving in Hollywood soon. She wondered what Avery Lewis's house looked like. Poor Helena. Word had come early on in the fighting that Fen was dead—it had taken him all of two months to get himself married and killed. Who knows what their life would have been like if he had survived? They were both a couple of children and neither one had any money.

Helena's mother, her Aunt Frances, had not made a brilliant marriage either. Still, she had never seemed unhappy that she was forced to make do with less. Nick had never heard her complain about the fact that her older sister had been the one to inherit Tiger House, or marry a man who made oodles in bobbins and spools, while she had virtually nothing. It hadn't occurred to Nick that her aunt might have wanted things to be different. But thinking now of Helena's strange, mad dash to get married again, her need to have someone of her own, as she had put it, made Nick wonder if Aunt Frances had ever wished she'd been the one in the big house.

Perhaps it didn't really matter. After all, Nick couldn't

remember a summer that Aunt Francis and her mother weren't in each other's pockets. Even after Helena's father died, when the Depression came. And even when her own father died and her mother was so unwell. Nick stopped herself. She didn't want to think about that right now.

She pulled two of the eggs out of their brown-paper bag and cracked them on the window sill, revealing the shiny white skin. No, everything was new now, just waiting to be discovered. And she would. She and Hughes would do it together. She was hungry for it, she would stuff the world whole into her mouth and bite down.

1945: December

Nick was lying on the floating dock when she heard Hughes pull up in the old Buick. She tried to concentrate on the music coming from the porch across the yard, so she wouldn't hear the coughing engine or the slap of the screen door as her husband entered the bungalow.

Count Basie's piano. The worn wood from the dock shed tiny splinters into the back of her yellow bathing suit. Her big toe skimmed the top of the canal. She waited.

When Hughes didn't come outside, Nick felt relieved. She heard the shower start inside the house as he washed away the dust and paint from mothballing the warship in Green Cove Springs. She imagined his body, the blond hairs on his arms covered in a fine layer of what was once the shell of the *U.S.S. Jacob Jones*. She could picture him slicking his hair back under the water, turning his face up to the spray, his eyelashes like cobwebs catching fine beads. Would he be thinking of her? She wondered this only briefly. She knew he would not.

The cottage was giving off its evening song: the sound of water rushing through the cheap pipes, and scratchy jazz. Nick hated that cottage, hated its same-ness. A rented pre-fab, it was just like all the others surrounding it: boxy, with a kitchen and bedroom at the front, and a large living room and dining area to the rear, with windows onto a back porch.

The bungalows sat in rows on either side of a dusty drive, each separated by its own plot of land. All the kitchens looked out onto the drive and at any time, any number of the servicemen's busybody wives could be seen peering out. Nick had made it a habit to walk out to the drive in her bathing suit at least once a day, just to watch the kerchiefed heads quickly disappear, one by one, as she stared them down. It had become something of a game, to see if she could catch one polka-dotted head, frozen in the beam of her racy bathing suit, cut higher at the thighs in the French style. This brightened her day.

Each bungalow on her side also had a good-sized back-yard stretching all the way down to the salty canal, which served as a byway for St. Augustine's fishermen and, from time to time, kids fooling around in rowboats.

But theirs had one thing all the others didn't have: a dock, tethered into the silty bank, which swayed with the movement of the water. Unlike the rest of the development, it didn't have the look of better times to come, of new lives being started over in cheap boxes. The wood was gray and perfectly weathered, perhaps rescued from an old piece of siding or a fisherman's ramp. Nick loved the dock, like nothing else in that Florida town. Sometimes when she was lying there with her eyes closed, she was almost sure the hammered planks had come free from their soft purchase and that she was floating away, down the canal and out to sea, back home to her island up north. Then she would open her eyes and see the ungainly house at the other end of the lawn, and realize it had only been a passing fishing boat, causing the dock to pitch from side to side.

Nick passed her days stretched out there in the Florida sun, listening to the records that had arrived from Cambridge in a trunk lined with old newspaper, and trying to shock her neighbors. Sometimes, she tried out new recipes from a book she had bought in town, *The Prudence Penny Regional Cook Book*. It was divided into chapters: Pennsylvania Dutch, Creole, Mississippi Valley, Minnesota Scandinavian, and Cosmopolitan, and called for ingredients whose presence on the page continued to startle her.

Before they left Elm Street, Nick and Helena made a small bonfire and burned their expired ration books. Helena had always had a hard time figuring out which stamp went with what food, and would sometimes return with a can of creamed spinach instead of chicken because she had mixed up the days. And while Nick had liked the challenge of rationing for a while, it had eventually grown tedious, like trying to put together a jigsaw puzzle that was missing a piece. Now, she could cook whatever she liked, without having to figure out a substitute. But she found it difficult to concentrate on the recipes, and sometimes would give up halfway through the honeyed ham or oysters Rockefeller, and go lie on the dock in the sun. Later, she would throw the remaining ingredients together into some kind of casserole.

Hughes never said anything, but she knew he was dismayed by her uneven cooking. Now, listening to the shower, she tried not to think of dinner, once again left undone. She also tried not to think about her husband, who had himself become something rationed.

The orchestra's horn section broke in and she slapped her foot in time against the coming tide, making little splashes of canal water fly up onto her calf. Her eyes were shut and her yellow bathing suit was losing the heat it had absorbed from the afternoon's sunbathing. A breeze was whispering up from the water and she could hear a small rowboat passing.

In the house, the water stopped running. Silence, except for the sound of the music and the children a few houses down, complaining about being called to dinner. Nick turned her face to the west to catch the last heat of the day on her cheek.

"Hello."

Startled, she lifted her head. Shading her eyes, she saw Hughes standing on the lawn, freshly showered and wearing the white shirt she had ironed earlier in the day.

"Do you want me to make you a drink?" she asked, not moving.

"No, I'll make it myself." Hughes walked over to the Tiki bar and, pulling a bottle of no-name gin out of the cupboard, poured two fingers-full into a tumbler.

"There's no ice out here," Nick said. "Too hot." She lay her head back on the warm planks and shut her eyes again.

"You haven't forgotten that Charlie and Elise are coming for dinner?" There was a note of resignation in his voice, as if he knew she had forgotten, as if she couldn't but have forgotten. As if all she did was forget and not remember.

Nick stiffened, but kept her eyes closed.

"Who? Oh yes, your friends," she said. "No, I haven't forgotten." She had. "I bought shrimp from the shrimp boat."

She heard Hughes sigh into his drink.

"Well, I know you're bored of it, but for a dollar a bucket, it's really all we can afford until the next paycheck." Nick got up and dusted herself off. "Especially if we're entertaining."

"I thought you said you missed having dinner parties," Hughes said quietly.

He stood facing her, holding his glass. His blond hair had turned dark from the shower, and the setting sun lit him from behind. To Nick, it seemed as if his shoulders were almost squared against her, like a fighter.

"I do," Nick said. "I mean, I did say that. Darling, it's just that I don't know them and you—" She broke off when she saw Hughes staring at her like she was some kind of slow child.

She felt the strange juxtaposition of emotions, so familiar now. She wanted to take his drink out of his hand and smash it into his face, grind the glass against his skin. She also wanted to beg for forgiveness, and then be forgiven, like when she was a child and her mother's cold punishment would pass into clemency.

"Never mind," Nick said. "I'll go in and fix the supper. What time did you tell them?"

"Eight, sharp," Hughes said.

Nick didn't go in and fix the supper. Instead, she stood smoking in the kitchen, letting cold air leak out of the icebox as she studied the vegetables. Cucumber salad, she decided. It would go well with seafood. She shut the door, leaning against it. She looked down at her legs, which were getting brown from her daily doses of sun. She'd had to buy the bathing suit in town, for a small fortune. She hadn't realized the heat would still be strong in winter. On her island up north, the sun would already be a muddy, washed-out color, her bathing suit long packed in a cedar trunk to hibernate.

She heard Hughes turn off the record player and head toward the kitchen. Nick began busying herself with the shrimp, peeling and de-veining the pink moons. She used to love them. Now, they ate them almost every other day.

"Why don't you turn on the radio?" Hughes asked.

She held up her slippery hands. "You do it, I don't want to hurt it."

Hughes had bought her the radio the week before and Nick had a vague feeling of animosity toward it. He had taken a Saturday afternoon drive alone and returned with a box. She didn't ask why he drove without her on the weekends, or where he went. He would just stare at the sky through the screen door and then pick up his keys. The first time, she hadn't even realized he was going until she heard the engine start. She walked to the door and looked up at the cloudless expanse, the dusty drive, the road beyond, to see what in it had made her husband want to drive away. But as far as she could see, there was nothing. Only the old green Buick flatlining down the straight Florida road.

Then one day, the radio had appeared, like a spy, from wherever it was he went to get away.

"I thought you'd want to hear something other than your records," he had said by way of explanation. "You may even be able to hear programs from London."

"London?" she had asked, wondering why he thought that was important to her. But he was already on his way to the shower, her voice echoing in the empty kitchen.

Nick looked up from the shrimp. Hughes hadn't switched the radio on, but he was fingering the silver knobs. He had elegant fingers with neat, square nails. Everything about him was like his hands, tailored and clean, the color of pine. Nick watched him gaze at the dials, run the tips of his fingers over the brown covering of the speaker. She wanted to eat him, he was so beautiful. She wanted to cry or melt or gnash her teeth. Instead, she peeled the skin off another shrimp.

"They look good," Hughes said, coming up behind her and putting his hand on the small of her back.

Nick had to grip the counter with one hand to keep herself still. She smelled him, Ivory soap and bay rum, so close to her skin, but not touching it. Touching it through the fabric of bathing suit. She wanted his hand on her neck, or her arm or between her legs.

"I'm sure it will be delicious," he said.

She knew he was sorry he'd been nasty about the shrimp. "Oh, well," she said, suddenly feeling lighter again. "I know it's awfully repetitive. I suppose it's partly because I sleep so late and can't seem to get up in time for that early market. Are you sorry you have such a lazy wife?"

"I have a lovely wife," he said.

She was about to turn to him when he took his hand off her back. She would have caught it, pulled him to her, maybe even begged him, but he was already moving away.

Nick watched him head for the screened-in porch, his long legs moving like a sleepwalker. The invisible imprint of his hand burning into her.

When she had finished with the shrimp and put them in the icebox to cool, Nick went into the bedroom and carefully removed her bathing suit. She showered in the small bathroom off the bedroom. When she opened the closet, a cockroach as big as a sparrow came flying out, ten times bigger than any she'd ever seen up North. Water bugs, one of the servicemen's wives had called them. Nick didn't scream, she wasn't even surprised by them anymore.

Running her hand across her dresses, she stopped at a cotton sundress with cherries and a sweetheart neckline. Slipping it on and surveying herself in the mirror, she took out her sewing scissors and cut off the straps. Without them, her breasts sprang to attention, the heart-shaped top just clearing her nipples. She brushed her dark hair back, still glossy despite the sun. She looked strong and healthy, and a little less severe with her new nut-colored skin setting off the yellow flecks in her eyes. She felt proud of the effect.

She dabbed her wrists and cleavage with perfume and went barefoot back into the kitchen.

She pulled a bottle of white wine out of the icebox and brought it out to Hughes, who was sitting on the porch looking out over the canal.

"Would you open this for me, darling?"

Hughes looked up at her and took the bottle and the corkscrew out of her hand. He began peeling away the foil.

"That's quite revealing," he said to the bottle.

"You took me to the Yacht Club dance in this dress, don't you remember?"

He looked up, a half smile that didn't quite reach his eyes. "No, I'm sorry, Nicky, I don't."

"Oh, come on," she said. "There was that funny, ugly little man leading the band who thought he was Lester Lanin. And he made some comment about the cherries and you almost hit him."

"Did I?"

Nick sucked in her breath. "Well," she said, "it is a bit different. I did cut off the straps. But I think it's more sophisticated this way."

Hughes pulled out the cork and began freeing it from the screw. "Won't you be cold?"

Nick stared at him, her head pounding out a hot little rhythm, like the angry horns in Count Basie's orchestra.

"Goddamn it, Hughes," she said slowly. "It's goddamn Florida. I will not be cold."

Hughes didn't look up, didn't even flinch. He handed her the bottle. She took a swig, not bothering with a glass, and walked out to the lawn.

❖

Nick wasn't sure how long she'd been there when she heard the knock at the door. Only that the bottle was almost half empty and her dress was damp from the grass. With some difficulty, she roused herself and moved unsteadily toward the porch. Walking through the house, she saw Hughes was already shaking hands with the couple at the front door. Nick didn't realize she was still barefoot until she reached them.

"Hello," she said, laughing and looking down at her feet. "Well, you have a shoeless hostess. I do hope you won't take it as a sign of indifference. I was out in the yard. It's too damp for shoes."

"I've always thought a barefoot hostess is a mark of the highest regard," the man said, extending his hand. "Charlie Wells. And this is my wife Elise."

His eyes were round and black, like the jet beads her mother used to wear to the theater, but his brown hand was warm, if a bit rough to the touch. Nick knew it was from the ship, and that Hughes's hands had also hardened from the chipping and painting, preparing the *Jacob Jones* to be docked. But Charlie's calluses also reminded her that he'd been an enlisted man. He'd eventually gotten a battlefield commission, but he hadn't started out that way. Not like her husband. A mustang, Hughes said they were called. "One of the brightest men I served with, though," Hughes had told her. "They were smart to bring him up."

While the man was dark and slender, his wife looked blond to the point of albino. And she was wearing a pale-pink dress that, in Nick's opinion, wasn't doing her any favors. Still, she had a sort of soft femininity that gave Nick a small prick of envy.

"What can I get everyone to drink?" Hughes asked.

"Come out to the porch," Nick said. "Our silly bar is outside, so Hughes won't have to walk as far to bring you your Scotch." She led their guests through the house back to the porch. "Really, we live out here. That's the lovely thing about Florida. Do you have a porch, Elise?"

"We do," she said. "But I'm hardly ever out there. I'm not really . . . well, I'm not crazy about the outdoors."

"That's a shame," Nick said, rolling her eyes, but only inwardly. "Do you like Count Basie? I'm on a sort of a kick at the moment."

"I don't really know. Charlie's the one who knows about music in our house."

"Do you have 'Honeysuckle Rose'?" Charlie asked.

"I do indeed," Nick said, skipping off to the record player. "Are you a fan of the blues? Hughes always says it's too melancholy."

"Life is melancholy. Why dwell on it?" Hughes said, returning with the drinks. "Anyway, this stuff isn't the blues, it's swing."

In the fading light, Nick saw he had removed her wine bottle from the lawn. "Oh, you think you're so clever," she said, laughing.

"You must think I'm clever, too. You married me, after all," Hughes said, returning her smile, and offering her a martini.

"Have you ever heard Robert Johnson?" Charlie asked. "That's real blues. Southern blues. Not for the club set."

"What do you have against the club set?" Nick asked, turning to face him, happy to rise to the bait. Happy for something to happen around here.

"I have nothing against the club set, except maybe their musical taste," he said, giving her a quiet smile.

Nick was about to reply, but thought better of it. Instead, she stared at him a moment, wondering just how drunk she really was. She could hear the beetles singing in the night. The rustle of the palm at the corner of the lawn. Her lily-of-the-valley perfume mingled with the soft, Southern night air. She heard Hughes talking about Elise's hometown, in Wisconsin, somewhere. And the sound of the horns.

Next to her, sitting in the rented chintz-covered chair, was this man giving her a smile full of cathouse jazz and motel rooms.

"Excuse me for a minute," Nick said rising, her hand on the arm of the chair to steady herself. "The kitchen calls."

"I'll help you," Charlie said.

"It's really not necessary," Nick said, picking up her martini and holding it against her like armor.

"I'm a whiz in the kitchen. Ask Elise."

Elise stared at her husband, impassive. But she didn't, Nick noticed, offer to come in his stead.

Nick didn't dare turn around as they walked back inside. She opened the icebox and pulled out the peeled cucumber.

"Could you slice this for me?" she asked, handing the cucumber back.

"Knife?"

"In the drawer under the sink," she said, retrieving the shrimp.

"From the shrimp boat?" Charlie asked, eyeing the bowl.

"Yes," Nick said, laughing.

"Which one?"

"What do you mean, which one?"

"The five o'clock?"

"Yes, what other one is there?"

"The morning shrimp boat," Charlie said, slicing the cucumber, a little too thick for Nick's taste. "Seven a.m., sharp. It's the best one and you get more shrimp."

"And how in the world would you know this?" Nick asked, giving him a mocking smile.

"I always buy the shrimp. Elise doesn't like the canal."

Nick busied herself making a lemon sauce, whisking a yolk into the pool of juice at the bottom of the bowl.

"I'll show you one morning, if you like," Charlie said. "Cucumber's done." He approached her with the cutting board and stood motionless behind her.

Nick stopped whisking.

"Do you have any Robert Johnson records?" Nick asked.

"I do," Charlie said. "Would you like to hear them?"

"Yes," Nick said. "And the shrimp boat, too. I'd like to know about that."

"Fine," he said.

Nick began whisking, the sauce turning a thick pale yellow.

"Your cucumber," he said.

"I liked them," Nick said, clearing the plates.

"He's a good worker," Hughes said, staring into his Scotch. "Some of the men don't seem to care one bit whether the work on the boat gets finished. Mostly, those are the ones without families."

"Nothing to go back to, I suppose." Nick turned on the tap. She eyed Hughes. "But Charlie, I liked him. He said he'd show me the good shrimp boat."

"Did he? Well, Elise doesn't seem much for the out-doors, does she?"

"A bit milquetoast," Nick said.

"She's quite lovely, though."

"Did you think so? I thought she might fade into the wall

and we'd be searching for her all night." Nick scrubbed at a plate. "He's pretty dashing, though."

"Yes, well, you're not alone. He has many admirers at the lunch canteen."

"I imagine she must have a hard time with that."

"Oh, I don't know, he seems quite devoted to her."

"Really?"

"You did seem to have a good time. I'm glad," Hughes said, swirling the remnants of his drink around in his glass. "I don't want this to be too dull for you."

"This is our life. Why would it be dull?"

"Our life," Hughes said slowly, an almost imperceptible sigh escaping his lips. "Yes, I suppose it is."

"What do you mean, you 'suppose it is'?"

"I don't know what I mean, maybe I've had too much to drink."

"Well, I've had too much to drink," Nick said, turning to face him, "and I want to know what the goddamn hell you mean, you 'suppose it is'?"

"Yes, you're right." Hughes stared straight back. "You have had too much to drink."

"So I've had too much to drink. So what? I've had too much of everything, goddamn it."

"I wish you wouldn't swear so much."

"I wish you were the man I married." Nick was shaking. She knew she had said too much, but it was like cliff-jumping.

When she was a girl, she and Helena and a couple of boys would go up to the old quarry to test their nerve. The granite had run out years before and the quarry had been abandoned to the groundwater, its depths unfathomable. They would each take turns, starting from an old oak stump that served as their marker, and running without stopping until they were in the air, plummeting off the cliff. The boys who were really scared would skid like marbles at the edge. But Nick always jumped.

Then again, there, she had known the lay of the land.

Hughes finished his Scotch in one quick swig and poured himself another. "I'm sorry if you feel disappointed."

"I don't want you be sorry."

"Go to bed, Nicky. We can talk when you've sobered up."

"You're the person who's supposed to . . ." She stopped, unsure. "You're my husband."

"I'm well aware of that, Nick." His voice seemed angry, spiteful even.

"Are you really? You don't seem aware of much these days."

"Maybe you'd be better off alone, maybe I'm not up to the job of being anyone's husband."

"At least I'm trying," Nick said, suddenly afraid. "You . . ."

Hughes stood, and in an instant seemed to be towering. His palm pressed against the table, his knuckles white around the empty glass. "You don't think I'm trying, Nick? What do you think I do every day, every second? That boat, this place, this house, this life: you think this is what I want?"

Nick looked at him. And then with one swift move, she yanked the radio cord out of the wall. One minute the radio was in her hand, and the next, it was hurtling through the air.

Hughes didn't move a muscle, he just stood, his words hanging about him and an emptiness in his eyes.

The radio missed him and smashed into a corner of the wall.

"And what? You think that," she pointed at the springs and plastic lying in a heap, "you think that's what I want?"

"I'm going to bed," Hughes said.

"What's the point?" Nick ran her fingers through her hair. "You're already asleep."

Hughes left early the next morning. Nick pretended to be sleeping. The curtains were drawn and the room was stuffy. They both liked to sleep with the window open, but Nick had left it shut when she had finally come to bed, refusing to afford herself even the pleasure of the cooler air. It would be horrible and it was horrible, not least because it was stifling.

When she heard the engine turn over, she rose, not even bothering with her dressing gown. She sat at the kitchen table staring into her black coffee. She toyed with the idea of throwing her things into a case, calling a taxi, and fleeing back home. But when she mentally arrived in Cambridge, she was lost, the future yawning out in front of her. And he would still exist somewhere, somewhere else, and she wouldn't have him. So she just stared at the coffee.

She tried to think of her parents' marriage, but it was no use; she wasn't aware of what went on behind closed doors, in dark stairwells, at parties when she was left at home, on midnight walks when the world slept. They had seemed happy. But her father had died when she was still so young, and what she could remember of the two of them together were fragments: a diamond brooch presented in a green leather box at Christmas; her mother running her hand over her father's whiskers; the intermingling smell of Royal Yacht tobacco and L'Heure Bleue.

Her mother hadn't wanted her to marry; she thought they were too young. She had forced Nick to go on dates with other boys, boring dances with a sweaty-palmed neighbor trying to hold her hand under the table. But when it became clear that she and Hughes were meeting in secret, her mother gave in. Better she be married if anything happened, she had said.

They wed on the Island, at the church where she had been christened. Small, with beautiful stained-glass windows. The reception was at Tiger House. They had some overly strong punch and tea-sandwiches and a sweet white cake with candied violets on it.

Nick, feeling strange and sick, had escaped to the upstairs drawing room. Sitting on the gray silk Sheraton sofa, she began pulling the orange blossoms out of her hair. She wondered if she'd ever be able to go back downstairs. Maybe she'd waste away on this sofa, like a sort of Miss Havisham; the orange blossoms would wilt and petrify, the chocolates set out on the side table would become brown, old stones.

And then Hughes had appeared in the doorway in his morning coat. Without a word, he came over and sat beside her. Nick continued to toy with the small scented sprigs, not daring to look at him, ashamed. He had taken her chin in his hand and turned her face to him. And in that gesture was everything, everything that wasn't dead and stale and confining.

He took her hand and led her to the maid's bedroom in the back. The window was open and the yellow-checked curtains were blowing in the harbor air. Lifting her voluminous skirt and petticoat, he knelt and put his face against her, inhaling her, but remaining still. Minutes seemed to pass before they heard footsteps in the corridor. Hughes turned his head toward the open door, but remained pressed against her. The downstairs maid passed by the door and stopped, paralyzed and flushing, before their tableau. Hughes had stared at the woman a moment, as if he wanted her to see them, see what was happening and changing between them, keeping still, before kicking the door shut.

It was ten o'clock, the sun was on its way to its apex, and Nick was still wearing her nightgown. The coffee stood cold beside her motionless hand on the breakfast table. She thought she could detect the lingering odor of last night's shrimp, although it could have been the shrimp from Wednesday, or Sunday for that matter.

She had found the remnants of the radio carefully wrapped in tissue outside the front door, like a baby left on a doorstep. She had half expected to find a note pinned to it reading: Unloved and Unwanted.

Damn him, Nick thought, damn him to hell.

They were supposed to be different, different from all the people who didn't want things and didn't do things and who weren't special. They were supposed to be the kind of people who said to hell with it, who threw their wine glasses into the fireplace, who jumped off cliffs. They were not supposed to be careful people.

But if only he weren't so beautiful. If only she didn't want him so much.

She heard an engine outside and slowly rose, moving toward the kitchen window.

Charlie Wells was slamming the car door shut, a stack of records tucked under his arm. Nick ran into the bedroom and shut the door. A sensation from the night before—his hand on the soft interior of her thigh under the dinner table, a silent interloper—came back to her. How could she have forgotten that?

Her heart pounding, she found her dressing gown and checked her appearance in the mirror. She looked thin and unhappy. Goddamn it, she thought, I am thin and unhappy, so what?

Charlie was knocking on the screen door. Nick straightened her back and went to greet him.

"Hello," she said, looking at him through the screen.

"Hello," he said, smiling back at her. "I'm sorry for dropping in on you like this, but I was wondering what to do with my morning and I thought to myself that I'd like to spend it listening to Robert Johnson. And then I thought, maybe you would, too. I'm playing hooky."

"Ah, and Hughes told me what a good worker you were."

His hand, seeking her out while she'd fiddled with her napkin.

"Yes, your lieutenant is a very serious man."

"He is," Nick said.

Charlie stood there, jostling the records under his arm. He was wearing a pair of khakis and a chambray shirt, dock shoes and that cathouse smile.

Nick picked at the grime lacing the screen.

"Look," he said, finally. "Maybe I've been too impetuous. You're probably busy and I'm being a nuisance."

Nick looked at him thoughtfully. "No, I'm not doing anything that a little music wouldn't improve." She pushed the door open and stood aside. "Please."

Charlie stepped in and put the records on the table.

"Stay here and make yourself at home. I'm going to put on something a little more practical. One has to be serious about music after all," she said, finally throwing him a smile.

In the bedroom, Nick put on her green-striped sundress and some red lipstick. She went back to the kitchen and began fixing a fresh pot of coffee. She stood with her back to the counter watching Charlie thumb through his records at the breakfast table. Some of the cardboard packaging was worn, disintegrating at the corners. Hughes would never let anything he cared about be so ill-used, she thought. All his tools were kept clean and carefully returned to their cases when he was done with them. He even kept his toothbrush in a special case in the bathroom cabinet. And yet it moved her, all that care and intensity for a screw-driver or a toothbrush.

"I think we'll start your education with this one," Charlie said.

Sitting in one of the chintz chairs, Nick gripped her coffee, as Charlie put the needle to the vinyl. The music was rougher than the blues she was used to, but it had a certain back-porch quality. It was like a piece of drift-wood, all worn down and muddy-colored. But with the sun shining on the green lawn and the palm trees bowing and straightening in the breeze, it couldn't make Nick sad. In fact, it made her feel light-headed, like she might blow away with it.

The damp coming off the grass beckoned to her and the porch seemed to float up and away from the house, moving over the canal. The skirt of her dress ballooned and Nick laid her head against the back of the chair. The lonely appeal of a mourning dove sounded somewhere through the haze.

Nick didn't know how long she had been drifting like that, but when the music stopped, she forced herself to open her eyes. Charlie Wells was sitting in his chair looking at her, sizing her up, as if he were trying to catalogue her.

"Did you like it?"

"Yes, it has a sort of tonic effect, doesn't it?" It was all she could find to say, without saying what was really in her heart. Something about fleeing, something about this horrible cottage, about a broken radio and Hughes's hand on the small of her back.

Charlie didn't answer, inspecting his fingernails. After a moment he looked up, as if whatever it was he had been thinking had passed. "Are you hungry?" he asked. "Because I'm starving."

"I suppose I could make up some sandwiches. Our cupboard's rather shameful at the moment. I'm a bit of a sporadic shopper," Nick said.

"Never mind the sandwiches. I'll take you to lunch in town."

"What an awfully grand offer," Nick said. "A little too grand, really."

"That's all right. I know a Spanish place in the old town, tapas. Not so expensive. Have you ever eaten tapas?"

"I don't even know what that is," Nick said, laughing.

"It's good. You get to taste all sorts of different small dishes," he said. "I ate octopus once in Spain, before the war. I had never even seen a real octopus, but there I was, eating it. Sometimes a thing like that, a thing you've never even imagined in your head, can go down surprisingly easy."

The rusting Clipper, which Charlie said he had borrowed from "one of the boys," rolled toward town along the flat road. Next to them, the canal opened up into a large waterway, dotted with fishing boats and clapboard shacks.

The car felt close, almost intimate. Nick found herself pressing her ankles together, knees touching, like her mother had taught her to do when sitting with a boy. She smoothed her hair back and willed herself not to look at him. But as she listened to the whirr of the tires moving over the road, her mind returned to the dinner table.

It hadn't been a noisy, clumsy, mean advance, like the man on the Havana Special. It had been silent, the hand sliding under the hem of her skirt, pushing her knees apart slightly. His thumb brushing the interior of her thigh, making little concentric circles on her flesh.

She knew if she closed her eyes she could imagine that it was Hughes's hand, quiet but insistent, the way she remembered it.

She had poured more wine, rising in her seat a little to reach the others. Some of it spilled on her grandmother's white linen tablecloth. All the while, Charlie had kept his eyes on Hughes, continuing their conversation about the lousy food at the canteen, chuckling at Hughes's jokes. It had made her feel sad, to see Hughes nodding his head, his blue eyes crinkled at the edges in a smile. But it also took her breath away, made her feel drunker, powerful.

Nick had been unable to resist a glance at Elise, who had kept her own eyes on Charlie. She wondered if Elise suspected, if maybe she was used to it, the way they said you got used to the air-raid siren. You wait, knowing it's coming, then try to keep your ears covered until it's finished, when you can curse it in safety.

In the car, Nick pressed her knees tighter together. She should have stayed home. She should be lying on her dock, listening to Count Basie, thinking about getting ready for the officers' picnic that night.

But then she remembered the radio, wrapped carefully in tissue, and the heavy cookbook full of ingredients she hadn't bought, and she leaned her head against the car window and closed her eyes.

She tried to remember the last time Hughes had taken her to lunch. Sometime before the war. Always the same thing about money, as if they really were poor. It wasn't that she minded so much about the money, exactly, but she hated the way things always had to be discussed and weighed, and in the end he always decided anyway, leaving her with the impression that she might as well have been a wall. It was exhausting and it made her reckless. When she had wanted the yellow bathing suit, she had telegrammed her trustee and asked for the money in secret. Then she had lied to Hughes about how much it cost, ripping up the tag on her way home and scattering it on the roadside. All for a goddamn bathing suit. Somehow she loved that suit even more for it.

Still, money was money, and at least they had it. She thought of Helena and the recent telephone call. They had been writing to each other regularly over the past couple of months, an exchange of cheerful, if not mundane and—on Nick's side at least—somewhat untruthful letters. But when Helena rang her last week, long-distance from Hollywood, Nick knew something was up. It seemed her cousin's marriage had changed her already limited circumstances for the worse; Helena, or more precisely Avery Lewis, wanted to sell the little cottage on the Island for cash. The news confirmed Nick's suspicion that the man was a charlatan and she told Helena as much, making her cousin cry down the scratchy telephone line. She told Nick that Avery wanted to invest in a film venture, some B-movie nonsense. Nick had reminded Helena that she wouldn't even have the house if it weren't for Nick's father, hoping to shame her into dropping it. And Helena had relented, saying they would just

39

have to find the money another way; of course Nick was right. Nick had been furious when she hung up and she told Hughes she thought they'd better get to Hollywood and see what was going on out there. Hughes had, of course, reminded her that cross-country tickets were costly and Nick had stayed in a black mood, refusing to do the shopping for days.

"Where are you?" Charlie Wells's voice brought Nick back to the car, the warm air drifting through the open windows.

"Oh, just away somewhere," Nick said. "I'm a bit tired from all the wine last night."

"Let's park, we can walk from here," Charlie said, pulling up alongside the old Spanish fort that had once served as a lookout.

The restaurant was in one of the crumbling colonial buildings that lined the narrow cobbled streets of the old town of St. Augustine. It was dark inside, with a low ceiling, and Nick wondered how many other women Charlie had taken there.

"I'll choose for us, if you don't mind," he said.

Nick waved her hand. "Please. I wouldn't even know where to begin."

When the waiter brought the wine, Nick put her hand over her glass. "I don't think I'll have any."

"You must," Charlie said. "You can't have tapas without wine."

"Well, just a little then," she said, removing her hand.

The table was small, their knees were almost touching under it, but Charlie hadn't made a move toward her, leaving Nick vaguely disquieted.

The little fish and meat dishes were at once salty and

spicy, oily and sharp. Their chins were slick from the sauces and Nick was compelled to lick her fingers at one point.

"I feel so native," she said cheerfully. He had been right about the wine and she tipped her glass toward him for more.

"You look a bit native with that tan," Charlie said, laughing and pouring.

"This is the first time I've been brown in the winter," Nick said. "I've been working very hard at it."

"Well, I'd say it's been worth the effort. All the boys on the ship have quite a crush on you."

"Do they? I've hardly seen them."

"Once is enough," Charlie said. "I'd been told, but I had to see it to believe it."

Nick knew he was lying; she wasn't the type that had seamen swooning, but she felt herself flush anyway.

"Don't be embarrassed," Charlie said, grinning at her.

"I'm not embarrassed, I just don't know . . ." Nick hesitated. "Well, I guess I am a little embarrassed."

"Doesn't your lucky bastard of a husband give you compliments?"

Nick didn't say anything, just looked down at her dirty napkin.

"All right, all right. I'll stop teasing you. Let's order some coffee."

The waiter brought thick coffee in small chipped cups and it tasted like nothing Nick had ever had at home.

"It's Moroccan," Charlie said. "They filter it twice, and they put cardamom in it, that's what gives it that flavor."

They sipped their coffee in silence, listening to the sound of dishes banging in the kitchen.

"I feel so tired," Nick said, as she swirled the silt at the bottom of her cup. "Like I could sleep forever."

"Do you want to go back?"

"I think I'd better. Otherwise, I might end up like Rip Van Winkle and sleep at this table for a hundred years."

"I doubt they'd mind," Charlie laughed.

"I suppose it wouldn't be the worst place. At least I'd have something nice to eat when I woke up."

"I wanted to show you where the good shrimp boat comes in," Charlie said. "But I guess we can wait on that."

"First, I'd have to be able to get up early enough," Nick said. "And maybe one lesson is enough for today."

Nick leaned her head out the car window, letting the wind take some of the heat from the wine out of her cheeks. If she'd been alone she would have gulped at the air, let its saltiness blow her whole insides clean, but she didn't want to do that in front of Charlie.

She could feel his gaze slide over her from time to time and she knew he wanted to touch her.

The car turned into their driveway and Charlie switched off the ignition. The cooling engine dinged and Nick rested against the door frame, listening to the crickets thrumming in the stiff swamp grass around the bungalows. Sweat had dampened her neckline and she could feel the back of her knees sticking to the vinyl. Charlie put his hand on her thigh. She looked at him. He pushed himself along the seat, reaching around the gear shift, to get to her. She didn't move closer. He seemed to be searching her face for something and she wondered what he saw there. He slid further, his arm outstretched to catch her to him, but his pant leg caught on the gear and he had to stop to fiddle with it.

Nick almost felt like laughing. It was like watching a desperate contortionist. He pulled at her, trying to get her to move closer to the middle, but she remained still. She could hear him breathing heavily. He finally got one leg around the gear shift and was on her, pushing her back into the corner. Nick thought about how strange they must look to the busybodies who were no doubt watching from their kitchen windows. Now they really would have something to talk about.

He was covering her neck with his mouth, leaving a wet trail around her collar bone. Nick felt too hot, from the wine and the sun and the sound of the crickets, whose song suddenly sickened her. She pushed back at him. But he was tearing at her now and using his full weight against her, one hand up the skirt of her sundress, the other clawing at the straps at her shoulders.

"Stop," she said. "It's too hot."

Charlie wasn't listening, or hadn't heard, and Nick wondered if she'd actually said it out loud. She pushed at him, harder this time, but it didn't seem to make any difference. He ripped the top of her sundress, sending a dozen tiny cloth-covered buttons flying around them.

Nick found the door handle behind her and released it, sending them both tumbling out onto the driveway.

She lay flat on her back, with her dress fanning out around her, feeling an uncontrollable urge to laugh. She covered her ripped top with her hand and tried to push the humming laughter back down, but it refused to go. She clamped her free hand over her mouth, but it was too late. Tears began streaming down her face as she gasped for breath, laughing and choking into the dusty ground, the force of it threatening to rend her apart. Charlie sat next to her, looking very angry and overwrought, which made her laugh even harder. He pushed himself off the drive. He stood glaring at her, his face red and sweaty.

43

"I'm sorry, it's just . . . oh dear," was all Nick managed, before dissolving again.

"Bitch," Charlie hissed, "you're just a damn tease." He kicked dirt at her before getting back into the car and slamming the door.

Nick just lay there laughing and holding her stomach as the car peeled out, watching the dust particles make twisters up into the shafts of sun.

She spent the rest of the afternoon making the tomato aspic that she had promised to bring to the officers' picnic in Green Cove Springs that evening. It had completely slipped her mind until she saw the hand-written recipe on the counter next to the icebox, calling for her mother's stock and a little Knox gelatin. It had seemed suddenly so important, possibly the most important thing in the world, that aspic, and Nick threw herself into the task with intense concentration.

She roasted the leftover bones and peeled the vegetables. She watched the stock carefully as she reduced it to a thickened consommé. She boiled the tomatoes and strained them and poured her mixture into the pewter fish mold that had been sent from up North with the rest of her belongings. She then placed it in the icebox to set and went to get ready.

Nick had thrown her ripped dress in the laundry hamper and was fastening her pearl earrings when she heard the Buick cough and spit its way up to the house. She applied a bit of powder and checked her appearance. A Good Lieutenant's Wife looked back at her. Hair neat and in place, a yellow cotton sweater covering her shoulders and buttoned over her bosom. A little lipstick and no rouge. She walked

44

out into the kitchen and almost bumped right into Hughes. They both hopped back a bit, startled.

"Hello," Nick said, glancing only briefly at him, before fixing her gaze to the floor.

"Hello," Hughes said quietly. "I'm going to shower and change. We don't want to be late."

"I made the aspic," Nick said. "And I'm wearing shoes this time." She looked at him and saw his expression soften. "I think it may be the most glorious aspic I've ever made."

"Thank you," he said.

They regarded each other for a moment, then Hughes turned toward the bedroom and Nick's heart sank. She heard the shower start and she tiptoed toward the sound. The bathroom door was slightly ajar, to let the steam out. Through the opening she watched her husband stretch and soap himself, rub shampoo into his blond hair. He really was golden all over, she thought, realizing how long it had been since she'd seen him naked in daylight. She was so close to him and yet he didn't even sense her presence. Nick wanted to cry. Instead, she went back into the kitchen to see if the aspic had gelled.

She pulled it gently out of the icebox, so as not to break its continuity, and marveled at its perfect color, like a bright tomato swimming pool. She carefully pressed her finger to the top to check the firmness. It pushed back and Nick let out a sigh of satisfaction. She chose a platter and slowly turned the mold over, lifting it away to see the perfect fish-shaped gelatin gleaming and winking back at her. She selected her favorite cloth, with the little Dutch boys printed on it, and covered the platter. She picked it up gingerly, and began heading out to the car.

Nick wasn't sure if she'd caught her heel or the dish had just slipped from her grasp, but, before she could react, it was tumbling, the aspic bouncing and breaking into tiny ragged cubes across the green and white linoleum floor. A piece of it squished between her toes. Nick stared at her foot, her smudged yellow patent-leather sandals, the red splotches melting in the warm air. Her legs gave out underneath her and she dropped to the floor. Then she hung her head in her lap and cried, her sobs breaking out of her violently, like painful hiccups.

Hughes came rushing out of the bedroom, his white shirt unbuttoned and his hair damp from the shower. Nick looked up. Rasping and shivering, she spread her hand out, gesturing at the mess around her.

"It's ruined," she cried. "It's ruined and I don't know how it happened. I wasn't careful enough."

"Hush," Hughes said, crouching down and wrapping his arms around her. He pressed his face into her hair. "Darling, it doesn't matter. We'll fix it. Don't cry, we'll fix it."

He put his hands around her waist and pulled her up, leading her to the kitchen table.

"Sit down, sweetheart. I'll take care of it." He picked up a bowl and carefully gathered up every piece that hadn't yet melted. "It's perfect. Look, Nicky."

"Oh god," Nick said, peering into the bowl at the broken and glittering remains of gelatin. "It's disgusting."

"No, it's the most beautiful aspic in the world. Every man is going to be green with envy that I have such a creative wife," Hughes said, smiling at her. "Darling, please. It's going to be all right."

"It's not all right, Hughes. It's really, really not all right," Nick said, pressing her face into her hand.

"It will be all right," he said, prying her hand away and turning her chin to face him. "I'm sorry. Our life is lovely.

You're lovely and I'm going to be a better husband to you. I'm going to take care of you, darling, I promise."

"Hughes," Nick said. "Hughes, please, I want to go home."

"I'm going to take you home, Nick," he said. "And everything will be all right."

1947: February

Nick sat smoking in the kitchen, half-listening to a program about birds and rubbing her drum of a belly. She looked out over the backyard, which, like her stomach, was hard and asleep. Here and there, a sparrow picked hopefully at the unyielding ground. After a commercial for Bromo Seltzer, the announcer broke back in.

We're back with Miss Kay Thompson reading from Winfrid Alden Stearns's seminal manual New England Bird Life, *which has been delighting bird lovers for over sixty years.*

A woman's voice, husky with a New England twang, drifted up through the radio.

The whippoorwill is a bird belonging to a family peculiar in many important respects, and of such singular habits that superstitions no less dismal than ridiculous have attached to its mysterious manners. But the whippoorwill has a number of amiable and admirable traits, among which are its parental affection and its conjugal fidelity.

Nick checked the meringues baking in the oven. Hughes had become positively obsessed with meringue, following a recent work luncheon at a French restaurant. So strange, the desires he picked up when he was away from her. It never ceased to amaze her to find out that he suddenly loved this or that, when only that same morning he had left the house a fairly well-known quantity. But, despite these small, surprise passions, she did feel she knew him better. Or maybe she knew their marriage better; she was beginning to learn that the two weren't the same thing. Such an ugly, mediocre word, compromise, Nick thought. But things had become smoother, like a creaky door whose hinges had finally gotten greased. And Nick had paid for that with compromise.

When they came home to Cambridge, he had bought her this house. Nick had thought that perhaps they could go live at Tiger House, if only for a little while, to wash away the hot, stale Florida air. But Hughes had immediately put his foot down.

"I can't work there, Nicky," he told her over dinner in their temporary apartment on Huron Avenue. "And we're not asking my parents for money."

Hughes had gotten a job as an associate lawyer at Warner & Stackpole, where his father worked. And then in February, he had found the house. "Built by the first woman architect to graduate from MIT," he told her. She knew this was supposed to be an incentive for her to love it. She could see herself through his eyes: difficult, combative, someone who would have something in common with this disruptive female pioneer, who was probably a lesbian anyway.

The way he had taken her through the rooms—touched the door frames and spread his arms wide in the kitchen to show her where the counter would be—she had known he was buying a place to put her in. A place for her to be perfect in, where all her strangeness would be sucked out of her, or at least hidden. She had been sick with the thought of it.

As she unpacked their boxes, dusted off wedding silver, hung his shirts, she imagined herself running away to Europe, renting an apartment on the Champs-Élysées or the Via Condotti, drinking small dark coffees and dancing in the cafes until dawn. But aside from buying a very expensive set of French lingerie, she made no move to get away, except in her head. If she knew he was trapping her, she also knew that she loved him, or rather she had him under her skin, like a fever. Wherever she went, she would be sick with him. She wasn't sure how it had happened, but she had stopped fighting it. And just like that, as if her capitulation had broken the dam, he had begun to see her, to really see her.

"You're amazing," he said one day, when he came home to find the table set with the good linen and silver, and Nick patting down a round, rosy side of beef she had gotten cheap from the butcher.

Another night, he touched her knee under the table, after she had prepared an impeccable dinner of cold cucumber soup, lamb chops and roast potatoes, and floating islands for a partner at the law firm he wanted to impress.

"You're a lucky man to have a wife that can really cook," the partner had said. "A man like that can go far."

Hughes had taken her dancing at the Spring Ball in Boston, and pressed himself against her, his arm wrapped tight around her waist.

"I could get drunk just smelling you," he whispered in her ear. "You always smell like home."

When he made love to her, he held her face in his hands and watched her.

"Tell me you're happy," he said once. "I want to know I've made you happy."

So the little things were done, done perfectly. And in between, she read her books and listened to her music and thought up plans for them. And she thought that maybe when he felt that everything was good and safe, maybe he would wake up and want to be free again, with her.

Then there was the talk of a baby.

"I don't want one, Hughes," she told him one night at dinner, over the remains of a peppered pork chop. "Not now, at least."

"Everybody wants a baby," he said.

"That's a ridiculous thing to say." She brushed some scattered pepper off the white tablecloth. "And anyway, we're not like everyone else," she added quietly.

"Nick," he said. "I know this isn't how you imagined things. It's not how I thought things would be, either. But then there was the war."

"The war, the war. I'm sick of it." She stood to start clearing the plates. "That can't be the excuse for everything."

Hughes caught her wrist.

"I'm serious, Nick. I really want a family."

"Well, I've got some news for you, Hughes Derringer," Nick said, wrenching away from his grasp. "I'm serious, too."

"I want us to live our lives. Just live them." He was searching her face. "Can't you understand that?"

"Don't talk to me as if I were a child."

"Then don't act like one."

His tone had changed from passionate to chilly in an instant, and a silence—a dangerous one, Nick knew from experience—lay between them.

"I'm not trying to make you angry," he said finally. "I want a life . . . Maybe not exactly like everyone else's, but not complicated, either."

"A baby," she said, "is going to be complicated."

"I want to make something, something good and real."

"We already have something good and real. Why can't you see that?" She looked at his face; it already looked weary. She tried to get a grip on the heat rushing through her, the feeling of desperation causing her legs to shake.

"It's just . . ." She sat down and put her hand over his. "Oh, Hughes, we'll have to be so careful with a child. Our life, it'll be . . . careful."

"Not careful," he said. "Deliberate."

Nick thought about him, the way he always returned his cuff links to their right box, instead of putting them in the *vide-poche* on his bureau, or the way he never lost the covers for his Swiss Army knives, the way most people did the minute they got them home. All the little things she had always found so moving. Hughes wanted to be careful, he took pleasure in it. He wanted life just the right temperature, not too hot, not too cold. But Nick wasn't sure she could survive all this smoothing down.

"I don't know, Hughes," she said finally. "We're still young. We could do things before we have a baby." Yet even as she said it, she felt the weight of the house he had bought her and knew it might already be too late.

"What things? Travel? I've been abroad, the world's no better out there than it is here. And anyway, we can always travel as a family."

Nick thought about Europe, about wrought-iron balconies and large windows and the feel of a foreign language on her lips.

"I don't know if I can be that careful, deliberate, whatever you want to call it," she said.

*

Nick pulled the meringues out of the oven and set them to cool. She had to extend her arms at full length to place them on the rack, taking care not to knock her large belly against the counter. She stood back and admired her handiwork; they were large snowy-looking things, peaking and dropping along the ridges, lovely, it was true, but she preferred macaroons. Grittier with their bits of coconut.

After their conversation about the baby, Hughes hadn't brought it up again. But when Nick found out that same month that Helena was pregnant, he had paid for her train ticket from Los Angeles.

"It will be nice for you two to see each other again," he told Nick. "Anyway, I'm not so sure about that Avery fellow."

"I couldn't agree more," Nick said.

Nick knew Hughes was thinking that seeing Helena happy in her pregnancy might change her mind about a baby, but she didn't care. She hadn't seen her cousin in the seven months since they had packed up and left the house on Elm Street, and she missed her. She also felt a sense of unease about her; Helena seemed so bowed and tired every time she talked about Avery and his plans for the two of them.

Helena arrived in Cambridge in May, just when the lily-of-the-valley was spreading across the yard in a blanket of glossy dark green and delicate white. Nick picked a small bouquet to take when she met her train at South Station.

"Helena, my word. You don't look the littlest bit pregnant," Nick said, laughing and hugging her close when she descended onto the platform.

"Really? I feel huge." Helena was wearing a sky-blue suit, made from some lightweight wool, or one of the man-made blends that were all the rage.

"You look positively glamorous. Don't tell me you're in the pictures now, too."

"Dear Nick," Helena said, smiling. "You haven't changed a bit. Still lying through your teeth every chance you get."

Nick handed the porter a quarter from her red leather purse and took her cousin by the hand. "Hughes has even given us taxi money, so we'll be traveling in style."

"Oh, it is good to be home," Helena said. "You don't know how happy I am."

"Well, I know how happy I am." Nick waved at an idling cab. "I've almost been completely transformed into the perfect housewife. I'll need you to examine my head later. Come on, let's get home. Lunch and wine await."

When they arrived at the house, Helena went to freshen up in the guest room, while Nick set the small round table in the garden room and began fixing a tuna salad. When she came back down, Helena had removed her little blue hat and her blond curls brushed her shoulders. Her face looked rosy and plump, like an advertisement for Christmas.

"Well, pregnancy does agree with you, I'll say that for it," Nick said. "What is it, three months, now?"

"Four," Helena said, seating herself at the green Formica counter. "Or at least that's what the doctor told me. I'm not sure I trust him, though. I think he may be a bit of a quack." She sighed. "But Avery says that all the good actresses go to him, so . . ."

"The only thing good actresses do is have abortions,"

Nick said. "You really should come back here and have it. You could see Dr. Monty."

"I thought Dr. Monty was dead," Helena said, laughing.

"No, sir. Alive and kicking and still pinching the nurse's bottom." Nick looked at her cousin, then turned back to arranging the lettuce on the plates. "Hughes wants one."

"A nurse to pinch?"

"I wish it was just that. No, a baby."

Helena smiled. "It's not a death sentence, you know. It's actually quite nice."

"So they tell me. Oh, Helena, can you see me elbow-deep in dirty diapers? He's already got me chained to the stove. What more does he want?"

"Oh, stop pretending you don't love him." Helena spread her arms out around the kitchen. "All this."

"Of course I love him," Nick said. "I just thought it would be a little more exciting."

"Marriage is a haven," Helena said quietly. "You'll never be alone again."

"Not marriage," Nick said. "Life." She looked out the window and then turned quickly back to her cousin. "I mean, think about Elm Street. We could do exactly as we pleased and no one expected anything of us. I even miss those horrible ration books. I wish it could be like that now, for me and Hughes. Not all stuffy and respectable. Sometimes I want to rip my clothes off and go running down the street stark naked and screaming my head off. Just for a goddamn change of pace."

"That was the war, not real life," Helena said. "And it wasn't all good."

Nick sighed, remembering Fen. "You're right. I'm being

a twit." She forced a smile onto her face. "Enough of this. Darling, why don't you pour the wine. It's right next to you on that funny counter Hughes designed."

"He really has bought you a lovely house," Helena said, filling the two small jelly glasses Nick had rescued from their apartment.

"Yes, a lovely house for a good wife," Nick said, bringing the knife down on a stalk of celery. "I shouldn't say that, it's nasty. But damn men, anyway."

"Nick, you really are impossible. You want too much. It's like flying in the face of God, as Mother used to say."

"And Avery?" Nick asked, suddenly piqued with Helena's stoicism. "Is he everything you want? Is god so damn pleased with you both?"

"We're living in a rented house," Helena said, thoughtfully. "I would like to have one of my own. Then again, it is a lovely little bungalow, with a spare room for when the baby comes."

"You can be so dense sometimes, darling," Nick said, putting the knife down on the cutting board. "I want to know about your husband, not your living arrangements."

"Oh." Helena seemed to withdraw slightly from Nick's gaze. "Well, I don't know. The same as usual, I guess."

"Lord, Helena, you're slower than molasses in January." Nick felt like hitting her on the head with the celery stalk. "What is the same as usual?"

"Nick, he's not like other men, you know. I mean, he's an artist, really."

"What on earth are you talking about? Avery isn't an artist, he sells insurance, for god's sakes."

"Yes, to earn his living. But his real passion is films," Helena said, peering into her glass like she was looking for something. "Actually, he's very meticulous about it. You see, he has this collection."

Nick walked over and sat down next to her cousin. "A collection."

"Yes, well actually, you see he had this friend, this actress, and she was very good and very talented and very beautiful. And they were going to make films together, she was going to be the star and he was going to raise the money, but then, well, then someone killed her and he was just absolutely heartbroken. It changed everything for him."

"I see." And Nick did think she was beginning to see just what Avery Lewis was all about. "That all sounds very dramatic."

"Well, yes," Helena said. "And he didn't feel like he could go on. And then he met me and he realized that he didn't have to do it alone. You see, he's dedicated himself to showing the world the talent that she was. So, he's started this collection. Of her."

Nick could barely believe what she was hearing; Helena could be guileless at times, but she wasn't a complete idiot. "So, how is he doing with all that? Showing the world what a talent his ex-mistress was, I mean?"

"I knew you wouldn't understand," Helena said, jerking her chin. "Most people don't. It's a work of art, someone's whole life. Like if I collected everything about you in order to capture your essence. And he's going to make a film. That's what Avery is doing."

"Essence, my foot." Nick tried to make eye contact with her cousin, but she wouldn't look at her. "Honestly, Helena." She shook her head in wonderment. "I knew something hinky was going on out there, but I didn't realize he had you convinced it was art."

"You're being unfair," Helena said. "He may be unusual, but what's wrong with that? He loves me and, Nick, he understands me. I owe him my support."

"Your financial support, you mean." Nick saw her cousin's face color, and she felt her passion receding. She put her hand on Helena's shoulder, saying gently, "I'm sorry. I don't mean to be critical. But really, darling. This is cracked, you can see that, can't you?"

"Nick, he's my husband. And my second at that. I don't plan to get a divorce and move on to number three."

Nick pulled Helena to her and put her cheek against her soft hair. "We could ask someone at Hughes's law firm."

"I'm having a baby."

Nick drew away and looked at her for a moment, and then slowly nodded her head. "Right. Of course, you are."

The whippoorwill may be in the brush where it was hidden during the hours of light, or it may have stolen close to the house. It may even drop unperceived on the house-top, and cry out with sudden vehemence in the middle of the night, sending a shiver down the spine of those susceptible to ominous impressions or superstition.

Nick felt the baby kick, like a very small flash of lightning running down her belly. She began sorting through the mail. In one pile, she put the bills for Hughes to look at when he returned from work. In another, she put their social correspondence, which she would have to reply to tomorrow, after the ironing.

"Oh, god, life is boring," she said to the empty kitchen.

Nick knew that Hughes wanted a girl, but a boy wouldn't have to deal with all of life's mundane details. He would call the shots, do whatever he pleased. He would be strong and determined and independent, without having to apologize or bake cookies he didn't even want to eat.

She stopped. "For crying out loud, cheer up," she told herself. She found these black moods coming over her more and more frequently these days. Dr. Monty had said it was normal to feel off during pregnancy.

"Many women feel a bit down during this time," he said, his hand lingering a little too long on her knee as they sat in his little office off Brattle Street. "It's very normal, Mrs. Derringer. It's a big change for any woman, but a welcome one."

Last week he had recommended she start reading more enlivening books, eyeing Kant's *Observations on the Feeling of the Beautiful and Sublime* suspiciously. "Many of my patients have found pattern-making very uplifting. Industry, that's what I recommend," he said, assurance leaking out of his voice.

And Nick had gone and bought a book of patterns, for day dresses. It was sitting upstairs in her dressing room, still wrapped in its brown paper.

She put a finger to the meringues. They had cooled. She brought over the black tin lined with wax paper and gently started placing them in it, taking care not to break their peaks. She wondered what Helena was doing at that moment, how she was dealing with life with a baby. Ed was four months old now, and Nick kept telling herself that her cousin must be awfully busy with her son. But she couldn't help feeling that during their brief chats on the telephone, Helena sounded increasingly far away, like she was underwater.

Each time, it made Nick a little sorry, although not entirely, for the way they had parted at the end of Helena's visit. After their first conversation about Avery, they had stuck to happier subjects. But the night before Helena went back to Los Angeles, Nick couldn't help bringing him up one last time.

"You don't have to go back to him, you know," Nick said. Hughes had gone to bed and they were finishing off what had already been a little too much wine.

"I want to go back to him," Helena said, not looking at her.

"You don't owe him anything. I know you think you do, but you have a right to be happy, too."

"I don't think you're really one to be dispensing marital advice."

It was the first time in their lives that Nick felt something akin to contempt in Helena's voice, and it took her aback.

"I just want you to be happy." She felt her own temper rise.

"You don't know anything about it." Helena looked directly at her. "Nothing makes you happy except what you don't have. You've never known how to do anything but to take and take and then ask for more. You have everything and you act like it's nothing. So how would you know what makes me or anyone else happy?"

Nick was stunned. "I guess I should be glad that we're finally telling the truth," she said, tasting metal in her mouth. "Since we're not mincing words, your neediness is what makes you so goddamn self-centered that you can't see past your sorry little world. I'm supposed to be happy just because I have more than you? For heaven's sakes, listen to yourself."

"No, you listen to yourself," Helena said, rising. "I'm going to bed."

They had made their apologies in the morning, and kissed warmly at South Station, but the episode had left Nick wondering how well she did know her cousin's heart.

The birds are in full cry during the breeding season, after which the cry is seldom, if ever, heard. This being the principal indication of the whippoorwill's presence, it is therefore difficult to say at what precise time they do depart, so silently and furtively do they slip from our midst.

Nick slid her mother's silver letter opener under the fold of the first letter in her pile. There was no return address and her hand shook as she tried to pull the card out. She knew it would just be an invitation to a cocktail party thrown by the wife of one of Hughes's colleagues, or a note from a neighbor on the Island reporting on her hydrangea, but she felt her mouth go dry, nonetheless. Ever since The Letter, as she thought of it, she found this dread creeping up on her, when confronted by an unknown sender.

"Don't be a silly goose," she told herself firmly, but felt unconvinced.

She had to put the card down and stare out the window for a minute before she could read it.

> *Nicky Dear,*
> *Tea on Wednesday?*
> *4 p.m.*
> *Love, Birdie*

Nick laughed with relief. Just tea, just Birdie. It was fine. She felt elated, high. Hughes would be home soon, she had baked his favorite cookies and they were having a baby. It was fine. Everything was just fine.

The Letter had arrived on a Tuesday five months ago, during an unseasonably cold September. She had been on the fence about whether to take the pot-roast out of the freezer or make a run to the butcher for lamb chops before Hughes got home, erring on the side of the pot-roast, because it meant she would have time to go buy some new gloves in Harvard Square instead.

She thought, I'll just open the mail first, and then decide. It was the third letter in her pile. It was a bulky brown envelope, almost a parcel. It was addressed to Hughes, but it was hand-written instead of typed, so she knew it wasn't a bill. Also, it had been forwarded on from the base in Green Cove Springs, and she was afraid that it might be a letter from Charlie Wells, perhaps an act of revenge for her behavior after their lunch together.

The minute her hand felt the expensive correspondence paper inside, however, she knew it couldn't be from Charlie. The first thing she noticed was the initials at the top, ELB. Frowning, Nick scanned down the card to the slanted, elegant script.

> *I know I said I wouldn't write.*
> *The world's not on fire anymore. But I still love you.*
> *I wanted you to know that, wherever you are.*
> *Besides, everyone deserves to be happy.*

Nick reached her hand back into the envelope and pulled out a silver skeleton key attached to a brass plate that read: Claridge's Room 201.

The key was heavy and the plate so smooth. Nick rubbed her thumb over the shiny brass, leaving a greasy smudge.

She looked at her thumb and it suddenly seemed fat and dull and dirty. *Common hands*, as her mother had told her as she massaged butter into her fingers at night, *that's what every lady must avoid*.

Nick picked up the card and read it again, deciphering every line, measuring it, trying to decide which word meant something, and which had just been pressed into service to connect those that carried weight.

There were few that weren't significant, she decided. "That" and "to be" were the only spares, and even they couldn't be done without. *Besides, everyone deserves to be happy*.

"Oh, god," she said, as the full weight of the words, the stationery, the heavy key, hit her. "Oh, god."

She put her head down on the counter and tried to cry, but nothing came out. She watched her breath as it steamed up the Formica before vanishing again.

After a while, she sat up and straightened her back. She passed her hand over The Letter again. Leaving the key on the counter, she picked up the thick, creamy card and walked into the bar in the garden room, where she mixed herself a martini and upended it into her mouth.

Then she mixed another. After she had drunk the second one, she looked at the card again. *The world's not on fire anymore. But I still love you*. She mixed herself a third, this time letting three olives drop into the glass. Then, with The Letter in one hand, and the martini in the other, Nick walked into the living room, where the fire she had lit earlier that afternoon was now smoldering and spitting.

She sat down on the embroidered low bench in front of the fireplace and took one last look.

I know I said I wouldn't write.

Then she threw The Letter on top of the sagging logs, where she watched it curl and slowly, slowly turn to ash.

She stayed there, twirling the stem of her glass between her fingers, feeling hypnotized by the fire. Then she rose and walked slowly into the library. Taking out her address book, Nick placed a long-distance telephone call to Helena.

As she waited for the operator to connect her, she pulled a cigarette out of the box on the telephone table. Lighting it, she stared out the small bay window that made the library her favorite room in the house. The low branches of the ash tree outside the warm room scratched at the windowpane.

The operator told her to hold for her connection.

Nick sipped what was left of her martini.

"Pot-roast," she said to herself drunkenly.

By the time Helena's voice came down the line, Nick felt numb.

"Nick?" Helena's voice sounded scratchy.

"Oh," she said, suddenly surprised to be talking to her cousin.

"Is that you?"

"Yes, yes, it's me." Nick found words difficult. *But I still love you*.

"How are you? Is everything all right?"

"No, it's not all right," Nick said. "I . . . I was just suddenly missing everything. Do you remember our little house on Elm Street. And how hot it was the first summer?"

"Yes," Helena sounded hesitant. "Nick, what's wrong? Is Hughes all right?"

"Hughes is Hughes," Nick said. "No, I just was sad for our life before. That's all. I would give anything to be back in that house right now, washing out our stockings in that horrible little bathroom. Do you remember when my last pair just disintegrated, on the hanger over the tub? And we came back and found only a tiny pile of brown dust? And we had a little funeral in the yard?"

"Yes, I remember. And we played the 'Moonlight Sonata' for them."

"That's right, that's right," Nick said, running her hand through her hair. "I'd forgotten what we'd played."

"That was it," Helena said. "And then I drew a line on your leg with your eyebrow pencil, but it came out pretty wobbly."

"Yes, and I had a terrible time getting it off." Nick lit another cigarette. Wind blew against the windowpane.

"Darling, have you been drinking?"

"Yes, a martini, or three." Nick laughed, but it sounded more like a fork on a tin cup. "I'm sorry, darling, I just wanted to talk to you, talk about something from before."

"Are you sure you're all right?"

"Yes, yes. I have to go now. Goodbye, Helena."

"Goodbye, Nick. Write to me soon."

Nick put the receiver down. "Goodbye," she said to the quiet room and the wind whistling past the ash tree.

Nick went to bed early that night, complaining of a headache and crying herself to sleep while Hughes ate soup in the kitchen by himself. But the next night, when he arrived home, she was prepared.

She had put on her red shantung dress, the one she had worn to the 21 Club during the war, and had her hair set in Harvard Square. She prepared steaks and mashed potatoes and peppered green beans. She fixed vodka martinis and the pitcher was sweating on the marble top of the bar when her husband came through the door.

She met him in the front hall and took his briefcase out of his hand.

"Feeling better?" he asked, kissing her forehead.

"Much," Nick said. "Go into the sitting room. I've prepared cocktails."

Hughes looked at her, saw her hair, her dress. "What's the occasion?"

"A great occasion," Nick said, disappearing through the dining room toward the bar, his briefcase heavy as lead.

Her hand shook as she poured the martinis and she had to swab up the tears of vodka that had dribbled down the glasses. She placed them on a silver tray with olives. Nick stood back and looked at them, marveling at how something could look so clean and be so poisonous at the same time.

Patting down her hair, she picked up the tray and walked carefully through the long garden room, her high heels clacking out a rhythm on the tile floor. When she reached the living room, she saw Hughes sitting in his blue wing chair, looking expectantly at her.

Nick set the tray down gently on the side table next to him. She handed him one glass and took the other for herself.

"Hughes, I've decided . . ." She stopped. "I think we should have a baby. I want a baby."

Hughes put his glass down and stood, taking her in his arms.

"Darling," he whispered into her hair, sending off the acrid odor of hairspray. "It is a great occasion."

"Yes," Nick said.

"I knew you'd want one. I knew you'd change your mind and that you'd want one, too."

And with that, something hard and pure that had been living inside her, a dream that perhaps had begun in the maid's room of her mother's house the day she married, shattered, and dissolved into her hot blood.

DAISY

1959: June

Daisy would always remember that summer as the summer they found the body. It was also the summer she turned twelve and had first been kissed, near the old ice cellar, where they now kept all the rusting bicycles. But that first flutter of skin on skin had paled in comparison to the excitement of death. When they stumbled upon it behind the tennis courts, they weren't even sure what it was at first. Just a large lump covered with a dirty travel blanket, with something sticking out of it that looked like a man-of-war.

It had started out like every other June she could remember. Two days after her birthday, her mother packed up the station wagon and they drove the two hours to the ferry in Woods Hole. They fought about the radio station. Her mother said that the Clovers were all right, because they sounded like real music. But, she told Daisy, she didn't understand why all the music seemed to have lost its poetry. And she hated the word chick. Daisy smirked to herself.

On the boat, her mother bought her a coffee, with lots of milk. Her mother always drank hers without anything in it, bitter. *Young girls must learn to drink coffee, but jangly nerves are unbecoming.* "Just a drop," she told the man in the white cap serving it from the bare steel counter. He gave her mother a queer look, but did as he was instructed, like men always seemed to do.

Daisy often wondered what invisible power her mother

had that made men do that. Daisy did what she was told, too. That was because her mother was a bit crazy and she knew better than to cross her, unless she really wanted to get it. But these men weren't going to get it, not really. And anyways, they were always a bit goofy around her, not like they were afraid, but like what her mother wanted was exactly what they had been waiting their whole lives to accomplish.

Daisy asked her mother about it once. Or rather, she asked her mother if she was pretty, because she had the vague notion that whatever power her mother had was something to do with her looks.

"Being pretty isn't really all that important," her mother said. "Men like it when you have *it*."

She smiled at Daisy when she imparted this piece of information. An inclusive smile, that made Daisy keep quiet. But privately, Daisy wondered who else had *it* and where they might have gotten it from. She thought about the movie stars she liked, but her mother didn't really look like Audrey Hepburn or Natalie Wood, she wasn't even pretty, exactly, so maybe that wasn't really *it*. But then Daisy didn't look like her mother, either. She was blond and blue-eyed, like her father.

For her twelfth birthday, her mother had taken her to the Nickelodeon in Harvard Square to see *Gone With the Wind*. When the beautiful Vivien Leigh, green eyes flashing, told Mammy that she wouldn't eat her breakfast, her mother had leaned over.

"She went mad during this picture," she whispered in her ear. "And you can see it in her eyes. You can see her breaking apart."

Daisy thought she could see it, too. But what she really thought about afterward was that her mother had eyes just like that and she wondered if her mother was really, truly going mad, just like crazy Vivien Leigh. Maybe that was *it*. That would not be so good, she decided.

They arrived at Tiger House in the late afternoon. The car was hot and sticky and the coffee had made Daisy feel hollow. The cedar-shingled house, turned silvery from the constant onslaught of sea storms, sat on a property that spanned the length of two streets, a fact that had always amazed Daisy. It started with a back driveway on North Summer Street that wound between a smattering of other cottages until it opened up at their own back lawn.

The front of the house was dominated by a double-storied, columned porch that looked out across North Water Street. On the other side of that road, a sloping front lawn led down to the small boathouse and rickety dock.

Daisy's great-grandmother had wanted a "bungalow," one of the simple shingled homes the off-Islanders built to summer in. But the necessity of a summer and a winter kitchen, then a conservatory for light, and a few extra bedrooms for weekend parties, had caused the original plans for the house to grow backward until what had been imagined as a boxy cottage overtook almost the entire back plot. It had been named by Daisy's great-grandfather, an admirer of the first President Roosevelt and an avid big-game hunter, with a particular passion for tigers. A large tigerskin rug, head and all, took pride of place in the green sitting room.

Pulling into the driveway and turning off the engine, Daisy's mother let out a big sigh. She was looking across a cluster of dusky tea roses at Aunt Helena's cottage next door. Aunt Helena and Uncle Avery were renting it out this summer, which meant they would all have to stay in the main house.

"She could at least have found some people who don't hang their laundry line in the yard," her mother said, in that voice that meant she was talking to herself. *Rhetorical*, her mother called it. *That means no one wants an editorial*.

Daisy had thought it sounded fun, everyone together; her mother and aunt and Ed. And her father, of course, when he came up on his trips from the city. But her mother didn't. Uncle Avery needed money for his collection, she knew; something to do with the movies, but she wasn't sure what exactly. When she thought of it, Daisy imagined a huge room filled with reels of film under glass. Her mother had been very angry about it all and she had seen her father trying to calm her down. But her mother had said, "God-damn Helena and her goddamn husband," before realizing that Daisy was standing at the door. She had looked at her with those green eyes, not flashing like Vivien Leigh's, but flat and cold, like broad beans. Then she slammed the door shut and Daisy couldn't hear anymore.

Her mother pulled Daisy's little plaid suitcase out of the back of the car and handed it to her.

"Don't forget to unpack those dresses so they don't wrinkle," she said, but Daisy was already racing off, dragging the case through the back door, letting the screen snap behind her.

She was anxious to get upstairs to her room and make sure all the things she had tucked away the summer before were still there. Her comic-book collection, the pink, striped shell she had found on the beach, and the special shampoo she had begged her father to buy her, So Glamorous! For Soft, Lustrous Hair.

She ran down the long hallway that led from the back of

the house to the front, catching her case on the worn runner every few steps. Just before the front door, the house opened up, with two large sitting rooms, one green and one blue, on either side. Their large screened-in windows looked out onto the front porch, and the harbor beyond.

As she crossed to the wide staircase, she caught a glimpse of Aunt Helena sitting in a chintz armchair in the blue room, wearing a soft, distracted expression on her pale face. Daisy had almost forgotten that her aunt and cousin had already arrived. She wondered where Ed might be lurking.

"Hi, Aunt Helena," she called over her shoulder, as she stomped up the stairs.

"Hello, dear one," her aunt called back. "Ed? Daisy and Aunt Nick are here, darling."

Daisy huffed into her beloved bedroom, with the twin brass beds and the pink rosette wallpaper she had been allowed to pick out herself. She threw her suitcase on the extra bed and flew to the window. Pushing up the sash and pressing her nose against the screen, she breathed in the air, heavy with ocean, but sweet, too, with the scent of the albizia tree flowering just outside. She fingered the gauzy, ruffled curtains. Then she went to her secret hiding place.

In order to keep nosy-parkers such as her mother or her cousin out of her business, Daisy kept her treasures at the bottom of an old bureau that, considered too bulky for everyday use, had been abandoned in the back of her closet. She pushed back the decoys, an old beach blanket and the enormous stuffed unicorn her father had gotten for her at the West Tisbury fair three summers before. She had been in love with unicorns that summer, but she had been unable to knock down the four bottles to win it. She had spent all her allowance trying, and when she had none left, her father had taken pity on her and handed the man two dollars for it. She had slept with it every night, admiring its golden horn and stroking its flowing mane. But the next year, she had stuffed it in the bureau, suddenly embarrassed by the cheap plastic eyes that stared dumbly at nothing.

Underneath it were the ten *Archie* comics; the matching Silver City Pink nail polish and lipstick she had bought at the five and dime on Main Street and snuck into the house under her blouse; six nickels she had earned sweeping the walk the summer before; a pair of oxidizing copper clip-ons, stolen from her mother's jewelry box; and the picture of her parents on their wedding day. After taking stock of all this, she put the blanket and the unicorn back in their place and shut the drawer. As she was emerging from the closet, she saw Ed standing there, staring.

"Hello," Ed said.

"Ed," Daisy said, a little breathless. "I was just looking at my unicorn."

"It's all right. I know that's your hiding place." Ed looked at her in that strange, impassive way he had that made Daisy feel as if he were looking right through her.

"What are you doing in my room? Sneaking around as usual, I suppose." She pushed her hip out and tried to flatten her eyes, the way her mother did.

"I wasn't sneaking," Ed said. "I came to say hello."

"If you weren't sneaking, then how would you know about my hiding place?"

"I know everything about this house," Ed said, picking some imaginary dirt out from under his thumb nail.

"Oh, aren't you just cool as a cucumber," Daisy said, and stamped her foot on the braided rug. "You don't know everything, Ed Lewis. I bet you don't know even where my secret strongbox is." She immediately regretted having said anything about the strongbox.

"It's in the trapdoor in front of the wine cellar," Ed said, not looking up from his nail. "Actually, you're not the only one who has secret hiding places in this house."

"And what is that supposed to mean?"

Ed just arched one eyebrow.

Daisy was infuriated. "You really are an imbecile. You'd better stop poking around my stuff, Ed Lewis. I mean it. If you don't, I won't pick you as my doubles partner for the round-robin."

The threat was a real one, Daisy knew, and it had the desired effect of silencing her cousin. But she found she couldn't stay mad at him for long. She was secretly glad to see him, even if he was irritating.

"Anyway," Daisy said, shifting her weight. "Let's go down to the Quarterdeck and see who's around. I want to check my bike."

"I'd rather walk," Ed said. "You can't really look at any-thing when you're on the bike."

"We're not ten anymore. We can't just walk everywhere."

Ed was silent.

"All right, well . . . fine then," Daisy couldn't think of any more threats. "But just get out. I'm going to change."

When she heard Ed heading down the stairs, Daisy yanked off the sundress and sweater her mother had laid out for her that morning and pulled on her green checked shorts and a white cotton blouse. She slipped into her boat shoes, and looked at herself in the mirror. Her mother made her keep her hair in a bob—*long hair is common*—but Daisy really wanted to grow it so she could have a ponytail that swung around her shoulders.

Her legs were still a bit too pale for the shorts and her blond hair was curling around her face with sweat.

Only horses sweat. Men perspire and women glow.

She knew her mother disapproved of the shorts, but Daisy thought they made her seem older. She looked like a baby anyway, just like the Gerber baby, in fact, with its curly blond hair and saucer eyes, so she needed all the help she could get.

"Hell's bells," Daisy whispered to her reflection. The minute she had heard Scarlett O'Hara say it, she knew that expression was for her. It made her feel grown-up. A signature expression, one that gave her the air of an impatient plantation belle.

On her way downstairs, Daisy could hear her mother's jazz coming from the record player; her mother's, and no one else was allowed to touch it. Daisy had a Chuck Berry record she had bought at the five and dime, but it sat unopened in her room.

She found Ed in the blue sitting room, staring out onto the front porch, where her mother sat with Aunt Helena. He turned and put a finger up to his lips.

"Helena, I don't understand why you let him do it to you, I really don't," her mother was saying, pushing a black lock away from her face.

"Avery's just been working so hard," Aunt Helena said, her voice almost a whisper. "I don't mind. I . . ." She stopped, then said: "Things have been, well, a little off lately. There was an incident before we came with Bill Fox, you know, the producer. It was my fault, really."

Daisy hoped to hear more about the incident, but her mother didn't seem to care.

"He's a fool, your husband," she said. Her mother didn't bother to whisper. "He's a goddamn fool and he was lucky to get you in the first place."

Daisy looked at Ed. His expression was neutral, but his

eyes had darkened, ever so slightly, like they did when he was concentrating on something.

"Oh, I don't know," Aunt Helena said, and although Daisy could only see the back of her head, she knew her aunt was about to cry.

"Helena, this has been going on for years."

Daisy tugged at Ed's arm. "Let's go," she whispered.

Abruptly, her mother turned her head, peering in toward the window where they stood eavesdropping.

"Are you two off somewhere?" she asked, as if it were the most natural thing that they should be listening.

"We're going to the Quarterdeck," Daisy said quickly, going to the front door and walking out to the porch.

Ed followed slowly behind her.

"That's fine. Why don't you take fifty cents from my purse and buy yourselves some clams."

When neither of them moved, she added, "It's in the kitchen," and gave Daisy a look.

Aunt Helena kept her face turned away from them. She had a glass of Scotch in her hand. As long as Daisy could remember, her aunt had had a glass of Scotch in her hand. When Daisy smelled it from the decanters on her father's bar, or on his breath when he kissed her goodnight, a picture of Aunt Helena, blond and soft, would rise up in her mind. Normally, her father drank gin and tonics. Daisy knew because he let her make them for him sometimes. She loved the bar, with its collection of swizzlers, a rainbow of different-colored glass. The beautiful decanters, her grandmother's crystal, each with a silver plaque that had the name of the alcohol engraved in swirling script. Her father had taught her to put the gin in first, then the ice. *Finish it off with tonic water from the glass seltzer bottle, and squeeze a quarter of lime over the top and let it drop in.*

Daisy loved to watch the tonic fizz the second time when the lime hit it.

"Come on," Daisy said to Ed.

"Go on, Ed," her mother said. "Keep Daisy company. Your mother and I want to catch up a bit."

Without a word, Ed turned and went back into the house. Daisy followed him down the hall into the summer kitchen, which was a big, bright affair, with a big white oven that Daisy wasn't allowed to touch. It was lighter than the poky winter kitchen, which had long since been converted into a linen closet. Across the hall from the kitchen was a conservatory that looked out over the driveway and back lawn, bordered by her dead grandmother's blue hydrangeas. (Her mother said that the blue was rare and came from the way her grandmother had mulched them with coffee grounds.)

"I can't believe she didn't say anything about my shorts," Daisy said, pulling out her mother's wallet.

"Who cares about your shorts," Ed said.

"Oh, well," Daisy said uncomfortably. She started humming "Rockin' Robin." "You ready?"

Ed just looked at her. His eyes reminded Daisy of the silver skin of the small fish in the bait shop.

"Oh," she said. She scuffed her shoes against the baseboard of the counter. "I'm sure it's not that bad. People talk like that all the time."

"Who talks like that all the time?"

"Well, in the movies, anyway." She looked at Ed's eyes and wondered if he, too, were mad. "Anyway, the point is it's probably just talk."

People will talk. Ladies don't listen.

"You don't know anything," Ed said. "Not about Hollywood, anyway. Things are different there."

"Well, look, let's not think about it. Let's go, and we can skip the bikes and walk slowly all the way there, if you want."

At the Quarterdeck, kids were milling about, laughing and eating hot dogs wrapped in wax paper and fried clams from striped boxes, as the day unwound. It was just a shack, with a roof over the kitchen and a counter for ordering, but you could always find someone there you knew. Dozens of bikes were leaning against the clapboard sides of the shack and, on the stone wall across the road, groups sat chatting and eyeing each other up.

"I'll get the clams," Daisy said, the quarters hot in her palm. "You go find a spot."

Daisy gave the boy with acne her order, then put her back to the counter to get a better view of who was around. Looking at Ed amidst the other groups of kids, she felt a small pinch in her stomach. It wasn't that he was a square, really. In fact, lots of kids thought he was mysterious, even cool, coming from Hollywood, with his pressed dungarees and Ray-Bans. It was just that he was so different; the way he looked at people, the same way her mother looked at melons in the supermarket. Most people didn't even notice it. The ones who did stayed away from him. It didn't scare Daisy, it just made her feel sad and a bit restless.

When her order came up, she walked over to where Ed was standing and perched herself beside him on the wall. She picked out a fat clam and slipped it into her mouth, feeling the greasy batter shatter against its soft belly. Daisy could smell the fishing boats docked behind the Quarterdeck and she felt the breeze riffle her hair, making the down on the back of her neck rise up. Summer seemed to arrive at that moment, with its mysterious mixture of salt, cold flesh, and fuel.

She saw a tall boy, sandy-haired and slim, talking to Peaches Montgomery.

"Who's that guy?" Daisy asked, nudging Ed. The boy's spiky hair reminded Daisy of sea grass and she imagined him smelling like the inside of her riding hat: sweet, salty, and like leather.

"Tyler Pierce," Ed said. "He's fourteen, if you were wondering. Which I imagine you were."

"How do you know him?" Daisy said, ignoring the dig.

"I ran into Peaches when I was walking around town this afternoon, before you got here."

"Yes, and?"

"She was talking about him," Ed said.

Daisy looked at Ed, but he didn't continue. Instead, he carefully picked a clam out of the box and began inspecting it.

"Hell's bells, Ed. You're slower than molasses in January. What did she say?"

"I wasn't really listening," Ed said, crumbling the batter off the clam into his palm. "She knows him from home, I guess. And his family just bought a house on South Summer."

Watching Ed dig his nail into the flesh, Daisy turned the information over in her mind. She stared at the boy a little more and wished she had a ponytail. Peaches had a ponytail, the color of fudge. It swung from shoulder to shoulder when she moved across the tennis court.

Peaches Montgomery was a real waste of space, in Daisy's opinion. Always preening and prancing and mincing about. Her real name was Penelope, but Peaches said she had gotten her nickname because of the texture of her skin. *Like peaches and cream, my father always says.* Daisy didn't believe that for one second. But older boys liked Peaches.

Even the tennis instructors took a shine to her. Peaches had *it*, apparently.

She caught Daisy staring, and narrowed her slanty little eyes. *Almond eyes, my father calls them.* She sauntered over to where they were sitting.

"Hey, Daisy," Peaches said, moving her ponytail from her left to her right shoulder. "Hello, Ed." She threw the greeting in Ed's general direction, without really looking at him.

"Hi, Peaches," Daisy said.

"Did you just arrive?"

"Un-huh," Daisy said.

"I hear you all have to live in your house this summer," Peaches said, still not looking at Ed. "I guess that will be a crowd."

"I guess," Daisy said, viciously stuffing a clam in her mouth. "Are you playing tennis this year?"

"I sure will be," Peaches said. "My father's been training me all winter. You know how he is."

"Right," Daisy said. She hopped off the wall and did her best to throw her bob over her shoulder.

Ed just stared at Peaches. Peaches glanced at him, almost a wince, really, before making her way to the crowd of kids calling out her name.

"Peaches has gotten fat," Daisy said. "I bet I'll beat her at the tournament this year."

"Some men like that," Ed said.

"Who cares?" *Some men like that.* This was the first she'd heard of it. "If she has to drag her fat behind around the tennis court, I'll be able to run circles around her."

"I bet you will beat her," Ed said matter-of-factly.

"Thank you," Daisy said.

The still evening enveloped them as they walked up Simpson's Lane. It had no sidewalks, only the flowering bushes, stretching and bending over the white fences and skimming across the dusty way. It was hushed back there at that time of day, deserted by the well-heeled on their way to the Yacht Club for cocktails, or evening sailors on their way to Cape Pogue with their picnics. Not that the other streets were especially busy, but they seemed part of the real world. Simpson's Lane could have been a country lane leading to nowhere. It was a summer road.

Daisy idly picked a Pink Parfait and began plucking the petals off. Her mind was turning around Peaches and tennis, turning around the sandy-haired boy.

"She doesn't like you, you know," Daisy said looking up at Ed, who was ambling by her side and staring at the lit windows of the passing houses. "Peaches, I mean. You make her shiver." Ed seemed to be in a trance, unhearing.

"What did you two talk about this afternoon, anyway?" Daisy looked at him a little more keenly now. "I mean, she barely talks to any boy that isn't at least fourteen."

"This and that," Ed said softly.

The buzz of the crickets rose up and a foghorn sounded off the harbor.

"You didn't talk to her at all," Daisy said after a moment. Ed kept his gaze on the houses.

"So how did you know about all that stuff?"

Finally, he stopped and slowly turned toward Daisy.

"You were spying on her," Daisy said.

"I wouldn't call it spying," Ed said, his silvery eyes watching her closely. "I'm educating myself."

Daisy awoke sometime in the night. She thought it might have been the moon, echoing too brightly off the harbor. But then she heard the sound of Billie Holiday streaming up the stairs. She crept downstairs in her nightgown and bare feet and saw her mother and Aunt Helena illuminated by candlelight on the front porch. They were wearing only their slips, the silk straps straining against their curved shoulders.

Her mother was leaning in and listening with an intent expression to Aunt Helena's soft voice, a bottle of gin at her feet. Daisy moved closer to the window.

"I don't know," Aunt Helena was saying. "Maybe I'm just the wrong mother. Or I've let him spend too much time with Avery, I don't know. I just feel exhausted, Nick. Truly I do."

"Our children," her mother said softly. "Who knew they'd turn out so differently from us? Or maybe we wanted them to. I look at Daisy, so golden, just like her father. Sometimes, well, it's odd to say, but sometimes I'm hard with her because I feel like a stranger in a house of the good and the golden and the heavenly. Which makes me the devil, I suppose."

"Old Nick," Aunt Helena laughed. "Oh, dear. I wish I had more of that in me. And less of the good and the golden. Although I do think that part of me is disappearing little by little."

"And what's there to replace it?" Her mother poked Helena's shoulder.

"Other men?"

"You wouldn't dare."

"Oh, you think you're the only one, do you?"

Her mother looked at Helena and then took a drink out of her jelly glass, crushing the ice between her teeth. "Do you remember that horrible fat woman who lived next to us on Elm Street? The one with a different sailor every night?"

Helena was quiet a moment and then said: "Loretta. What was her last name?"

"She was a cautionary tale, if there ever was one," her mother giggled.

"And the little skinny enlisted boy, the pockmarked one who would howl like a wolf outside her window?"

Her mother snorted. "Stop it," she said. "I'll split and we'll wake our good little children."

"We aren't fit," Helena said, breaking into hushed laughter.

Daisy had been holding her breath so long she thought her rib cage might shatter. But she was mesmerized. It was as if her mother and aunt had been snatched away by goblins and replaced with fairies of some sort. They looked so beautiful to her, and so different, the movement of their heads and their hands in the low light throwing graceful, arching shadows across the wooden porch. They could have said anything, and she would have loved them. Just the lilt of their voices, the smell of their mingling perfume brushing the air, was like a love song. She wanted to be with them out there on the porch, under the too-bright moon, crushing ice and letting a strap slide off her shoulder. She wanted to be part of that enchanted world they seemed to have made with hurricane lamps and music and laughter. And then somehow they got confused with the image of the boy Tyler and the smell of the boat fuel near the Quarterdeck.

Daisy slowly turned on the balls of her feet, so as not to make a sound against the polished wood floor, and silently ascended the stairs to her bedroom.

1959: July

I

It was only two weeks into the tennis program, and July had barely begun to impress the full weight of summer onto the island, when Ed stopped showing up for their lessons. He would leave the house with Daisy every morning at eight and they'd walk together to the Tennis Club. But that was the last she would see of her cousin until noon, when he'd reappear to pick her up, and they'd walk back to Tiger House for lunch.

He didn't say where he went or what he did during the hours that Daisy spent skidding across the hot clay courts, working on her backhand. There was no point asking him; he would either say "this and that" or nothing at all.

Daisy had mixed feelings about Ed's disappearances. On the one hand, she didn't really care. The only thing she did think about during those morning hours was winning the singles tournament at the end of the season. As she crisped under the hot Eastern summer sun, as her thighs burned and her forearms hardened like the waxed rope bracelet tightening around her wrist, all Daisy concentrated on was making her opponent cry in a practice match, making her drop shot undetectable, her volley invisible, her step surer, making her swing move across her chest like a metronome.

Tick-tock, tick-tock, like a good little clock. Trying to hit the sweet spot every time. And not having her cousin there was just one less distraction.

But his absence was also a problem. He was always her partner for the end-of-summer doubles round-robin. Ed wasn't very good, but Daisy was strong enough to carry them, and while the doubles tournament was a bit of a joke, you had to play in it to qualify for the singles. Teamwork is God's work, or that's what that shriveled prune Mrs. Coolridge always told them in her lecture at the start of every tennis season. Normally, Ed feared not participating in the doubles round-robin, because it meant an automatic holdback the next year. But this summer, anyway, he didn't seem to care. For Daisy, not having Ed around meant she would have to suck up to someone new for a partner.

Because of her skill, Peaches would be the natural choice, but Daisy didn't want to give up the chance to beat her twice. Anyway, she knew Trinny, Peaches' stringy blond sidekick, would scratch her eyes out if she even tried to get Peaches to defect. Still, Daisy couldn't help imagining playing with her. Peaches moving across the court with her heavy, steady stroke, ponytail swinging, and Daisy moving into the servicebox to whip the ball into the ad court, invisible like a baby wasp in a piquet cotton dress. (The image instantly faded when she actually saw Peaches in person again, and then all she really wanted to do was slap her slanty little eyes out of her head with a hard backhand.)

The only other player who wasn't a total goof was the new girl, Anita. Daisy had been giving her a mental tryout for a couple of days when she decided to approach her. The points against her included the fact that she had pierced ears, not that Daisy really had anything against it, but she couldn't help remembering her mother's comments about the Portuguese girl who waitressed at the Yacht Club and who apparently dated too many boys.

Nice girls don't pierce their ears.

Also, Anita looked a bit like a Beat, with her very straight black hair and bangs cut across her forehead. But she could return a smooth backhand from the right side of no-man's-land, and as far as Daisy was concerned that far outweighed the pierced ears and the possibility of bongo-playing.

She had meant to ask Anita during their mid-morning break, when all the kids went to catch some shade under the back porch of the Club House. But as she made her way from the back courts to the large expanse of lawn, she spied her mother playing a match with Aunt Helena, who had turned the color of a Red-Hot Candy with the exertion. Her mother moved coolly across the court, spinning up tiny clouds of clay in her wake. Her skin was brown and her hair, normally a glossy black, was taking streaks of honey from the sun. Yet what struck Daisy most was how dispassion-ately she played the game. She didn't seem to feel any of the rage that drove Daisy back and forth from the base-line to the net, her body didn't seem to hum with the kind of energy that made Daisy feel like she would jump out of her skin. Daisy couldn't imagine how her mother could hold her racket so lightly, as if it weren't a weapon, how she could look at her opponent as anyone other than the enemy. She just seemed to go through the motions, even if they were perfect.

Daisy caught sight of Tyler Pierce sitting on the specta-tors' bench in front of the court. Tyler, whose sea-grass hair had been accompanying her in her daydreams, was follow-ing the game with what seemed to be intense interest. She thought about going over and talking to him, telling him that the woman who played such a cool game of tennis was her mother, but she was afraid they would tease her later for fawning over an older boy. Reluctantly, she went up the steps to the Club House porch, and leaned over the white-painted railing, watching Tyler watch her mother.

Her concentration was broken by something cold and wet on her arm. Daisy turned to see Anita smiling at her, pressing a glass of lemon water against her shoulder.

"Hello," Anita said, holding the glass out for Daisy.

"Hey," Daisy said.

Hay is for horses.

"She's far out, isn't she?" Anita said, scanning the court where her mother and aunt were now picking up stray tennis balls.

"Who?" Daisy said, confused by Anita's sudden appearance and the shock of the chilled glass on her skin.

"The dark-haired one."

"That's my mother," Daisy said, squinting her eyes at Anita, but taking the lemon water anyway.

"Really? You don't look anything alike."

"I know," Daisy said, feeling irritable and crowded. Anita was standing so close their shoulders were touching. "I look like my dad."

"Oh," Anita said. She sipped out of her own sweating glass. "Well, I'm sure he's nifty, too."

"I don't know about that," Daisy said, shifting her feet.

Daisy had to admit that Anita's bangs, cut straight across her forehead, were glamorous, in some old-fashioned way. Like the photograph of that 1920s film star she had found in one of her mother's scrapbooks. "Look, I've been meaning to ask you, do you want to be my partner for the doubles tournament?"

"Sure," Anita said, as if it were nothing at all.

"We'll have to practice a lot," Daisy said severely. She felt suddenly quite cross with Anita for being so cool about the offer. "I mean, like every day."

"We're already playing every day. But sure, why not? Can I come over to your house?" Anita asked.

"I guess," Daisy said, caught off guard. She wasn't sure she wanted her hanging out at her house. She wondered what her mother would say. "We should get back. Break's over."

"I'll catch up with you," Anita said, still staring at her mother.

As Daisy walked back across the lawn, her mother waved from the court.

"Hello, Daisy."

"Hello, Mummy," Daisy said. She could feel her own racket like a sleeping weapon in her hand and wondered again about her mother's perfect game.

As the week wore on, Daisy avoided having to invite Anita over by staying back at the end of the session. She was leaning against the chain-link fence that separated court seven from the grassy paths and marshes that led up to the Ice Pond, when her cousin rattled the metal behind her head.

"How's your backhand coming along?" Ed said, mimicking the clipped tones of Mrs. Coolridge.

"Hell's bells, Ed, what on earth are you doing here?" Daisy said, spinning around and lacing her fingers through the aluminum. Ed towered above her and she had to peer up into the sun to meet his eyes. "If Mrs. Coolblood catches you, you're dead meat."

"You're supposed to walk me home, now," Ed said. He was wearing his tennis clothes, still pristine except for his shoes, which were muddy and scuffed. His blond hair was the color of bleached wheat.

"You're such a baby," Daisy said. "Why don't you just tell your mom you don't want to play?"

"Because I'd hate having to spend the morning with her," Ed said, without any real passion. "Come on, let's go for a walk. I found a good path to the pond, one that no one knows about."

"I'm hungry," Daisy said. "Let's go back home. Mummy's making deviled eggs."

"I stole two cigarettes," Ed said. "From Tyler Pierce, actually."

Daisy imagined smoking a cigarette with Tyler Pierce behind the old ice cellar in the backyard, his hand in her short blond hair.

"All right, but let's make it quick. I might starve to death."

"Only the Chinese are starving to death," Ed said.

"Hell's bells," Daisy said.

"You should stop saying that," Ed said. "It doesn't sound grown-up."

"As if you'd know anything about that," Daisy said, opening a side door in the fence and joining Ed. "Come on, hurry."

When they were safely behind the tall marsh grass and cluster of old oaks that made up the lush backlands of Sheriff's Meadow, Daisy slowed her pace. Now Ed was leading her, and Daisy noticed that whatever it was he was doing during his mornings off had tanned the back of his neck.

"We have to go left behind the old shed," Ed said, taking Daisy's hand and pulling her deeper into the undergrowth.

"There's nothing behind the old shed," she said, feeling cranky and hungry for lunch. "I don't want to get my shoes all muddy tromping around in the marsh. Besides, there's hundreds of mosquitoes back here."

"No, there's a path I found," Ed said. "It leads to an old shelter. We can smoke the cigarettes there."

"I thought you said cigarettes were disgusting," Daisy said. "And anyway, how did you steal them from Tyler?"

"From his tennis bag. And the cigarettes are for you."

"You have to promise to smoke one with me, or I'm going home right now." Daisy stopped, her tennis dress caught on a raspberry bramble.

"It's this way," Ed said, carefully removing the cotton from a thorn.

They had reached the dilapidated shed that belonged to a defunct camp house off the Ice Pond. As they moved off the well-worn path, they passed a stone marker whose face had been eaten by lichen. Daisy would have stopped and picked at it if Ed hadn't kept his grip tight on her wrist. He pushed through a cluster of bushes, pulling her in his wake. Normally, she would have told him to stop yanking her around, but she wanted to know what he got up to on his secret mornings. Also, she liked him like this, when he was purposeful and had things to show her, instead of just mooning about staring at people and making them feel weird.

They emerged onto a small winding path, bordered on both sides by a wild, high hedge. The air was still and quiet, and only the sound of crickets purring in the heat broke the *hush-hush* of their feet in the damp grass.

"Hell's bells," Daisy said before she could check herself. "Ed, how on earth did you find it?"

"Just walking," Ed said, but with a slight inflection in his voice. He sounded pleased. "I knew you'd like it. I knew you'd understand it," he added, looking at her intently.

"Is there a clearing anywhere?" she asked.

"A ways up."

"Well, let's smoke the cigarettes here," Daisy said, putting her hand on his arm, feeling the ropy muscle underneath.

"Let's go a bit further," Ed said. "The shelter's just around the bend."

At the next turn stood an old rotting oak, its roots resurfacing like a winded swimmer. Daisy put her back against the tree's crumbling bark and slid down to rest on one of them.

"I'm tired. Let's do it here. I hope you brought matches," she said.

Ed handed her a cigarette and pulled out a pack of matches embossed with the words the Hideaway. She put the cigarette to her mouth and felt the dry tobacco stick to her lips. Ed carefully lit the match and moved it slowly toward the end of the cigarette. It wouldn't light.

"You have to breathe in at the same time I put the match up," he said.

Daisy did as she was told, watching the end hiss, and then glow brightly.

"It hurts," she said. She tried to inhale, like she'd seen girls do in Harvard Square, quick hiccups of breath, followed by gray-blue streams flowing evenly between their red lips. But she couldn't seem to get the hang of it. Anyway, it was bitter and made her feel slightly sick, like when she drank too much coffee. "I don't think I can finish it."

Ed was staring down the path.

Daisy tamped the cigarette out against the root, and sat feeling strange, and a bit sad about Tyler. Maybe she could pretend to like it if he asked her. She started kicking at the meadow grass growing up around the tree until she realized it was staining her shoe. Beyond the grass was what looked like a small clearing.

"So where's this shelter?"

"Over there," Ed said. "Do you want to see it?"

"Yeah, but then I want to go home and eat deviled eggs."

Ed led the way past the oak tree, beyond a thicket of honeysuckle, toward the clearing. Off to the side was a wooden shack, buckling under the weight of the humid air and its own decaying wood. It looked like a bus shelter, with a slanting roof and open front, partially obscured from their view.

"Creepy," Daisy said. "Is this where you hang out all morning?"

"Sometimes." Ed's tone was noncommittal.

Daisy walked around the shelter to get a look at it head-on. It was fairly deep, with brambles and some old trash —beer bottles and candy wrappers—peeking out of the recesses.

Along the back, Daisy spotted what looked like a plaid travel rug.

"There's a picnic blanket, or something, over there," she said, kicking some dirt in its direction.

Ed came up alongside her and squinted into the shelter.

"Somebody's been having a picnic in your secret place."

Ed was silent.

Daisy moved toward the shack until she stood under the roof, peering at the blanket. It was lumpy and stained with something that looked like chocolate sauce. Then she saw the man-of-war, its tentacles oozing out of a moth-eaten corner and squishing up against the back wall. "There's something under it," she said, her heart beginning to beat fast. "Maybe somebody's sleeping."

95

Inexplicably, Daisy was suddenly reminded of the man with a face like Walt Disney who had rubbed his private parts when she passed him outside the ladies' room at Bonwit Teller, his mouth making a perfect O, like a fish. She hadn't mentioned the man to her mother, about how he had grunted and then wet his pants right outside a bathroom, the small dark stain blooming on the front of his trousers. Instead, she spent five minutes fingering the red Mary Janes in the girls' shoe section, until her mother relented and bought them for her.

"I don't think anyone's sleeping," Ed said, walking into the shelter, as Daisy began to back away.

"Yes, I think so," she said. "We should go. I don't like it here."

Ed caught her arm, his hand pushing her rope bracelet painfully into her wrist. Daisy stopped moving. Ed took a step toward the humped tartan blanket, and stooping over it, reached out.

"Don't," Daisy said, but she felt like she was trying to talk underwater.

Slowly, he raised the rug.

The fathers were called in. Daisy heard her mother on the phone to Boston.

"Goddamn it, Hughes. She saw it."

Her mother paused and Daisy could hear a faint buzz coming from the receiver, her father's voice.

"Well, they're not sure. There's some talk that it may be somebody's maid. Apparently, she's one of the Portuguese girls."

Her mother paused again.

"Well, I didn't see it," her mother said, running her

ringed fingers through her hair. "No, I didn't ask her. I don't know what to do, honestly. You have to come here. And Hughes? You call Avery and you get him on the next god-damn flight down here. No excuses. That boy's already way too much for his poor mother, and this certainly isn't going to help."

Daisy was put in a hot bath with Epsom salts. Her mother sat on the powder-blue toilet, drinking a cup of black coffee and watching her. Daisy wasn't sure exactly what she was looking for and it made her uncomfortable. Should she be crying? After all, a girl was dead. But she didn't feel like crying. She wanted to talk to Ed about it, but she hadn't seen him since she had run into the house, flushed and shaking with excitement, tearing through the rooms to find her mother and tell her to call the police.

"Where's Ed?" Daisy finally asked.

"I don't know," her mother said, stirring from the seat and kneeling next to the tub. "We have to wash your hair too, baby."

Daisy couldn't remember the last time her mother had called her that. Had she ever called her baby? She couldn't be sure. But it sounded nice and Daisy surrendered will-ingly as her mother began to rub the shampoo into her hair, massaging her scalp and wiping back the suds that built up on her hairline.

Her mother turned on the tap and gently pushed Daisy's head back under the stream of warm water, humming 'The Itsy Bitsy Spider' under her breath.

"All done," she said, holding out a towel to gather her in, like she sometimes did at the beach when Daisy came screaming out of the water, rigid with cold.

Daisy adjusted the towel. Her mother gripped her shoulder and stared at her, but said nothing.

"Let's get your pajamas on," she finally suggested, in a forced, cheerful tone.

"It's only two o'clock, Mummy," she said.

"Oh, yes," her mother laughed. "Well, put on whatever you like, I guess."

Downstairs, Daisy found her mother in the summer kitchen staring at a chicken on the counter. Sun streamed through the yellow polka-dotted curtains, making the room look like the inside of a bright lemon.

Her mother stood motionless, both hands gripping the polished wooden counter, peering at the uncooked bird like it might sit up and tell her something important.

"Mummy?" Daisy wondered if this was it. Her mother was finally cracking up like Vivien Leigh.

"Oh." Her mother turned and smiled. "I was thinking we might have chicken for dinner. When your father gets here, I mean. But I don't think I'm hungry. Are you hungry?"

"No," Daisy said. Actually, she was starving. She had missed lunch and now it looked like dinner might be off, too.

"Maybe just some sandwiches. Egg salad or cucumber?"

"Egg salad," Daisy said.

"Darling, would you make Mummy one of those lovely gin and tonics you make so well for Daddy?"

She was in the green sitting room, carefully measuring the gin from the crystal decanter, when she heard the back door slam. She thought it might be Ed. But as she made her way down the hall, glass in hand, she realized it was her aunt who had returned. Daisy stopped where she was, and stood still, listening to the disembodied voices coming from the kitchen.

Little pitchers have big ears.

"Where was he?" Daisy heard her mother say.

"I found him at the sheriff's office," her aunt's voice replied.

"What on earth was he doing there?"

"Apparently, he was there when the police arrived, with the . . . the body, the girl, I mean. Why he didn't run away with Daisy, I don't know. But then he went ahead and told the policemen he'd been going there for days. He hasn't been at his tennis lessons, as it turns out." Here Daisy heard her aunt pause to catch her breath. "And the police took him back to the station so that the sheriff could talk to him and see if he'd seen anyone suspicious hanging around there."

"Well, where is he now?" Her mother sounded exasperated.

"He's still there," her aunt said. "It was the strangest thing. He wasn't upset, he wasn't even happy to see me. He was just sitting in this chair in the sheriff's office, calm as could be. Well, actually, he was almost smiling. And then he said, 'Don't worry, Mother, everything's going to be fine.' As if he'd just solved an arithmetic problem instead of finding some poor girl strangled. I'm embarrassed to say, Nick, it chilled me to the bone. My own son. Smiling about a dead girl."

"Yes," her mother said in a half-whisper.

"And then the sheriff, he said he would be happy to drive him home when Ed had finished helping them. Helping them! How on earth could my twelve-year-old son help them? And then the sheriff winked at me, which I took to mean that this was a boy thing, or something. Is that what it means? I mean, is it a boy thing? Oh, heaven help me. I wish Avery were here."

"I think we both need a drink," Daisy's mother said. "And when Hughes gets here, he'll know what to do."

Daisy took her cue to enter the kitchen.

"Here's your drink, Mummy."

"Thank you, darling," her mother said. "Would you mind terribly making a Scotch for your aunt, too?"

"Oh, Daisy," her aunt said, advancing toward her. "Oh, dear girl. You poor, poor thing."

"I'm all right, Aunt Helena," Daisy said. Would her words chill them to the bone, too? Should she weep, or swoon like they did in the movies? "I'll just go get your Scotch."

She did not get the Scotch. Instead, she hot-footed it out the front door, with some vague notion of going to the sheriff's office and demanding the release of her cousin. Although they weren't really keeping him there, were they? She was working through this thought as she opened the front gate and turned toward Morse Street.

"Hello, Daisy."

Daisy nearly fainted when she heard her cousin's voice behind her. "Hell's bells, Ed Lewis. You really scared me. Where did you come from?"

"I was hiding out here," Ed said calmly, "waiting for you."

Daisy held her hand over her heart, as if that would slow the beating. And yet, she had never been so glad to see anyone in her life. "Oh, Ed. Where did you go?"

"I didn't go anywhere. You're the one who ran away."

"Yes," she said. "It was that horrible tongue." The tongue had looked like a melted grape Popsicle, twisting out of the girl's surprised, waxy mouth. "But I thought you were behind me."

"No, I wasn't. I stayed."

Something in the tone of his voice made Daisy stop listening to the sound of her own blood and look more closely at him. "What's wrong with your eyes?"

"Nothing's wrong with my eyes," Ed said.

But there was something wrong. They were still silver fish, but now they were alive, like the little minnows that swam between her toes at low tide. She wondered when that had happened. She tried to think back to before they found the body, but she couldn't remember.

"Look, we can't talk here," Daisy said. "They're all going crazy inside. And my father's coming and so is yours. And they know about the tennis."

"I know." Ed didn't seem bothered.

"Well, we're in a whole heap of trouble, thanks to you, Ed. Are you hungry?"

"Not really," Ed said.

Daisy felt exasperated with everyone who wasn't hungry. "Do you have any money?"

"The sheriff gave me two dollars. For helping out."

"Good. You can buy me a cheeseburger. But we should go by the harbor, so they won't see us."

Daisy stayed silent until she wolfed down the cheeseburger, careful not to let the grease pooling in the wax paper drip on her green shorts. They were sitting on a bench by the ferry, away from the crowd at the Quarterdeck. Ed was still in his tennis clothes, but they had been soiled in patches, and his blond hair stood up in spikes. He was gently swinging his long legs, letting his tennis shoes scrape on the gravel under their feet.

"Did you tell them about the cigarettes?"

"No," Ed said. "Don't worry about the cigarettes. They didn't see them. And if they do find them, they'll think the murderer smoked them."

The murderer. Daisy hadn't really thought how the girl had gotten that way. Just, that she was that way. When Ed had lifted the blanket, it had taken her a minute to really see anything. And when she did, it seemed to take ages before her feet would start moving. But, thinking back, Daisy understood that, of course, someone else had done that to the girl.

Half of the girl's face looked like it had collapsed or something, with the man-of-war swimming out from her dark curly hair. The eyes were open and bulging like a frog's, the fat tongue running between her teeth. And her breasts. Besides the tongue, that had scared Daisy the most. She had never seen naked breasts before, except her mother's. But these weren't like her mother's; there was something wrong with them. There were bits missing, as if someone had taken a cookie cutter and stamped out her skin, leaving oval-shaped impressions that stared back at Daisy like sticky eyes. It was at that point that Daisy's feet had begun to move.

"A murderer," she said, slowly. "Do they know who?"

"No," Ed said. "But her name is Elena Nunes. They found her identification card under her body. She's the Wilcoxes' maid."

"What about the man-of-war?" Daisy still couldn't figure how it had gotten there. Had Elena Nunes been swimming?

"What man-of-war?"

"The one on her head," Daisy said, "you know, where it was squashed up."

"That was her brain, and scalp," Ed said.

"How do you know that?" Daisy whispered.

"I was with the policeman when he reported it to the sheriff," Ed said. "He said, 'That guy bashed her brains in so hard some of it popped out of her head.'"

"He said that? He said it popped out of her head?" Daisy felt butterflies in her stomach.

"But she was strangled, too. That's why her neck was black." Ed's voice had a hush to it, like the way they spoke in church.

"I can't believe it. I can't believe we've seen a murdered person, Ed."

"I know," Ed said.

"Do you think the murderer will come after us now? Maybe we've been marked for death." Daisy had read a story like that, where red crosses appeared like molten lava on the foreheads of the victims.

"No," Ed said. "I think it makes us special."

1959: July

II

When Daisy's father arrived at Tiger House, order seemed to follow. Within twenty-four hours, he had pulled some strings with a friend from his club and gotten Ed enrolled in a summer Scouts program, while her mother had resumed cooking for the household, preparing for their annual summer party, and generally being less distracted. She even started working in her garden and packing beach picnics for her father, who himself had taken over managing all the phone calls and visits from concerned friends and nosy neighbors.

News travels fast. Bad news travels faster.

Only Aunt Helena seemed immune to his plan-making. Uncle Avery wasn't coming.

"He won't do it, Nick," Daisy's father had said. "Something about that idiotic collection of his. Frankly, he didn't seem all that concerned. He said something odd about it being character-building. That fellow is a real piece of work."

"Damn man," her mother had said.

Aunt Helena, who had been standing by during the conversation, didn't say a word.

*

Daisy's mother had been skeptical when Daisy had told her, almost tearfully, that she needed to go back to her tennis lessons. Even one day, she explained, would put her behind.

"She's almost hysterical about it," she heard her mother tell her father through the closed bedroom door. "It worries me. I think it's a bit unnatural. I mean, why would she want to go back there, after everything that's happened?"

"She's just determined," Daisy's father said. "She wants to win the tournament, that's all."

"I don't think it's healthy." Daisy heard a rustling in the room, as if her mother was tidying the bedclothes. She had a habit of doing that when she was nervous or distracted.

"I think it will take her mind off it," her father said. "Let's not make more of it than is necessary. We don't want her summer to be ruined because some lunatic chose to garrote a maid."

"Aren't you a cold one, Hughes Derringer." Her mother's voice had the quality of glass. "I'd say it's ruined the summer for all of us. Some cut-up, bashed-in maid found by our daughter."

"You know what I mean."

"Well, I'm not sure I do. Then again, it's always you two, and I'm the odd man out. I guess I shouldn't be surprised that you agree with her."

"Don't start in on that again. You know that's not true."

Daisy heard more rustling.

"I hate it when you speak to me like that." Her mother's voice had dropped and Daisy had to press her ear against the door to catch it. "Like I'm tedious."

"You're not tedious. It's just . . . you confuse me sometimes, Nick."

"Oh, are we telling the truth now?"

"We could give it a try."

"In that case, I could say the same thing about you."

She heard her father sigh and the bedsprings creak, as if he had sunk heavily into the mattress.

"What do you want me to say?" he said after a while. "Do you want to keep her out of it?"

"I don't know. I just want us to agree, that's all." Then her mother said: "It's this murder. It frightens me."

"Come here."

Daisy felt like eons passed before either one of them spoke again.

"It's hot in here." Her mother sounded breathless. The bedsprings creaked again.

"Wait. Don't move."

"I . . ."

"Your skin . . ." Her father's voice trailed off. "Can I? I mean, do you want . . ."

"Yes."

"Nick, I . . ."

"No, it's all right. Don't say anything." Then: "Wait, Hughes, we haven't made a decision yet. About Daisy, I mean."

"All right, but you better decide quickly."

"I suppose it's all right," her mother said, almost whispering. "You're right, it shouldn't ruin her summer. And she is so serious about that tournament."

"She's a winner," her father said.

Flushed, Daisy went to her room and laid her tennis dress on the spare bed, smoothing out a wrinkle in the collar.

She had to admit that her mother had been right in some ways. At times, when she was pounding the ball back over the net, the image of what they'd seen, the smell of the rotting shelter, would suddenly come to her and she would feel dizzy and disoriented, like the time she got sunstroke and vomited in the Gilchrists' swimming pool.

But on her first day back, she felt like a movie star. Everyone wanted to talk to her about the dead girl. They all crowded around her on the Club House porch, offering glasses of lemon water, penny candy, and promises of new racket strings in return for the story.

"Did you know she was dead when you first saw her?"

"Was she all white, like a ghost?"

"Did you faint? I would've fainted dead away."

This last was from Peaches, which was typical given that Peaches always had to make everything about her. Of course Peaches would imagine herself fainting dead away, to be carried off by some obliging boy in tennis whites. As if Peaches were light enough to be carried away by anyone. But this time, no one paid her any attention. Even Tyler seemed annoyed by her.

"Let Daisy tell the story," he snapped back.

Daisy felt a strange glow and leaned in closer to Tyler. She could smell his particular odor, leather and sweat, but also clean. She gave him a look of gratitude.

"It was weird," Daisy said. "She just didn't look right. And her head was lopsided. Ed says it was bashed in with a rock. Or that's what the deputy told him."

A collective gasp rose from the group.

"Ed was very brave," Daisy continued, feeling loyal and proud of her cousin. "He's the one who lifted the blanket."

"It's just like a movie," Anita said approvingly.

"I think you were brave, too," Tyler said.

Daisy felt her breath catch in her chest in a small hiccup.

"If I had a little sister, I'd want her to be just like you."

Peaches smirked, returned to her former glory.

Anita invited herself over after the lesson. Daisy, still thinking black thoughts about Tyler and Peaches, found herself agreeing, even though she wasn't sure it was such a great idea. She just hoped her parents would be at the beach. And that Aunt Helena wasn't acting too weird.

"I think it's absolutely thrilling that you found the girl. It's like a Nancy Drew story."

"I thought you said it was like a movie," Daisy said, feeling mean-spirited.

"It's both, all rolled into one. And even better because it's true."

Daisy was silent.

"She was the Wilcoxes' maid," Anita said, throwing a glance at Daisy.

"I know that," Daisy said, irritably.

"My grandmother says Mrs. Wilcox fired her last maid for stealing."

Daisy stared at her. The corners of Anita's lips were curled up a little at the corners.

"Stealing what?"

"I don't know. But my grandmother says it was probably Mrs. Wilcox's fault. She said it's a bad mistress who can't keep her help."

The idea of Elena Nunes stealing made Daisy feel heartsick. She changed the subject.

"Do you live with your grandmother?"

"No, I just stay with her during the summer. My mother's an actress and she's always away in the summer," Anita said.

"Your mother's an actress?" Daisy was beginning to think

Anita was a lot more interesting than she'd given her credit for.

"Un-hunh. In the theater. She's doing *The Crucible* right now, Off Broadway."

"What's that?" Daisy asked.

"It's a play about the Salem witch trials, although my mom says it's really political."

"Oh," Daisy said. They had reached her driveway on North Summer Street. "Come on."

Daisy led Anita into the summer kitchen, which had grown stuffy in the day's heat. There were some bologna sandwiches in the icebox and a note on the counter from her mother telling her that her parents were picnicking at the beach.

"Here." Daisy handed Anita the plate and grabbed a pitcher of lemonade, her mother's special recipe. Presumably, one of the sandwiches was for Ed when he got home, but she didn't care. "We can take this out to the front porch."

As they passed the blue drawing room, Daisy saw Aunt Helena asleep in her chair.

"Take these out," she told Anita. "I'll be right there."

She walked over to her aunt and put her hand on her shoulder. "Aunt Helena?"

Her aunt didn't move. She could hear her snoring lightly, her soft mouth slightly open. The tumbler in her hand had tipped where it rested in her lap and a dark stain spread on her navy sundress.

"Aunt Helena," Daisy said, a little louder this time. She shook her gently.

Her aunt opened her eyes and seemed to be trying to place Daisy.

"Aunt Helena. You look really tired. Don't you want to go upstairs and lie down?"

Without a word her aunt stumbled out of the chair and disappeared toward the stairs. Daisy watched her climb the staircase, leaning heavily on the curved banister.

"That's my aunt," Daisy said when she returned to the porch. "She's really tired. I think it's the heat."

Anita didn't say anything, just looked at Daisy while she took a bite out of the sandwich.

"She's related to your mother?" Anita asked, chewing.

"Un-huh. I mean, she's not her sister. She's really her cousin. But I call her aunt."

"My mom has some acting friends she calls her sisters. But I don't call them my aunts," Anita said.

As she ate her sandwich, Daisy wondered if, from inside the house, she and Anita looked like her mother and her aunt, glamorous and feminine, having grown-up conversations about plays and New York and dead bodies.

By the time Ed got home from the Scouts, Daisy had shown Anita her secret hiding place, with the *Archie* comics and the pink shell. She had even shown her the unicorn, and Anita hadn't laughed. She had admired its mane. They were playing War on the floor of Daisy's bedroom when Ed walked in, wearing his funny khaki uniform and bandanna around his neck. In the shorts, his legs looked like pale stilts.

"Hello," Ed said.

"Oh," Daisy said. "Hi."

Anita jumped up. "Hi, I'm Anita. I guess you're the one that found the body."

Ed didn't say anything, just stared at Anita.

"Daisy's told me a lot about you," Anita said, smiling at Ed.

That wasn't true. Daisy felt a bit disgusted with Anita.

"How's the nerd brigade?" Daisy asked.

"It's actually quite interesting," Ed said. "We spent the day at Gay Head, looking for arrowheads."

He bent down and carefully placed a small pointed gray stone next to Daisy's pile of cards.

"It's for you," he said quietly. "I'm the only one who found one."

Daisy suddenly felt sorry she had been so mean. "Thanks."

"Wow," Anita said. "Cool."

"And I got to use my new knife," Ed said, turning the red Swiss Army knife Daisy's father had bought him in his hand. "Cutting saplings."

"Do you have to swear allegiance to the flag and all that?" Anita asked. "My mother says all that stuff is brainwashing."

Ed looked at her more closely now. "No, Mr. Reading doesn't believe in that. He says he's a renegade and that the Massachusetts Scouts won't even allow him to be a real leader, at least not by their rules. We follow the traditional methods of Thomas Seton, the way of the Indians."

"Indians are cool," Anita said. "Did you know they don't believe in God?"

Daisy felt annoyed listening to the two of them jabbering away over her head.

"What are you talking about, Mr. Reading doesn't believe in God?"

"Not everyone believes in God," Ed said. "A lot of people in Hollywood don't."

"You two are crazy," Daisy said. "And if he's not really a Scout leader you won't get any merit badges, then."

"That doesn't matter," Ed said. "I'm learning how to do ancient woodcarvings and use my knife on rabbits, like the

111

Indians in Gay Head do. Survival techniques. It's much more useful."

"You're killing rabbits?" Daisy was horrified.

"They don't suffer. You wring their necks first."

"So you really have to choke them?" Anita seemed fascinated.

"Well, actually, you just dislocate the neck," Ed said evenly. "You hold it and then pop its neck back. After that, you hang it by one of its hind legs and cut its head off, to let it bleed out."

Daisy suddenly felt dizzy.

"Are you all right?" Anita asked. "You've gone all pasty."

"I don't feel so good," Daisy mumbled. She felt the bologna rise in her throat.

Ed watched her.

"I think I'm going to throw up," Daisy said, getting up. She put her hand over her mouth and ran.

In the bathroom, she vomited into the powder-blue toilet.

Over the next two weeks, preparations for her mother's party took up more and more space in the house. Little American flags were scattered across the dining-room table waiting to be sewn onto their ribbon; invitations, with "Tiger House" printed on the front and overlaid with a long, sinuous Indian tiger, covered her mother's desk; wooden crates packed with the best crystal had been hauled up from the basement and lined an entire wall of the green sitting room; scraps of paper with telephone numbers, addresses, and names, some of them crossed off, floated around the rooms like large dust motes. Soft bags filled with silver to be polished lay in heaps across the counters of the summer kitchen, while her grandmother's embroidered linen could be found draped over chairs and sofas, awaiting attention from the housekeeper. And the phone rang incessantly. It was either the flower man reporting that no peach-colored peonies could be found this time of year (white hydrangeas were settled on instead), or the man from Crane's warning that the engraved place names for the early supper might be delayed a day or two. Disaster had been narrowly averted, Daisy's mother announced to the household, when the man who painted the Japanese lanterns called back to say that he had finally found a truck with ample space to take the shipment over from the mainland in time.

The anticipation gave the house an electric quality and Daisy half expected the candlesticks and flags and spoons and forks to get up and start marching into place by themselves, like in *The Nutcracker*, when all the toys came alive after the people had gone to bed. She felt so infected with the magic of the party that she didn't mind the constant scolding not to leave her tennis racket lying around, or to eat on the porch so crumbs wouldn't attract ants into the house. She noticed that even Ed pitched in, constantly checking the mousetraps in the kitchen and the pantry.

And even though Daisy and Anita had wound up losing the doubles round-robin, she decided to ask her mother if Anita could come to the party. After all, it wasn't Anita's fault if she wasn't up to scratch.

"Yes, yes," her mother said distractedly, before looking up from one of her furious lists and adding, "but she can't come to the early supper."

"I'm not even invited to the early supper," Daisy said loudly.

"No, that's right." Her mother chewed her pencil and stared back down at her pad. "When you're sixteen . . ."

The early supper was reserved for her parents' closest circle of friends, who would come at six and dine with them before the party got into full swing. The meal seemed to cause her mother as much anxiety as the main event, although Daisy couldn't fathom why, given that she didn't even cook it herself, just fussed at the women she hired from Vineyard Haven to help.

"Simple," her mother always explained. "Simple, but tricky and impossible to replicate."

With the singles final set to take place the day after the party, Daisy was practicing furiously. She had started biting her nails again, a habit she had given up years before when her mother, in a fit of rage, had applied Tabasco to her fingertips twice a day.

Pretty is as pretty does.

She had even found herself crying at the end of each tennis lesson. She wasn't sure why, only that it felt so good to sit down and choke out the tears, biting the damp collar of her shirt between her teeth. At the end of the week, she played Peaches in a first-to-two practice set.

Peaches did her worst, winning quickly and handily by beating Daisy on her own serve. Daisy felt numb, and yet strangely, her heart was beating so fast she thought it might come crashing out of her chest.

"Not your best tennis," Mr. Collins said when she reached the Club House. The tennis instructor then put his hand on Peaches' shoulder. "Nicely played, Peaches. Very efficient. OK, girls, shake hands."

Daisy walked straight through and out the front door onto the street, dragging her racket behind her. She didn't even want to cry, just to be home under her own cool lavender sheets.

She heard the sound of feet behind her, but she didn't

speed up. Even if they tie me up and use Chinese water torture, Daisy thought, I won't shake hands with that fatso.

A warm dry hand caught her arm.

"Hey," Tyler said. "Wait up."

Daisy turned.

"Hey, it's OK," Tyler said. "Don't cry."

"I'm not crying," Daisy said and sped up her pace.

"All right, all right, you're not crying," he said. "Hey, come on. Wait up a little."

Daisy stopped.

"Look, I just wanted to tell you I think you played great."

"Don't be an idiot," Daisy said, furiously. "I lost."

"It wasn't even a real match," Tyler said. "You only played two games. And anyway, you looked great out there, just made a few mistakes, that's all."

"Did Mr. Collins send you? Because I'll tell you right now, I'm not shaking hands."

Tyler laughed. "You're a prickly one, aren't you?"

Daisy continued to eye him, pushing the top of her racket into the gravel.

"OK, OK. Look, I'm not Collins's spy. You just seemed to take it so hard, that's all." He held out his hand. "Give me your racket, it doesn't deserve that kind of abuse."

Daisy handed it over, the top now scratched from all the dragging. They started walking.

"You can't take these things to heart. Anyway, you're the better player."

"She still won," Daisy said, her voice cracking a little. "Not me. She's the better player."

"Nah, I was watching you. You're mean out there."

"Not mean enough."

"You're hotter, and she's colder, that's all," Tyler said. "Two different styles. But I prefer yours."

Daisy chewed her lip, turning this over in her mind. *I'm hotter, she's colder.*

"I can't believe she broke my serve," Daisy said.

As they turned down Morse Street, the heat of the match began to lift and Daisy realized with a swift, sharp happiness that Tyler Pierce was walking her home. The dusty sidewalk seemed to rise to meet her feet, and the white shutters looked as crisp and clean as fresh laundry against the cedar shingles of the houses. She smelled the honeysuckle trailing near the tips of her tennis shoes. She ached to put her hand in his; she couldn't imagine anything finer.

Tyler had her racket slung over his shoulder and she could see a sweat stain under his lifted arm. His hair was damp and pushed back down. He was pretty, like a girl, with his high cheekbones and long lashes. But really, he was a man with his sweat and his tan, strong arms, carrying her racket so lightly.

Daisy didn't take the shortcut on North Summer Street that led to the back of the house. Instead she walked the long way round to North Water Street, trying to think of something to say that didn't have to do with tennis or Peaches. She was still thinking when they reached her front gate.

"Well," Daisy said, slowly pushing the latch down.

"Well," Tyler said, smiling. He handed her the racket and looked up at the house. "So this is where you live."

"Un-huh," Daisy said, looking up too, wondering what it looked like through his eyes.

He passed his hand over the tops of the red roses climbing the fence, and the movement released the fragrance of the fat blooms.

"It's big," Tyler said. "It's nice."

"It was my great-grandmother's." Daisy couldn't think of

one interesting thing to say. She desperately cast around for some small tidbit to offer up to him. "It used to have two kitchens." She immediately regretted it. Why would a boy care about kitchens? "My cousin brought me a real Indian arrowhead from Gay Head. Do you want to see it?"

"Sure," Tyler said. "Actually, I'm kind of thirsty."

"Oh," Daisy said. "Do you like lemonade? My mother has a secret recipe."

"A secret recipe, huh? That would be great."

"Come on," Daisy said, leading him up the front path to the porch. "You can sit on the porch and I'll bring some out." She didn't want Tyler to see her Aunt Helena snoring in her favorite chair.

The house was still when she walked in. In the kitchen, she hurriedly poured the lemonade into two big tumblers ringed with bluebells. Walking carefully back, she checked the blue sitting room. There was no sign of her aunt. She turned on the old radio, loud enough so that music would float out onto the porch. The sound of Little Anthony singing about the tears on his pillow filled the room. She pushed the screen door open with her hip, relieved to find Tyler where she'd left him.

"Here." Daisy handed him one of the tumblers. She watched as he turned the rim slightly, looking at the bluebells etched into the glass, before drinking out of it.

She was memorizing him. His white collared shirt had the Tennis Club insignia stitched onto the breast, and droplets of sweat beaded up at his hairline. The laces of his tennis shoes were neatly tied, but not double-knotted, as if he knew there was no way they would come undone at the wrong moment. She liked the way he had looked at the bluebells, like every detail mattered to him.

"It's good," Tyler said, setting the empty glass down on the wrought-iron table between them. "What's the secret?"

"Only my mother knows," Daisy said. She almost added that her mother had promised to tell her when she was older, but stopped herself. "Do you want to see the arrowhead?"

"Sure," he said, but he was looking out onto the street.

"I'll be right back."

Daisy tore up the polished stairs to her room, pulled out the unicorn, and began rummaging through her secret drawer. She sifted through the shells and money cluttered at the bottom, but she couldn't find it. Had she put it in there? Frantic, she tried to think. What had she done with it after Ed had given it to her? Anita had held it for a minute, but she had given it back. She looked under her bed and on the nightstand, then, getting down on her stomach, under the painted radiator below the window, but there was only a dead fly and an abandoned spider web.

She decided to go back down, afraid that if she spent any more time looking, Tyler might give up on her and leave. She hopped the stairs two at time and barreled out to the porch.

There, she found her mother leaning over Tyler and whispering something in his ear. She was wearing a pair of poppy-colored shorts over her strapless bathing suit. Her dark hair, still wet from her swim, brushed Tyler's cheek.

Daisy froze. Slowly, her mother straightened and smiled at her.

"Hello, darling," her mother said.

Daisy knew her mouth was open, but no words would come out. She looked at Tyler, who was smiling up at her mother.

"Daisy," her mother laughed. "Are you all right, darling? Cat got your tongue?"

"I was looking for my arrowhead," Daisy finally said. Heat was rising from the very tips of her fingers and spreading across her cheeks, like a sunburn. "What have you done with it?" she demanded too loudly.

"What?" her mother was still laughing, as if she were being ridiculous.

"Where is it? You shouldn't have touched it. It wasn't yours. Ed gave it to me." She stamped her foot, causing the bluebell glasses to shiver on the iron table.

"Daisy," her mother said a bit sternly, now. "I haven't done anything with it. I only put it in your top drawer so you wouldn't lose it."

"I wanted to show it to Tyler," she said, trying to push back the tears threatening to spill out. She felt confused and changed tack. "What were you talking about?"

"Well, now don't be mad," her mother said, her smile returning as she glanced at Tyler. "But I was telling him the secret recipe for the lemonade. He pestered me so."

"It's true, I did," Tyler said, beaming up at Daisy's mother. "Mrs. Derringer said you were the only one who she could really tell. But I told her you wouldn't mind, seeing as we're friends and everything."

"Well, I expect you to do something very nice for Daisy, now," her mother said, her hand resting lightly on Tyler's shoulder. "To make up for tricking me into telling you."

"Anything," Tyler said.

Daisy watched the exchange in agony. She recognized her position in this game: she was the spectator watching a rally from the bench.

"I think," Daisy's mother said, winking at Daisy, "that you should be her escort for the party we're throwing next week."

This clearly was not the kind of task Tyler was expecting,

but he smiled at Daisy gamely, saying, "Of course. I'd be honored."

Daisy wanted to die, to sink into the floor and disappear. She had been angry with her mother before, but at the moment, she hated her.

1959: August

I

The day of the party, Daisy's mother appeared in her bedroom at 6 a.m., ordering her out of bed like a military general in a green silk dressing gown.

"I can't believe you're still sleeping," she said, pulling back the sticky sheet. "Early bird catches the worm. And the girl has to clean the rooms, for heaven's sakes. You all know that. Do I have to do everything myself?"

Daisy wanted to point out that if the girl was cleaning the rooms, then she wasn't doing everything herself, but her mother had already marched out.

Daisy stumbled downstairs to the kitchen, where she found her father and aunt sitting bleary-eyed at the kitchen table. Her father's stubble cast a shadow across his jaw as he sipped his coffee. Her aunt, encased in voluminous yellow, was staring morosely into her own cup.

"What's for breakfast?" Daisy asked.

At the mention of breakfast, Aunt Helena groaned and put her head down on the table.

Her father smiled and stood up, tightening the belt around his flannel bathrobe.

"Ah, Daisy, my sweet, aren't you a sight for sore eyes. Come over here and give your old man a kiss."

Daisy walked obediently over to her father, who put his arms around her, kissing the top of her head. Her father smelled like sleep and something sour. Daisy wriggled out of his arms, squinting up at him.

"Everyone's feeling a bit out of sorts. Except your mother, of course. Nothing save a natural disaster could stop her at this point," he said, chuckling. "How about some scrambled eggs for my best girl? Not sure I'll be able to do them as well as Mummy, but I'll give it a go."

"OK." Daisy sat down. "Can I have some coffee, too?"

"Coffee?" Her father stopped and turned back toward her, brandishing the frying pan in his hand. "When did you start drinking coffee?"

"Mummy lets me have a little with lots of milk."

"Mummy has some interesting notions." He didn't sound convinced. "I suppose it's all right. I'll pour a drop into a mug and you put in the milk. Deal?"

"Deal." Daisy walked over to the icebox and took out the bottle of cold milk.

"Daisy, dear," she heard her aunt's muffled voice behind her, "will you pour me a glass of that lovely milk? In fact, just bring the whole bottle."

Daisy looked at her father.

"Crikey, Helena," her father said, laughing.

"It's your fault, Hughes. You and your whiskey sours."

"Well, you didn't have to drink ten of them," he said.

"You didn't have to keep pouring them. You know how I love whiskey sours."

"I think the secret's out."

"Well, I'm paying for it now. Badly done, Hughes." Her tone was petulant, but Daisy could see she was trying not to smile.

She brought her aunt a glass and the bottle of milk. Her

aunt pressed the bottle against her forehead. Daisy thought about the strange effects parties seemed to have on adults, like Christmas when there were no rules. Her father and aunt, in their pajamas at this hour, acting crazy. It reminded her of the grown-up movies her mother sometimes took her to, where the adults said things to each other and everyone in the audience laughed, except Daisy, who couldn't see what was so funny.

In any case, the party had obviously taken hold of Tiger House and Daisy felt it coming over her like a fit of temper. In the distance, she could hear her mother opening the windows in the front rooms, to air them out. This was followed by the clattering of serving dishes, and intermittent exclamations of "Goddamn it."

Ed arrived in the kitchen, freshly showered and wearing neatly pressed dungarees. Aunt Helena made a visible effort to sit up when he entered, but Daisy saw him cast a disapproving glance over her anyway. She suddenly felt annoyed.

"We're all having breakfast in our pajamas," she told him imperiously.

"The Indians rose with the sun to hunt their breakfast," Ed said coldly.

"Well, go have breakfast with the Indians, then," Daisy said.

"Ed," her father broke in. "Scrambled eggs?" He said it in his normal voice, but Daisy noticed his hand had gone still over the pan and the eggs had begun to smoke.

"No, thank you," Ed said, staring at her father for a moment before turning away. "I'm going to check the mousetraps."

Her cousin left the kitchen, but his disapproval remained, poisoning the air of camaraderie.

"Well," Aunt Helena said, rising with a sigh. "I better go and get dressed. Your mother probably needs help."

"Soup's up," her father said, placing the plate of eggs in front of Daisy.

Daisy had just shoved a slightly burnt forkful into her mouth when her mother entered the kitchen.

"Daisy Derringer," she said sharply. "Get your foot off that chair. And what's this bottle of milk doing out? It will spoil." Her mother picked up the bottle and looked around. "What's all this mess? All these pans and dishes and glasses."

"People have to eat," Daisy's father said, putting the pan into the sink and walking over to her mother. "Even soldiers get breakfast before going into the field."

"People do have to eat." She tried to slip out of his embrace. "But people don't have to drink so much and then laze about the next morning when a hundred and one guests are arriving in twelve hours."

"Laze about, indeed. It's 6:30, for God's sakes. Decent people are still in bed."

Daisy watched her parents over her breakfast. Her father was smiling down at her mother, who was fidgeting like Daisy did when someone was trying to put sun lotion on her.

"What's the point of hiring the girls if you won't let them do the work for you?"

"Just clean up the goddamn dishes, Hughes," her mother said, leaving Daisy and her father to the bright, messy kitchen and the plate of cooling eggs.

By midday, the house was in a frenzy. The intense heat was making the cut flowers wilt, despite constant baths by one of the girls, who stood guard with a pitcher of ice water. Also wilting in the heat were the Top Liners, the ragtime band her mother had hired from the mainland. They had arrived in some disarray and were now cooling their heels out back behind the ice cellar. As far as Daisy could glean, they had suffered some kind of rock attack on their way over and her mother had ordered them to hide themselves.

"They're stoned," her mother had exclaimed when Daisy's father brought them from the ferry.

"I wish I was stoned," her father had said.

"Well, go find yourself a gin bottle and get to it, if it'll keep you out of the way," Daisy's mother had replied acidly. "Although I think Helena has a head start on you."

On the front lawn, across North Water Street, men in overalls and undershirts were erecting the bandstand and hanging the small cloth flags, lanterns, and tigers on poles around the perimeter. There seemed to be some difficulty in getting the angle of the stage right, given the slope of the lawn down to the harbor.

"They say that every year and every year they manage," her mother said in Daisy's direction, but to no one in particular, after inspecting their work.

Ed had disappeared somewhere and despite all the commotion, Daisy felt bored. She had been instructed to sweep the front walk, which she hadn't done. Instead, grabbing one of the tea sandwiches from the kitchen, she retreated up to her bedroom, where she fell asleep in the noon heat.

She was awoken some hours later by her father's anxious voice.

"Daisy," he said shaking her gently. "Sweetheart, have you seen your mother?"

Daisy shook her head slowly.

"It's four o'clock. I can't find her." Her father looked around her room as if he expected her mother to jump out from behind the closet door or something. "Hmm. Well, if you see her, tell her it's four. She may have lost track of time." Her father patted her leg and walked out.

Daisy slowly roused herself and wandered downstairs. The house had been transformed. Her grandmother's linen lay smooth and crisp on the dining-room table, with chilled silver buckets overflowing with bunches of happy-looking hydrangea and sweet peas in the center. Outside, the bartender, his stiff collar soaked with sweat, was setting up his wares, polishing the ice bucket with a soft chammy cloth. The heat was still unbearable, and the oyster shucker hired to man the raw bar was fussing with the ice chests, his green visor casting a pall over his worried face.

Daisy peeked into the blue sitting room, where a half-finished glass of Scotch beaded on the side table. She didn't find her mother in the green room either, or the kitchen, which was just as crazy as Daisy had left it, with the girls trying to devise a way to cool down the consommé.

"Have you seen my mother?" Daisy asked.

When she got no response, or even any indication that they had heard her, Daisy raised her voice. "Have you seen my mother? My father's looking for her."

Her voice came out a little louder than she had intended and all the women stopped talking, although none of them looked her way.

"She may have lost track of the time," Daisy added more softly, feeling embarrassed.

One of the girls, her dark hair clinging to her face, wiped her hands on her striped apron and said, "She's out there," waving in the direction of the back lawn. "With the music men."

The others looked at the girl who had spoken and then turned their attention back to the large bowl of consommé.

Daisy headed out the back door, taking care not to let the screen bang too loudly on the frame.

She found her mother behind the old ice cellar with the Top Liners. The musicians were drinking beer from the bottle and inspecting their instruments. Her mother was lying on her back in the grass with her shoes off staring up at the sky.

"Mummy?"

Daisy's mother turned her head without lifting it and looked at her.

"Darling," she said in a voice that suggested she had been sleeping, although her eyes were open. "Hello."

"Daddy's looking for you. It's four o'clock."

"Is it four o'clock? My goodness, I need to get ready." She made no move to get up. "It's just so lovely and peaceful here."

Daisy looked around and saw only the driveway and the graying ice cellar.

"Oh." She shifted her feet. "Well, should I tell Daddy I found you?"

"No, no. That's all right, sweetheart. Give Mummy a hand up, will you." Her mother stretched her arms to the sky.

Daisy clasped her mother's hands and gave a tug, but she was dead weight. "You're too heavy," Daisy said.

Her mother giggled. Daisy stole a glance at the musicians, but they weren't paying any attention, just twanging strings and cleaning mouthpieces.

"All right, all right, one more time. I promise I'll help," her mother said.

Daisy did as she was told and pulled again. Her mother pushed herself up and dusted her skirt off.

"I suppose we have to shake a leg, now," she said, propelling Daisy in front of her toward the house. "Run along and start your bath. I'll come and check on you before the guests arrive for supper."

"I'm not a baby," Daisy said. "I don't need checking on."

"Of course you're not a baby," her mother said, distractedly. "Go on, now."

From the bottom of the stairs, Daisy watched her mother ascend, twirling her skirt and humming some unknown tune.

Later, Daisy sat on her bed, freshly washed, smelling her damp hair. She loved the smell of her special shampoo, like honeysuckle and jasmine, with the faint odor of salt that never left her in the summer.

She heard her mother's step as she approached the third-floor landing.

"Daisy," she called. "Oh, good, you've bathed," she said when she entered her bedroom. Her mother was wearing her dressing gown, but her hair was already dry, swept back in black glossy waves.

"The guests will be here soon, so you'll need to keep yourself busy until supper is over. All I ask is that, for god's sakes, if you're going to go and play, you don't wear your dress for this evening. The girls should have made you children sandwiches, which you should eat in the kitchen."

"Where's Ed?"

"I don't know, darling. But I have a favor to ask you. I want you to help Aunt Helena get dressed. I have Daddy to help me, but your aunt might need some help with her jewelry, or her hair, or whatever else. All right?"

"All right," Daisy said, watching her mother. Her dreamy mood seemed to have dissipated and she was back to her brisk, businesslike self. "Where's Daddy?"

"Daddy's getting himself dressed. Now, shoo and help your aunt."

Daisy put on her bathrobe and went down to the second floor.

"Aunt Helena," Daisy said, knocking on the bedroom door. When there was no answer she turned the knob and pushed it open.

It was one of the larger, bright rooms at the front of the house, papered with large bluebirds in golden cages resting on flower-covered vines. But the striped upholstery was almost hidden from view by mountains of clothes strewn willy-nilly over every piece of furniture. On the floor, dresses, which had been stepped out of and left where they fell, lay like wilting blooms on the rug. Beyond, windows looked out on a calm blue harbor.

Aunt Helena sat at the dressing table, her hands motionless on its glass top, surrounded by makeup pots and open lipsticks.

"Aunt Helena?" Daisy moved slowly around the discarded clothing.

"Oh, Daisy, sweetpea," her aunt said, not bothering to turn around. "I can't seem to get this rouge to go right."

In the mirror's reflection, Daisy saw that her aunt had placed two stripes of rouge, like welts, on her cheekbones and made some half-hearted effort to rub them in. Sweat glistened on the fine blond hairs covering her upper lip.

"Do you want some help?" Daisy asked. "Mummy thought you might."

"I bet she did," her aunt said, something hard creeping into her soft tones.

"I could do your rouge; I've watched Mummy do it a thousand times."

"Oh, I suppose that would be nice," her aunt said, sighing finally. "Thank you, sweetheart. You really are a dear."

Daisy located a handkerchief abandoned among the makeup and, finding a clean patch, dipped it into the pot of cold cream.

She gently rubbed the rouge off her aunt's face and then wiped the remaining cold cream away.

"OK, now you have to suck your cheeks in," she instructed.

Her aunt gave Daisy a glance in the mirror and did as she was told. Then she puckered her lips and starting making goldfish noises with her mouth.

Daisy started laughing. "Not like a fish, Aunt Helena."

"Oh, really?" her aunt said, in mock surprise.

"Stop it," Daisy said, giggling.

"No, I'm sure this is how they do it in the *Ladies' Home Journal*."

"No, it isn't," Daisy said, laughing harder. "You're just being silly."

"Me, silly? No, no, Daisy, dear, it's the latest fashion. Goldfish glamour. I'm telling you, it's all the rage."

"Aunt Helena," Daisy said, "quit it."

"All right, all right, I'll be serious."

Her aunt put her lips back to normal and Daisy picked up the rouge. She passed her middle and forefinger across the waxy surface and then slowly rubbed a blushing circle on the apple of each of her aunt's cheeks.

"You know, dear, I do know how to put on rouge."

Daisy spread the color out from the edges, up the length of the cheekbone.

"It's just sometimes everything seems so unimportant and impossible."

She saw her aunt's eyes well up in the mirror.

"So . . . I don't know . . . pointless."

Daisy felt an overwhelming urge to run out of the room, away from the fat tears that were collecting in her aunt's glassy blue eyes. But she knew her mother would be mad, and between the two, she decided she'd rather face Aunt Helena.

"There." Daisy stood back, pretending to be keenly inspecting her work. "That looks nice."

"So, which lipstick?" Her aunt spread her hand over the collection of gold tubes. "Midnight Garden, Tickle Me Pink, Atomic Red, Lobster Bisque? Oh, do you see what I mean? Exhausting."

"Lobster Bisque, definitely," Daisy said, wiping the tip of the lipstick off with the hanky. She started to apply the color to aunt's lips, but she goofed it and some of the Lobster Bisque ran outside the edges.

"I'll do it," Aunt Helena said. "I think it was choosing that was the hardest part."

When her aunt had finished, she replaced the top carefully back on the tube, but managed to knock a little silver box off the tabletop, sending what looked like tiny white Smarties into her lap. She quickly scooped them up and put them in her pocket.

"So which dress are you going to wear?" Daisy asked, looking around the room.

The sound of Vic Damone, whom Daisy loved, drifted up the stairs from the record player.

Ohhhhhhhh, the towering feeling, just to know somehow you are near.

"What do you think?"

"I think that one," Daisy said, pointing to one spread out on the bed. Navy blue, with lobsters printed on its full skirt. "To go with the Lobster Bisque."

"I agree," Aunt Helena said, suddenly sounding cheerful and definite. "I was thinking that would be just the ticket."

"Do you need help getting into it?" Daisy smoothed the skirt of the dress with her hand, still thinking of her mother.

"No, sweetest lamb, I'll be all right."

She waited while her aunt struggled into the girdle, her fleshy bottom pushing upward, like a wave cresting, before finally disappearing under the tight garment. The dress provided less resistance, and Daisy helped fasten the hook into the eye at the top of the zipper.

I've often walked on this street before, but the pavement always stayed beneath my feet before.

Her aunt turned to face her and, laughing, twirled, lobsters flying among the caged bluebirds.

Daisy laughed too, and thought how she had never really noticed how pretty Aunt Helena was, like a blond Olivia de Havilland, with her plummy cheeks.

People stop and stare; they don't bother me, for there's nowhere else on earth that I would rather be.

The music suddenly stopped and the sad, sultry tones of Julie London took up where Vic Damone left off. Julie was crying a river again, something she did often whenever Daisy's mother was in the mood.

Daisy heard her step on the stair, her tap-tap with its precise, small rhythm, marred only by some faint hesitation before each foot landed. Her mother rapped lightly on the door before turning the handle. Daisy saw that Aunt Helena hadn't heard her approach, and she turned quickly at the sound, her cheeks still flushed.

Now, you say you're lonely . . .

When the door opened, Daisy's mother stood in a frothy gown of periwinkle-blue muslin embroidered with gold tigers. Her dark hair was brushed back, revealing pale round sapphires clipped onto her ears. Daisy noticed with wonder how the sapphires were almost the exact same color as her silk underskirt.

"Mummy," Daisy said. "You're beautiful."

Her mother laughed, her red, red mouth widening in pleasure. "Helena, do you remember this?" She spread her skirt out and twirled, like Aunt Helena had done only moments before. "I had it made out of that bolt of cloth Grandfather brought back from India. I thought it'd be a laugh."

Her aunt stared. "I thought you were going to make cushions out of that. For Tiger House, you said. You said there wasn't enough to make two dresses out of it."

"Well, yes," Daisy's mother said, fiddling with the muslin overlay. "Cushions are boring. Anyway, it's a dress now." She winked at Daisy. "And look at you, don't you look charming."

Watching her mother's lips spread over her white teeth, her arm move in a perfect arc to adjust the strap of her dress, Daisy felt like she was looking at a panther or some other beast which had just finished its dinner and was licking its chops in satisfaction. Maybe, Daisy thought, that was the it her mother had been talking about. Something wild and beautiful and hideous all at the same time.

She couldn't bear to look at her aunt, with her wrinkled dress and her Lobster Bisque lips.

"Doesn't Aunt Helena look absolutely lovely, darling?"

"Yes," Daisy said. She felt angry with her mother. "I'm going to get dressed," she mumbled, fleeing the room.

Upstairs she took her bathrobe off and looked at herself in the mirror. She wondered what her breasts would look like when they finally arrived. Now, they were just suggestions of a breast, like the unfinished sketches her mother had taken her to see in a museum once. She thought about the Wilcoxes' maid and her bitten breasts. She looked away. Rummaging in her closet, she pulled out her dress for the party. It was a white linen pinafore with large stiff ruffles rising from thick straps, and a red silk sash. Her mother had relented and let out the hem, so the full skirt now fell two inches below her knee and it made her feel more grown-up. As she brought the dress over to her bed to lay it out, Daisy saw a piece of her mother's stiff stationery lying near her pillow, a small, round pin encircled with pearls sitting on top.

> *For my darling Daisy,*
> *I know you'll be the prettiest girl at the party.*
> *Pin it to your sash.*
> *Love, Mummy*

Daisy felt a rush of love for her mother, and the angry feeling in her stomach, and the image of her mother's red lips drawn over her teeth, faded.

After struggling to get her dress on, she examined herself in the mirror again and sighed. She still looked like a baby. Locating the Silver City Pink lipstick in her hiding place, she returned and applied the frosty, shell-pink color. She was puckering and smacking her lips when she saw Ed come up behind her.

"Your mother won't like it," Ed said.

"Who cares?" Daisy said, but she wiped the lipstick off on

the back of her hand. "How many times do I have to tell you, Ed Lewis, not to sneak up on me?"

"I didn't sneak up on you. You could see me in the mirror," he said. "You look attractive."

"Hell's bells, who says 'attractive'?"

"Who says 'hell's bells'?"

"Don't ask stupid questions. What time is it?"

"Six-thirty," Ed said, looking at his Swiss Army watch, a present from Aunt Helena after she'd seen the care he took with his knife. "Tyler's coming at eight."

Daisy rolled her eyes. "I know that. Did I ask?"

"No, but that's what you were thinking," Ed said, matter-of-factly.

"Why do you always think you know what I'm thinking? You're such a know-it-all."

He was silent and it made Daisy want to slap him in the face. Because that was the thing about Ed: he did know what she was thinking.

"And," she continued, "it's creepy. That's why you don't have a girlfriend. So what if I like Tyler? At least I have someone to like."

"Yes," Ed said, thoughtfully.

Daisy turned back to the mirror and fiddled with the pin on her sash.

The prettiest girl at the party.

She saw Ed looking at her, in that way of his, like she was a butterfly pinned on velvet. "Why do you like him?"

"What do you mean, 'Why do I like him'?" Daisy said. "All the girls like him. Even Mummy thinks he's hand-some."

"Because he's handsome," Ed said, more to himself. "That's why you like him."

"Not just that, he's a really good tennis player." Daisy

stopped. She felt stupid. "I don't know. Why are you being so weird?"

"So, because he's handsome and he's a good tennis player."

"Look, Ed, you just wouldn't understand. When you like a girl, you'll know what I'm talking about." There, Daisy thought, that'll fix him. She felt very grown-up.

"How will I know unless you tell me?"

Daisy could see his mouth working in concentration and was reminded again of her mother's carnivorous smile.

"It's just a feeling," Daisy said, wanting the conversation to be over now. "Like why you like ham sandwiches better than peanut butter, only more."

"Like sandwiches."

"Oh, crikey, not like sandwiches, but kind of." Daisy was beginning to feel sorry for him, he was acting so dumb and he did seem so interested, even if she couldn't shake the feeling that he was making fun of her, or something. "When I see him, it's like when I'm playing tennis. I get that same shivery feeling and everything else kind of disappears."

"Oh," Ed said. For once, he looked away first. He put his hand over his heart, like he was feeling it beating.

"What's wrong with you?"

"Nothing. I'm just thinking."

"Well, I'm bored," Daisy said. She flopped down on her bed, pulling out the skirt of her dress. "What should we do?"

"We could check the mousetraps," Ed said. "I found a dead one this morning. Its mouth was open like it was screaming."

"That's disgusting. That makes me sick to my stomach, Ed Lewis."

"We could go spy on the adults. They're probably all seated for supper now."

"They're boring." Daisy swung her legs, hitting her heels against the brass side-rail of her bed. "Oh, all right," she said finally. "I guess there's nothing better to do."

Daisy started down the stairs before him, but Ed put his hand on her shoulder and gently stopped her. He put his fingers to his lips.

"You have to walk on the balls of your feet," he whispered. "That's how the Indians snuck up on the animals they were hunting."

He pushed himself in front of her and tiptoed noiselessly down the staircase to the second-floor landing.

Daisy copied him the rest of the way until they came to the double doors that connected the dining room to the blue sitting room. They stood, listening to the sound of clinking glass and silverware against china that seemed almost indistinguishable from the conversation.

The proximity to the dinner party made Daisy afraid to breathe, in case she gave them away. She looked at Ed. He was leaning casually against the wall behind one of the doors.

". . . looks lovely. Where on earth did you get those sweet little flags?" Daisy heard Mrs. Smith-Thompson's high-pitched voice.

"Oh, we've had them for years," her mother said.

". . . You know Nick," her father's mellow tones broke in.

"I surely do," Mr. Pritchard said, and laughed.

"One of the Portuguese girls that worked for Mother made them," Daisy's mother continued.

"Speaking of Portuguese girls." This was Mrs. Pritchard.

"What on earth do you make of the situation with the Wilcoxes' maid?"

"Oh, Dolly," Mrs. Smith-Thompson scolded. "Really . . . not dinner conversation . . ."

"I don't care a whit if it's dinner conversation," Mrs. Pritchard said. "I've been absolutely agog to talk with Nick about it and I've held my tongue as long as humanly possible."

"And we all know that's saying something," Daisy's father said.

Laughter erupted from the table and for a minute conversation was drowned out.

"Awful," Daisy heard her aunt saying.

". . . the poor children . . ."

"Now, seriously, though." Mrs. Pritchard's voice rose above the din. "Ten to one, Frank had his hands up that girl's skirt."

"Dolly," Mrs. Smith-Thompson hissed.

"Oh, for heaven's sakes, Caro, don't be such a ninny. We all know he had a taste for the staff."

"It's true," Mr. Pritchard said. "Dolly's right. Frank was never really discreet about it."

"I'll give you that," Mr. Smith-Thompson said. "And he's got an awfully bad temper. I thought he was going to punch me in the nose when I beat him at the rummy tournament at the Reading Room last summer."

"I'll punch you in the nose right now, if you feel you've missed out," Daisy's father laughed.

"I think you're all being unfair," Mrs. Smith-Thompson said. "Frank's never been anything but a gentleman to me."

Mrs. Pritchard snorted.

"What do you think, Hughes?" Mr. Pritchard asked.

Her father didn't answer right away. Then he said quietly,

but firmly, "I think he and the girl were definitely up to something."

"Aha," Mrs. Pritchard exclaimed. "I knew it."

"Why do you say that so definitely?" This from Daisy's mother.

"Remember when I came down in June, to prepare the boat?"

"Yes . . ."

"Well, I went for a drink at the Reading Room afterward . . ."

"Thirsty work," Mr. Pritchard laughed.

"Let him talk, Rory," Mrs. Pritchard said.

"I was walking home, it must have been around ten or so, and I passed the Hideaway."

"Don't tell me you frequent the Hideaway, Hughes," Mrs. Smith-Thompson broke in.

"Don't be ridiculous, Caro," Mr. Smith-Thompson reprimanded. "No one we know frequents the Hideaway."

"You can set your mind at ease, Caro, I have never even stepped inside the place," Daisy's father said. "I was just on my way home, coming down Simpson's Lane, and I saw Frank and that girl coming out ahead of me. I didn't want Frank to know I'd seen him, so I just slowed down and stayed as far behind them as I could."

Daisy felt the hair on her arms stand up as she listened to her father. She thought of Ed's Hideaway matches. And then the stained tartan blanket, the woman, that purple, jellied mass leaking out of her head, flashed before her, and she had to put her hand over her mouth to try to quiet her breathing. She looked at Ed, but he was standing pale-faced, fixated on the door.

"I can't believe you didn't tell me this." Daisy's mother sounded shocked.

"Heavens to Betsy," Mrs. Smith-Thompson said. "We are never having that man over to dinner again."

"You can bet your bottom dollar we certainly aren't," Mr. Smith-Thompson responded.

"Still," Mrs. Smith-Thompson said, "I'm sure Frank wasn't the only one. You know how those girls are. She was trying to catch herself a big fish. But more likely than not, there was a score of minnows, as well."

"I think that's a horrible thing to say." Daisy's mother sounded angry. "The poor, stupid girl probably loved him."

There was a silence.

"Anyway, it's not really about Frank Wilcox, is it?" Her mother's voice had a brittle quality to it.

"Nick's right," Mrs. Pritchard said. "After all, there's a murderer in our midst."

"Chills. It just gives me chills," Mrs. Smith-Thompson said. "But—"

"I grew up on this island," Daisy's mother interrupted. "Helena, too. It's where I married you, Hughes. It's where all the good things . . . It's not how it was supposed to be." Her mother stopped. "What's happening to us?"

"Oh, Nick, my dear," Mrs. Pritchard said. "I'm sure they'll find whoever did it."

"Dolly's right," Mrs. Smith-Thompson said. "In the meantime, I don't think we should talk about it. Not on such a lovely evening,"

"No, we shouldn't talk about it." Daisy's mother was speaking a little too loudly now. "Because then we'd actually have to think about it. Think about who we live with . . ."

"Who needs more wine?" He father's tone sounded jovial. "Caro, your glass looks a bit on the dry side? Rory?"

Daisy heard a small creak and turned to see Ed stalking out of the room. She tried to follow him, but the necessity of doing it quietly slowed her down. When she got into the entrance hall, she didn't see him. She wanted to ask him about those matches he had. She was frightened. She looked for him upstairs, and then outside, but he had disappeared.

Daisy was eating an oyster when Anita showed up. She had waited on the front porch awhile, before her parents and their guests moved out to the lawn. Then she planted herself by the raw bar and made the man with the visor shuck her one Wellfleet after another, ignoring the group of people waiting patiently for their turn.

"Hey, lovely," Anita said. "Got one for me?"

Daisy turned and her eyes nearly fell out of her head when she saw Anita was wearing black. Daisy's mother would rather kill her than let her wear black, and she felt a pang of jealousy.

"Where did you get your dress?".

"Oh, my mother bought it for me in New York, on her tour. I like yours too. Black and white. 'Dark needs no candles now, for dark is light.'" This last Anita said with a flourish of her right hand, holding the pose for a moment. Then she turned to Daisy, "We're a pair."

"Oh," Daisy said, feeling a little sorry for Anita. "Anyway, I've been looking for Ed, but he's disappeared."

"Really? Do you think he's been kidnapped?" Anita reached for one of Daisy's oysters.

"No, he hasn't been kidnapped."

Anita slurped at the juice pooled in the shell. She looked around. "Neat party."

The Top Liners were in full swing and the music seemed to make the low-hanging moon even brighter against the darkening sky. White dinner jackets swam in a sea of dresses, dusty shades of pink and lavender, beige silk and powder-blue linen. Blond heads leaned in pleasure toward their darker-haired companions. The sound of ice skimming off lowballs and laughter cut through the music. A firefly glanced the air near Daisy's arm. The light from the Japanese lanterns, swaying on invisible metal wires, made everything beyond them disappear into the night.

"Do you think we could sneak a glass of champagne?"

"No way," Daisy said. "My mother would kill both of us."

"Too bad."

"Hello, girls." Daisy's father came up behind them. "Having a good time?"

"Hi, Daddy." Daisy thought her father looked like William Holden in his dinner jacket. "This is Anita."

"A pleasure," her father said, stooping to shake Anita's hand. "So, what do you think of the party?"

"Absolutely smashing, Mr. Derringer. A real ringer."

"Good." Daisy's father chuckled. "Now, what are you girls drinking? I'm sure the bartender could whip you ladies up some Shirley Temples."

"That's simply charming," Anita said.

"OK," Daisy said, sighing.

They followed her father to the bar. "On second thought." He turned to them. "How about just a tiny drop of wine in some water? Wouldn't that be a little more fun?"

"Yes, please." Anita sounded practically winded by this suggestion.

Daisy's father raised his hand. "Two drops of wine in two glasses of water for these young ladies." Daisy saw him wink at the bartender. "Now, just this one, all right? Why don't you go on down and listen to the band."

Daisy and Anita, carefully holding their glasses, made

their way down to the bandstand. They stood off to one side watching the musicians, while couples danced on the wooden platform. One woman had taken her heels off and was dancing on the soft grass with her husband, who, still wearing his shoes, was slipping in the evening dew. They were laughing and clasping each other's shoulders tightly to keep balanced. Seeing them made Daisy laugh, too, forgetting everything that had happened in the house. She noticed that the banjo player was staring straight at her. She stared back and then he smiled and a thrill shot through her. For a second, Daisy thought she would swell up the size of that yellow moon and burst. Then she heard her mother's voice calling her back to earth.

"Darling," her mother said. "Look who I found."

Daisy turned and saw her mother holding Tyler's hand, pulling him toward them. Tyler, wearing a white dinner jacket and with his hair brushed down neatly against his head, was staring at her mother's gauzy dress.

Daisy was still so full of the beauty of the evening, and a feeling of general goodwill, that she didn't even mind that it took him several seconds to bring his gaze to hers.

"Hello," he said, smiling.

"Hello." Daisy felt like she was in a movie, that this was the moment where boy meets girl and all is right with the world.

"Hey," Anita piped in. "You look awfully buttoned up."

"I think he looks lovely," Daisy's mother said.

"Thanks, Mrs. Derringer. You look lovely, too."

"That's very nice of you, Tyler. How do you like Daisy's pin?"

"It's lovely." He seemed to have gotten stuck on the word.

"Well," Daisy's mother said after a moment, "you kids have a nice time. I have to go find Daisy's father and make sure he's not being carried off by some vixen or other." She patted Tyler's shoulder, and gave Daisy a wink over his head.

"Did you just get here?"

"Yup. But you could hear the music all the way down North Water Street. It's really a swell party."

"Absolutely charming," Anita said.

"What are you drinking?" Tyler squinted at their glasses.

"My father got the bartender to give us some wine with water in it," Daisy said, feeling extremely sophisticated.

Tyler looked toward the bar. "Your dad seems pretty cool."

"He is." Daisy said a silent prayer of thanks to her father.

"He's a riot," Anita said.

"I saw Peaches earlier. She said she was coming with her parents."

"That's news to me," Daisy said sharply.

"'Double, double, toil and trouble,'" Anita said.

"Well, she seemed pretty keen. You two are facing off tomorrow. The grand match." Tyler grinned at her.

Daisy bit her lower lip. "Un-huh."

"Aw, don't worry. You're going to trounce her."

"Un-huh," Daisy said. She didn't want to think about the tennis right now; fierce sunlight and green clay.

"Let's go see if we can sneak some champagne," Tyler said, after taking a second look at the bar.

"Daisy's mother . . ." Anita began.

"No, it's all right," Daisy said, quickly. "But I don't know how we're going to do it. I don't think the bartender will give us any."

"That's all right," Tyler said. "It'll be a laugh, even if we don't get away with it."

As they crossed the lawn to the bar, the band struck up
"Poor Little Rich Girl."

You're a bewitched girl, Better take care.

"Daisy . . . Woo-hoo there, Daisy."

Daisy recognized the voice and her spine went stiff.
Coming toward her was Peaches, swathed in a dress of pale
pink netting that matched the rose she was wearing in her
hair.

"Oink, oink," Daisy whispered to Anita.

"She looks like a giant Pepto-Bismol," Anita said.

"Hey, Peaches." Daisy shifted from one foot to the other.

Peaches glanced at Anita, her eyes widening a bit at her
black dress, and then cast her gaze over Daisy. She gave
Daisy a small smile. "Well." She turned and pretended to
be surprised to see Tyler standing with them. "Why, is that
Tyler Pierce I spy?"

Daisy rolled her eyes.

"Hello, Peaches," Tyler said. "I like your rose."

Peaches patted her hair. "My mother grows them. Pink
Parfait. That means Perfect Pink in French. She won a
competition with them last summer." She smiled at Tyler,
showing teeth Daisy thought looked awfully horsey in the
moonlight. "So where were you kids off to?"

"Well, if we let you in on our secret, you'll have to swear
fealty to the cause."

"I love a secret," Peaches said. "I'm surprised you didn't
know that about me, Tyler Pierce."

"Swell," Tyler laughed. "We're going to try to steal some
champagne from under the bartender's nose. Want to join
the mission?"

"Lead the way," Peaches said, taking Tyler's arm.

Daisy could have ripped that rose right out of her hair
and stomped on it. She looked at Anita.

"Don't worry about that slug. You'll get your chance tomorrow," Anita said. "I can loosen her racket strings if you'd like."

"Forget it," Daisy said. She fingered the pearl pin her mother had given her. "Come on."

They followed Tyler and Peaches to the bar.

Tyler turned to Daisy. "It looks like he's keeping those bottles pretty well guarded back there."

"That's all right," Peaches said. "My father lets me have a glass of champagne at parties. I'll ask."

They watched as Peaches walked up confidently and exchanged several words with the bartender, who dutifully began pouring two glasses. That's what her mother had been talking about, Daisy realized. That's what the it is, she thought, and she felt like crying. She didn't have it, and she never would. No one would ever love her, or kiss her, let alone pour her a glass of champagne. She was doomed.

Peaches walked back carrying the two glasses. "Here, Tyler," she said handing him one.

"Aw, come on Peaches," he said. "Couldn't you get four?"

She looked blankly at him.

"That's all right," he said. "You girls can share with me. But let's take it somewhere where your parents won't see."

"We can go to the old ice cellar behind the house," Daisy offered.

"Swell," Tyler said.

"Swell," Daisy said, taking Tyler's arm and smiling sweetly at Peaches.

They sat on the back lawn and poked through the musicians' cases, abandoned on the grass. Anita blew idly through an extra mouthpiece she found in the trumpet player's case, while Daisy took her first sip of champagne from Tyler's glass. She imagined she could taste his breath, sweet, left over from where he drank. But the champagne was bitter and it burned her throat. She ran her hand through the warm grass. She wanted to take her shoes off, like her mother had done when she was lying in that same spot earlier, but for some reason it felt like getting naked, so she left them on.

Peaches took her champagne in small sips, her pinky finger sticking out as she held the coupe.

Anita put the shiny mouthpiece down and lay back, stretching her arms above her head. "'How silver-sweet sound lovers' tongues by night, like softest music to attending ears,'" she said to the sky.

Daisy smirked at Tyler and handed the glass back to him.

"Damn fine, champagne," Tyler said, emptying the rest into his mouth.

For a moment Daisy felt embarrassed for him; the way he talked about the champagne, and then the rough way he drank it, seemed phony. Daisy hummed along with the music to make the feeling disappear.

"So, Tyler," Peaches said, tipping her head at him coyly. "Are you going steady with anyone?"

Tyler laughed. "I never kiss and tell."

"Oh, come on," Peaches said.

"Geez, Peaches, you really know how to make a guy thirsty," he said, slapping his forehead in mock embarrassment.

Daisy loved him again.

"All right then," Peaches said. "How about dancing? Do you dance, or is that a secret, too?"

"I'll tell you, I'd rather have another glass of champagne."

"Well, I suppose we can do that, too." Peaches rose and gave Tyler her hand. "Come on."

Tyler looked at Daisy and shrugged, as he took Peaches' hand. "I guess we're getting more champagne."

Daisy shrugged back because she didn't know what else to do, but she felt a pain in her chest at how easily he had agreed.

"I hate her," Daisy said, passionately, after they were out of sight. "I don't think I will ever hate anyone more."

The sound of "Sweet Georgia Brown" floated over them.

"She's a drag," Anita said. "But just think how wonderful you'll be tomorrow when you beat her. That's what I keep thinking of."

"I might not beat her. Anyway, don't say things like that, you'll jinx it."

Daisy wondered what had become of Ed. "I'm not going to wait behind this old ice cellar forever," she said, finally. "We'll miss the whole party."

"They'll be back soon." Anita sat up and scooched closer to Daisy. "Do you want me to read your palm? One of my mother's friends taught me how."

"No thanks," Daisy said.

"Come on, we can find out if you're going to win."

"I told you to stop jinxing it." Why was everyone so annoying tonight? She felt like getting on her bike and riding away into the darkness, up Pease's Point Way, with the air from the harbor whistling in her ears. "Let's go find them," she said standing up. "I'm getting bitten by mosquitoes just sitting here."

She walked along the side of the house, Anita following slowly. Daisy kicked at little pebbles along the way, taking a queer pleasure in the thought that she was scuffing her white sandals. The path between the house and the fence was narrow and gloomy, and the party glowed brightly across the street. It gave her the same odd feeling as a dream she sometimes had, where she tried to call out, but no one could hear her.

She was relieved when she emerged onto the front lawn, taking in a big gulp of night air. Something—a small sound perhaps—caught her attention. Then she saw them. They were standing on the porch, Tyler's head bent down to Peaches' lips, his hand resting lightly on her shoulder. A painted lantern swayed above them, a Japanese woman combing her hair, and for a moment, Daisy wondered how she had been able to grow her black hair so long and make it curl in such perfect loops at her feet.

It was a quiet kiss, with only Peaches' Pink Parfait quivering in the soft breeze, but Daisy's ears were filled with an intense rushing sound, like being under the ocean when it was both hushed and deafening at the same time. Her pulse hammered. She opened her mouth, but just like her dream, nothing came out.

She watched Peaches' arm slide up to Tyler's neck. She wanted to move, knew she should, but she felt weirdly fascinated. And yet, she was also aware of a strange kind of not-thereness. She was suddenly so thirsty.

Peaches pulled her face away from Tyler's and let out a soft sigh. It pierced Daisy. She quietly moved back around the corner on her tiptoes, like an Indian, and, pressing herself against the side of the house, put her hand on her chest to stop the pain. She thought of Aunt Helena's smeared makeup and of her mother's big red smile and the couple dancing with their shoes off in the wet grass. She started crying.

You'll be the prettiest girl at the party.

DAISY

Anita nearly fell over Daisy in the darkness. She looked at her, and then peeked out around the corner.

"Ohhh," she whispered.

Daisy tried to stop the tears by rubbing her eyes furiously, her knuckle squishing into the soft, damp skin. The sour leftovers of the champagne caught in her throat.

Anita lifted the edge of her skirt and unpinned a white handkerchief from the hem. "My grandmother made me take it," she said. "Just in case."

Daisy couldn't look at her. She felt ashamed. She wanted to be like Scarlett O'Hara, to stomp her foot and toss her head and go marry somebody else. But she was scared. She had smelled fear on her opponents before, an actual odor that was part rust and part wet earth, but for the first time she could smell it on herself. Part of her wanted Anita to go away, but she was also afraid to be left all alone there. In the distance, she could hear the sounds of laughter and tinkling glass.

Anita took a corner of the handkerchief and gently started dabbing Daisy's eyes. Daisy was grateful for the cool feeling of the linen on her hot skin, and the comforting smell of lavender water and starch. She felt her friend's hand on her forehead, her index finger tracing her brow, then Anita's face loomed large in the darkness, and her dark eyes seemed to grow bigger. All at once Daisy felt Anita's lips on her own. She could taste the saltiness of her own tears mingled with Anita's breath, felt her hair brush her cheek, and the soft down on Anita's upper lip. Daisy's head felt light and her heart beat once, in a long, exhausting rush at her rib cage that left her trembling.

Daisy pushed Anita away, hard, and saw her stumble and lose her balance on the path, but she didn't care.

She started running, running toward the light of the party, crossing the street to the sloping lawn beyond, weaving through crowds of smiling guests, trying to pick out the shade of her mother's dress among the riot of color. The music had stopped. The musicians, on a break, were smoking cigarettes along the side of the fence. She found her father by the bar, and grabbed at his sleeve.

"Where's Mummy?" Her own voice sounded odd, high-pitched and out of tune, like the old piano that sat moldering in the basement.

"Daisy," her father said, his smile fading. "What's wrong?"

"Where's Mummy? I need Mummy."

"I don't know, sweetpea." He looked down the lawn. "I think she said she was going to the boathouse to cool off for a minute."

Daisy tore down the slope toward the little boathouse that sat at the edge of the harbor. She heard her father calling her name, but she didn't care. The only thing she knew was that she had to find her mother.

When she reached the boathouse where they kept the life preservers and kerosene lamps and other odds and ends, she heard the faint sound of running water. Her mother must be in the outdoor shower they used to rinse the salt off after swimming. Daisy, breathing hard, slowed to a trot as she circled around the front of the boathouse, almost tripping over her mother's dress, discarded in the grass.

At the steps that led down to the beach, she was startled to see the trumpet player, toweling off his hair, his undershirt clinging to him.

"Hi there." He smiled at Daisy.

"Hi," Daisy said, unsure whether to keep going or stop completely.

"Just been for a swim. Hot night." He continued to dry his hair, looking at her.

"Oh," Daisy said. It seemed like he wanted to chat and she felt like she should be polite, but it was weird being so close to him there, in the half-darkness. With just his under-shirt on, Daisy could see the dark hair fanning out underneath his raised arm. She waited for a minute. "I'm looking for my mother," she said. "I have to go now."

"Un-hunh." He smiled slowly. "Sure."

Daisy edged around him and started walking toward the far side of the boathouse. She turned back once and saw him still looking at her, his face partially hidden in shadow.

When she rounded the corner, she could make out the vague outline of the outdoor shower and the hump of the *Rosa rugosa* bush that grew around it. Over the whirr of the water, she heard her mother's voice, humming a tune from earlier in the evening.

She picked up her pace, moving toward the sound. Then she stopped in her tracks. Directly in her path stood Ed, his faced pressed up against the wooden slats that gave the shower privacy. One palm was outstretched on one of the planks above his head. He was still, like always, but some-thing about him reminded Daisy of the squirrel she had seen in the Cambridge Common once, its muscular little body twitching uncontrollably. Rabid, her mother had said.

Maybe she was wrong; maybe her mother wasn't in the shower. Or they were playing a game. Her brain felt sticky: Peaches' arm circling Tyler's neck, Anita's face growing closer in the darkness, the trumpet player, drying his hair. "A gentleman doesn't kiss and tell. Cleanliness is next to godliness. Children should be seen and not heard." She chanted her mother's lessons, as many as she could remember, strangely comforted by the repetition.

Ed turned at the sound of her voice—first his head and then, dropping his hand from the slats, his whole body. He looked at her. Daisy looked back. They stood like that for a minute, their eyes locked, Ed's face frozen, like a mask.

"Mummy?" Daisy called loudly, her eyes never leaving Ed's. She was no more than six feet away, but her mother didn't hear her over the sound of the water.

Ed started to move toward her and, for a split second, Daisy felt afraid. And then he was right there, taller than she remembered.

"Curiosity killed the cat," he said quietly, so close now that she could feel his breath on her cheek.

Daisy's heart pounded, once, twice. She was breathing hard. She swallowed. "But satisfaction brought it back." Her voice sounded harsh and low. She felt her legs shaking. She dug her heels into the soft ground to hide it.

Ed cocked his head, looking at her as if he were making his mind up about something.

"What are you doing looking at my mother, Ed Lewis?" Daisy finally whispered. "Are you a sex maniac? Like Mr. Wilcox?"

"Don't talk about Mr. Wilcox." His voice was hard and flat.

"Those matches, the ones from the Hideaway . . ."

But before she could finish, Daisy saw her father rushing at her from behind Ed. He'd come from the other side of the boathouse, and his speed made her panic.

"Daisy, get away from him."

He didn't say another word to either of them, just grabbed Ed and hauled him off toward the beach.

Daisy stood where she was, watching them in the distance, her father twisting Ed's arm as he brought his face inches away from her cousin's. Words drifted up.

"If you ever . . . my wife . . ." Her father was jerking Ed's body as he spoke. ". . . I will tell them . . ."

Her father stopped talking as if he were expecting a response. Then she saw Ed, whose expression hadn't changed, bend his head toward her father's ear. By the time his lips had stopped moving, her father's face seemed to have gone a shade paler in the moonlight.

"Daisy?"

Her mother's voice made Daisy jump.

"Mummy." Daisy rushed at her, squeezing herself against her damp body. Her mother felt cool and clean, and Daisy wanted to climb inside her arms, her lap, her skin.

She put one arm around Daisy, using the other to adjust the strap of her slip, soggy from having been put on while she was still wet.

"What on earth is going on?" Her mother looked at Daisy, and then down toward the beach. "What's your father doing? Is he the one who's been hollering like some alley cat?"

Daisy saw that only her father remained at the end of the lawn, staring out at the harbor lights. Suddenly, she didn't care about Ed being a sex maniac, or her father's craziness.

"Mummy." She started crying, choking against the silk, inhaling the faint odor of her mother's lily-of-the-valley perfume and the sea.

"Darling, what is happening?" Her mother sounded exasperated.

"Oh, Mummy." Daisy rubbed her face against her mother's slip. "Everything's awful. It's all wrong. Tyler kissed Peaches. And then . . ."

"Oh," her mother said. "Oh, I see." She sighed, and smoothed her hand across the top of Daisy's head. "Why don't we go into the boathouse for a minute, darling, and you can tell me what happened."

The boathouse smelled of linseed oil and mildew. A discarded towel lay in a heap near the picnic basket. Her mother pulled down two of the yellow boat cushions hanging on the wall. She sat down cross-legged on one and patted the spot next to her. In the gloom, Daisy could see her mother's hair was only slightly wet, her dark glossy curls still brushed back from her forehead. The sapphires in her ears glinted as the beacon from the lighthouse on Chappaquiddick swept through the small windows, momentarily illuminating their faces.

"So," her mother said, as Daisy sat down on the second cushion. "What's all this?"

Daisy put her head in her mother's lap, feeling the warmth of her hand on the nape of her neck. "I saw them," she said quietly. "They were kissing on the porch. Our porch. And Peaches had this horrid rose her mother wins competitions with. And she put her arm around him. And . . ."

"A rose?"

"It's not about the rose," Daisy said, impatiently. "It's that I know I'm better than her. I just know it."

"I see. Well, it's not always about choosing the best person," her mother said. "Sometimes . . ." Her mother stopped, her hand going still on Daisy's neck. "Sometimes people just get lonely, and then they do funny things."

Daisy thought about this. "But Tyler chose her. I wanted

him and he chose her." She buried her face. "Oh, Mummy, I could just die. How could he? Why doesn't he love me?"

"I know it hurts, darling. It's so hard to be young and have all this wanting."

"But when you were young, you loved Daddy and he loved you back. You got what you wanted."

"First of all, we were older than you are. And then, well, we were very lucky." Her mother sighed.

"I want to be lucky," Daisy said.

"You'll be better than lucky." Her mother brushed Daisy's hair off her forehead. "You'll be strong. And all the Peaches and Tylers in the world won't be able to hurt you."

Daisy was silent. She thought about growing tall like a giant and crushing a very small Peaches under her foot.

"Besides," her mother said matter-of-factly, "Peaches is a very nasty young girl."

"I know." Daisy sighed. "But he loves her."

"Darling, I doubt very much that Tyler loves Peaches. Boys are just like that. Peaches is fast, and boys that age just take what's offered to them."

"Oh, and then, Mummy, something else happened . . ." Daisy stopped, thinking about Anita's big eyes and the taste of her breath. "It's so awful."

"What else happened?"

"Anita. She was giving me her handkerchief, and then, Mummy, she kissed me."

"Oh, well." Her mother laughed. "That is interesting."

"It's not funny." Daisy sat up. "Why would she do that? She knows I love Tyler and that I wanted him to kiss me."

"No, you're right, it's not funny," her mother said, but she was still smiling. "Anita's just a theatrical girl. And, frankly, Daisy, her family's a bit wonky. You know that."

"I don't care. I hate all of them."

"Darling," her mother took Daisy's face in her hands, "I want you to listen to me. I'm going to tell you this because someday it may be very important for you to remember." Her mother's face was serious, her big green eyes like snake skin. "If there's one thing you can be sure about in this life, it's that you won't always be kissing the right person."

1959: August

II

Daisy unscrewed the wooden press from her racket and laced her fingers between the strings, pulling on the gut. It was eleven in the morning and the sun was already burning her bare shoulders, the dust from the clay court creating a haze around her.

She placed the press on the spectators' bench near the post and looked up at the tennis club's big, cool porch, where her mother sat chatting with Mrs. Coolridge. She was nodding her head slightly at something the director was saying. Unlike her father, who had given her a good-luck kiss earlier that morning, Daisy's mother looked fresh, as if the party had never happened. She saw Mr. Montgomery whispering into Peaches' ear. Daisy turned back to the court.

She scraped her Keds against the clay and then used the top of her racket to knock them clean. Peaches came down the steps, her ponytail catching the sun. Daisy pushed her headband higher up on her head, and wiped the gathering sweat off her top lip with the back of her wrist.

She pretended not to watch as Peaches sat on the bench, pulled a chammy out of her bag, and began polishing the already gleaming frame of her racket.

She's cold, I'm hot. She's cold, I'm hot.

Daisy looked up at the porch again. Her mother's eyes were on her, a small line creasing the smooth skin between her eyebrows. Mrs. Coolridge was now shaking Mr. Montgomery's hand, smiling at something he was saying. The voices were just a murmur and they made her feel like the hot rectangle of clay was a world away. Her head ached from the glare and she could hear a faint ringing in her ears.

Hot enough to roast an ox.

There was a small stirring on the porch. Daisy saw Mrs. Coolridge turn her head and squint toward the dark interior of the Club House.

Ed stepped out, his eyes flicking momentarily over the program director, before taking a few easy strides toward her mother. Daisy breathed out. She hadn't seen him since the night before and, although she couldn't say why, exactly, she was glad he was there. Her mother looked up and smiled at Ed, who pulled one of the wooden deck chairs closer and sat down. Daisy fingered the arrowhead in the pocket of her dress. It was rough, like a small piece of coral, against her thumb and forefinger.

Mrs. Coolridge descended.

"All right, girls, you know the rules. First to win two sets," she said.

Daisy made a small crescent in the clay with the rubber tip of her shoe.

Mrs. Coolridge dug in her pocket and pulled out a quarter. "Daisy Derringer, you will call the toss."

She looked up at the sky, wide and blue and bright.

Mrs. Coolridge spun the coin up. It glinted in the sun.

"Heads." *Heads I win, tails you lose.*

Mrs. Coolridge caught the quarter in her palm, and slapped it on the back of her hand. "Heads."

Daisy thought she could hear her mother say something, but she wasn't sure.

"Daisy?" Mrs. Coolridge eyed her impassively.

"I'll take first serve."

"Peaches?"

Peaches jerked her head toward the far side of the court and Daisy watched as she made her way around the post. Daisy picked up two tennis balls and stuck one in her pocket, before walking across the clay to the center mark.

Standing at the baseline, she watched Peaches spread her feet wide and drop her body low, shifting her weight from one foot to the other. It was if the whole world had gone quiet, except for crickets rubbing their wings together in the heat. She stared at Peaches' feet and the angle of her right hip, which was jutting a little toward the alley.

Daisy tossed high and dropped her racket behind her right shoulder. She could see the ball was straight, even though it hurt her eyes to look up at the sun. Bringing her racket up, she hit a can-opener, slicing into Peaches' body on her backhand side, feeling her right foot come down with a hard thud as her weight moved forward.

Peaches was late stretching for the backhand, and the ball didn't make it back over the net.

Someone clapped from the porch.

Daisy moved to serve to the ad court.

"Fifteen–love." Her voice sounded small in the open space.

On the second serve, she hit slightly wide and the spin on the ball brought it straight into Peaches' body. She squinted to make sure Peaches had missed it before turning her back on her opponent and repositioning herself.

"Thirty–love."

She sliced her serve again, but this time Peaches was

ready for her, hitting a low ball that forced her to the net. Daisy slid up and tried to volley into no-man's-land, but Peaches was already there. She returned with a slightly weak forehand, and Daisy skittered backwards, her racket already dropped low at her left thigh. She hit a backhand straight down Peaches' alley. Her heart pounded as she watched Peaches stretch for the ball. Stretch and miss.

Daisy knew the game was hers, she could taste it now, feel it vibrating in her muscles like the thrumming in the brush behind her. She pulled out the collar of her dress and blew down it, feeling the sweat running down her stomach cool under her breath.

Peaches positioned herself close to the alley, already protecting her backhand. It was a mistake and Daisy knew it.

Always punish a weakness.

Daisy felt her feet move instinctively toward the center, the ball go up, the racket drop back, arc, and then slam a cannonball, flat and hard, down the T. It was in. Too late, Peaches shifted her weight, reaching for the forehand. Her wrist turned slightly as she made contact with the ball. It caught the top of the net and dropped back into her own servicebox.

Daisy's fingers reached for the arrowhead in her pocket. She looked up at the porch and saw Ed, a small smile curling his lips. Her mother was still gripping his arm tightly, even though the game was over. Daisy passed her hand over her face, which was feverish and smooth to the touch, the sweat so thin it slid right off.

They switched sides. Peaches gave almost as good as she had gotten, winning the game, although Daisy managed a couple of points. They continued like that, back and forth, tit for tat, each winning on their serve. At times Daisy felt like they were dancing together, tight and uncomfortable, like when she danced with the boys from the Park School at Mrs. Brown's class, their faces in frozen concentration as they tried not to step on her toes. The soles of her feet ached when she stopped running, but as she slid and skimmed across the court, her arm muscles straining to give power to her shot, her thighs extending, she felt no pain.

She watched Peaches move, watched the ball move, but her mind had almost disengaged. Images of the dead girl, of Peaches and Tyler under the Japanese lantern and of Ed's white knuckles as they listened at the dining-room door, spooled through her head. And Daisy played to make them disappear. If she hit harder, reached further, moved quicker, they would fall like ducks in a row.

So she hit harder and moved faster, hit and ran and hit and ran, until she broke Peaches' serve. She took the set. Then she took her next game, and the next until there was only one last game for her to win. And she was going to win, and once she did, she would never be hurt again; she would be armored for life.

At 30–40, Daisy watched Peaches maneuvering for her serve. As she made contact, the ball looked sluggish, and Daisy was already on the move. She chipped the return to Peaches' backhand, moving quickly through the shot to set up for a volley. Peaches' expression changed as she saw Daisy charging the net. As the return came back, Daisy delivered the final blow—a hot, sharp volley to Peaches' forehand. It may as well have been Timbuktu. It was over.

Daisy let her racket drop to the clay, with a soft thud. She stood on the hot court looking at Peaches. Her ponytail was in disarray and her round face was bright pink, as if she had been slapped. For a moment, Daisy felt sorry for her, and somehow sorry for herself, too. But then her mother was there, taking Daisy into her embrace, and she was panting into her mother's cotton blouse. She felt Ed standing close by.

She knew she had to go shake Peaches' hand. But she just wanted to enjoy the cool shade of her mother's body and the blankness in her mind.

The mills of the gods grind slowly, but they grind exceedingly fine.

HELENA

1967: August

I

Helena padded over to the mirror and looked at her reflection in the early morning sun. Her blond hair stood up in a ball of graying frizz, like a hideous crown. She was reminded of a line in one of Nick's poetry books. Somebody's something had been "exquisite and excessive." Excessive indeed. A whole box of Nick's books had been accidentally shipped to Los Angeles when they had left Elm Street after the war. She had meant to send it directly on to St. Augustine, but when she never quite made it to the post office the first week, or the second, she began to rummage through the volumes.

She looked in the mirror again, pushing her heavy breasts up with both hands, then turning to view them in profile. She let them drop. She looked at her cheeks, once apples, now just plain-old round. Delicate frown lines snaked across her forehead, papery in the brisk light.

The room she had woken up in was nothing if not bright and cheerful, with its airy volumes and starched, glad colors. Yet, somehow, it depressed her. It felt accusatory. She had grown up in this kind of shimmery, reproachful eastern light, but she did not feel bright and cheerful.

Helena sighed. It was never any good all this thinking about things. Too much thinking and then too much not thinking had started most of the trouble, anyway. It was why she had woken up in this room with the bluebirds on the wall in someone else's house.

She sat down at the dressing table. Her eyes trailed across the smudged glass surface, resting on a photograph of herself standing between Hughes and Nick. Nick had put the picture there. They were facing into the sun and her own eyes were partially hidden in the shadow of her browline. Nick was looking off to the side, as if something there had caught her attention, putting her features into starker relief.

Helena nudged the frame a little, and then a little more until it clattered to the floor. When she bent to pick it up, she saw the glass was broken. She pulled the photo out and straightened up. She looked at the picture a while longer before taking up the small sewing scissors on the top of the vanity and, ever so slightly, trimming an edge of Nick's face from the photograph. She held it out and inspected it. Then she cut away another sliver, erasing her lips and the tip of her nose. But it still didn't look quite right, so she just went ahead and cut Nick's face out entirely. Satisfied, she put the picture back in the frame and brushed the broken glass into the wastepaper basket.

It was only then that she remembered: it was her birthday. She was forty-four.

"Aunt Helena." Daisy came rushing out of the kitchen as Helena approached the door. "Oh, no. We were going to bring you breakfast in bed. We're too slow, Mummy," Daisy called over her shoulder.

"Tell your aunt she's not to come into the kitchen." Nick's voice had a mock seriousness to it that made Helena cringe.

Daisy turned back to her aunt, smiling. "Well, you heard the general. Stay there and I'll get your tray and keep you company on the porch." She kissed Helena on the cheek. "I almost forgot to say it. Happy, happy birthday."

Daisy was wearing a pair of minute shorts, and a tee-shirt. Helena could see the outline of her niece's nipples through the fabric. Daisy's breasts were small and pointy, and Helena thought of her own, heavy in her hands only minutes before. The girl was tiny, so light and blond, like her father. Helena was reminded of something Nick had said once about living in the house of the good and the golden. She understood what her cousin had meant. It was unnerving.

Daisy set the tray down on the rickety white table on the front porch. Eggs Benedict. Toast. One slice of cantaloupe, with a wedge of lime. Orange juice.

"Ta-dah," she said, spreading her hands over the tray. "Mummy's making you your birthday surprise."

It wasn't really going to be much of a surprise, if Helena judged correctly. When they were younger, she had loved angel food cake. But she had lost her taste for it years ago, although no one had bothered to ask her. So she ate it every year, and every bite tasted of disapproval.

Helena dipped her fork into the hollandaise sauce and licked it. She had to admit, one thing you couldn't reproach Nick for was her cooking, when she got around to it. The sauce was delicious and creamy, shot through with lemon.

"This is just too sweet of you, dearest," she said. "Really, you shouldn't spoil me so."

"It's your birthday. Everyone deserves some spoiling on their birthday."

"Well." Helena cut into the English muffin. "So, when did you get down last night?"

"I just made the last ferry. Ty couldn't get away from work, but he said there's no way he's going to miss your birthday celebration tonight."

"Mmm. So, anything new on the wedding front?"

"I'm sure there is, although no one tells me," Daisy said, laughing a little too gaily. "I'm so sick of this wedding, I could cry. I'd rather elope, but you know how it is. Mummy and Tyler won't be stopped. They always have their heads together, conspiring over flowers or music, or some other detail. And if we're not here, then the two of them are on the phone at all hours of the day plotting."

"Well, I suppose they just want it to be beautiful for you." Helena took a bite of her poached egg. "Although," she swallowed and shot Daisy a look out of the corner of her eye, "it is unusual for the groom to be so interested in all the trivial comings and goings."

"Not very manly, I agree. I keep telling him so. But I suppose I should be flattered that he's so excited. Anyway, the wedding's boring. What are you going to do for your birthday?"

"Oh, I don't know. I hadn't really thought that much about it."

"It's too bad Ed can't be here," Daisy said, taking a sip of Helena's juice.

The gesture shocked her. It was so like Nick, so cavalier, so entitled, and she found that she wanted to slap the glass out of Daisy's hand. She willed her hands not to shake.

"Maybe we could go to the salon and have our hair done."

"I'm not a doddering old woman, Daisy. I am still capable

of making my own hair appointments." She heard the acid in her own voice.

"That's not what I meant," Daisy said. "Of course you can. I just meant my treat. Just something fun to do."

"I'm sorry, dearest. I didn't sleep very well. Woke up on the wrong side of the bed, I suppose." Helena sighed. It was very tiresome, all these little cover-ups, but she had to be careful. She had to be cheerful and, above all, well. She straightened her spine. "Perhaps you're right. The salon might be just what I need."

When Daisy went off to ring Shelley's in Vineyard Haven, the sole hairdresser on the Island, Helena turned to her cantaloupe. She knew she was supposed to have eaten it first, like everyone else did, like she had always done, but she decided that she didn't care. It was her birthday after all, and this small act of subversion gave her pleasure.

She pierced one of the squares of melon that Nick had no doubt cut with perfect precision, and bit into it. Its sweetness astonished her. She was reminded of the first time she had eaten melon in California, not long after she had moved there. Avery had taken her to the Cabana Club Café at the Beverly Hills Hotel for breakfast. It was 1945 and Helena had never eaten breakfast out; she didn't even know people did that. And not by pools, anyway; maybe in some dark, dingy diner if you were a traveling salesman. They had brought her a slice of cantaloupe, or at least she thought it was. Maybe it was honeydew. Either way, when she bit into it, it sparkled—that was the only way she could describe it. She'd never tasted fruit like that, and after all the wartime rationing in the East, she thought she had died and gone to heaven. Or maybe some glamorous version of Mars.

That's what Los Angeles had been like those first couple of months. Everything was new and startling and alien.

Avery had written to her while she was still in Cambridge to tell her that he'd found a house, but when he picked her up at the train station, he informed her that they would be living in the guesthouse of a famous Hollywood producer. (The Producer. Even after she knew his name, Helena always thought of Bill Fox as The Producer, like a character in a script.)

Of course, the ceremony at City Hall hadn't been so great, but then again, she had told herself, Avery was very busy and weddings weren't all they were cracked up to be. She'd worn a cream-colored hat that the shopgirl at Bullock's had convinced her to buy. She didn't know where that hat was now.

After the justice of the peace had pronounced them wed, Avery had taken her back to the guesthouse on Blue Sky Road. She had been staying at a small hotel, and although the bungalow was small and dark, she was so relieved to be finally settled that she didn't notice some of its less appealing features. He took her into the bedroom, where laid out on the bed was a strapless dress embroidered with silver thread. The inside was lined with cream-colored satin, with the same satin detailed in a panel on the left hip. Helena laughed out loud. Nick was so proud of her dress with the cherries; if only she could see her now.

Avery held up the dress and Helena stripped down to her slip, with only a momentary feeling of shyness to be suddenly undressed in front of her new husband, and stepped in. It fit perfectly.

"How did you know my size?" Helena was practically breathless with pleasure.

"I've taken your measurements," Avery said, giving her a small wink. "I told them you had the same numbers as Jane Russell, only a little shorter." He took her hand and spun her around. "Perfect. Now I want to take you out on the town and show you off."

He'd taken her to Ciro's. Helena had never seen anything like it. The outside was plain and drab, just a block of concrete with a neon sign. But inside it was like a jewel box, with its small stage swathed in gold curtains and its huge, tiered chandeliers. She saw Marlene Dietrich with some French actor, and Jimmy Stewart, and a fat, fierce-looking woman in a huge hat, who Avery told her was a well-known gossip columnist. She had to keep herself from whispering "Who's that?" at each table they passed.

"I want to introduce you to Bill Fox," Avery said. He didn't say it at the time, but it was, of course, The Producer who had gotten them the table at Ciro's.

"Well, well," The Producer said when Avery introduced them. "So this is your Jane Russell."

"Didn't I tell you, Bill?"

"Yes, you did. Well, well." He nodded in what seemed to be appreciation.

Helena felt as beautiful as any woman in there. Not fat, or too pale, or slow-witted. She wasn't the Helena whose house was always smaller, or whose father was always poorer. She was a blond Jane Russell in a silk-lined gown that fit her like a glove. She was charming.

"Hello, so nice to meet you," Helena said, extending her hand. "I'm just thrilled with the house. Thank you so much for letting us live there."

"Guesthouse," The Producer corrected, running the tip of his finger over the half moons of his mustache. "Yes, well, Avery and I have an old friend in common."

"Oh." Helena looked at Avery, who just smiled back at her.

"All right now, you kids enjoy yourselves." The Producer turned back to his table.

173

Avery pulled on Helena's arm. "We're in the back."

Helena stood there for a moment, unsure whether the conversation was really over.

"Oh, and honey," the Producer said, without turning around. "Don't forget to return that dress to wardrobe by Monday."

Daisy was waiting in the car with the motor running when Helena came out to the driveway. Helena looked across the fence at what had once been her own house. The one Nick had taken away from her. Stolen from her, really. A young couple with no children now owned it and had put up a new white picket fence to keep in their dog, an animal with a sweet temper, a mutt most likely. Its tail was always wagging and its fur was soft and black. She liked that dog.

Daisy called to her and Helena tore her eyes away from the cottage and walked toward the car. The "Bug," as Daisy referred to it, was small and cramped, the color of a sunflower. She always felt like she had been twisted into a pretzel after a trip in it.

Opening the passenger door, she was greeted by the sound of Bobby Kennedy's unmistakable faux-Brahmin tones coming over the radio.

It should be clear by now that the bombing of the North cannot bring an end to the war in the South.

"You know, I've never understood those Kennedys," she said as she adjusted herself in the small seat. "With that silly accent. No one has that accent."

Daisy turned the dial. Some tinny-sounding music replaced the news program. Helena sighed and Daisy released the clutch and reversed at a terrifying speed through the back road until they hit North Summer Street.

Helena noticed that her niece had kicked her flats off under her seat. She crossed her own legs at the ankles, and then felt like a priss. Why did she feel so old?

It wasn't just Daisy. After all, at twenty, she was just a baby, really. She looked across at her niece's profile, the wind ruffling her short blond hair. It was amazing, she thought, how unaffected Daisy seemed by her mother these days. When she was young, she was always watching Nick. You could almost see how afraid that child was of not being able to live up to her. And now, she was so carefree, so un-bothered. In a way she treated Nick like Hughes did, with a sort of indulgence. Then again, Helena reminded herself, she was going to be married. She was young and attractive and she had gotten her man. What was there to worry about? She had mooned after that boy for years, played the little show-off, and then subsequently ignored him until he came around to her way of thinking. Helena chuckled. Daisy was relentless, she had to give her that.

She wondered if they were having sex. Probably. People seemed to jump in bed with each other at the drop of a hat these days. Of course, when she was Daisy's age it wasn't that people weren't doing it, but they had the good manners to feel ashamed about it. She had waited to go to bed with Avery until they were married, and she hadn't even been a virgin.

They hadn't slept together on their wedding night, because they'd both drunk too much champagne. Frankly, she'd been relieved. Sex with Fen had been an unsettling experience. He seemed so in awe of her body that it left her feeling like a child's playhouse. And then, of course, the memory of their love-making had somehow gotten tangled up with his death, so that by the time she married Avery the whole idea of it was fairly repulsive.

But going to bed with Avery was completely different. When they finally did, he whispered "my wife, my movie star," the whole time, which made Helena feel strange, but sexy. Afterward, Avery lay tracing the outline of her breast and looking at her with his hooded eyes. Hazel, Helena had remarked, realizing she actually hadn't known their color before that moment.

"I like that you're not a virgin, all that fuss," he said. "But I did think you'd be a little more experienced."

"Oh," Helena said, at a loss.

"I want you to talk when we make love."

"Oh."

Avery laughed. "You don't have to be ashamed, Helena. Not with me."

"I'm not ashamed," Helena lied.

He took her face in his hands and his expression became more serious. "Promise me, you'll never try to hide who you are."

Helena kept her eyes turned away, but she felt a glow spreading through her. "People just don't talk like that where I come from."

"I know where you come from," Avery said. "All those East Coast snobs, like your cousin. But you're away from all that now. We can be who we want."

"They're not snobs," Helena said.

"No, no, you're right." He smoothed down her hair. "You just make me want to protect you. I don't want anyone to make you feel like you're less than what you are. Do you know what I mean?"

She did know.

"I want to show you something," Avery said, sitting up.

He guided Helena through the living room to the dark

wooden door leading to what he had offhandedly referred to as his office when he'd first given Helena the tour.

He opened the door to reveal a cramped, square room with only a small window set off to one side to let the light in. Tacked to one wall were two large posters. One showed a man in a trench holding a smoking gun, with a red-headed woman in a torn green dress clinging to his leg. "Paid in Blood" was written in big red block letters across the top, and the tag line read: "The Mob wants him . . . She needs him . . . But you can't hold a man like this!"

The other was for a picture called *Eyes Through the Keyhole* ("He sees you when you're sleeping"). Helena had never heard of either of the pictures, but they sounded like the kind you could see at the double-feature.

On the floor, underneath the posters, were two piles of women's clothes. The only furniture in the room was a gray metal filing cabinet, a desk covered with stills, and a chair. Stacked against the walls were boxes with what looked like junk spilling out; Helena could make out an empty perfume bottle, a hairbrush, and a thumbed copy of *Mrs. Parkington*.

"What is all this?" She was particularly disturbed by the hairbrush. Was someone else living here?

"I want to introduce you to Ruby," Avery said, spreading his arms wide like a pastor.

"I'm sorry, who's Ruby?"

"She's my twin," he said, entering the room and lovingly touching the poster of *Paid in Blood*. "Don't worry." He turned back to Helena, who was rooted in the doorway. "She died."

Helena said nothing, just looked at him; she suddenly had no idea who this man was.

"Listen, I need . . . no, I want to tell you everything." He ran his hands through his hair, then looked at her. "Can I?"

Helena nodded, but she felt afraid.

"Before I met you, Ruby and I were married. Not married like you and I, at City Hall, but married in our souls. She was beautiful and talented, and she taught me how to be free. Look." He picked a photograph off the desk and held it up. A woman with smoky eyes and hair curling around her shoulders lay looking away from the camera. "This is her. This is Ruby."

Helena had to admit she was glamorous, lovely really. She felt a little ill. "What happened to her?"

"They killed her," Avery said.

"Who?" She wasn't sure she wanted to know.

"All of them. The world and all its sordid jealousy." Avery sighed and sat cross-legged on the floor. "They found her body in her automobile, in some alley off Sunset." He looked at the photograph again. "Someone had strangled her. The cops said it looked a like a pick-up gone wrong. Called her a prostitute, a whore. They're the ones who're scum. Ruby would never have sold herself. Never."

Helena felt like she was drunk. Or in a dream when you know you're in your house, but it isn't your house. She clutched the filmy robe she had bought for their wedding night closer around her body.

"Avery, dearest, let's go back to bed. I'm cold." She thought that maybe, if they left this awful room and shut the door, they could pretend none of this had ever happened. Go back to the bedroom and rewind the clock.

Avery's expression changed. "Poor little mouse, I've frightened you." He got up off the floor and took Helena in his arms. "I know this is a lot to take in, and maybe it sounds crazy. But I need you to trust me."

His arms warmed her and she thought of him whispering "my wife, my movie star," as they made love.

"The thing is, she died while she was making a film. And I'm going to finish it. All I need is to raise some capital to buy it off the studio." His words were coming out quickly now, almost if he were reciting something from memory. "I'll use a double, like they did for Jean Harlow in *Saratoga*. But she'll need to really understand Ruby, to know her. That's what this is for. I'm putting her back together."

"Avery . . ." She pulled out of his embrace.

"Wait, wait," he said, clasping her hand and holding it to his chest. "Don't push me away. Please, Helena." His eyes looked desperate and so sad. "Haven't you ever felt alone? Like you didn't belong to anything or anyone? Like you might go crazy with all the things you wanted?" He shook his head. "Don't say you haven't, because I know. I knew it the minute I saw you in that hardware store. All that pain, all that pretending that everything was all right, when you were dead inside. It's been the same for me. We're a pair, Helena. We can make it right. We can save each other."

Helena looked at him. Yes, she knew what that felt like, all right. Always the nicer one, the poorer one, with nothing of her own. The pretty girl who boys knew they could fondle without repercussions, too scared and humiliated, too small, to tell on them. Always saying thank you for every little kindness shown to her, even with Fen, as if she didn't deserve it. She deserved it. She deserved to be happy. And now, with Avery, with her husband, she wouldn't have to do it alone anymore.

On the way to Vineyard Haven, Daisy made a quick stop to run an errand and Helena watched as her niece set her parcel carefully in the backseat, adjusting it fussily until she was sure it was in just the right position. Helena saw shades of Hughes in the gesture, his deliberateness. Hughes was nothing if not careful. Where Nick was careless with money, people, anything that wasn't hers, really, Hughes rounded off every corner he came across. Outwardly, his manner was solicitous and charming, but, she thought, there was something missing underneath. It was as if he had reserved a part of himself somewhere inside, untouched, and kept his own mysterious counsel there. Helena would have felt pity for Nick, if it weren't so comical. She was chained to a man, the only man, it seemed, who failed to respond to the charms that worked so well on others.

Still, Helena sympathized with Hughes, even if she didn't understand him exactly. She understood about keeping one's cards close to the chest. She had learned the hard way that when people know too much they inevitably want to save you from yourself. One of Nick's little prescriptions for her, for example, had been the removal of all the pills in the house, to the point where one couldn't even find an aspirin in case of a headache. It drove Helena crazy. As if by removing the pills Nick could remove her appetite, as if she had any control over Helena's desires. Anyway, the pills weren't the problem. Not anymore, at least.

At first, Helena had tried to help Avery put order into the collection of Ruby's things, catalogue them, as it were. But she had been too clumsy, even broken the perfume bottle, and her help had only ended up frustrating him. So she left him to work alone in the early evenings, when he returned from his job at Sunshine Insurance.

After a month or so she found her routine. Most mornings, she busied herself with making breakfast, tidying up, doing the marketing, ironing and starching Avery's shirts, setting her hair. But this only took her to about two o'clock. There was no cooking to be done, because Avery liked to eat out, even at a dumpy diner if there was no money, or just go out for a drink instead. Yet she lived for those evenings with her husband. This was when he seemed to come alive. Sometimes Bill Fox invited them out, and she would watch Avery with pride. Women and men alike seemed to lean toward him when he spoke, the way plants lean toward a sunny window. He always knew the right thing to say, the right compliment or tease, and, just when she would start to think he had forgotten her, he would catch her eye, give her a special smile, let her know that they were in it together.

Still, her afternoons were problematic. To pass the time, Helena began reading Nick's books, although they eventually ran out, too. She walked around the grounds of the compound for hours, until she knew every inch like the back of her hand. Sometimes, she would catch a bus and ride it around until supper, but she didn't like the way the men looked at her. She also wrote letters to Nick. Aside from her cousin, she didn't have any close friends. Not anymore, anyway. In the very beginning, she had written to Fen's sister and some of his friends' wives, but her letters went unanswered. It was as if her old life back East had ceased to exist. Then again, she told herself, the war had scattered people.

One morning, she woke up to find a bottle of pills on her nightstand, with a note attached.

For my Little Mouse.

When Avery returned from work, Helena knocked on his office door.

"What are these?" she asked when he opened up a crack, his hazel eyes heavy from squinting in the darkness.

"A little gift," Avery said. "I mentioned to Bill Fox that you were finding the days a little dreary here while I'm working so hard and he recommended these. He gives them to some of his biggest stars. For sleeping. And dreaming, too, my love." He gave her a wink.

"Oh." Helena turned the bottle around. The prescription was in her name written by a Dr. Hofmann. "Nembutal. I don't know, Avery. We've never taken pills in my family."

"When you have a headache don't you take an aspirin or a tonic?"

"I suppose."

"It's the same thing, only these aren't for headaches. They're for beautiful little mice who have hardworking husbands and who feel lonely. I know you feel lonely. I'm only trying to help. Of course, you don't have to take them if you don't want to."

"I suppose I do feel a little, I don't know, useless. I was thinking of joining that ladies' reading group I told you about."

Avery laughed. "I need you here. You aren't useless; you help me more than you can know. I've worked harder since we were married than ever before. For the love of God, don't abandon me now for the ladies of the reading group."

Helena laughed, too. "All right, dearest. I promise I won't abandon you." But she put the pills in the back of the bathroom cabinet.

A week later, after she'd finished her chores, Helena found herself sitting alone at the kitchen table listening to the tick of the wall clock in the empty house. She considered writing to Nick, but hadn't yet received a reply to her last letter. She had tried to play down her money troubles, but Nick's silence still felt like a slap in the face. As she watched the second hand complete its circle, she began to get angry. She thought about the shadows under Avery's eyes when he came home from work and all the effort he was putting into his project. And Nick, who had everything. She knew they couldn't really afford the long-distance call, but she decided to phone her cousin, anyway.

To her surprise, when she heard the sound of Nick's voice, Helena felt all her resentment disappear. She had forgotten how much she loved her cousin's laugh and Nick seemed genuinely glad to hear from her. She told Helena some crazy story about putting on a bathing suit and taunting her neighbors in the driveway, and for a while she forgot all about the clock and its revolutions. Finally, Helena screwed up her courage and asked about selling her cottage.

"Avery . . . well, actually both of us . . . we thought it might make sense." It wasn't fair to put it all on Avery. It had only been a suggestion, as he had pointed out. "It's just, things are a bit tight. And it doesn't make sense to hold onto it when we really need the money now."

"You want to sell the cottage?" Helena heard her cousin's voice go cold.

"It is mine," she said, quietly.

"Goddamn it, Helena. What are you thinking? My father built that cottage. And now what? Your husband thinks you should just sell it because you're short of cash?"

"Nick, you don't understand." She could feel tears pricking her eyelids.

"Helena, it was your mother's house. How could you?"

"Never mind," Helena said, the receiver shaking in her hand. "Of course, you're right. I'm sure we'll figure something out."

But after she hung up, she went into the bathroom and pulled out the prescription bottle. Filling a cup with water from the tap, she swallowed one of the small yellow pills. Then she lay down on the bed and waited while a tingling, numbing sensation crept up her limbs. Just when she began to feel like a child's eraser, everything went dark.

She woke that evening feeling heavy, and one martini at the Mocambo had her stumbling on Avery's arm. He had been wrong about the dreams; there were none, only a kind of deep nothingness. Still, it whiled away the hours at the house on Blue Sky Road. Later, there were others, the heavy golden opiates, like sugar in the blood, and the amphetamines, with their bustling buzziness.

When Helena became pregnant, she finally met the Dr. Hofmann who filled the blank stretches of her day. He looked exactly as she had imagined him, which surprised her. Fine silver hair had receded halfway from his forehead to reveal a shiny pate sprinkled with liver spots. His eyebrows were jarringly dark and bushy. He had a kindly face and a distracted, avuncular manner.

"Now, Mrs. Lewis," he began, looking over some papers in a folder, presumably hers. "Now, you're expecting, yes? Well, you'll have to stop with the Nembutal and the, uh," here he paused as he read. "Yes, the Demerol and the Dilaudid, too. Definitely the opioids. And the Benzedrine."

He looked up at her. Helena sat quite still. She had worn gloves to the appointment, thinking that it was something Nick would do, but her palms itched a bit and she wondered if it would seem strange if she took them off now.

"Whatever anxiety you've been feeling, Mrs. Lewis, may disappear with the birth of your child, making the medication unnecessary. We've seen that before. However, if, during the pregnancy you feel the need to take something, take a half or quarter of a Nembutal. That should be sufficient."

"All right," Helena said, feeling unsure.

"Now, let's have a look at you," Dr. Hofmann said, patting the metal table with stirrups.

Helena did manage to stay off most of the pills. She vomited quite a bit in the first few weeks, most likely morning sickness, and found it difficult to sleep, which she read was common during pregnancy. But she had plenty to do to prepare for the baby. She ordered several books of patterns from the Sears Roebuck catalogue, and sat all day sewing romper suits in all sizes and colors, remembering not to favor blue or pink too much.

She also began planning a trip East to see Nick and Hughes.

"I haven't seen her in so long, dearest, and I won't be able to go after the baby's born," she told Avery, trying to cajole the $140 for the round-trip ticket out of him.

"Well, Mouse-Face, I'm just not sure that it's the best use of our money. We need it all for the project, you know that. Especially since you refuse to sell your house."

"But maybe I could convince her, if I see her in person."

"I'm still not sure why it's necessary to convince her."

"It's complicated." Helena put her hand on Avery's arm. "It's family."

"Jesus," he said, pushing her hand away. "I thought I was supposed to be your family." He shook his head. "If you want to leave me, leave."

"Dearest . . ." Helena said, feeling desperate.

"Forget it. If you want that train ticket so badly, get your uptight bitch of a cousin to pay for it."

When they returned from Shelley's Salon an hour later, Helena's right eye had begun to twitch.

"Aunt Helena, I'm sorry," Daisy began, but Helena

refused to look at her. In fact she hadn't spoken one word to her niece on the whole car ride back.

She could hear the record player inside the house. It was Sinatra, "Somethin' Stupid." Helena laughed. Her eye twitched back.

They followed the music to the blue sitting room where they found Nick, wearing some silky white tunic, singing along and swaying, a glass of champagne in her hand. She was spilling little frothy drops onto the carpet as she moved.

Hughes was fixing a drink at the bar.

The twitch in Helena's eye was going full throttle now and she pressed her index finger against it.

Nick turned, still mouthing the words to the song, her face caught in an expression of surprise when she saw them standing in the doorway.

"Oh my god," she said, her hand flying up to her mouth, as she tried to hide her laughter. "What on earth did that crazy Shelley do to you, Helena?"

"Oh, Mummy," Daisy said, breaking into nervous laughter herself. "That woman is a danger . . . poor Aunt Helena . . ."

"Poor Aunt Helena, indeed." Nick laughed out loud now, and Helena noticed how one smooth lock of her cousin's dark hair fell over her eye, as if on cue. "For christ's sakes, Daisy, are you trying to do your aunt in?"

"I think it looks lovely," Hughes said, smiling kindly at Helena.

Helena touched her hair. It was awful. She had known it the minute Shelley had finished with her. She looked like a poodle caught in an electrical storm. She wanted the floor to swallow her up. She wanted to take her sewing scissors and cut out the whole house and everyone in it.

"Well," Nick said, "the good news is you can wash it out."

Helena just stared at her cousin.

"Or not," Nick said cheerfully. "Anyway, I suppose there's nothing for it, you ladies most definitely need a glass of champagne."

"I," Helena said, enunciating lowly, the way she had learned in the hospital, to keep the rage out of her voice, "don't think I should."

"Oh, for heaven's sakes, Helena, it's your birthday. Of course you can have one glass of champagne. Or ten if you want. You look like you might need them."

"No thank you," Helena said, continuing to press her finger against her eye. "I could, however, use an aspirin."

Nick looked at her a minute before answering. "Well, darling, I don't think we have any."

No one said anything. Helena could feel Daisy's eyes on her, hear her niece's little intake of breath. She continued to look straight at Nick. Finally, she nodded and, turning on her heel, walked back down the hall.

"Helena . . ." she heard her cousin call after her.

"Just let her go, Nicky," she heard Hughes saying.

"I was just trying to be festive, goddamn it. It's been five years, for heaven's sakes. When is she going to forgive me?"

Helena walked into the kitchen and opened the icebox. She pulled the bottle of champagne off the shelf and removed the silver spoon before taking a generous swig. After carefully replacing the bottle as silently as possible, she looked around her. The afternoon sun beat in through the windows, the yellow walls glowing smugly. In the corner next to the stove, under an aging tea towel printed with little Dutch boys, was the angel food cake. Helena went over and lifted the cloth. She stared at the golden, fluffy surface of the cake with its hole in the center. She smiled to herself. She pushed her finger into the soft, sugary surface, until the tip of her nail hit the plate underneath. She put her finger in her mouth and tasted the fleecy sweetness. She gritted her teeth.

Discarding the tea towel next to the stove, Helena picked up the plate and walked out the back door, guiding the screen until it rested noiselessly against the frame. She padded softly across the lawn, the plate pressed to her chest.

"Here, boy," she cooed when she reached the white picket fence.

The black dog bounded across the lawn, trampling part of a flower bed he had been sniffing when she called. Helena reached across and scratched the delicate spot behind his ear. He wagged his tail.

She leaned over the fence as far as she could, the pickets poking into the flesh of her belly, and placed the plate on the grass. Snuffling, the dog began to tear at the angel food cake, swallowing hunks of it whole.

Helena felt calm for the first time that day, serene even. She watched until he had finished.

"Good boy," she said softly to his expectant, upturned face. "That's a very good boy."

1962: November

She could hear them outside the door. She hadn't heard that voice in a long time, but it was definitely The Bitch. The Bitch and The Producer. First The Bitch said something, then The Producer. The Bitch, The Producer. Like a game of tennis. The Bitch and The Producer were playing tennis. Helena laughed, and then tried to muffle it with her pillow. They mustn't hear her.

"What do you mean you don't have a key?"

"Well, well. Mrs. . . . ah . . . Mrs. Derringer, is it?"

"Yes, it is." The Bitch did not sound pleased.

"Yes. Well, Mrs. Derringer, I don't generally make a habit of keeping a key to someone else's house."

The knocking started again. "Goddamn it, Avery, open this door. Helena? Are you in there, darling?"

"Now, Mrs. Derringer. I don't think Avery is in there."

"What do you mean? Where the hell is that man?"

"Like I said over the phone, I don't keep tabs on my friends. But I can't say that I've seen him lately."

"Well, Mr. Fox. It is Mr. Fox, isn't it?" She sounded very cool now. But she could do cool better than anyone. That's why she was The Bitch; Avery had been right about that. "I don't want to tax you, but if you could make a very big effort, just this once, and try to remember the last time you did see him."

"Well, well. I'd have to say it's been a couple of weeks."

"A couple of weeks?"

"Maybe a month."

"A month. You must be joking. Where the goddamn hell has he been for a month?"

"Well, now, Mrs. Derringer, I couldn't rightly say."

"You couldn't rightly say."

"No, I couldn't."

"That's just fine, Mr. Fox. You don't have to say anything. Here's what I say: I will find Avery Lewis by myself, and when I do, he will have been up to no good. And I will create the biggest scandal you've ever seen and everyone in your town will know that he was doing it on your property. Under your roof. Now, if you do not produce a key to this door right this instant, I will call the police and have them knock it down. I did not travel two thousand miles to be stopped by you or anyone else. Do we understand each other?"

Score one for The Bitch. Helena bit her pillow.

"Well, well. Mrs. Derringer."

There was a silence, and Helena thought she might have dozed off, but then she heard The Producer start again.

"Now, I think I did hear that he was auditioning actresses for his film project. I believe he rented a space somewhere for that purpose, that business purpose, you understand. And, well, that's where he might be."

"I want the address. And get me that goddamn key."

"Like I said, I don't have one. But I'll get the gardener. I think he might be able to help us out here."

"That is a fine idea, Mr. Fox."

Then Helena really did drift off. It was the Dilaudid. Or the Demerol. She couldn't remember which one was on the nightstand. She heard a faint banging, somewhere in her dream, and then a very cool hand on her forehead.

"Darling, oh Helena."

Helena opened her eyes. It was her. Was she crying? No, because The Bitch didn't cry. What did The Bitch ever have to cry about?

"Darling? Can you hear me? It's Nick. Oh, my poor Helena. I'm getting you out of here."

Helena was too sleepy to tell her that she didn't want to go anywhere. Not with her.

"Avery."

"Don't worry about anything right now. Please. I'll take care of everything."

Helena nodded. She didn't know why she nodded, she just wanted the talking to stop so she could go back to sleep. She was so tired. She closed her eyes, but she could still hear the tennis.

"Jesus Christ. We need to get a doctor."

"It's just the pills, Mrs. Derringer." The Producer was there, too. "She'll be fine after she sleeps it off. But if you're worried I can call Dr. Hofmann. That's Helena's . . . uh . . . Mrs. Lewis's doctor."

"Are you out of your mind? Look at her. And you're even crazier if you think I'm letting that quack anywhere near her. Where's the telephone?"

Helena was back in Tiger House, it was summer and the linen curtains her grandmother had made were fluttering on the landing. Out the window, she could see her mother and father having tea on the lawn across the street with her aunt and uncle. A breeze had lifted her mother's hat and she was trying to keep it pinned down while holding her tea cup in her other hand.

Her shin hurt where Nick had kicked her. She didn't

know why she was the one who had gotten kicked. It was Nick who had been naughty. She had promised Helena a surprise, and then taken her to Main Street where they were tarring the road. Helena had watched in horror as Nick reached down and pulled a strip of the warm tar off the road and popped it in her mouth. Then Nick had tried to make Helena put some in her own mouth. Helena had refused and Nick had called her a baby. She had thrown a piece of tar at her, staining Helena's dress. Helena had cried, knowing her mother would be furious, and told Nick she was going to tell. That's when Nick had kicked her in the shin as hard as she could.

Now, Nick was looking for her. But Helena had hidden herself behind the curtains on the landing. She could hear her grandfather downstairs.

"Ah, there you are, you devil child," Helena heard him say to Nick. "What mischief have you been getting up to?"

"Nothing, Grandfather."

"Is that tar on your teeth?" She heard her grandfather laugh. "Old Nick. You really are the devil. Well, never mind that. I wanted to show you what I brought back from India. Isn't it beautiful?"

Helena desperately wanted to see, but was still wary of giving up her hiding place.

"See those tigers? When you and your cousin are old enough, I'll have dresses made for you both. What do you say to that?"

"I love it," Helena heard Nick say, a little breathless.

"All right, then. I'm going to the Reading Room for a drink. Don't tell your grandmother."

"I won't, Grandfather." And then a little louder: "I hate tattletales, more than anything."

"So do I. Well said."

Helena waited a little while, until it was quiet again, and then looked over the banister. Nick was standing there in the hall, her head slightly to one side. Helena sucked her cheeks in and out until enough saliva collected on her tongue. She leaned over the banister as far as she could and let the spit ball go, watching until it landed with a satisfying pat on her cousin's head.

When Helena opened her eyes, she could still hear her. But the room was different, it was big. She could tell because the distance from the bed to the wall was vast. And the walls were mint green. There was a nightstand, but her pills weren't on it, only a glass of water. She wanted to reach for it, her mouth was dry, but she didn't want them to know she was awake.

"I've called Dr. Hofmann. He gave me a list of what she's been taking, and frankly, Mrs. Derringer, I'm surprised she hasn't overdosed yet. It's quite a cocktail."

"I see. And did this doctor, or whatever he is, say why she was taking these pills?"

"The usual list: anxiety, depression, insomnia, listlessness."

"All of it?"

"Well, in my opinion, some of the pills may have brought up other symptoms that were then addressed with further prescriptions. I can't be entirely sure, not having followed her case myself. It appears that she was taking the medication at fairly reasonable doses for a significant period of time, but in the last three years or so she has been taking them at what I would term an abusive level."

"Goddamn it. If I find her husband I am going to strangle him myself. And that goddamn quack along with him."

"Yes. In any case, you do understand that she can't be taken off the medication directly."

"You can't possibly be suggesting that she keep taking these pills?"

"That is exactly what I'm suggesting. If we remove the drugs completely, the withdrawal could kill her. Now, I must reiterate my strong feeling that your cousin should be in a hospital. The doses have to be given in a precise and regulated manner, and are best handled by someone with experience. I'm not sure a hotel is really the most suitable place to deal with a situation this grave."

"I'm not putting Helena into a hospital. I think the doctors in this town have done enough."

"We are not all monsters, Mrs. Derringer."

"Dr. Monty recommended you, and I have faith in him. But I can't say at this point it extends much further than that, as I'm sure you can understand. Now, what do I have to do?"

"As you wish. I have written out a list of the new prescriptions, when they are to be administered and at what dose. I'll give you the number of a private nurse. This does not mean Mrs. Lewis won't exhibit symptoms of withdrawal, but they should be controlled. Nightmares, irritability, vomiting, sweating, possibly seizures. These can all be expected. Do you understand?"

"Yes." The Bitch didn't sound so cool now. "When will she be able to travel? I want to take her home as soon as possible."

"Definitely not for a week. Maybe two. Now, let's start with the phenobarbital. In your cousin's case, while she seems to have consumed largely opioids, the barbiturates are the most worrying . . ."

Helena didn't want to hear any more. She wanted Avery.

Where was he? He would never come back, not if The Bitch was around. She had been waiting, waiting, waiting, for him. But he hadn't come back. He said he had found Ruby. But it wasn't Ruby. It was someone else. She was blond. Ruby had red hair. She remembered telling him that. She couldn't be Ruby, because Ruby had red hair. And Avery had said he would make her hair red. That was it. He was going to do screen tests. And he had found the Ruby. And he said she had to sleep and when she was feeling strong, she must call The Bitch and get the money. Once and for all. And then he would be back. And now she was here. Had she called? She couldn't remember. But if she had the money, where was Avery? Why hadn't she just given Helena the money? How many times had she begged for the money? The Bitch didn't care. She took Ed. She had said that Ed needed to go to school. Because he was different. And now Avery had left her because she had failed. She had not gotten the money, and she had let them take Ed, and now Avery didn't love her.

"Shhh. Darling, it's all right. I'm here with you. Oh, Helena, don't cry."

She didn't want her; why wouldn't she go away?

"It's time to take your medicine. The doctor says it will make you feel better."

There was the cool water. And then there was darkness.

Elm Street. Through the screen door, Helena could see Nick reading on the back steps.

"I've mixed up the days again. It wasn't the day for meat. I have some canned corn, or at least I think it's canned corn."

Nick looked up from her book, arching one of her eyebrows. "I wouldn't expect anything less."

Helena laughed. "Oh, stop it. I know I'm hopeless. But this time I have a good excuse." She pushed the door open and sat down next to her cousin. "I met someone. At the hardware store. They didn't have any needles for the record player, by the way. All the metal is going to the troops. Mr. Denby really gave me the stink-eye, too, like I was some kind of German spy."

"Maybe we can sharpen the one we have, somehow. It really is too boring. Canned corn and scratched records."

"Don't you want to hear about the man I met?"

"Do I? What's his problem? Flat feet, or just light in the loafers?"

"Don't be mean. He works for the Office of War Information, in Hollywood. Isn't that exciting?"

"Thrilling, darling. Does he have any record needles? Now that really would be exciting."

"No, but he's invited me to dinner. And he thinks I'm beautiful, like Jane Russell."

"Jane Russell, indeed." Nick looked at her and then laughed. She threw her book on the grass and put her arms around Helena. "You are beautiful. Very. In your own way. But not like that trampy Jane Russell."

Helena leaned her head against Nick's. "A date."

"Yes, a date."

"I haven't been on a date since Fen." Helena lifted her head and looked at her cousin. "Can I ask you a big favor? May I borrow your stockings? I know they're your last pair."

"You may have my stockings, darling. My contribution to the war effort. This calls for a celebration. Get out the gin and the jelly glasses and I will go find those damn stockings."

Helena was already sipping her gin when Nick came back into the kitchen, her mouth turned down in a vaudeville version of sadness.

"Darling, I have some bad news. I think you better come with me."

Helena followed Nick back into the small, cramped bathroom. On the curtain rod above the bathtub hung an empty hanger. Helena looked at Nick, who pointed solemnly to the bottom of the tub. She peered in at what appeared to be a pile of brown dust.

"It appears the stockings have gone on to a better place," Nick said.

"Well, for heaven's sakes." Helena looked up at her cousin. "They disintegrated? That's just . . . tragic."

"I know."

"What on earth should we do?"

"Well, I think we should give them a decent burial."

"It's only Christian," Helena said.

"I will prepare the ground, you should choose the procession music, since they were to be yours, darling." Nick scooped up the dust pile and held it in her skirt.

Helena chose a record and when Nick gave her the nod from the yard, Helena put the worn needle to the vinyl.

She saw Nick throw her head back in laughter when the music floated out the window.

"Oh, Helena, I do love you," her cousin called to her. "The 'Moonlight Sonata'? Really, you're too much."

Helena opened her eyes. For a moment, she thought she was alone. The room felt so empty. Her palms itched, the soles of her feet itched, she ached. Her pillow was wet through. Had she been crying? Then she smelled cigarette smoke. It made her sick. And she could hear snuffling somewhere behind her.

"Yes, I found him. It was all so sordid, he was shacked up with some tramp in a hole in town. You should have seen his face when he opened the door. So goddamn smug, like he was expecting me."

Helena held her breath. The Bitch was talking about Avery. She had to listen very carefully, she couldn't fall asleep again.

"Hughes, we have to sell the cottage. No, we can't afford it. He named his price and I accepted. There was nothing to be done for it. She can live off the rest. We'll still have to pay for the hospital and for Ed's school."

Helena felt a peace coming over her; Avery had gotten the money. Now he would come back for her. It was all going to be all right.

"Well, what else can we do? Don't you think I feel sick about it? I could kill him. The worst is that he got what he wanted in the end. And don't even get me started on that vile Fox man. The money from my father's cottage is going straight into his pocket. Remember all that 'collection' business? Well you should have seen the sad little garage sale in their house. Like some goddamn shrine. It was disgusting."

She was snuffling again.

"I hate myself for abandoning her to him."

The Bitch and all her pious self-pity, as if she wouldn't have chewed Helena up and spit her out a long time ago if it weren't for Avery.

"Did you make the arrangements? Yes, and what did Dr. Monty say? Hughes, I know Dr. Monty's an idiot, but he's our idiot. At least she'll be in a decent, respectable institution where she can get some help, until she's strong enough."

What was she up to now? Avery wouldn't let them take her away. She mustn't get upset.

"Well, we can talk about it when I get home. What did the school say? Oh, for heaven's sakes. It's just boy antics. You're too hard on him. Yes, you are. The poor boy was waiting and waiting for someone to pick him up for the holiday and no one came. It's enough to make anyone want to cause a little trouble."

Ed, her baby. She was talking about Ed. What holiday? The school holiday. Something about a plane ticket. A plane ticket for Ed. To come home. Was it Thanksgiving already? Oh, she had failed again. How could she be so stupid? But Ed had been cruel to her. He had. But it wasn't his fault. He was her child and she had failed him. It was because of what he had seen. The dead girl. No, that wasn't right. The dead girl came after. She wanted her pills. Why wouldn't The Bitch give her another pill?

"Bill's having a party." Avery was sitting on the floor of his office, promotional stills of young actresses spread out in front of him. "A party for some very important people. And you know how beautiful Bill thinks you are. So he was wondering whether you might adorn his party. And, well, he'd pay."

"What do you mean? What does that mean, Avery?" Helena felt very cold.

"No, no, no. Nothing like that," Avery said, catching her expression. He got up and put his arm around her shoulder. "He just wants you to be there, have a glass of champagne, talk to some of the people. Don't you know how stunning you are? Don't you know people would pay just to look at you?"

"I don't believe that."

Avery laughed. "You don't understand Hollywood, my sweet. But that's what I love about you. Almost fifteen years, and you're still pure and new." He put his mouth to hers.

"Mother?"

Helena turned to see her son standing in the doorway. His body almost filled the frame of the low door. When had he gotten so tall?

Avery pushed Helena away and looked at her accusingly. "Why is he always looking at us? Why does he have to skulk around doorways?"

"Avery."

"Ed, what goes on between a man and a woman, two people who are in love, is private. They are free. Do you understand that? It is not for you to look at and watch like some peeping Tom."

"Avery," Helena said again, sharply. "Don't." She turned to Ed. "I'm sorry, dearest, I hadn't gotten around to asking him. Avery, Ed wanted me to ask you if he could help with your work. He's almost thirteen and he wants to help. He knows how hard you work."

"I'm not a peeping Tom," Ed said. "I'm doing research, like you."

Avery looked hard at Ed. Then he slowly nodded his head as if he had decided something. "All right. You're turning into a man, I can see that. A man has the right to work and be free and create. I believe that."

Helena had an unsettled feeling in her stomach. "Avery, I don't want you showing him the pictures of you-know-what. Please. And, Ed, you must also do your school work. I don't want you locked up in some dark room all day."

"No, Mouse. If Ed's a man then I will treat him like one. He's *becoming*."

Ed stood there looking at his father, but Helena couldn't read his expression. Perhaps this had been a terrible idea, she thought, looking at the two of them and then the room, with its yellowing posters and the disintegrating clothing.

She didn't want her son to see those gruesome crime-scene photos. But she wanted them to spend more time together, that was true. They had never been close; Avery had always treated their son like he was some kind of irritating appendage of Helena's. She decided then that she would take Ed to Tiger House again that summer, get him away for a while, away from Avery, let him play tennis and run around with Daisy, so things didn't get out of hand.

"Now, son, I want to speak to your mother privately," Avery said. "And don't think I won't know if you're listening."

When Ed had left, and Avery had waited to make sure he was really gone, he turned to Helena.

"So you'll go to Bill's party?"

"Yes. As long as it's not anything . . . I don't know. Anything strange."

"Unless men wanting to look at a beautiful mouse is strange."

"Avery . . ."

"Listen. I want to talk to you about something else, too. Dr. Hofmann called. He said you hadn't renewed any of your prescriptions lately. He's worried, and so am I."

"It's just they make me so tired. And Ed's not a baby anymore. I can't send him off to play or keep him in his room. He might need me for something. And the pills, it's like my head doesn't work right."

"Ed's a man now, my love. What was that whole conversation we just had? We both need you rested and well. I'll take care of Ed."

"Dearest, I don't really want to take them anymore. I don't think I need them. Remember when I was pregnant and afterward? I wasn't taking them, and I was fine."

"You're free to do whatever you want, Helena. You've always known that. Just promise me you'll be on good behavior for that party. If you're not rested, it will show in your face and Bill will be disappointed. Just think about it."

Helena nodded. She would take one, maybe, but just for the party. After that she wasn't taking them anymore. They didn't make her sleep now, anyway, unless she took a lot. And then she felt sick. While she'd known for some time that it was bad, it hadn't seemed to matter. But now her hands shook and her heart raced in a way that frightened her. And sometimes she couldn't remember things. She definitely wouldn't take any when she was at Tiger House. She knew Nick would disapprove, and it would be harder to hide if they were all living under the same roof. If she felt unwell, she would have a whiskey, like everyone else in her family.

"Well, well," Bill Fox said later that evening, as he opened the heavy, carved door to the villa. "I thought it might be you. So I said to myself: 'Why don't I open the door myself and make our Jane Russell feel welcome.' Nothing like a personal greeting, is there, honey?"

"Hello, Bill." Helena hated The Producer. He was always promising things to Avery and then changing the terms. But the Demerol was going some way to making her feel less spiteful toward him.

"Now, isn't that a lovely dress. Hits you in all the right places, of which there are so many." He winked. "Come on in."

Helena was wearing a fitted teal sharkskin dress she had

made from a pattern book Nick had sent her for Christmas. Her heels echoed on the Batchelder tile as she followed Bill through the vaulted hall out to the terrace.

Men in white tails were serving flutes of champagne on silver trays to the guests—a few actresses Helena had seen with Bill before and a group of older men, whom she assumed worked in the business in some capacity or other.

The sun was setting, red behind the hills, and Helena leaned against the wrought-iron rail and breathed in the night air. It was different up here, at the villa. Lighter, airier. So far away from the cramped guesthouse and its drawn curtains, and yet just up the hill. She could smell the perfume from the orchard below. The Anna apples, the Eureka and sweet lemon trees, the Valencia and blood orange.

"Have a glass of champagne, honey," Bill Fox said, motioning to a waiter. "It is beautiful up here, isn't it?" He followed Helena's gaze onto the orchard. "My first wife. She loved fruit trees."

"Really?"

"Really." Bill Fox leaned in close, his hand fluttering on her thigh. "Do you love fruit trees, too?"

Helena remembered how one night, when she and Avery had been drunk, they had snuck out and stolen some of the fruit. It was only a couple of apples, which hadn't been ripe, anyway. But she remembered wishing Nick was there. It was exactly the kind of escapade Nick would have loved.

"Yes, I like them." Helena moved a few inches away.

"Well, well. You're not shy, are you, honey?"

"Bill, why would I be shy? We've known each other a long time."

"That's right. We're like family. You and me and Avery. And let's not forget our dear, departed Ruby. She's one of the family, too."

Helena saw one of the young actresses, Vicky or Kiki, or something, staring at them.

"Is that your girlfriend?" She pushed her elbow in Bill Fox's side.

The Producer turned and looked at the young woman. "My girlfriend? Oh, I think I'm a little old for girlfriends these days. Couldn't keep track. Besides, the girls keep getting skinnier and skinnier. I like them more like, well, like you, honey. Round, soft."

Helena reached for another glass of champagne. "Excuse me," she said. "I have to go powder my nose."

In the bathroom she washed down another pill with the water glass left out for guests. She wished Avery were with her. She had only been to Bill Fox's house a handful of times over the years, and never without her husband. She wondered how much Bill Fox was paying him. She hoped it was a lot. She couldn't believe he had wanted her there. He had always been free with his hands, but never more so with her than anyone else. And he was old now. He had already seemed old when she had first met him, in Ciro's, with his silver hair. Now he had liver spots on his cheeks and hands like a crone. She shivered. She just had to look pretty and be pleasant and then go home and sleep.

Much later, she found herself alone with Bill Fox on the terrace. Everyone had left, without her noticing, somehow. She had been in conversation with one of the actresses, who was complaining about the casting couch. Her main objection, it seemed, wasn't about the sex part, but about the fact that she never got dinner afterward. Helena was nodding and drinking, and drinking some more. Then the girl floated away and it was just her and Bill Fox on the terrace. She knew what The Producer wanted. She had known all night.

It didn't take a genius. He was leaning against the frame of the French doors, smiling at her.

On the way to the guesthouse, Helena tripped on one of the steps and twisted her ankle. Bill Fox caught her elbow.

"Careful, honey," he whispered.

"Why are we going to my house?" She couldn't remember.

"You'll be more comfortable there."

"Avery," she said.

"He's gone out, honey. He's working, remember?"

She didn't remember.

In the bedroom, he wanted the light on.

"I want to look at you. I want to see what I'm paying for. I haven't had to pay since I was sixteen." He chuckled.

Helena joined in, although she knew the joke wasn't for her.

The Producer was moving over her, grunting. He was out of breath. He was old. Helena wanted to laugh at the old man who needed a nurse more than a roll in the hay. But she knew he would be angry, and then they wouldn't get their money. So instead she let him rasp away, while she watched the wall.

"You really are a slut," he coughed in her ear. "I always knew it."

He was getting close now, she could tell.

"Mother?"

Helena's body went stiff as a board. The sound of The Producer and the light and the bed, all swirled like a pool of water going down a drain. No, it wasn't possible.

"Mother?"

Ed. How could she have forgotten about her son? She pushed The Producer off her, so hard that he fell off the side of the bed, panting and coughing. She sat up, covering her breasts with her arm.

Ed was standing in the doorway in his pajamas. She wondered how she could have thought he looked tall. He was just a boy, but his eyes were flat, hard. He looked at her, more as if he was curious than afraid or angry.

"Ed," she said, but found she had nothing else to say.

Ed looked at The Producer, who was peeking over the side of the mattress now. His clothes were too far away for him to get to without exposing himself.

"Now, son," he started.

"I'm not your son," Ed said, matter-of-factly. "You shouldn't be here. My mother isn't well."

"I was just . . . Well, well." The Producer, too, seemed at a loss.

But Ed didn't move. He stood there, stock-still, until the old man made a dash for it, grabbing up his clothes and fleeing. Helena would have laughed at his cowardice in the face of a young boy if her heart wasn't breaking.

"Ed, dearest," she began, when he was gone. She had covered herself in the bed sheet. She wanted to hold her hand out to him, as some kind of peace offering, but the gesture, just the idea of it, seemed somehow grotesque. "Your father, dearest. He's been working so hard for so long . . ." She stopped. She couldn't explain this to her son.

"I understand," Ed said. "Research."

And with that, he left her alone in the lit room.

Helena awoke to the sound of a radio.

A bus carrying a group of young civil-rights activists bound for Birmingham, Alabama, was attacked Tuesday afternoon outside Anniston.

Her nerves felt like glass, her head was throbbing. But she no longer felt sick to her stomach and she found she could sit up without feeling dizzy. She reached for the pitcher and poured herself some water. It tasted sweet and lemony, and she gulped it down, before pouring herself another.

"Helena?"

Helena looked up to see Nick standing in the doorway.

"How are you feeling, darling?"

"My head hurts."

"Oh, darling, you're back with us. In the land of the living." She crossed the room and sat down on the edge of the bed. "You didn't speak for days. I was wondering if we were ever going to hear your voice again."

Nick tried to take Helena's hand but she pulled it away.

"What is it?"

"I want to see Avery," Helena said.

"I see." Nick looked down, fidgeting with a corner of the sheet. "I don't think Avery will be coming, darling."

"You mean you won't let him come. Does he even know where I am?"

"No, I don't think he does." She saw Nick's face, a mask of soft pity.

"Don't look at me like that. I don't want your pity; I want to talk to my husband."

"Darling, we're going home. You haven't been well. We need to get you well and we want you back with us, Hughes and I. I've missed you and I don't want to be without you anymore."

Helena laughed, a hot, shallow shuddering through her lungs. "You've missed me?"

"Yes, Helena, I've missed you. I want . . ."

"You want, you want." Helena's skin had begun to itch

again and she wanted to tear it off with her nails. "And what about what I want?"

"Helena, for heaven's sakes. Be reasonable, darling. Do you really want to go back to that awful house and be all alone?"

"I'm not alone. I'm married, if you've forgotten."

Helena watched Nick's eyes go a shade darker.

"I haven't forgotten." Nick's voice was cold, now. "But it looks like your husband may have."

"Don't say that." Helena felt her strength dissipating. "I know he's not perfect, like your saintly husband. But I want to speak to him."

"No," Nick said slowly. "No, I'm sorry, darling, but I can't let you. Not now, anyway."

"You can't keep me prisoner. You can't stop me from being with Avery."

"I am not keeping you prisoner. I'm trying to protect you, and I don't give a goddamn what you say."

"Oh, I know you don't. Avery was right all along. You've never cared about me, not really. I'm your shadow, there to make you look better, and I can have your scraps, when you've finished. But I can never have something of my own. It just kills you, doesn't it?"

"How can you say that to me?" Helena saw Nick's eyes go shiny. "I love you. Don't you know that?"

"Well, I don't love you. Not anymore."

"You're not well, darling," Nick said, rising from the bed and crossing the room to the door. "I know you don't mean that."

Helena could hear her crying in the other room. And, even though it hurt her a little to know it, she was glad.

1967: August

II

After her escapade with the neighbors' dog, Helena had tried to brush out the horrendous wig of hair, but it hadn't done much good. So she had lain down on the chaise longue in her room and fallen asleep, awaking some time later to a knock on her door. The sun was making its way down to the water, and she could hear the hum of the beetles on the front lawn. The grass had been brown for some weeks now, burnt out by the long hot summer.

"Helena," she heard Nick call softly. "Can I come in, darling?"

Helena sighed.

Nick didn't wait for an answer, of course, she just pushed the door open slowly and poked her head in.

"I don't want to fight. Not on your birthday."

Helena looked at her. There were so many things she couldn't say to Nick anymore that it made it almost impossible to say anything at all. Even the small pleasantries, or minor concessions.

"We're not fighting," she said. She felt tired.

"I've brought you something. A peace offering, and a gift. Can I come in?"

"Of course you can come in," Helena said. "It's your house."

Nick pretended she didn't hear the last comment. She was carrying a brown parcel under her arm. On the side table next to the chaise longue, she put down a small white pill.

"I found an aspirin." She looked at Helena as if she expected her to jump up and rejoice.

"Thank you," she said. She kept her hands in her lap, clasped tightly around her book.

"And I wanted to give you your birthday present. Before dinner." Nick placed the package next to her.

Helena waited, hoping she would leave and not make her open the present and pretend gratitude in front of her.

"Go on, darling, open it. I'm feeling pretty clever about it." Nick smiled one of her winning smiles.

Involuntarily, Helena found herself smiling back. She picked up the parcel and tore the paper, revealing carefully folded fabric: light-blue muslin, embroidered with gold tigers. She pulled it out and unfolded a dress, knee-length and fitted at the waist, with a bell-shaped bottom.

"I used one of your old patterns, with a little tweaking, just to update it, and had it remade for you. What do you think?"

Helena gingerly touched the cloth. It was beautiful.

"Do you love it?"

"Yes, of course."

"Oh, I knew you would. Hughes worried that you might not, because it had been my dress, before. But I told him Grandfather had brought it back for both of us and I had been selfish in taking it. I know it was selfish, darling. I'm sorry." Nick clasped her hands together.

"You said you were going to make cushions out of it," Helena said, careful not to sound reproachful.

210

"Oh, I know. I know, and I made a dress. Well, I said I was sorry, and I am." Nick looked up at the ceiling for a minute and Helena could tell she was trying to keep her temper. It made Helena smile inwardly. "In any case, darling, I'm just thrilled you love it."

Helena placed the dress over her lap and smoothed the fabric with her hand.

"Well," Nick said, finally, when Helena remained silent. "I guess I'll leave you to it. I have to go prepare for your birthday dinner." She stood and then turned. "Oh, I forgot to tell you. I'm sorry, darling, but your cake appears to have been stolen, if you can believe it. Must have been one of the neighborhood boys. We looked everywhere for it, but it's just vanished. The strangest thing. I am sorry. I know how much you love angel food."

"Amazing," Helena said.

Nick walked to the door. "I really do love this room," she said. "I've always loved it, especially those bluebirds." Then she shut the door softly behind her.

Helena fell back against the chaise longue. God, she hated her. The worst part of it was that she also missed her. She was charming and she was fun and awful, all at the same time. It wasn't that she didn't want to forgive her cousin, it was that she just couldn't. She had gone too far. Helena had only ever really wanted one thing and Nick had ruined it.

"Why do you believe she's stronger than you?"

"I don't believe that."

"If she's not stronger than you, then how could she take your husband away?"

"She's one of those people who gets what she wants. And she decided I had made a mistake."

"Who are these people who get what they want? Why do you feel like you aren't one of those people?"

"Because I'm not a fool, Dr. Kroll. I know what the world's like."

"And what is the world like, Mrs. Lewis?"

"The world is cruel to the innocent."

"And you are innocent?"

"I was, yes. I know I was."

Helena could hear them downstairs. Tyler, it seemed, had arrived. She caught his voice, and then Daisy's laughter. It was a specific kind of laughter, the kind girls made when someone they loved told them something charming about themselves.

Helena put on her girdle and then looked at the dress lying on the bed. Of course Nick would think it was all right to give her something she had already worn, something used. She had intended to throw the dress in the waste-paper basket. But she knew they would worry, they would think she wasn't well again. So the dress could just go to the back of the closet, and it could stay there until kingdom come, for all she cared.

But looking at it, lying there on the bed—blue the color of evening and the perfectly stitched gold tigers—she began to have second thoughts. She picked it up and slipped it over her head, zipping up the side. It fit perfectly, she had to give it to Nick.

She crossed the room to the vanity and looked in the mirror. The dress matched the color of her eyes, and for a moment she wished Avery could have seen her in it.

"I love you," he'd say. "My movie star."

She closed her eyes and imagined him, holding out his arms to her. She would fall into him and he would pull her very close.

Helena opened her eyes and looked at herself, standing in the blue dress in the middle of the room. No, she decided, she would wear it after all. This dress was made for her; tigers suited her very well. In fact, tigers were just perfect.

"You say soul-mates. If that is the case why do you think your husband hasn't come to visit you here?"

"Because he doesn't know where I am."

"I see. Why is that?"

"Because she won't tell him. She paid him off to stay away."

"And why do you think he would accept that? Why would he accept money to give up his wife?"

"He needed the money, Dr. Kroll. For something he's been working his whole life on. The most important thing to him."

"So you are expendable."

"I don't really think I know how to answer that question."

"Why is that, Mrs. Lewis?"

"Because you make it sound like he had a choice, which he didn't."

"It wasn't a choice?"

"No. She had a choice. But we didn't."

"Aunt Helena?" Daisy was tapping on her door.

What was this, Grand Central Station? Why couldn't she just be left in peace for one blessed moment?

"Yes, sweetest lamb? What can I do for you?"

Daisy opened the door, and, just like Nick, peeked around.

"I have a surprise for you."

"Really, now what would that be, dearest? I feel like I've been spoiled enough today."

She heard Daisy whispering behind the door. Helena turned back to the mirror.

"Hello, Mother."

Looking up, she saw her son standing in the doorway. He took her breath away, he was so handsome.

"Ed, dearest." She rose to go to him, but found herself hesitating, stopping just a few feet in front of him. "Well, this certainly is a surprise."

"I know," Daisy said, pushing in behind her son. She was always doing that, touching him, bossing him around, as if there were no barriers between them. Helena envied her. "Isn't it just the best? Ty drove him in from the city."

Helena saw Ed turn to look at his cousin. As always, his expression remained relatively unchanged, although Helena detected a kind of softness there. Again, she wondered if her son was in love with her niece. But she knew that wasn't quite it. Something else, but she couldn't put her finger on it. In any case, it suited her fine.

"Ed has been very mysterious with his comings and goings, but I managed to pin him down." Daisy was practically beaming over her coup.

"Happy birthday, Mother." Ed crossed to Helena and kissed her on the cheek. The kiss was neither warm nor cold. She wouldn't call it perfunctory, but it was close.

"Have you been very busy with work, dearest?"

"Yes, Ed Lewis, what have you been up to?" Daisy stamped her foot in mock outrage. "I tried your office a hundred times and they said you were away on business. Now, what kind of business does a market researcher have to do away from the office? I thought you all sat in basement dungeons, poring over figures."

"Housewives in Iowa," Ed said, looking at Daisy. "How they feel about Hoover's latest model."

"Dearest, all the way to Iowa and back for my birthday? Well, I couldn't be more touched." Helena tentatively put her hand to his cheek. He was so pale, as if he hadn't seen the sun all summer long.

"Well," Daisy said, looking from one of them to the other, "I should probably go help out Mummy. You know what she's like when she's preparing a dinner. Don't get up to anything naughty without me," she sang over her shoulder, with a wave.

Ed watched Daisy leave and then turned back to Helena. "What happened to your hair?" Unlike Nick, Ed wasn't mocking her; he seemed genuinely curious.

Helena laughed. "I'm afraid I had a little run-in with the hairdresser. Daisy's treat. I suppose I was feeling a little blue this morning."

"Why would she think that would make you feel better?"

"Oh, Ed, I don't think she thought it would turn out like this." Helena walked over to the mirror and patted her hair. "Did you say hello to your Aunt Nick?" She tried to make her voice sound light, but she watched her son's face in the mirror.

"I haven't seen her yet." His expression was impassive.

"It's nice that Tyler could make it for the dinner. I know how well he gets along with the family, especially your aunt."

Helena gazed down at the collection of lipsticks on the vanity, trying to decide on a color that would complement the dress. She chose Catch-Me-Coral. "Although, I must admit, I do wonder sometimes if it makes Daisy uncomfortable. He does dote so on Aunt Nick."

"Yes," Ed said. "He's watching her."

"I'm not sure how I would feel as a young bride-to-be, if my beloved paid so much attention to someone else, even if it was my mother." Helena applied the lipstick, and then leaned back on the stool to inspect herself. "Then again, Daisy's so lovely, she'd never say if it hurt her."

"What are you trying to say, Mother?"

"Nothing," Helena said, turning around to face him. "I just wouldn't want to see Daisy get hurt, that's all. Nor would you, I imagine."

"No," Ed said. "I wouldn't let that happen."

"Of course you wouldn't." Helena stopped and pretended to fiddle with something on her dress. "It's just that your Aunt Nick, well, she can be stubborn when she thinks she's right. Sometimes, people like that need to be forced to see how dangerous their behavior can be. Do you know what I mean?"

Ed was silent, watching her.

She swiveled back to the mirror, smoothed her hair down one last time, and fastened her pearl earrings. "There," she said, patting her knees and looking at her son in the reflection. "Shall we go down and join the others?" She tried to give her best impression of Nick's hundred-watt smile, all wide pleasure and glittering eyes. But, in the end, she just felt like she was baring her teeth.

"What about your son, Mrs. Lewis. You said you two haven't been close in the last few years. Why is that? Is that because of your husband?"

"No. He's a teenager. I don't think teenage boys have much time for their mothers, in general."

"I see."

"Why are you looking at me like that?"

"I'm not sure I agree with that assessment."

"For heaven's sakes, Dr. Kroll, I don't know."

"I think you do, Mrs. Lewis. You said he began to communicate less after he found a dead body, some summers back, is that right?"

"I said that I thought it might have scared him. I suppose he became a little quieter after that summer, but Ed has always been different. I know that's a dirty word here, but I don't see anything wrong with not being like every other blessed person."

"Does it upset you to think he is different from other boys his age?"

"What did I just say?"

"You seemed to think I might not approve, which leads me to believe that you are not entirely comfortable with the idea."

"I suppose you're just much more clever than I am, Doctor."

"Mrs. Lewis, I'm here to help you. I realize that your coming to us wasn't entirely your choice, but from our time together I can safely say that you are, at the very least, extremely unhappy. People who are unhappy are considered unwell. We must find a way for you to feel better. Do you understand?"

"So that I can be free."

"If you like."

"I suppose it did use to bother me that he wasn't like other children his age, Ed I mean. But I think he has a *peculiar inner strength. I think he was meant for great things. Many unusual people do great things."*

"You think he's special."

"Yes. Special. And strong. Strong is the most important."

❖

The dinner table was decorated with small vases of pink cosmos, and a little gold paper crown sat on top of Helena's plate. On Ed's arm, she made her way into the blue sitting room, where everyone had gathered for cocktails, except for Nick, who she could hear humming in the kitchen. Daisy, wearing a thin sundress printed with ivy, was sitting on Tyler's lap, while Hughes told some joke.

"Aha," Hughes said, when he saw her in the doorway. "What can I get for our lovely birthday girl?"

"I suppose one glass of champagne wouldn't hurt."

Hughes poured the glass and handed it to Tyler, who ferried it over to her.

"Happy birthday, Aunt Helena," he said, handing her the coupe. He was wearing his usual uniform, khakis and a striped Oxford, rolled up at the sleeves. The perfect little son-in-law.

"Thank you, Tyler. It really was so lovely of you to bring Ed with you for my little celebration."

"It was my pleasure. Nick knew how much it would please you and Daisy wouldn't let up until she'd tracked him down. Where was it, sport? Iowa? Housewives and Hoovers?"

"Yes," Ed said, "housewives and Hoovers." Helena was taken aback by the cruelty in her son's expression. For a moment, she had the strange impression he was going to tear Daisy's fiancé limb from limb.

Even Tyler shrank back a bit.

She looked at the two of them a moment longer, before taking a sip of her champagne. "Absolutely delicious."

"You know, I think I hate dinner parties," Nick said, entering the room. She was still wearing the white silk tunic from the afternoon. "I'm locked away in a hot kitchen while everyone's being witty and lovely without me."

"Poor darling," Hughes said. "We really must stop forcing these things upon you."

"Yes, Mummy, we all know how much you hate dinner parties," Daisy said. "What a faker."

"Oh, laugh if you will, but you know I only started cooking to make your father love me. Pathetic, isn't it?"

"Well, it worked," Hughes said, crossing the room to her.

An image of Nick and Hughes, before they were married, came to Helena: Of them standing in the road in front of the house. Nick was calling to Helena, and Hughes was next to her, his arm around her cousin, looking at her like he couldn't believe his luck.

"I, for one, am with Nick," Tyler said, brushing his hand through his hair and smiling in that boyish, crooked way that drove Helena crazy. "It's not only unfair to her, but to us as well, because we miss out on her company."

"Oh, you are a cool one, Tyler Pierce," Daisy said, narrowing her eyes at him. "If I don't watch out, you're going to turn into some kind of lounge lizard on me."

"At least I won't be at a loss for words."

"God forbid," Helena said.

At the dinner table, Helena donned the crown. The minute it was on her head, she wanted to take it off again, but thought it would appear hostile. So she sat there, feeling foolish, instead.

"The last tomatoes of the summer," Nick said, as she placed their plates in front of them.

The red flesh of the tomato startled Helena, it was so bright, glistening almost indecently against the bone china. The room was still for a minute, with only the sound of forks clinking against their plates.

"You'll never believe who I saw at Morning Glory Farm," Nick said, finally. "That disgusting toad of a man, Frank Wilcox. Shopping or some such nonsense, with his new wife. Who, by the way, looks twelve and stunned by just about everything."

"I didn't know the Wilcoxes had divorced," Helena said.

"Oh, you bet they did. She took her family's money and made a run for it after that whole business with the maid."

Ed looked up from his plate. "I didn't know he was still around."

"Neither did I," Nick said. "But there he was, large as life. You know, it was odd, but seeing him made me furious, for some reason."

"I hadn't thought about all that in forever," Daisy said, putting her fork down.

"Well, we never told you this, you were so young. But Frank Wilcox was fooling around with the girl, what was her name? Your father saw them."

"We know," Daisy said. "We were listening at the dining-room door when he told you."

"You scamps," Nick said. "Honestly, can a person not have a private conversation anymore?"

"You were talking with five other people, Mummy. It wasn't exactly private." Daisy took a bite of tomato.

"Frank Wilcox took me to a dance one summer, before the war," Helena said. "And he got quite rough on the car ride home. Nothing happened, mind you, but it was a feeling that something might have, if you know what I mean."

"We do," Nick said.

Helena remembered his hands, pinching her. They were mean hands. She had found tiny bruises on her skin the next day.

She caught Ed looking at her, his expression unmoved.

"What I can't believe is that they never found the person who did it," Daisy said.

Helena saw Hughes and Ed exchange a glance. Not a very friendly one either, she thought.

"I'm not sure it would have made any difference," Hughes said. "The damage was done."

"How can you say that, Daddy? Of course it would have made a difference. That poor woman. There has to be some justice for her. Someone has to be punished."

"My girl, the firebrand," Tyler said.

"Daisy's right," Nick said, thoughtfully. "Maybe it would have helped. Somebody should have been punished."

"That's not what I meant," Hughes said.

"I know, darling," Nick said, softly. "I know what you meant."

"Well, anyway," Daisy said, looking at Tyler, "that was the summer I fell in love with you. And you had the nerve to kiss Peaches Montgomery, you rat." Her adoration was palpable, heavy and sweet like the angel food cake.

"I had very bad taste in the '50s," Tyler said, winking at her.

Nick laughed. "Really, Ty, she is too awful."

"All right, all right." Tyler held up his hands. "I admit, it was a mistake. But I fell in love with you, too, that summer, in a way, even if I was too much of an idiot to know it." He looked at Daisy. "At least with your family. With all of this."

He held up his glass. "A toast to the Derringer-Lewises. Thank you for saving me from eternal boredom."

"Hear, hear." Hughes raised his glass. "And to our beautiful Helena. Happy birthday. And many happy returns of the day."

"Happy birthday, darling," Nick said, leaning over to touch her glass to Helena's.

"Thank you, thank you, dear ones," Helena said, touching her crown. "I wouldn't be here, for yet another splendid birthday, without you all."

"You seem very happy today."

"Yes, my son came to see me. It was lovely to see him. He's grown up so much. It frightened me a little bit."

"How long has it been since you last saw him?"

"I'm . . . not really sure. The pills, you see . . ."

"You lost a lot of time with the pills."

"Yes."

"How does that make you feel?"

"Well, I don't feel guilty about it, if that's what you're trying to make me say. I was very tired at the time."

"I'm not trying to make you say anything. Can you remember the last time you saw your son?"

"Well, it's hard. I do have memories of him as a teenager, younger, though. But then she sent him to school and I didn't see him anymore."

"She, meaning your cousin, Nick."

"Yes."

"You feel she took him away from you."

"Just par for the course. But I'm not going to keep complaining about that, as we discussed. It's in the past. As you say, she was doing what she thought was right. But it was

*so lovely to see him today. He's different, more . . . more of
a real person, I guess."*

"In what way?"

"He's very self-possessed, which is a good thing, I think."

"What do you mean when you say 'self-possessed?'"

"I don't know. He doesn't discuss his feelings."

"And this is something you think is a positive trait?"

"I don't know. I said 'self-possessed.'"

"You also said he doesn't discuss his feelings."

"I've never been good at word games, Dr. Kroll."

"All right. How does your son feel about your being
here?"

"I don't really know. He said I was unwell. And that it
was all right. He seemed curious about the hospital, I suppose."

"Is he protective of you?"

"I've never thought about it. No, not really, I guess. He's
very protective—if that's the right word—of my niece,
Daisy."

"What do you think he feels about you?"

"I don't know. Like I said, he's very . . ."

"Yes, self-possessed. You said earlier that it frightened
you, how much he'd grown up. Why did it frighten you?"

"I don't know why it did, but it just did. He seemed
stronger than I remembered."

"You've said in the past that strength is a characteristic
you hoped he'd have."

"Yes. It's good to be strong. Strong people get what they
want, you taught me that in one of our first sessions."

"I don't think that's what I meant."

"Yes, you did. Only strong people can fight off other
strong people. I don't want my son devoured."

"You feel you were devoured?"

"Yes, I do. But I guess, seeing him now, I am sure that if anyone's going to do the devouring in Ed's life, it's going to be him."

"And this makes you happy?"

"Yes, Dr. Kroll. This makes me happy."

There was no dessert, of course, but Hughes brought out a crystal decanter filled with port.

"Anyone for a nightcap?"

"I don't know," Nick said. "That wine was awfully heavy."

"Oh, go on, Nick," Tyler said, placing his hand lazily on Nick's shoulder. As if it were nothing. "It's a party."

"Helena, darling?" Nick's expression was solicitous, but Helena could tell it was a test.

"No, thank you," Helena said. She had never really cared for port, anyway.

"Aunt Helena, I almost forgot," Daisy said. "Your present, your real one. But we all have to go into the sitting room."

"You know, Daisy," Nick said, "I think Helena may have had enough of your presents for one day."

Daisy rolled her eyes. "Daddy? I need your support."

"I shall be the bearer of the port," Hughes said gaily. "Let us sally forth."

He was certainly having a good time.

"All right, dearest lamb," Helena said, putting her palms down on the table and pushing herself out of her chair. "Whatever you say."

"Yes, dearest lamb," Tyler said, offering Daisy his hand, probably still warm from Nick's shoulder, "let's sally forth."

Daisy batted Tyler's hand away. "You all go ahead, I'll be right back."

They made their way back into the blue sitting room.

"Helena, would you like something other than port?" Hughes asked.

"Oh," Helena said. "I'm not sure if I should."

He looked a little pained and glanced at Nick, who made a small shrug of her shoulders. Helena laughed to herself; they were all so ridiculous.

"A Scotch? It is your birthday."

"You're right. It is my birthday. Make it a Scotch." Helena smiled sweetly at Nick, who looked away. She was feeling sharper, more awake, than she had in some time, and it felt good.

Nick walked over to one of the big windows, placing her hand on the screen. "Summer's over. You can almost feel fall in the air, can't you?"

"I like fall," Helena said. "It always smells like change to me."

"Does it?" Nick looked at her. "I don't know. It smells like death to me, all those wet leaves rotting."

"They're the same thing," Ed said.

"That's quite a morbid thing to say there, Ed." Tyler looked slightly disgusted.

"Why?"

Tyler opened his mouth, and then just shrugged, taking a sip of his port.

"No, I suppose Ed is right," Nick said. "The seasons and all that. But it makes me sad. I've never liked either one of those things, change or death."

"But you're the devil, you're going to live forever," Helena said. "Old Nick, just like Grandfather said."

"Thank you, darling, you're too kind."

225

"Aren't you? You could have fooled me." Helena tried to laugh, but it sounded harsh, even to her.

"Well," Nick said, "I suppose I am. So what? I'm not going to apologize for it."

"No, no, of course not." Helena took another sip of her Scotch.

"I suppose that would suit you, would it?"

"Why would what suits me ever be an issue?"

"Oh, christ in heaven, Helena, why don't you just come out and say whatever it is you have to say."

"I don't know what you're talking about, dearest."

"Fine, have it your way." Nick was shaking her head in a way that made Helena want to slap her. "I may be the devil, but goddamn it, I'm your devil and you'd better get used to it."

The room had gone quiet. Tyler was looking at the floor and Ed had his eyes on Nick. Hughes, on the other hand, had disappeared. Typical, Helena thought.

"OK, everyone," Daisy said, coming into the room with a slim square package under her arm, oblivious, as usual. "Ta-dah." She handed it to Helena. "Daddy? Get back in here, we need you. Where's he gone?"

Helena tore at the wrapping paper with a vehemence that surprised even her. It was a record. The cover showed some sort of hazy, hippy man, with his head turned. "Van Morrison Blowin' Your Mind!," it read in fat, sausage-like writing. Helena laughed out loud, and held it up for the rest to see.

Nick put her hand over her mouth, trying to stifle her own laughter, her eyes locked with Helena's. "Daisy, darling, really. Do you think that's appropriate for your aunt?"

"Oh, don't be such fuddy-duddies. It's not about drugs," Daisy said, taking the album and heading for the record player. "You have to hear this song, Aunt Helena. It's called 'Brown-Eyed Girl.' It's about you.' She squinted at Helena. "Except, of course, you have blue eyes." And then Daisy started laughing, too. "Oh, well, never mind. I'm not really doing so well, today, am I?" She put the needle to the vinyl.

A little drum beat and then the sound of a guitar, like calypso. Helena smiled. It was a good song, a glad song, the kind that made you want to be happy, even if you didn't feel like it.

Daisy took Tyler's hand and started to do a little twist. Eventually, she held her hand out to Ed and pulled him toward her, the three of them forming a small circle.

Helena watched them, a little band of young gypsies, with everything in front of them. Even her son, sometimes so serious, doing his version of Daisy's Chubby Checker–style twist.

She looked at Nick. Her cousin held out her hand. Helena sighed and then took it. Nick pulled her up and put her arm around Helena's waist.

"We are old fuddy-duddies," Nick said.

Helena leaned her face against her cousin's soft cheek and felt an indescribable longing. Over Nick's shoulder, she could see the kids smiling at them. All except Ed. She was glad he didn't pretend. She needed him. She had set the ball rolling and now she needed him to be strong and true.

She could smell her cousin's perfume and thought about those wet leaves she had been talking about. How could she still love Nick, after everything? Helena's head felt like it might split; it was too much to think about. She couldn't bear it. So instead, she just held Nick, tight, as if it might be the last time.

HUGHES

1959: *July*

I

The phone was ringing in the house.

Afterward, when Hughes would go over the moment in his head, he would swear he first heard it ring as far as a block away. But, then again, that could have been his memory playing tricks on him. What he did remember clearly was the feeling of dread that arose in him at the sound.

He had been ambling slowly down Traill Street, passing his hand through hazy clouds of gnats suspended in the warm July air. It was late afternoon and, after a morning of unproductive work on a client's estate, he had taken off early and caught a showing of *Laura* at the Nickelodeon in Harvard Square.

That was one of the things Hughes loved about summer in the city. He could leave the office and no one asked, or cared, where he was. With his family far away on the Island, he experienced a sense of weightlessness that was rare in his daily life. He would eat dinner alone in the kitchen, a sandwich, or a steak if he felt like cooking, and then he would go up to the study and read until he fell asleep on the single bed. He only went to the bedroom he shared with Nick to change his clothes.

When he did, it felt like a ghost town. The picture of Daisy in the silver frame on his bureau, the cuff links in the blue china bowl, the perfectly straight pillows on the bed, all seemed to belong to someone else's life. He wondered sometimes, looking around at the room, what an archeologist would make of all this, of him. How would he be described? A man who kept his shoes shined, his socks in order. A man who loved his family. Was that him? When he was in the study, he knew better who he was, and this soothed him.

Recently there had been a sense, tugging away at him, that something was wrong. He noticed it sometimes when he was driving to work, or when he was reading, and would find himself having to stop what he was doing until the feeling passed. He couldn't put his finger on it exactly; something akin to fear, but it wasn't quite that. He knew it had to do with Nick, with losing her. But he hadn't lost her, though sometimes he would imagine that he had. The thought sickened him, like the sound of a bone breaking.

And when he heard the phone ringing in the house, as he walked his street on that summer afternoon, the same disquiet came over him, an alarm ringing in his head.

It had started a month ago, early June, shortly after Nick and Daisy had arrived at Tiger House for the season, and he'd gone down for the weekend to prepare the boat. After scrubbing *Star* down and checking the dinghy's hull and rigging for any damage, he went for a drink at the Reading Room, where he played two rounds of rummy and drank three gin and tonics, staying later than he had intended.

Still not tired, he had decided to take a stroll by the harbor, to breathe in the ocean and watch the lights dotting

Chappaquiddick. When he reached the Yacht Club, he went in and stood out on the stringpiece, listening to the hum of the outboard motors passing by. He loved the Island. Sometimes he wondered, had he and Nick moved back here after the war, as Nick had wanted to, if things would have turned out differently. He thought of Nick, at home, perhaps getting ready for bed, the small sigh that escaped her lips when she sat at her dressing table at the end of an evening. He looked back out at the dark water and pushed the idea out of his head.

He took Simpson's Lane, because it was the quietest way. He liked how it had remained almost a dirt path when everything else on the Island was changing. He was thinking about this when he reached the corner, and saw Frank and the girl coming out of the Hideaway, her dark head leaning on his shoulder.

Startled and not wanting to be seen, Hughes held back. He watched them walking away, and, unsure of whether to continue, decided to kill time with a cigarette. As he smoked, he tried to rearrange his surprise. It wasn't the obvious implication that confused him. It was more that it was an odd thing to do, for Frank to be so careless. Anyone who had happened to see them would have known something was going on, and the Island was a small place; everybody knew everybody. You couldn't just walk down the street flying your secrets at full mast. And if you were stupid enough to do that, you knew it would be around town in two seconds flat.

Hughes stamped out his cigarette and headed toward home. As he approached the back drive on North Summer Street, he saw Ed, or the shape of him, really, standing there. And beyond the boy, Frank Wilcox again, still with his maid, this time engaged in some kind of intimate conversation. Hughes's first thought was to wonder how Ed had managed to sneak out of the house so late without anyone noticing. He quickly forgot all about that when he saw the boy start moving toward the couple, like a cat, silently, keeping to the far edge of the sidewalk near the privet hedges lining the street. Frank and the girl turned down Morse Street in the direction of the tennis courts, Ed following in their wake. The boy stopped a moment and leaned down to pick something up from where Frank had been standing, before turning the corner and disappearing out of sight.

Hughes stood there feeling foolish. The idea of following Ed who was following Frank seemed like some kind of ridiculous caper. But what choice did he have? He couldn't very well let Ed go after them, especially knowing what they were likely to get up to.

Hughes made up his mind to grab Ed and haul him back to Tiger House. He started toward the corner, but when he reached Morse Street it was empty. He jogged to the end and turned onto the overgrown path that ran down the side of the tennis courts toward Sheriff's Meadow. He waited briefly and listened. He could hear footfalls ahead of him.

The path was one that few people used anymore, since the town had cut a real trail to the meadow from Pease's Point Way. As he made his way along it, the warmth of the night pushed the scent of untouched plant life up around him. The low moon provided a little light to see by, but not much, and Hughes had to tread carefully so as not to trip on the low branches and roots.

When he came to the run-down shed off the old Ice Pond, he stopped again. It seemed as good a place as any to take a girl who wasn't your wife for a roll in the hay. But after listening for a moment, he decided it was empty. He looked around for a sign. He was in the backlands of the meadow now: ahead was the marsh, and to either side was only thick undergrowth; neither seemed particularly likely spots. Hughes's shoes were getting wet in the soggy ground, and he cursed under his breath. When he found Ed, he was going to give him a good talking to for this wild-goose chase. *If he found him.*

He was considering just calling it a day and waiting for the boy back home when he heard the *hush-hush* of feet off in the bushes to one side. He tried to peer through. He couldn't see much, but the feet were definitely moving away from him. *Shit.* Hughes pushed through the thicket, covering his face to keep from getting scratched by the brambles.

He emerged and found himself on a winding path, set on both sides by a wild hedge. The smell of honeysuckle hung heavy, and Hughes found himself thinking of the first time he kissed Nick, outside her mother's house after a dance. She had been leaning against the side of the house, pressed lightly into a mass of flowers that was growing up a trellis, and forever after, the odor had been linked with her in his mind.

Hughes came to a clearing, and here he stopped dead. The moon had risen slightly. In an old shelter off to one side was Frank Wilcox, pants down around his ankles, pumping rhythmically into the girl, who was facing away from him. Frank had pushed the girl's head down to the side with his hand, and was using it as a sort of leverage.

In the middle ground stood Ed, his back to Hughes. The boy wasn't making any noise, but Hughes could see his right arm moving up and down at a frantic pace.

Jesus Christ, Hughes thought. *Jesus fucking Christ.*

He approached Ed as quietly as he could and reached

out his hand, clamping it hard on his nephew's shoulder. The boy's arm stopped, but other than that, he didn't move a muscle. No gasp or little jump of surprise. He heard the sound of the zipper going up, and then Ed turned around. There was no expression on his face and Hughes felt himself wince. He put his finger up to his lips and then pointed in the direction of the path. Ed waited a moment, looking at him, and then headed back toward the courts.

Hughes stayed silent on the way, furious, just watching the boy's unhurried steps in front of him. But when they hit the street, he swung Ed around to face him.

"What the hell do you think you were doing?"

"I'm not a pervert," Ed said, matter-of-factly.

"I'm not so sure about that," Hughes said. "I mean, Jesus Christ, what were you thinking?"

Ed just stood there, his eyes strangely flat. Hughes couldn't guess what was going through the boy's mind, but he also knew that he had done some weird stuff when he was Ed's age and had felt pretty crummy about it at the time.

"Look," Hughes said, deciding to take a different tack. "It's normal to wonder about these things."

"What things?"

Jesus. "Men and women."

Ed was silent.

"When I was your age, there was this girl I really liked . . ." He wasn't sure where he was going with this.

"I don't like Frank Wilcox. I don't like the girl particularly, either."

Was the kid dense? Hughes tried to keep his voice even. "What I'm saying, Ed, is that you can't go around spying on people in the middle of the night. Especially like that. I mean, Christ."

"I wasn't spying."

"I think we both know what it was you were doing."

"It was research."

"That is not research." Hughes was getting angry again. "And what you saw was not a pleasant sight."

"Why does it have to be pleasant?"

The boy's tones were neutral, but Hughes had the impression that Ed was taunting him. "Look, I know things aren't easy at home, with your father . . ."

"Don't talk about my father," Ed said, and here Hughes detected an edge.

"Look . . ." Hughes began.

"I'm trying to educate myself," Ed said. "About people, what's inside them."

Hughes stopped. "I'm sorry, what do you mean 'what's inside them'?"

"I do a lot of research. Research other people don't want to do." Ed was looking at him intently. "It's not all pleasant."

It was the way he said it, a slight inflection, perhaps; Hughes felt a chill come over him. Something was very wrong here. "What do you mean?" he said slowly.

"For example," Ed said. "I know about your letters. The ones from that woman in England. Eva."

Hughes felt his breath being sucked out of his body. Then the adrenaline. Eva. This couldn't be happening. His brain felt fuzzy, primal. He moved toward Ed and took the boy by the collar, pushing his face close to him. So close, he could smell the kid's shampoo, and his sweat. "What the fuck did you just say?" His own voice sounded strange to him, quiet and cold.

"The letters," Ed said in a rush, as if Hughes's proximity excited him. "The ones you keep hidden in the basement."

"The letters I keep hidden in the basement." There was rage, like a stink coming off him. "My letters. You little bastard." He was going to tear the kid to pieces. He could feel it. He wasn't going to be able to stop himself. Then: Nick. He had to think. Hughes forced his brain to work. Finally, and with what seemed like impossible effort, he let go of Ed.

"No, Ed," he said evenly, "I don't think you found any letters. I don't think you know anything." He looked at him. "I think you're a pathetic little boy who's been caught jerking off to two strangers going at it. That's a sad story. That's the kind of story that makes people think: 'What a confused, messed-up kid.' And then they start to think about other things, like maybe he's too unstable to be out and about, that sort of thing. Do you see what I mean?"

"I don't think I'm confused," Ed said, not taking his eyes off Hughes. "But then again, I guess I could always ask Aunt Nick. Maybe she'd know."

Hughes nodded his head slowly and then backhanded the kid, hard, sending Ed flying across the pavement. Ed touched his hand to his lip, but stayed down.

"Get up," Hughes said.

When Ed rose, he grabbed boy's face and turned it from side to side. There was no blood.

"Get home now, and don't wake your mother." His voice sounded hoarse, as if he'd been running in the cold. "And don't you ever threaten me again."

Ed looked at him. He didn't cry, or mock him, or whine about the blow. Just cocked his head slightly, before turning and walking back down Morse Street toward home.

When Hughes returned, the house was quiet and he went to check on the letters. He had been keeping them in a toolbox underneath his workbench in the basement, a place he knew neither Nick nor Daisy would ever have any reason to look. When he lifted the tray of stray nails and screws, he found them seemingly undisturbed, Eva's beau-

tiful, creamy stationery stacked neatly in a pile. He picked
up the one resting on top.

> *Southampton, March 3, 1945*
>
> *Dear Hughes,*
>
> *As I write this, you are probably tossing and turning
> somewhere across the Atlantic, while I am sitting here
> at my dreary desk, still dreaming of that magical steak
> we ate last week.*
>
> *I must say, it felt very liberating and slightly
> scandalous to celebrate my divorce in such a manner.
> Champagne and steak! What would the War Office say?
> Who cares. I am a lost woman now, and am thoroughly
> enjoying it.*
>
> *A friend of mine has agreed to lend us her house
> in Devon the next time you get leave. It's just a little
> cottage, but we don't need anything bigger than a bed.
> I can't even boil an egg (will you care?), so never mind
> about a kitchen. We shall walk around naked all day
> and I will throw myself at you every chance I get.*
>
> *Hughes, I'm not sure I can stand all this happiness.
> Please, please stay safe. There's so much sadness around,
> it scares me. I know that sounds a bit dramatic, but
> I can't help it. The world's on fire, after all. Just come
> back to me quickly.*
>
> *Love,*
>
> *Eva*

Hughes carefully put the letter back and then took the
whole pile upstairs to his office, where with a heavy heart
he locked them in his desk, slipping the key into his pocket.

*

He didn't tell anyone about the incident and as the days passed, he tried to put the episode into perspective. Ed really was mixed-up, without a real father figure, and was probably just acting out, he told himself. He was a kid. He was going through some bizarre, albeit slightly unnatural, stage of growing up. It was all going to be fine. Hughes went back to the city and his lazy afternoons and sleeping in the study. Still, he kept thinking about Frank and the maid, about the letters, and about Nick.

The phone was ringing in the house. Hughes got to the front door and turned the key in the lock. His heart hammering, he bounded up the two flights to the landing and into the library. He picked up the cold black receiver.

"Hello?"

"Hughes. Thank god." It was Nick.

"What? What's happened?"

"It's Daisy. She and Ed found a dead body."

Hughes leaned back against the wall, his hand on his chest.

"Goddamn it, Hughes. She saw it."

"Who?" He felt like he couldn't breathe.

"Well, they're not sure. There's some talk that it may be somebody's maid. Apparently, she's one of the Portuguese girls."

"Whose maid?"

But he knew who it was. There was no use pretending anymore.

1944: December

Even though Christmas was over, the train station still carried that whiff of holiday excitement. You could almost smell the pine in the air. People milled past Hughes, a moving canvas of anticipation. A pretty Wren in a gray coat with jingle bells sewn onto the hem tinkled by, lifting his spirits, if only for a moment. He had missed the train to London and now faced the depressing prospect of spending one of his three precious liberty days back aboard the *Jones*.

Stepping out into the streets of Southampton only made him feel lower. The Germans had bombed the hell out of the city, so that its most prominent feature was now a snaking mass of metal from the station to the docks, a landscape of tracks, towers, and cranes. The buildings looked like a collection of ruins, jagged blackened structures reaching skyward. But it was the staircases leading nowhere that disturbed Hughes the most. They seemed to be everywhere, futile against the blown-out backs of the houses; he had learned to keep his eyes on the pavement when he went into town.

Still, it was better than Le Havre, where they had just left off an entire motorized division. The French port town had taken such a beating during its liberation that the *Jones* had been forced to continue to England to reprovision, instead of going straight back home.

Hughes made his way back to the docks and headed for

the Red Cross canteen, where at least you could get a coffee that wasn't just lukewarm sludge, and maybe a doughnut, and stare at the Red Cross girls in their pale-blue overalls.

Inside, a long line made him curse his luck all over again. Hughes was about to chuck it in and go in search of a pub instead, when he heard Charlie Wells call out to him.

"Derringer." Charlie was standing midway along the line, motioning for Hughes to join him. "I thought you were on a train to London. What happened, decided the charms of Southampton were too good to be missed?"

"I missed the damn train," Hughes said, ignoring the men grumbling behind him about line-cutters.

"Ah, well, you can come out with me and the boys. You might learn something."

"Go to hell."

"Ha," Charlie clapped him on the back. "Don't be sensitive. Come on, we need to put some hair on that chest of yours. It'll get you out of that stiff collar, at least."

Hughes wasn't in the mood for Charlie. In fact, he hadn't been in the mood for much lately. He hadn't seen Nick in three months, and Christmas had been a dismal affair, with the *Jones* pitching fitfully all the way from the Brooklyn Naval Yard, a frozen turkey, and cranberry sauce that tasted like sweet red piss. He was sick of these wretched, destroyed cities, harbors that were always blowing like shit, and the seasickness that never seemed to get better. When he'd seen the army boys disembark in France after ten days on the Atlantic, he couldn't help laughing to himself. They'd been the color of pea soup. But, then again, it could have been the thought of an enforced march against the Germans in mid-winter.

"Lieutenant Derringer."

Hughes turned to see Commander Lindsey behind him. Like Hughes, he was wearing his dress blues. "Captain."

"I'm glad I ran into you. You're going to London, I believe. Three days' liberty?"

"Yes, sir, but I missed my train. Doesn't look like I'll be leaving until tomorrow now, sir."

"Missed your train, did you?" Commander Lindsey rubbed his finger over the top of his lip, which he had a habit of doing when he was thinking over a problem. The first time it happened, Hughes had thought his captain was telling him that he had something on his face and he had mimicked the gesture, until Commander Lindsey had demanded to know why the hell he was so twitchy.

"That's unfortunate," the captain said. "I have a dispatch here that has to get to the Naval Control Room by tonight. Lieutenants Wilson and Jacks have already gone on, I suspect."

"Yes, sir. I think they did make it to the train."

"Right. Well, Lieutenant, maybe we can kill two birds with one stone, so to speak. I'll have a word with the Brits and see if they have a dispatch driver they can spare. Maybe we can get you to London tonight, after all."

"That would be terrific, sir."

"Get your coffee, Lieutenant, and be quick about it. I'll meet you out front."

"Thank you, sir."

"Mr. Wells." Commander Lindsey nodded at Charlie, before turning on his heel and walking toward the canteen door.

"Annapolis bastard," Charlie said when the captain had left. "Always walks like he has a stick up his ass."

"You got your commission. Besides, you shouldn't be so sensitive," Hughes said, grinning at him.

"Let's get the coffee," Charlie said, scowling. But his face lit up again when a Red Cross girl with a big chest turned to serve them. "Anyway," he said, "I'm not sure what London has that I can't find here." Charlie winked at the Red Cross girl, who smiled back.

Hughes laughed. He was already feeling a damn sight better.

At the Royal Navy's Admiralty House, in one of the city's remaining municipal buildings, Hughes waited in the lobby while Commander Lindsey went to speak with his British counterpart. The hustle and bustle of the post reminded him of the train station, but without all that Christmas business, which was a relief. He had sent off a letter to Nick two weeks before Christmas Day, hoping that it would get to her on time. He hadn't known what to say, except that he loved her and missed her; he couldn't write about what he was doing or where he had been or was going.

The year on active duty had been like living in suspended time. There was the world he had left behind, and this other place he had slipped into: the constant explosion of depth charges from the K-guns shaking the ship; the pale faces of the crew in the battle-station red lights; zigzagging across the Atlantic in total blackout, decoding messages until you thought your eyes would drop out of your head. Nick was still living in the real world, a place you could dream about sometimes when you took up the bunk chains to get some sleep. But where he was, you couldn't talk about, let alone explain.

"Lieutenant Derringer."

Hughes looked up and saw Commander Lindsey. It took

him several seconds more to realize that the person accompanying him was a woman; she was wearing breeches, an oversized hacking jacket, and what looked like flight boots. At first, he couldn't tell how old she was. But as they got nearer he saw from the girl's brow, shining below a mass of tightly pinned hair, that she was about Nick's age.

"You're in luck, Lieutenant. Dispatch Rider Eva Brooke here has a delivery to make herself in London." Hughes thought he detected the beginnings of a smile tugging at the corners of his captain's lips.

"Sir," Hughes said. He looked at the girl. "Miss Brooke."

"Mrs. Brooke," the woman said in a voice like a church bell.

"I beg your pardon. Mrs. Brooke."

"Right, then. Lieutenant, this dispatch is for Lieutenant Commander Napier at the Admiralty Citadel. See that it gets to him before you enjoy the sights."

"Yes, sir."

Commander Lindsey turned to the young woman. "Mrs. Brooke."

"Commander." The young woman gave his captain a sharp nod.

They made their way out of the building and around to a lot in the back filled with rubble from neighboring buildings. A group of boys were showing off their shrapnel collections to each other. One of them had a black eye. It made Hughes's head feel light, like vertigo.

"I suppose I won't be needing this," Mrs. Brooke said, throwing her motorcycle helmet in the backseat and eyeing the car with disgust, before opening the driver's side door and getting in.

"What do you normally drive?"

"A motorcycle," she said. She gave Hughes a wry smile.

"Yes, I got that," Hughes said. "Which kind?"

"Do you know anything about motorcycles?"

"No."

"That's what I thought," Mrs. Brooke said, and released the clutch, backing the car out of the lot. She honked twice at the boys, who scattered like pigeons.

Hughes ran his hand over the dashboard. "A Daimler. German."

"Very perceptive. Are you always this clever?"

Hughes looked at her; she was staring straight ahead. "Not always. I have my moments."

"Well, we did have a General Motors factory until the Luftwaffe took a sudden and rather noisy fancy to it."

"They're funny that way." Hughes patted his breast pocket, reassuring himself he had put his toothbrush in there. He had several extra collars in his coat jacket, and that was it for his liberty provisions. "So what are you delivering to the Admiralty?"

"This bloody car, if you can believe it. Apparently, they lost a couple in air raids last week." She turned to Hughes. He noticed that her eyes were almost exactly the same shade of brown as her hair. "I don't mean to be unkind, but I don't think the Royal Navy would waste their precious petrol taking just a letter all the way to London. Even for you."

They began to leave the vestiges of Southampton behind and the road opened up, dead winter fields on either side.

"Why didn't your commander take the letter himself?" Mrs. Brooke asked after some time.

Her voice really was like a church bell. Hughes thought of the chimes of St. Andrew's on the Island, where he and Nick had been married. Nick's naked body flashed inadvertently through his head, like a bright, hot streak of light.

"He's got a girl in town, I think."

"Ah, yes, the proverbial girl in town."

"You sound like you don't approve."

"I don't approve or disapprove. It's just a cliché, that's all," she said.

"I'm not sure that's the worst thing to be, a cliché," Hughes said.

"Aren't you? I think it's just about the worst possible thing in the world."

"Everybody wants to pretend they're different, but we're not. We're all the same." He thought about the *Jones*, two hundred seamen and twelve officers, two hundred and twelve men shaking from the depth charges.

"How awful for you, to think like that, Lieutenant," she said, and her voice had a softness to it that irritated Hughes. "And call me Eva. I'm not sure I can bear to hear 'Mrs. Brooke' for the next three hours."

"Where is your husband, then?" Hughes pitied the poor fellow.

"I can't really be certain," she said. "Last time we saw each other he had been in North Africa."

"He's in the navy, too?"

"Yes." She sighed.

Hughes fell silent. He didn't think he could handle listening to a soliloquy about Mr. Brooke, which was bound to follow that sigh. Then again, you could never be sure, especially about a girl who rides motorcycles. He leaned his head back against the seat and stared out the window.

"Are you from here?"

"When you Americans say 'here,' I'm never quite sure where you mean."

"Here," Hughes said, passing his hand in front of the windshield. He was getting impatient with her snotty little attitude.

"Hampshire? No," Eva said.

Hughes watched small circles of fog appear and fade on the window with his breath. Outside, the gun-metal sky hung dully around them. He pulled his Zippo out of his pocket, and started flicking it with his thumb, listening to the rhythmic click of the steel.

"So, where are you from?" Eva finally asked, as if she were resigned to conversation.

"Cambridge, Massachusetts," Hughes said, thinking of his mother and father rambling around their big house all alone.

He had written to his mother, too, letters full of good cheer and optimism about winning the war. It disgusted him a bit, the tone of those letters, but she had been so angry when he went off that he felt it was his job to present things in the best possible light. He imagined her now, on her fainting couch, her fists balled in fury as she read them.

In the distance, he saw what looked like seagulls with very black heads. He watched them circling and thought of German planes and the ocean. He thought of Le Havre and wondered where that division was now, and how many had already been cut up by the Panzers, and how many had frostbite and how many would be escorted by the *Jones* one day, back across the Atlantic, home. Listening to the sound of the motor vibrating underneath him, he dozed off.

When he woke, the glass was steamed up. He reached into the pocket of his coat and found his pack of Lucky Strikes.

He cracked the window a bit and put a cigarette in his mouth.

He turned to Eva and offered her one.

"Oh, yes, please," she said, and for the first time she looked like what she was, a young woman, delighted by the prospect of tobacco.

"How old are you?" Hughes asked, lighting one and handing it off to Eva.

"Twenty-four," she said.

The open window brought in the sharp scent of wet grass and dead leaves.

"What made you want to be a dispatch rider?" He pulled lazily on his own cigarette, feeling more relaxed than he had in some time.

"Why would you ask that?"

"The obvious reason," he said.

"Yes, of course. Then I suppose the answer must be equally obvious."

"Excitement?"

"Yes, and also . . . I don't like the idea of being stuck."

"I'd give anything to be stuck in one place right now," Hughes said.

"Not just in a place. I don't know, just stuck in anything, really." She said it firmly, but Hughes had the strange impression she might cry.

Her hair had started to come unpinned, curling up round her face and neck, and Hughes saw that she was, in fact, attractive, if it weren't for the breeches and the ill-fitting jacket. Her hands on the wheel looked very small and he had an urge to see her wrists, which he imagined to be birdlike.

"So you have your motorcycle and you can ride away whenever you like, is that it?" He exhaled into the car.

"Well, it's not all that cavalier."

"I guess it must be nice for your husband to know you're doing your part, fighting alongside him, so to speak."

"Oh, is that what husbands like? I've never been very good at knowing about those things." She sounded contemptuous. "Is that what your wife does, her part?"

"In a way," Hughes said, looking hard at her. He didn't like her tone. "She exists. That's enough for me."

"How charming."

Hughes ignored the comment.

"She must be quite a marvel, your wife, for her very existence to give you such comfort."

"She is."

Eva looked at him. She seemed unspeakably sad suddenly. "Oh, hell," she said, turning back to the road.

They passed a few minutes in silence. Jesus, she was prickly. "How far away are we?" he asked.

"We're not far now." Her voice had returned to its former clarity, all business.

Hughes felt relieved. "I've never been to the Admiralty Citadel," he said. "What's it like?"

"Oh, you know, maps and things. All very busy in there."

He lit another cigarette. "What are you doing for New Year's Eve?"

"Are you asking me out?"

"What?" Hughes felt his cheeks go a little hot, like a girl. "No, it was just a question."

"Oh, don't get so excited. I was only joking," she said and gave him a sly smile.

Hughes laughed. She was a strange bird, this Eva Brooke, like some kind of actress playing a million different parts.

"I'm not sure yet," she said, "perhaps with my family. I have a couple of days' leave."

"Oh," Hughes said.

"But your commander said you had three days. I'm sure there will be dances, if you're looking for something to do."

Hughes was silent.

"What's that face? Don't you like dances?"

"Not very much right now, I guess. They remind me of my wife." He thought of Nick in her dress with the neckline like a heart. He liked that dress.

"Oh my," Eva said, "you really are smitten. We'll have to see what we can do about that."

It was at that point that Hughes decided to shut up for the rest of the trip.

When they hit London, Eva's driving became more careful, as she maneuvered to avoid parked cars, fire trucks, and general debris. It was still strange to go from one bombed-out city to the next, with only rolling fields and the odd village in between. As they passed what had once been the Dunhill shop, he was reminded of his last visit to London, before the war. He had come with his college crew team and they had made a somewhat drunken visit to stock up on cigars in anticipation of a win against their English rivals. Now all that was left was its sign, leaning up against a pile of rubble.

"Goddamn Germans," he said. "Look at this place."

"Yes," Eva said, "it does feel sometimes like the whole world's on fire, doesn't it?"

They parked and Eva put her service card on the windscreen, flicking it disdainfully against the glass. "I'm not sure what they'd do about it, anyway," she said, more to herself than Hughes.

She walked briskly toward the Admiralty Citadel, a large

concrete blockhouse, with a square tower and firing positions, like something out of the Middle Ages.

"Charming, isn't it?" she said, giving him a smile.

Hughes noticed that she'd managed to put lipstick on at some point and her hair was tidied. When had she done that? Did she really think a little lipstick was going to detract from her badly fitting clothes? Still, there was something sexy about it. He didn't know if he had actually ever seen a woman in breeches before.

They showed their papers to the guards at both the entrance to the building and the stairwell, going down several flights underground. Eva seemed to know her way around. When they reached a certain level, she took a corridor and then another. They had to squeeze past several naval officials who were pulling maps out of drawers in heavy wooden chests. A white phone on one wall rang doggedly, before a Wren picked it up. It reminded Hughes of the *Jones* belowdecks. Dark and cramped, with green-painted concrete and steel. Finally, they got to the entrance of the operations room, which was heavily sandbagged, and again showed their identification.

Inside, a large map adorned the whole back wall, showing U-boat locations and the movement of the Allied convoys. In front of the map was a metal walkway, with Wrens going back and forth, moving the markers in and out of place as locations were called from the floor. It made Hughes feel ill to see how close those convoys were to the black markers. On the ship, you only had the depth charges, and although they went off constantly, rarely did they hit anything. You knew they were there, the submarines, probably lurking close by, but since you couldn't see them, you could still imagine you were safe. Sometimes, anyway. Eva had been right, the Citadel was all "maps and things, all very busy," but being there, her comment took on a different and sinister meaning.

A lieutenant commander approached him.

"I believe you have a dispatch for me, Lieutenant." The man's eyes seemed to look right through him.

"Commander Napier," Hughes said, coming to attention. "Yes, sir." Hughes pulled out the envelope and handed it over.

The lieutenant commander said nothing, only nodded and then walked away. Hughes looked around and saw Eva chatting with some officer, her head thrown back in laughter, her curly hair in danger of falling out again. He wondered if he should wait. It seemed rude to leave without saying anything after that long, strange drive, but he also felt it would be better, somehow.

He took one last look at the map, and then walked out past the guards at the door. He stood in the corridor, unsure if they had come left or right down the hall. He had just decided on left, when he felt someone squeeze his arm.

"You didn't think I was going to abandon you to the terror of dancing alone, did you?" Eva said.

Hughes couldn't say why, exactly, but a wave of relief washed over him.

Somehow, they managed to find a taxi, something Eva insisted on, which was all right because Hughes had just gotten his pay. But when she told the driver to take them to Claridge's, he momentarily panicked. Seeing his expression, Eva just laughed.

"Don't worry, I'm not going to force you to buy me dinner, Lieutenant. My family keeps a room there."

She seemed to have metamorphosed once again since

they had reached London. She was more relaxed, less fractious or sad or whatever it was. She pulled the pins out of her hair in the taxi and popped them into her jacket.

Hughes didn't ask what her family did to be able to keep a room at Claridge's, but he also didn't really care. The possibility of seeing the hotel where everyone, including his hero Churchill, stayed was good enough for him.

When they pulled up in front, he smiled. The stately entrance was piled high with sandbags, exactly like the operations room at the Citadel, as if there was no difference here between work and leisure. And as at the Citadel, Eva strode purposefully through the lobby, her funny boots clacking against the polished black-and-white-marble floor. This time, though, Hughes didn't feel the need to keep up. He looked around at the tiered chandelier, and the comfortable-looking club chairs. There was an unnerving portrait of an extremely stiff-looking woman hanging over the fireplace, which in its turn glowed warmly. He joined Eva at the front desk.

"Good evening, Lady Eva," said the older man behind the desk.

Lady Eva? Just who the hell was this girl?

"Good evening, Winson," Eva replied.

"Not too cold a drive for you today, I hope." He held out a key attached to a brass plate that read: Claridge's Room 201.

"Traveled by automobile today, I'm afraid."

"Very good," the man said.

Eva turned to Hughes. "The lift's this way," she said, taking his arm and guiding him back through the lobby.

"He seems like a pretty efficient fellow," Hughes said, smiling down at her. "Lady Eva."

"Yes, Winson's indispensable," Eva said, ignoring the mention of her title, "if only for his witty conversation."

They stood in front of the elevator. "I just need to take a quick bath and get out of these clothes," Eva said. "Then I'll buy you a drink at the Causerie."

Hughes disengaged her hand from his elbow. "I should wait down here," he said, feeling a bit foolish. "And then I'll buy you a drink."

"Don't be ridiculous," Eva said. "Nobody waits in the lobby." She pushed him into the elevator.

The attendant kept his eyes on the ceiling and pulled the inner door shut.

As they approached room 201, Hughes stopped, and held his ground. "Look, I'll just wait outside here. And don't tell me nobody waits in the hallway."

"They'll think you're a deviant," Eva said. "Or my lover, waiting for a signal. But suit yourself."

"Jesus," Hughes said, hurrying into the room behind her.

Once inside, he took in the curving burl wood cabinets and plush carpet, cursing himself. Eva was trouble, but he had already known that, if he was honest with himself. He thought of Nick, sharing that drafty rented house with Helena on Elm Street, and felt guilty. He shouldn't be here. But he also knew he wanted to be here, and if he felt guilty, it was because he wasn't really thinking about Nick at all.

"Sit here," Eva said, pointing to a cream-colored arm-chair.

Hughes kept standing.

"Don't be foolish," she said. "Here, you can read this to keep you busy." She handed him a copy of the *Illustrated London News*.

The cover story was about the Ardennes Offensive raging in Belgium and the terrible weather conditions. Hughes thought again of the division they had left off in Le Havre. He sank into the chair and ran his hands through his hair.

"I won't be a tick," Eva called from the bathroom and Hughes looked up to see a flash of the green marble sink disappearing as she closed the door.

He heard her turn the taps, the sound of rushing water. He should really leave. He could go down to the bar and wait for her there.

Instead, he flipped through the paper. He started to read a story about how families in London had made do over the Christmas holiday, managing to find clever ways to make rock buns and mince pies with their rations. It made him hungry. He wondered what Nick had eaten for Christmas. She had been with his parents, and their cook, Susan, was quite cunning when it came to black-market foods, or at least that's what Nick had written him, with no little envy in her tone. Nick had a rapacious appetite for life, which didn't sit well with rationing and making-do. He chuckled at the image of her carefully saving up her butter rations for a pie crust. She was impatient and sometimes excessive, but that's what had attracted him from the start. The belief that the world was hers for the taking. That, and her strange vulnerability. It had mesmerized him when he'd first met her, made him want to be a part of all that she promised. But he didn't feel so strong anymore, and yet she remained unchanged, a fact he found disquieting.

Hughes heard Eva splashing and singing in the bath. This was ridiculous. He got up and went to the polished desk in front of the window. He would write her a note telling her to meet him in the bar. He picked up the pen and took a sheaf of the hotel stationery from the box. But Hughes realized he didn't know how to start. "Dear Eva," or just "Eva," or "Mrs. Brooke"? Maybe just nothing. Just: "Down at the bar," but that seemed a little rude. He stared at the paper and then picked up the pen and wrote:

> *Awaiting your ladyship at the bar.*
> *Hughes*

He smiled, looking at it. That will get her goat, he thought to himself. But as he bent to place the note on the pillow, where he felt sure it wouldn't be missed, he heard the bathroom door open. When he turned, there she was, standing naked as the day she was born, framed by the rich black tiles behind her.

"Hello," Eva said.

It took Hughes a minute for his brain to register that he was actually seeing her. She was small and pale, with beautiful, heavy breasts, which hadn't been noticeable beneath that big jacket. Heavy hips, too, like a miniature hourglass. The tips of her hair were plastered to her wet shoulders. But it was her bush, large and dark and full, that his eyes fixed on. He had the odd thought that it was so unlike his wife's, which was like a flat vine growing up a trellis.

Eva was staring at him, her eyes candid, hands still at her sides, without the slightest hint of embarrassment. And for some reason, this made him very angry.

"Put some clothes on," he said coldly, crumpling up the note in his hand.

"Was that for me?" she asked, gesturing toward the balled paper. "What did it say?"

Hughes refused to turn away; it would be a sign of weakness. "For Christ's sake, Mrs. Brooke, cover yourself up." He was furious, but his tone was flat.

Eva shook her head, as if she pitied him. "We're back to Mrs. Brooke, are we?"

"We're not back to anything," Hughes said, feeling his

hands begin to shake. "You are Mrs. Brooke, a fact you seem to be forgetting."

"Trust me, Lieutenant, I haven't forgotten." Eva walked unhurriedly over to the wardrobe and opened it, running her hands over the clothes, as if she couldn't decide what to wear.

Hughes knew he wouldn't, or couldn't, leave, so he looked at his feet while she dressed.

"All right then, I'd say I'm decent enough even for the vicar," she said finally. The line was witty, but her voice sounded tired.

He looked up. He was strangely disappointed to see her all covered up in blue wool, a belt cinched around her waist.

"Don't tell me you're not going to buy me that drink now," she said, as if he was the one who was being unreasonable. "Besides, you look like you might need it. Your face has gone all pale. I hope you're not unwell."

Hughes felt like slapping her. But he'd be damned if he was going to be backed down and humiliated by some girl who couldn't keep her clothes on.

"I think I do need it," he said, trying to sound light. "It's not every day women throw themselves at me."

He watched as Eva's face colored. It gave Hughes some small measure of satisfaction.

"Yes, well, I can see why," she said tightly. "If you behave like a silly schoolgirl."

Hughes opened the door and Eva, gathering her handbag from the desk, walked out into the brightly lit hallway.

"We're going to the Causerie," she said. "They serve smorgasbord and you can eat all you like for the price of your drinks."

"Sounds like a good deal," Hughes said. He had decided he would buy her one drink and then get the hell out of there, go find a Red Cross where he could spend the night.

"It's to get around the price restrictions, you see. It's all very daring."

The room was awash in pink and green, with a buffet table off to one side covered with plates of meat and smoked fish, beans and other small, warm dishes. A waiter greeted them.

"Lady Eva, good evening," he said. "A table for two?"

"Yes, please," Eva said, craning her neck around the waiter. "Perhaps the one in the corner over there?" She motioned with her bag.

Their table was next to a window, but the view was hidden by the blackout curtains drawn against the pane. The waiter pulled out a chair for Eva, and Hughes sat down across from her. He quickly rose again.

"Excuse me," he said.

"Of course," Eva said, knitting her brow.

Hughes walked back out into the lobby and inquired about the lavatories. Inside the gentlemen's room, he tried to pee in one of the stalls, but realized he didn't really have to. He zipped up his trousers and went out to the row of marble sinks. An attendant turned on the taps for him and handed him a small cake of soap. Hughes ran his hands under the warm water and looked in the mirror. He recreated Eva's body in his mind, the dark hair between her thighs. He had acted like a prig, he realized, and he was slightly ashamed. He remembered her eyes, her unequivocal gaze on him. There had been no seduction in her expression, no lowering of the eyelashes, like he'd seen girls do when they were flirting. No terms of intimacy. Just a naked purity, and he realized it was that simplicity, or honesty, or whatever you wanted to call it, that disturbed him.

Besides Nick, he had never seen another naked woman,

not fully naked, except for a few French postcards. With his wife, it was her beauty and volatility that gave him pleasure; it was as if he never knew if he were going to get her until the last minute. That's how it was between them. She never came to him, the way Eva had. But it suddenly seemed childish, dishonest, and not a little tiresome, all the acting and role-playing they did.

"Sir?" The attendant was holding out a hand towel toward him and Hughes realized he had been standing there with the water running like an idiot.

"Thank you." Hughes took the towel and dried his hands before walking out of the room, and back to the Causerie.

When he returned to the table in the corner, he found a gin and tonic waiting for him.

"I didn't know what you liked, but I thought a gin and tonic was a safe choice, rather like the meat and potatoes of cocktails," Eva said.

"That's fine, thanks," Hughes said.

"Are you hungry?" Her voice was very polite.

"Not quite yet."

"Yes," she said. "It's been a busy day. I find that when things are hectic, one can lose one's appetite."

Hughes didn't say anything; frankly, he didn't know what to say. How do you respond to a girl who takes her clothes off in front of you one minute and then talks to you like your grandmother the next? He stirred the drink with the silver swizzle stick, mainly for something to do.

"Look," Eva said, finally. "I'm sorry if I behaved badly earlier. Things . . . well, things are rather strange for me at the moment . . ." She trailed off.

"Forget it," Hughes said, still stirring. "Don't mention it."

"No really, I apologize." She put her fingers over Hughes's other hand, and then quickly withdrew them when he looked up. She started fiddling with the doily under her cocktail glass. "I'm leaving my husband, you see."

"I see," Hughes said.

"No, you don't," she said, passionately tearing at the lace. "I'm not looking to trap you or anything. It's not like that. I suppose the whole business has just made me feel rather reckless."

"It's all right," Hughes said. He felt sorry for this motor-cycle-riding girl with a fancy name and a bad marriage. "Really, you don't have to say anything."

"Thank you," Eva said. She took a sip of her drink. "I'm fine, really," she continued. "I don't want you to think I'm some unhinged woman who goes throwing herself at every soldier's head. I just don't love him, my husband I mean, and I think it's better not to pretend."

"You don't have to convince me," Hughes said.

"I know that," she said. "But for some reason I want to convince you. Do you understand?"

Hughes felt something shift inside him. He realized what it had meant to her to show herself to him. He was embarrassed that he had read it as something dirty. He wanted to go back and do it again, only this time he would reach for her, he would let her know it was all right.

"I understand," he said quietly.

"When you get married, you always choose the best person in your circle, and then you pray to God that circle never gets bigger," Eva said. "But it always does, you see."

"Yes." He knew exactly what she meant. "Your circle got bigger, then, I guess."

"The world is bigger," Eva said.

"I don't know if my world is bigger," Hughes said, thinking about this. "But, then again, honestly, I don't feel sure

261

about much these days. Which is funny, because I was so damn sure when I went into this."

"Our war has been going on longer than yours," Eva said. "We've had more time to watch things get smashed up."

"And so your marriage."

"And so my marriage," Eva said, "is over." By now she had managed to rip some of the lace away from the linen doily. "God, I'm the cliché. Wartime bride and all that."

"No," Hughes said, reaching out now and touching her wrist. "No, I was the one who was wrong. Some people are different."

Eva smiled at him and Hughes's heart constricted in his chest.

"But you might want to give that doily a break." He grinned.

"Oh," Eva said. "Yes." And then: "Do you love your wife?"

"I do love her," Hughes said, not moving his hand from her warm skin. "But I don't want to talk about my wife right now."

"Of course," Eva said.

"I thought you were going to take me dancing," he said. "Show me the sights and all that."

Eva laughed. "You Americans are so forward."

"I know, we can't help ourselves. It's all those wide-open spaces and clean living."

"They have music here, in the ballroom. If you'd really like to dance."

"If your card isn't too full."

"As it happens," Eva said, "my card is completely empty at the moment."

After a few more drinks, Hughes found himself holding Eva in the ballroom, under all its French plasterwork and ornate mirrors, as the small orchestra played "We'll Meet Again." Her chin didn't quite reach his shoulder and she had turned her cheek away from him, so he found himself looking down at the curve of her profile.

"What did your husband say, when you told him?" Hughes asked, his voice lowered as if they were sharing a secret.

"He hasn't said anything. I only sent the letter yesterday." Eva spoke into his jacket.

He wondered if she'd ever loved her husband, and if she still loved him now, despite what she said. It made him afraid. Maybe there was someone else already. You could never tell with women. But he knew in his heart that was a lie, one he was telling himself so that wanting her didn't have to mean anything.

"Do you think you'll marry again?" He felt a small jolt of adrenaline as he waited for her answer.

"No," Eva said after a minute. "I won't ever marry again."

Much later, he held her in the darkness of the bedroom, the sheets tangled at their feet. He looked at the faint outline of his uniform draped over the desk chair. His hand traced the curve of her breast and he could smell the soap from her bath rising off her damp skin. It was so quiet. For a minute he missed the sound of the depth charges on the *Jones*. He wanted to hear her voice, but he was also afraid of what she might say, or what he might want her to say. So he said nothing, asked nothing, until a V2 flying overhead shattered the silence.

"It's midnight," he said finally. "It's New Year's Eve."

"Yes," Eva said.

"Maybe it's the year the war will end."

"Perhaps."

He could feel what was unsaid between them, as if it had been spoken.

Eva turned her head and looked at him, and her face was the last thing he saw before he fell asleep.

Hughes woke early with the distinct feeling that he was suffocating. He rose quietly and dressed. He pulled the blackout curtains apart slightly and saw New Year's Eve was gray, with a weak sun the color of urine trying to break through the cloud cover. He left without looking at Eva, letting the door close noiselessly on the latch.

The hotel was still; the only sound in the lobby was the soles of his shoes hitting the marble floor. Outside, he took a deep breath of damp, cold air and shoved his hands in his pockets and began walking.

The city looked ugly at that hour, dirty and broken. He wished the sky was clear and the air sharp, like it would be in Cambridge at this time of year. He tried not to think of Nick, but the more he tried, the more he thought of her. His wife, with her lovely smile, waiting for him. He hated himself. It was this damn war, turning everything upside down. You couldn't be one person one day and another the next, but that's what it did to you. He sure as hell didn't like the person he was this morning. He was weak. He had promised to love and protect Nick and instead he had betrayed her. She trusted him. More than that, she needed him. She loved him. He was disgusted.

He walked aimlessly for a while and then made his way toward Piccadilly, where he knew he would find a Red Cross. It was bustling inside. Hughes looked at his watch, 8:30. He waited in line for a cup of coffee and a doughnut, and then sat down at a small wooden table near the window. He drank the coffee and watched as the sun grew stronger. Then he ate his doughnut, dipping the end into the last drops in his cup. He began to feel better. He knew what he had to do.

He went to the counter and asked one of the girls for a pencil and a piece of paper and took them back to the table. He began composing a letter to Nick:

This letter might seem out of the blue and I don't want you to worry, but there are some things that I have to say. The war is making the world a strange place, and me with it. So, I want you to know that whatever happens, I love you. I loved you when we first danced together and you teased me about having two left feet. I loved you when I proposed, and you turned your face away from me. I loved you on our wedding day, when I found you hiding upstairs like some miserable kid. And more than anything, I've loved the idea of you as I've crossed back and forth across this damn ocean, waiting, praying to come home.

I'm not the same person who shipped off for training a year ago. Things have happened that I'm not proud of, that I wish I could take back. But I want to come back a man at least as good as the one who left you. I don't want to pretend anymore, that I'm the same or you're the same, or we're the same. I want to be honest with you.

But if I make it through this, I promise that I'll do

everything in my power to make our life a happy one, and to try and be the man you need me to be.

I love you, Nicky.

Hughes

Hughes folded the paper in thirds and slipped it into his breast pocket. He returned the pencil and took another coffee from the girl. The winter sun was now pale silver. Writing the letter had made him feel lighter, but he now found his thoughts turning back to Eva. He had left her without a word. He thought about that moment the night before, the way he had suddenly felt he knew her, not through experience, but intuitively. Hughes rubbed his eyes. He'd have to go back and explain to her that it had been a mistake. That they'd both had too much to drink and gotten carried away. That they'd been lonely and it had only been that loneliness that had driven them together. He couldn't be the man he wanted to be if he didn't do that. But he dreaded it, he dreaded looking into her eyes and telling her that it had all been for nothing.

He rose and left the canteen, making his way past the shops, some closed and shuttered, others still hopefully displaying wares to a public who wouldn't buy very much. He went into one and chose a pair of bright red calfskin gloves for Nick. He'd send them to her, but not with the letter. Later maybe, for her birthday.

Hughes found himself in Hyde Park, with its bare branches outlined against the sky. He sat on a bench and watched the people milling by. A G.I. had his arm around a girl, pulling her in tight as he leaned back against a tree. Hughes remembered it was New Year's Eve. He should have made provisions for a bunk at the Red Cross. He could do that after he'd seen Eva. He couldn't put it off any longer. He brushed himself off and headed back to Claridge's.

At the hotel, he didn't bother ringing her room. This time, he didn't hesitate at the elevator, but strode in briskly and waited impatiently while the attendant pulled the chain across. He just wanted the whole scene to be over as quickly as possible.

He knocked at the door of room 201. Eva opened it, and stood in the doorway in her dressing gown. He looked at her and then she stood aside to let him in.

"I didn't know if you'd be back," she said.

It wasn't an accusation, just a statement of fact, and Hughes knew then that he didn't care about his letter, or the war, or trying to be a better man. All he cared about was the way he felt when he was with her.

"Neither did I," he said. "But I am."

"Yes," Eva said, reaching for him. "You are."

When the sun had completely disappeared from the sky, and the sound of the V2s shook the night like fireworks, Hughes disentangled himself from Eva's sleeping body and rose from the bed. In the darkness, he felt his way over to the chair, where his jacket was hanging, and slipped his hand into the breast pocket. He pulled out the letter and ran his hand over the paper, as if touching it would tell him something. He went into the bathroom and switched on the light. He took one last look at his note to Nick, and then tore it up and threw the pieces into the toilet. He watched until they had all disappeared, pulled down into darkness with the pressure of the flush. Then he switched out the light and went back to bed.

1959: July

II

After Nick's phone call about the dead girl and the pandemonium at Tiger House, Hughes had been unable to think of anything else. He had gone over and over the situation all the way down to Woods Hole and then as he sat on the ferry, cupping his hot coffee in the ghostly illumination of the upper deck. He had barely managed to make the last boat, and the *Island Queen* had pulled out of dock just as the sun flashed and then winked out of sight, leaving ocean and sky in darkness.

Nick had charged him with getting Avery to come East to deal with Ed and Helena. But Hughes hadn't wanted him to come. He had hoped, when he telephoned him, to convince Avery instead to send for his wife and son. As usual, Avery had been cryptic and unhelpful.

"It's character-building," he said, after Hughes had told him about the dead body.

"I'm not sure that it is character-building," Hughes said. "I think you're missing the point here. Helena is very upset and we think it would be best if they were with you."

"And you think you know what's best for my family."

"I'm not suggesting that." Hughes felt like banging the receiver against the library table. He had to force himself to remain calm. "But the fact is, you're far away and maybe don't understand the situation as well as you could."

"What are you saying? That I don't take care of my family? I am far away, as you put it, because I am working for my family. Everything I do is for Helena and for my son, so they can know a life that isn't bound by the stricture of convention and servitude. Of course, I don't expect you to understand that."

"Oh, Jesus, Avery, stop being such a prick. Nick is worried. If you don't want them back in L.A. then why don't you come down to the Island, just for a week or so, if you can't get away for longer." He prayed to God the man wouldn't accept.

"That's not possible at the moment. I am at a critical point in my work."

Hughes was silent.

"But," Avery said, as if the thought had just occurred to him, "if you want to send the money for a plane ticket . . ."

"Go to hell," Hughes said, and slammed down the phone.

Nick had been right about Avery from the first. The man was a charlatan and had been trying to squeeze them for money from the minute he married Helena. One of the things Hughes loved about Nick was that he knew there was no way in hell she would ever give that man one red cent. She was a force to be reckoned with, his wife, and at times like this he thanked God for that.

With Avery washing his hands of the situation, Ed was Hughes's problem. But by the time the Vineyard Haven lighthouse came into view, he had a game plan, or at least the beginnings of one. He had to find something that would keep Ed out of the house as much as possible. Hughes had been in the Boy Scouts and remembered it as absorbing and exhausting: at best, it would be a good influence on the kid, and at worst, a distraction, at least until the summer was over. Meanwhile, Hughes decided he would stay on at Tiger House and keep an eye on things.

He couldn't be sure how involved Ed was in the murder of that girl. He might know something or he might not. Hughes didn't want to contemplate anything more than that. But he realized that the scene earlier that summer hadn't just been Ed acting out. The boy was dangerous.

As he walked down the gangplank, he spotted Nick waiting for him. She was leaning against the station wagon, the wind off the harbor blowing her green dress between her legs. She was lovely. In fact, she had only gotten more beautiful with age, as her bone structure became more pronounced. He wondered how he could have failed to notice that, and a sadness came over him, as if something had been wasted.

Nick was smoking a cigarette and had one arm folded across her chest, her hand cupping her shoulder as if she were cold. When he reached the car, he set his suitcase down and took her in his arms.

"You're freezing," he said, feeling the freshness of her skin.

"It's cold," she said into his neck.

"You get in. I'll drive." Hughes put his case into the trunk and walked around to the driver's side.

"You're staying," Nick said.

"Yes."

"Good," she said and lit another cigarette.

She was quiet as he navigated the car out of Vineyard Haven.

"How's Daisy?" Hughes finally asked.

"How do you think she is?" Nick snapped. She stubbed out her cigarette. "I'm sorry. It's been an awful day. Actually, she seems less shaken up than I am, frankly."

"I'm sorry. It must have been terrible for you."

"A dead body, Hughes. And not just some peaceful great-aunt, either. The poor thing was strangled and god knows what else."

"Jesus." Hughes took a cigarette out of the pack on the dashboard. He had a vision of Frank Wilcox pushing the girl's head down to one side as he took her from behind. "Have you talked to her? Daisy, I mean."

"She . . . well, you know how she is with me. I'm the ogre, aren't I?"

"Don't say that. She loves you. She looks up to you."

"She talks to you."

"She doesn't talk to anyone our age. She's twelve." Hughes smiled at the thought of his daughter. Such an intense little thing. Always worried about winning. He remembered taking her to the West Tisbury fair once, where she fell in love with one of the plush prizes. She spent over an hour and all her pocket money trying to knock down the four bottles to win it. Hughes knew the game was rigged. In the end, he paid for the damn thing outright, and it was a bargain. He knew Daisy would have stayed there all night until she succeeded.

"Well," Nick said, "she talks to Ed. Those two have been thick as thieves. He's been sneaking off and she's been covering for him. They even disappeared today, after everything that's happened."

"Where did they go?"

"I don't know. They told me they'd been down at the Quarterdeck, cool as could be. As if Helena and I don't have enough to worry about." Nick pushed her head back against the car seat. "God, I sound like a shrew."

"You sound like a mother," Hughes said, putting his hand on Nick's thigh.

"I wonder sometimes if there's a difference," Nick said and moved her leg out of his reach.

It was ten o'clock when they reached Tiger House, but the children weren't in bed.

"Daddy." Daisy raced down the stairs and leaped into Hughes's arms.

"I'm going to fix a drink," Nick said.

Over Daisy's head, Hughes watched his wife disappear into the blue sitting room. Her back was straight and she moved with her usual ease, but her grace was tinged with a sort of sorrow.

Hughes looked down at his daughter.

"How are you, sweetheart?"

"I'm starving," Daisy said. "We missed lunch. Ed bought me a cheeseburger, but that was ages ago."

"Hmm. Well, let's see if we can rustle something up."

He followed his daughter into the summer kitchen, watching her blond head bobbing along in front of him. It hurt his heart.

Hughes looked in the icebox. There wasn't much there and it made him feel guilty about leaving them on their own so much. Whenever Nick sank into one of her moods, the shopping didn't get done.

"How about some warm milk? It's not good to eat right before bed."

"All right," Daisy said, seating herself at the table.

Hughes pulled the milk bottle out and poured some into one of the copper pans that hung above the stove.

"How's your mother been?"

"Fine," Daisy said.

Hughes stirred the milk with a wooden spoon and poured in a little vanilla extract, something his cook had done for him when he was a child.

"Ed helped the sheriff and he paid him two dollars."

"Is that so? How did Ed help the sheriff?"

"I don't know. He was with the policeman when he reported it to the sheriff, I guess."

"Didn't he come back here with you?" Hughes turned to his daughter.

"Hello, Uncle Hughes."

Hughes looked up to see Ed standing in the doorway.

"Hello, Ed," Hughes said evenly. "I hear you've been helping the sheriff."

"Yes," Ed said.

"That's very good of you."

Hughes poured the milk into a mug and handed it to Daisy.

"You two should really be in bed, now. It's late." He put his hand on Daisy's shoulder and looked at Ed. The boy blinked first.

Nick was waiting at the bottom of the stairs. She handed Hughes a gin and tonic.

"Say goodnight to your mother."

"Goodnight, Mummy."

"Goodnight, Daisy."

Daisy started up, but Ed stayed where he was.

"You go on too, Ed," Hughes said.

"Goodnight, Aunt Nick," Ed said, but his eyes were on Hughes.

Hughes moved fractionally in front of his wife, feeling the hairs on his arm prickling a little.

"Goodnight," Nick said.

Hughes watched until Ed disappeared around the landing, before turning back to Nick. "Where's Helena?"

"Asleep," Nick said, nodding toward the sitting room. "What did Avery say?"

"I tried, but he won't do it, Nick," Hughes lied. "Frankly, he didn't seem all that concerned. He said something odd about it being character-building."

"Damn man," Nick said, pressing her tumbler against her forehead.

They both turned at the sound of a sigh from the doorway. Helena stood there, watching them, a Scotch clutched in her hand.

"I'm sorry, darling," Nick said, following Helena into the sitting room.

Helena walked over to the decanter and refilled her glass. "He's very busy," Helena said.

Nick looked at Hughes. He shrugged. Avery was Helena's problem. If she wanted to delude herself, that was her choice. He had other things to worry about.

Hughes settled himself in the wing chair, pushing aside a needlepoint pillow with a fierce tiger on its front. "So, ladies," he said, crossing his legs, "aside from a dead body here and there, how's the summer been going?" He smiled at them, but he felt exhausted already.

Helena looked at him as if she didn't understand the question.

"You can be so glib sometimes, darling," Nick said.

Her voice was light, but beneath her pretty green dress and her cocktails, Hughes saw a new fragility, like something splintering. He wanted to go to her, hold her, the way he'd held Daisy when she'd had nightmares as a small child, pressing her flushed little body to him.

He was struck by a memory of when they were first married, while he was waiting to be called up. He was in law school and he'd been having a particularly bad time with one of his professors, who thought he would never amount to much, let alone a good lawyer. He was walking home one evening, his mind heavy with potential failure, and as he arrived at their front gate, he felt a sudden rush of freezing water. Stunned and furious, he looked up to see Nick standing on the front lawn holding the hose, splitting her sides.

"I'm sorry, really," she said, obviously rejoicing in her own hilarity. "You just looked altogether too serious for your own good."

Hughes looked down at his soaked trousers and shoes.

"Oh, no, darling. Now, you're even more forlorn."

"I'm going to remember this," Hughes said. "One day when you're least expecting it."

But he went and sat on the steps, still drenched, and held Nick's hand until the sky turned dark and then, together, they went inside and shut the door against the world.

"Well," Nick's voice brought him back into the room, "there's the party. But I haven't done a goddamn thing about it, yet."

"Yes, I noticed from the icebox," Hughes smiled at her, but gently, in case she took it the wrong way.

"Oh that." Nick waved her hand in the air. "We've been drifting a bit, haven't we, darling?" She looked at Helena. "Playing Robinson Crusoe."

"Yes," Helena said, her words slurred and drowsy. "Drifting."

"I certainly know how that feels." Hughes wiped his damp palms on his trousers and finished his drink.

✿

Later, after making sure Helena made it upstairs, Hughes went into their room to find Nick readying herself for bed. He watched, arrested, as she pulled the earring off her lobe and placed it gently on a small velvet pad in front of her. She had always been very deliberate when she was getting dressed, but he could remember when she would throw her things around, clothes, jewelry, shoes, at the end of an evening together, in a sort of frenzied joy at being free of them. When had she gotten so careful, he wondered. He had the urge to go to her, to beg her forgiveness and make her swear not to leave him. But she wouldn't understand. She would think he'd gone mad. So, instead, he lightly touched her shoulder, before heading back downstairs to his office, jingling the small desk key in his pocket.

Southampton, July, 1945

Dear Hughes,

What can I say? I could say, Please, please, please don't do this. I could tell you what a false choice this is, making me choose between you and myself. How can I?

I can't, I won't marry again. I could tell you how definite this decision is, because, my love, it is. This is not about you. It's not about not wanting you for my husband, or having any doubts that you are the only man I could truly love with every fibre of my being. It's about me, about who I am. I know it's not a choice a woman is supposed to make. I know I should be thrilled that you would leave your wife and want to marry me, throw it all in for our love. But I don't want to be some-body's wife. I want you to come to me because you want to be with me, not as some harbour or safe haven from the rest of the bloody world. But honestly and purely, as we have always been, you and I.

You told me that if you were to hurt your wife (why can't I even write her name?), it would have to be for everything. That you needed to know I would always be there for you. That marriage was your version of honesty. But darling, why can't you see: we have everything, what difference will a piece of paper make?

I will always love you, Hughes, no matter what comes our way. I will always be there for you, richer, poorer, sickness, health. I swear it.

Please come back to me.

    Love,

      Eva

Hughes put the letter down and ran his hand through his hair. He stared at the pile. He should just burn them. He had always known he shouldn't hold onto the letters, that reading them and re-reading them wasn't going to change anything. And after a while, he had stopped reading them. But he knew they were there, that was the important thing. When the days seemed to stretch before him like an interminable forced march, their existence had been a reminder that once, the whole world had opened up and offered itself to him.

Now, something had changed; he was afraid, now. He wasn't sure if it was him or everything around him, the telephone ringing in the house, Nick waiting, cold and alone at the ferry. And the strange feeling this evening that Eva's letters were written to someone unconnected to him. It was like being awoken by the whistle of a departing train, and only then realizing you were supposed to be on it.

Hughes heard the creak of a floorboard out in the hall. His breathing quickened. He rose and went to the door of the study and peered into the darkness of the house. He thought he saw a shadow moving away toward the kitchen, but when he followed there was no one there. He latched the back door, which was swinging slightly on its hinge, and returned to his study.

The next morning Hughes and Nick walked into town together. Nick wanted to check the mailbox and Hughes needed to refresh his supply of Scotch, severely dented by Helena's ability to down the stuff. The day was going to be beautiful, clear and hot, but with enough of a breeze to keep the mosquitoes away.

"We should take *Star* out," Hughes said.

"Oh, not today," Nick said. "I feel like we should stay home after what's happened."

She was probably right, but the freshness of the morning was making him think that maybe his alarm over the recent events was overblown. He could almost forget the scene with Ed and Frank Wilcox and the maid, as they walked down the street, Nick swinging the French woven basket she used for errands.

"Besides," she said, "all the neighbors within ten miles will be ringing up wanting to know all about it."

"We should take the phone off the hook," Hughes said.

"Goddamn phone," Nick said. Then she sighed. "It might just make them come over instead."

"Good point. We'll let it ring. I don't want to listen to Caro or Dolly's hypotheses on the subject."

"No," Nick said.

On impulse, Hughes took her hand. She let him. It was warm.

"You know, darling, I've been thinking," she said. "Maybe we should get something for Ed, a boy thing."

"Why?"

"I don't know, he just seems to be running wild. Maybe he needs some fatherly attention."

"I'm not sure a present is going to help."

"Yes," Nick said, "I think he needs you to give him something. So he knows he has someone he can look up to."

"Jesus, Nick."

Nick withdrew her hand. "If you won't, I'll buy him something and say it's from you."

"Fine," Hughes said.

"I think a Swiss Army knife would be a nice present," Nick said. "So he can start the Scouts prepared."

Hughes couldn't believe it. Now he had to go spend his money on that little piece of work. And he certainly didn't want Ed to think he was bribing him for his silence.

This was getting ridiculous, he decided. He was going to destroy the letters. It was over and had been over for so damn long; he was the only one who hadn't been able to see it.

He thought of Eva, the last time he'd seen her, standing in front of Claridge's, wearing those breeches and not waving as his taxi pulled away. He'd only found the letter she'd slipped in his pocket once he was back aboard the Jones.

Dear Hughes,

There's nothing more to say, or at least, as you made clear, no more pleading to be done for my case. I am sorry you feel the way you do, but I wish you luck. And happiness.

As you requested, I won't write again. Be good to Nick. I finally managed to write her name.

Eva

And she had been as good as her word. She hadn't ever written again. She had known it for what it was, a failed wartime romance, a cliché. While he had remained blind, like a fool.

In the hardware store, Hughes picked out a red knife, fully loaded, with even the tweezers and the small bone toothpick. Maybe Nick was right. Maybe all the boy needed was a little guidance.

He carried this hopeful thought all the way back to the house and it lasted until he actually handed Ed the gift.

Ed turned the knife over and over, fixated on the bright, shiny thing like a rapt magpie.

"Thank you," he said.

"I'm glad you like it," Hughes said. "My father gave me one as a boy, before I started Scouts." This wasn't strictly true, but it sounded like a good thing to say.

"This is going to be very helpful," Ed said. Then he turned without another word and headed for the front door.

Hughes watched the boy through the screen as he went down the steps and out the gate. He cursed himself. There was something seriously wrong with that kid and he had just gone and given him a knife. He stepped out onto the porch. Ed had already disappeared from sight, but Nick was standing at the fence, deadheading the roses, her face flushed in the sun.

She was using her rusted clippers to trim the browning blooms from the stalk. She never kept those clippers in their case, and so the sea air had eaten away at the metal. But she was careful with the roses, gently pushing the branches aside with slim brown arms to get at the fading blossoms and errant shoots tucked away inside the bushes.

Behind her, the gardening basket had overturned, spilling red petals around her feet. Something about the scene was familiar, and he was reminded of the smell of the sea in the small maid's room upstairs.

Nick wasn't wearing any gloves and she must have pricked herself because he saw her suddenly pull away from the stem she was holding. Her brow furrowed as she inspected her finger and Hughes thought he saw her eyes tearing up in the bright light. But she didn't cry out.

He walked over to her and examined the small crimson dot where the thorn had pierced her flesh. He put her finger in his mouth. She looked up at him, squinting into the sun. They stood like that for a moment, not moving, each looking at the other, wordless. Nick put her other hand to his face. Then she slid her finger out and continued to cut away at the dead flowers.

Hughes found the mouse later that afternoon, when he went down to his workbench in the basement to repair a broken picture frame. The little thing had been crudely sliced open, its teeth exposed in a primal scream, the small toothpick sticking out of one eye. Hughes gently removed the toothpick, but his hand shook as he went to pick up the mouse. It was several minutes before he could bring himself to touch it, and even then, he had to look away when he put it in the trash can.

1959: *July*

III

A week after Hughes arrived, the heat wave that had been threatening the Island all summer finally hit. Hughes had gone back to the hardware store to buy fans for some of the upstairs bedrooms, only to find they had run out. The air inside the house was as still and dense as a swamp, suffocating. Outside, it was even worse, the sun burning skin and grass, turning the sand underfoot to lava. The delicate flowers from the albizia tree dropped in their dozens, creating a fetid carpet on the lawn and the front steps. The stone walk was littered with insect husks, brittle, as if the creatures had been flash-fried as they tried to crawl to the shade of the porch.

Strangely, the children didn't seem to notice, despite the fact that they were spending their days out in the relentless heat. Daisy, thankfully, appeared more or less unperturbed by the whole business with the maid, all her peculiar intensity focused solely on that tennis match. Ed, as he had hoped, seemed stitched up good and tight in the Scouts program.

Hughes found the sweltering temperatures were having an odd effect on him. They hadn't produced the kind of languor that Helena, who had enveloped herself in a boozy cocoon, seemed to be experiencing. It was more like a fever, when the skin is too sensitive to touch. He couldn't stop thinking about Nick. He found himself watching her almost obsessively.

They had made love the day after Hughes arrived at Tiger House, and it made him wonder when the last time had been. He couldn't remember; he only knew that the suddenness of his desire had caught him off guard. They had been arguing about Daisy resuming her tennis lessons. And then something turned. Nick mentioned the Portuguese girl, she was trembling. Then he was holding her, trying to comfort her, and her belief that maybe he could make it better, her damp face pressed to his shoulder, the very closeness of her, overcame him. He had found himself almost ripping her dress to get to her, tasting salt and lotion on her skin.

Since then, he couldn't get the episode out of his head. Whether it was the murder, or the heat, Hughes could see cracks in his wife's very polished exterior; a chink in her armor. Something fallible, almost unbearably real. Something he hadn't seen in a long time.

He was riveted. Touching her was like touching an exposed wire. And the shock, along with the soaring temperature, was making him feel like he was suffering an insane kind of heat stroke. Yet, despite all that, some part of Nick still seemed far away, out of reach.

One morning Hughes woke to find himself alone in their bed. Even though it was early, the air had no freshness to it and his pajamas clung to his damp skin. Out the window, he could see the sun tipping over the harbor, and the house was quiet as he made his way downstairs. He found Nick sitting in the dining room, a list dangling forgotten in one hand, a pile of invitations for the party in front of her. She was reading from a book of poetry, one he remembered from the early days of their marriage when she would read to him in bed. She had one elbow propped on the polished walnut of the table, and her lips were mouthing the lines, her hair falling in her eyes. The back of the house faced west and was darker at this time of day, but he could still see the sweat gathering around her neck and the damp edges of her nightgown. He stood in the doorway, wanting to go to her, but she seemed so perfectly complete that he felt like an intruder. He watched her for a while before going back upstairs to bathe.

He was the loneliest he'd ever been, as if not having rediscovered Nick would have been better. Whatever her own thoughts were, she hid them in a frenzy of party-planning. She sat at her desk, writing out menus she would end up discarding, making schedules and cataloguing things from some kind of master list, shaking out her hand every so often. He would offer his help, and she might send him on an errand, to the post office, say, for extra stamps, but it nonetheless left Hughes with an irrational animosity toward the party, or the post office, or the stamps, as if all these things were rivals devising obstacles to his wife's affections.

So, Hughes turned his attention to *Star*, spending his afternoons in front of the boathouse, sanding and repainting the hull a dark green and trying not to think of Nick.

The dinghy didn't really need any work after everything he had done in June, but he found that the repetition soothed him; the chipping and sanding, the lost hours spent drenched in sweat, running his hand over the wood as he looked for any rough spots, the acrid smell of primer. It was hot work, but when it got too much, he could just jump off the end of the dock into the cool harbor, the shores of

Chappy in front of him, his eyes watering from the sting of the salt and the sun.

Then one afternoon, as he was about to start on the second coat of paint, the sky opened up and it began to rain, big, heavy drops. Cursing, Hughes hurried to drag the dinghy into the boathouse, pulling the two saw-horses in after him. It was a flash storm, the kind that swept over the Island, only to clear almost as suddenly as it had begun. Hughes decided to wait it out. He took one of the beach towels hanging in the boathouse and began to dry the dinghy's hull. He was anxious to see the results of his labors.

The patter of the rain on the roof was broken by a tap on the side of the boathouse, and then Nick appeared wearing a red bathing suit and carrying a small hamper.

"Hello." She smiled that wide smile of hers. "I thought you might want a break," she said, gesturing to the rain that was falling on her. "I brought lunch."

Hughes wiped the damp off his forehead with the edge of his shirt, trying to think of something to say. He didn't know why he was so surprised to see her, but she had appeared like an idea that had emerged fully formed from his mind.

"Are you shocked that I walked all the way down here in only my bathing suit?"

It did have something to do with the bathing suit, but also with the wet hair curving around her ears, the long brown legs disappearing into red cotton and her bare feet with damp flecks of grass sticking to the delicate arches.

"No," he said, stupidly. "Seems pretty sensible."

"That's what I thought," Nick said, putting down the basket. "It reminded me of Florida, after the war, and that yellow one-piece I used to tease the neighbors with."

Hughes had no idea what she was talking about. Florida

was like a bad dream that he could no longer entirely remember, but her comment brought vague outlines of it back. He pushed the thoughts away; he didn't want to think about Florida or his sadness or Eva right now. He wanted Nick to take off her bathing suit so he could see her naked.

Instead, she unpacked the basket and produced two cheese sandwiches with mustard, and a shaker of martinis.

He watched as she pulled a boat cushion off the wall and sat down, tucking her legs neatly underneath her. Hughes sat next to her, but not too near. Nick poured the martinis into a couple of plastic cups and handed one to Hughes.

They sat in silence, Nick munching on her sandwich. Hughes looked at her out of the corner of his eye, wondering what she was thinking, wondering what had brought her down here to the boathouse, with her picnic and her red bathing suit and her bright smile. He had a strange vision of cracking her open, like a nut or a crab, to find out what was going on inside.

"Do you think the rain will break the heat?" she asked.

"No," Hughes said. "I don't think it's that kind of storm."

The chilled vodka sent a shiver over him. It was a perfect martini and he sat there thinking about that and about Nick and about the smell of the paint.

The boat winked in the stormy light, catching shades of the water off the harbor. Nick rose, her cup in one hand, and walked over to the dinghy. Gently, she pressed an index finger against the hull, and, evidently finding it dry, ran her hand over it, as Hughes had done only minutes before. She sipped from her martini, her lower lip rising to meet the rim. Then she sat down again, resting her head against the wall. The rain had begun to ease, but the soft rap of the drops against the roof was still audible.

"It's funny, isn't it," Nick said, after some time. "How much you hated being on that ship during the war, and how much you hated having to do all that work on it afterward. And here you are, spending all your afternoons working on a boat, all by yourself."

Hughes looked at her, but she was staring out at the harbor. He wanted to tell her something, but the language escaped him. As he struggled for the words, she rose and brushed the crumbs off her brown legs.

"Well, I'll leave you to it." She picked up the basket and the cups and, without even a glance backward, walked out, the white soles of her feet flashing against the gray floorboards.

And just like that, Hughes found himself sitting alone again in the boathouse, with nothing to say.

Hughes sweated into his freshly laundered shirt as he dressed for dinner that evening. They had a long-standing date with the Pritchards at the Yacht Club, and although he had tried to get Nick to break it, she had been adamant.

"Oh, Hughes, we can't. I know it's hotter than Hades, but we really do have to go. They have some tiresome house guest staying with them, and I promised Dolly we'd take some of the burden off of her. It was either the Yacht Club or here." She was sitting at her dressing table, wearing a yellow dress he had never seen before.

"Well, I suppose at least this way I won't have to restock the liquor cabinet again," Hughes said, looking away. "Helena's bar tab is about all I can manage right now."

"Don't be unkind," Nick said sharply. "There's nothing wrong with Helena that a good divorce wouldn't fix."

"You know it's not just that." He was feeling irritable.

"I don't want to talk about it," Nick said, adjusting her earring. "She's just tired."

Hughes didn't really want to talk about it, either. He knew it had gone beyond the whiskey and the heat; several times since he'd arrived, he'd seen Helena slip a pill from a silver box in her purse and swallow it when she thought no one was looking.

Nick picked up a bottle of her perfume, only to put it back on the dresser.

"It's too hot for perfume," she said, catching him staring at her in the mirror.

Hughes walked over and brushed his palm across her collar bone, watching her watching him in the reflection. Her skin was soft and slightly humid to the touch.

Nick sat completely still, barely breathing, her green eyes like wet grass, before pushing his hand away. "Don't," she said.

The Yacht Club was buzzing with the sound of clinking forks and laughter, a sea of blue blazers and rep ties.

"There they are," Nick said.

Dolly Pritchard was standing and waving, a look of mock pain on her face.

"Poor Dolly," Nick said as they headed toward the table at the back of the room, which looked out onto the harbor.

"What's his name, this guest?"

"Henry? Hank? I can't remember, he's someone from Rory's work."

"Another scintillating evening discussing the Pritchard family firm."

Nick laughed, and then quickly covered her mouth with one gloved hand. "Oh, I know. If I hear one word about investments I might have to throw my drink in his face."

"You throw the drink and run. I'll hold them off." Hughes lowered his voice as they approached the table.

"My hero," Nick whispered into his ear, and the soft heat of her breath made him hard.

Hughes guided her in front of him as they made the introductions, shifting his weight carefully.

"Nick, you look smashing," Dolly Pritchard said, clasping Nick's hand. "And Hughes, as dashing as ever."

"Hello, Dolly," Hughes said, kissing her cheek.

Dolly Pritchard always reminded him of Eleanor Roosevelt, tall and horsey, with an open manner and straight-forward mouth. Admittedly, she was more attractive, but she was one of those keen, no-nonsense types of woman for whom cheerful curiosity was a kind of dogma. Hughes enjoyed her immensely. It wasn't that he didn't like Rory, but he lacked his wife's zest. Rory Pritchard's father, Rory Sr., had started an investment firm that at first had handled only his family's money. Rory Jr. had grown it to include the kind of families that his father would have approved of. He was a smart fellow, there was no doubt about that, but he could also be long-winded when he got on the topic of the business.

"This is Harry Banks," Dolly said, putting her hand on their guest's shoulder. "Harry: Nick and Hughes Derringer."

"Harry's helping us design our new offices," Rory said, pulling out his wife's chair.

"One of architecture's bright young things," Dolly said.

Harry Banks looked a little young for an architect, even for a bright young thing.

"You'll make me blush, Dolly," Harry Banks said, smiling at his hostess.

"Tish," Dolly said. "You don't fool anybody, Harry. I doubt there's much that could make you blush."

Hughes suppressed a smile, but Nick laughed. "Oh dear, is this what you've had to put up with all weekend, Mr. Banks?"

"Harry, please." The architect smiled at Nick and Hughes noticed the man's eyes taking in his wife: her yellow, strapless dress, the curve of her breasts rising slightly from the foamy fabric. "And yes, Dolly excels at putting me in my place. It's a pleasure to watch her work."

"Smooth, Harry," Dolly said. "Now, what will everyone have to drink?"

Hughes ordered a gin and tonic for himself and a vodka martini for Nick, thinking of the cold thermos she had brought down to the boathouse. He didn't know what he was trying to offer, some kind of apology or signal of shared intimacy, and he looked at her face to see if she'd pick up on it. Her lips were parted in a slight smile, the white of her teeth barely showing. But as he watched her, her gaze slid over his shoulder and he saw her face harden.

Hughes turned and saw Frank Wilcox crossing the main dining room, steering his wife by the elbow. Etta Wilcox's mouth was set in a thin, hard line. Her husband, on the other hand, looked like he was doing an impersonation of himself, smiling widely, bestowing jovial glances on no one in particular.

The whole table had gone quiet and Hughes saw that all eyes were on the approaching couple. All except Harry Banks, who had the expression of a man who had missed the joke.

Hughes felt a hand on his shoulder.

"Hello, Hughes, Rory."

Hughes looked at Frank and tried for a smile. "Frank."

"Ladies," Frank Wilcox said, his smile deepening.

Nick just stared at him.

"Hello, Frank. Etta," Dolly said.

"Hello." Etta's voice sounded hoarse, as if it hadn't been used in a while.

No one bothered to introduce Harry Banks. Frank stood there in the building silence, and finally nodded his head and continued toward his table, as if it were the most natural thing in the world. Hughes saw him lean in and whisper something in Etta's ear, but her face remained unreadable.

Hughes looked down at his menu. "The sole looks good."

"Well, well—" Dolly began.

"Dolly, don't." Rory cut her off. And then: "I've never been that fond of sole, for some reason."

Harry Banks was looking around the table, a half smile on his face. "I seemed to have missed something awfully exciting."

"You haven't," Hughes said.

"You two are so buttoned-up," Dolly said, and then turned to Harry. "Their maid was recently found murdered. It's caused quite a stir, as you can imagine."

"Dolly." Rory's voice had an edge of warning.

"Oh, well. I suppose it's not polite dinner conversation. How boring." Dolly turned her attention to the menu.

Hughes looked at Nick, who had remained silent. He saw she was still looking at the Wilcoxes, now seated a few tables away from them. She pulled a cigarette out of her bag and Hughes leaned in to light it for her. Her hand trembled and he steadied it with his own.

Nick pulled her hand away and picked up her menu.

"The Chateaubriand is always good," she said in a cheerful voice that broke his heart.

After dinner, the conversation, predictably, turned to the weather.

"This heat," Dolly said.

"And no fans," Rory said.

"I read they're having a rash of suicides in D.C. from the heat wave," Harry Banks said, lighting a cigarette. "One man apparently ran all the way from his house to the Key Bridge, screaming about the heat, and then just jumped off. Middle of rush hour."

"Really?" Dolly said. "My word. You know, I heard somewhere that more people commit suicide on a Monday than any other day of the week."

"Work," Rory said. "They don't want to go back."

"Maybe it's just the monotony," Hughes said. "Every Monday's the same, so every month, every year's going to be the same, as well."

He felt Nick's eyes on him.

"Well, they need a thicker skin if monotony is their biggest problem," Rory said.

"I think that's the point," Hughes said.

"I don't know," Dolly said. "I can't say I relish monotony, but we all have to get on with it. I mean it's not all going to be adventure and excitement, is it?" She turned to Rory. "Sorry, darling."

Rory blew her a kiss.

"Well, it is your life," Harry Banks said. "You can make it as exciting as you want. Or not."

"Spoken like a true bachelor," Rory said.

"For shame, Rory," Dolly said. "It's not marriage that

makes life . . . well, tedious. Or, not just, anyway. It's every-thing. All the little things one has to do every day."

"I think it's about loneliness," Nick said. "And desire."

"Indeed," Dolly said. "Do tell."

Nick laughed. "No really. I know everyone thinks that desire is some sort of ridiculous silliness for young people. But who says? I mean without it . . . Well, that's the real reason people throw themselves off of bridges."

"I never realized you were such a romantic, dear," Dolly said. She turned to her guest. "What do you have to say to that, Harry?"

"I wasn't talking about marriage, although you're right, Rory. I don't know much about it." Harry Banks smiled at the table. "But when you talk about all those little, tedious things it makes me wonder: Why do it? I mean, why do what everyone expects of you? Who's watching?"

Hughes laughed out loud.

So did Dolly. "Look around you," she said, spreading her hand out across the room. "Everyone's watching."

The dinner wound down. Harry Banks went to get some fresh air, while Rory tried to get the waiter's attention for the chit. Nick had excused herself to go to the ladies' room and when she didn't return, Hughes went to look for her. Outside the club, the air was just as warm, but softer. He saw a couple drinking their wine by the large painted anchor that sat in the middle of the front deck. He walked toward the stringpiece. In the darkness, he made out the shape of two figures, their heads together. He recognized Nick's body, the way she held herself. She was leaning slightly against the side of the building and Harry Banks was tilted toward her, one hand against the clapboard siding.

Harry was saying something Hughes couldn't quite make out and Nick was laughing. Harry leaned in closer. Nick didn't move. It pierced him. It wasn't that he was surprised, exactly. It was the feeling that he was responsible for it, responsible for forcing her to find intimacy with strangers in dark corners, when it should have been so different for her. She was too good for this.

"Nick," he called softly.

She simply looked at him, before turning back to Harry.

Hughes watched for a moment longer, and then went back inside the club and waited for his wife to return.

He didn't touch Nick on the way home, although she walked easily at his side. She was so close that he could smell her soap, something floral, mixed with sweat. Her heels scraped along the road. He dug his hands in his pockets. She stopped on Simpson's Lane to pick a rose that was blooming over one of the picket fences.

As they rounded the corner onto North Summer Street, Hughes saw that the moon was hanging red and low in the sky. It was the heat that caused it to turn that color, something about the atmosphere, he couldn't remember exactly, but he thought of the old saying, "Red sky at night, sailors' delight. Red sky in morning, sailors take warning."

When they got to the back drive, Nick stumbled, her heel catching as she stepped off the curb, and fell into him slightly. Automatically, his hand went out to catch her, and he felt her body against him, her breast crushed against his open palm.

"Nick," he said.

"Sorry, darling. I think the martinis have made me a little clumsy."

"I don't care about the martinis," he said.

"Oh?" She kept walking, trying to pull out of his grasp.

"Stop," he said.

"What is it?"

"I want . . . I want to talk to you." He was still holding her.

"Let go of me," she said. "You'll make me lose my balance."

Hughes pulled her around to face him.

"Hughes." She wouldn't meet his eyes.

"Look at me."

"Don't." She raised her hand to push him away. He caught it, and felt the rose she was still holding breaking damply under the pressure of his grip.

"Nick."

"Whatever it is you have to say . . ."

"I'm sorry," he said.

"I don't know what you're talking about."

"You know what I'm talking about. I'm sorry. For everything."

"I don't care."

"I don't think that's true."

"It is."

They looked at each other and Hughes was certain she was about to break down, to let him in. He could feel her on the edge. He waited, but she remained silent.

Then he couldn't stand it any longer. "Enough," he said, and pressed his mouth against hers. Her mouth opened beneath his. "Enough, now," he whispered into the darkness.

But as suddenly as she had surrendered, she freed herself, and ran down the path, slipping from his grasp like water.

1959: July

IV

Hughes woke up the next morning with a headache, but also full of determination. Though it was still early, Nick had already risen. He stripped off his pajama bottoms, put on his bathrobe, and made his way outside, down toward the outdoor shower.

He slipped a little on the dew. The air was slightly cooler. The heat wave hadn't broken, but the heaviness had lifted a bit.

Hughes hung his robe over the wooden frame and turned on the water, letting it run over his head and shoulders until it swirled like a small tidal pool at his feet. He tipped his head back, pushing his hair out of his eyes, and looked up at the sky above him, a light blue that the morning sun was beginning to deepen. He could smell the wet grass and the damp bricks underfoot. He felt good. He also felt sad.

He thought about Nick running across the road in her red bathing suit, and wondered what was so much better about a bathrobe. They all acted like the strip of sidewalk between their house and the lawn across the road was private, belonged to them, when in fact you could run into any Tom, Dick, or Harry trotting between the two in your skivvies. At least Nick had the good sense to know it might be slightly shocking, even if she didn't really care.

Back at the house he found her in the kitchen. He had already planned what he was going to say, but when Nick saw him, she spoke before he could open his mouth.

"I'm sorry," she said, "I think I had too much to drink last night."

Hughes found himself momentarily confused; not only was an apology from his wife a rare thing, her words were also the kind that closed down the conversation. She was sorry, it had been the alcohol, everyone knows what that's like.

"I should be the one apologizing," he said. "I was boorish. I'm just . . . I don't know what's come over me, lately. Everything feels so, I don't know, different."

Nick didn't say anything.

"Look," he said, walking toward her, "I don't care about that. I don't want to talk about that. I want you to come on the boat with me today. I think the hull should be dry by now."

"All right," she said, slowly. "Daisy has her lesson until noon."

"No, just you. I'm inviting you."

Nick looked down at her feet and nodded. He could have sworn she was blushing slightly.

"You pack the picnic and I'll sort the boat out. Meet me down at the dock in an hour."

Then, before she could change her mind, Hughes walked quickly out of the kitchen. He met Daisy coming down the stairs. Her round blue eyes were full of sleep and her hair was mashed up in the back.

Hughes swooped her off the last step, up into his arms, and she let out a screech.

"Daddy, put me down."

"Sorry, sweetheart." Nick was right, she was turning into a sensitive little thing. "I was overwhelmed by this sleeping beauty on the stairs."

Daisy pretended to be offended, but he could tell she was secretly pleased.

Hughes headed upstairs to change. As he was passing Helena's room, she peeked her head out, but when she saw him she quickly withdrew it, like a turtle, and closed the door with a snap.

Down at the boathouse, he ran his hand over *Star*'s hull, checking to make sure it was bone dry. Satisfied, he pulled the dinghy down the lawn to the small strip of beach, where he began rigging her.

He stepped the mast, running the breast hook line and cleating it off. He slid in the boom and bent the sail. When he was finished tying and fastening, Hughes pulled out the oars, gleaming with varnish, and locked them in. He fetched the cushions and two towels from the boathouse and laid them on the dock in the sun to get rid of the faint clinging odor of mildew.

Then he sat down on the warm wooden planks, watching schools of minnows flitting in and out of the seaweed beneath, and waited.

He saw her as she made her way down the sloping lawn, tripping slightly against the incline. From that distance, she could be twenty, wearing a pair of poppy-colored shorts over a white strapless bathing suit, her short hair brushed from her forehead. She carried the picnic basket against her hip, tilting from the weight. When she reached him, she was a little breathless.

Hughes rose and took the hamper from her.

"Thanks," she said. "Phew, it's already hot."

"I think the heat's breaking a little," Hughes said.

"I don't know about that," Nick said.

They made their way to the beach where *Star* lay shining like a large green seashell. Hughes pushed the boat into the water, and Nick held her while he put in the daggerboard and rudder, and then handed him the hamper, cushions, and towels. He raised the sail and tied off the halyard, then, extending his hand, he pulled Nick in. Her calves, slippery from the water, slid against the siding and she used her palms to steady herself.

The day was bright and clear and as they sailed through the harbor the sun made little stars on the peaks of water. Hughes could feel the bridge of his nose crisping and he found himself squinting behind his sunglasses, already sticky with salt. His hand rested lightly on the tiller. It was a good day for sailing; calm, but not still.

Several midmorning swimmers were already walking the shoreline of the Chappy bathing beach, with its red-and-blue-striped bathhouses, and behind him Hughes could hear the bell on the dock ringing for the skipper of the *On Time*, calling him to make his way across.

"It's a perfect day," Nick said. "At least, here on the boat with the breeze. I packed deviled eggs. Do you want one now?"

"Not yet," Hughes said. "I'm going to delay my pleasure."

Nick laughed. "Why doesn't that surprise me?" She leaned back slightly and trailed her hand in the water. "I think it's in the genes, salt water. Whether you like it or not."

"Is that so?" Hughes smiled.

"Helena tells me that no one in California goes in the ocean. They only go in their swimming pools. Can you imagine? All that beautiful ocean and everyone in their pools."

Hughes didn't say anything. He was just enjoying listening to his wife talk. She had a way of making old ideas sound fresh, off-kilter, like she looked at things from a different angle than everyone else.

Nick reached out and removed his sunglasses. She blew on the lenses and then cleaned them off on the edge of her bright-red shorts.

"That's better," she said, placing them carefully back on his face. "Now you can see where we're going." She tilted her head to one side and looked at him. "Wayfarers. You look like William Holden, so glamorous, darling."

He steered the boat through the gut into Cape Poge Bay and made for the elbow.

When they neared shore, Nick jumped out and Hughes followed her into the water. Together, they pulled *Star* up onto the beach. Whenever they came here, they always chose the same spot, where the water was deep right from the shore, making the swimming better, but not so close to the gut that the current would pull you away. Nick's shorts were soaked through and she kicked them off before lying down on one of the towels.

"Do you want one of the cushions as a pillow?"

"No," Hughes said, "I'll use my shirt."

They lay side by side, the picnic basket above their heads. Hughes propped his cheek on his hand and looked at Nick, who had her eyes closed. Her skin was a kind of golden color against the white of her bathing suit. After a bit, she raised her head.

"Do you want a deviled egg now?" she asked.

"What else do you have in there?"

"White wine?"

"That's the ticket," Hughes said.

Nick reached in and pulled out the bottle, which she had

packed with a tea towel and ice. "You open it and I'll stick it in the water afterward," she said, handing him a corkscrew.

Hughes poured two glasses and gave Nick the bottle. He watched as she stood and tied a piece of string around the neck, with a small anchor attached. She dug the anchor into the sand and plopped the bottle into the water, where it quickly bobbed up with the current. Then she took out a little container of olives stuffed with pimento and offered one to Hughes.

The brine exploded into his mouth and he washed it down with a sip of the cold white wine.

"White wine and olives always taste like the beach," Nick said.

"The salt," Hughes said, closing his eyes.

"Yes. But also because they're both so clean."

Hughes could hear the beetles singing in the heat, and the gulls behind him in the dunes, where they made their nests. It was only eleven in the morning and he realized he'd missed breakfast. The wine was making him sleepy. Then he was dreaming about a race between a white horse and black horse, and the black one was winning, which, in his dream, pleased him. It had large nostrils and a braided tail that it held high as it ran. He was cheering for it. He felt Nick shifting next to him and he jogged himself awake.

She was sitting up looking out at the ocean.

Hughes followed her gaze and they sat for a while, not saying anything. Then he knew: this was his moment. He took a deep breath and jumped.

"I wrote you a letter once," he said. "I think the biggest mistake of my life might be that I never sent it."

Nick didn't look at him. "What did it say?"

"It said a lot of things." Hughes shook his head. Across

the gut, a fisherman was baiting his hook. "Things I probably should have told you a long time ago."

Nick was silent.

"I don't know how things got so . . . muddled. How it all passed."

"Oh, Hughes." Nick looked up at the sky and exhaled. "Because things do pass. Anyone who's lived just a little while knows that. Things just . . . go." She sounded so sad.

"That letter. It said that I loved you. Since . . . Jesus, I don't know how long. Since I first saw you, maybe."

"I can't . . . I don't know why you're bringing all this up."

"Nick, listen . . ."

"God, you're such a child." Nick stared at him, her eyes like flint. "You think you can snap your fingers and tell me you love me and conjure up some happy ending for us?"

"I don't know," Hughes said. "I don't know any other way. Do you know one? I mean, you tell me, how do people get their happy ending?"

She looked at him awhile. "All this time . . ." She shook her head and looked away.

"Say it."

When she turned back her eyes were wet. "All this time, you've been sleepwalking through our life. Do you think I'm stupid? You talk about letters. What about 'the world's not on fire anymore, Hughes'; 'come back to me, Hughes'? What about Claridge's, room 201?" She was shaking. "You were supposed to love me. Instead, you made everything, I don't know, blank. You turned my life gray."

Somehow, he wasn't surprised that she knew. It could have been Ed or she could have found the letters herself. Although he didn't know how she could have known about the room. It didn't matter now.

"Yes," he said. "Yes, I did all of that. And you have every reason to hate me. And if you do, if you really can't love me anymore, I'll go. Or I'll stay. Whatever you want." He stopped.

She was searching his face. The tears had stripped her own of its usual hard beauty, and now he detected something else there, some mixture of hesitation and longing.

"Nick. Don't leave me alone."

She was quiet and then she said: "Goddamn you to hell, Hughes," but she said it softly.

Then her hand was cupping the back of his head, running down the nape of his neck. She was close to him. He could smell the wine on her breath and feel the heat coming off her bare shoulders, where he touched her. Then there was the sand against them, and the glare of the sun and the flash of their skin together.

"Tell me you love me," he said into her. "And I can make it right. I swear to God I'll make it right."

"I love you," she whispered. "You'll never know how much. But I don't know if you can make it right."

Then she said something else, but he couldn't hear her. He couldn't hear anything except the rush of blood in his ears. He could feel the pulse in her neck quickening beneath his hand, like the harsh sound of his own breath. And she was moving underneath him, her face turned away. And then he wasn't looking anymore. He was blind, and could only feel it moving through him, through her.

Afterward, Nick rose and dove into the ocean. Hughes followed, reaching for her beneath the surface, but she was swimming a little too far out. She turned and faced the shore, treading water. He swam toward her, slowly this time, and when he got to her she put her arm around his neck and kissed him. She tasted like olives.

"I like the color of the hull," Nick said, nodding her head toward the dinghy.

"I did it for these," Hughes said, gently brushing his thumb over her eyelid. "The color of a garden snake."

Nick laughed and ducked under the waves, resurfacing with her head dark and sleek and round. "I think that's the first time anyone's called me a garden snake. That's a fine description." She began swimming back and then called over her shoulder. "Do you want those goddamn eggs now, Hughes Derringer? Or do I have to eat them all by myself?"

It was the kind of day that you didn't need to remember from a distance to know it was a good one. The bay was calm and the only things to see were the dunes rising across it, and the gulls coming out of the beach grass every once in a while to give warning to stay away from their chicks.

Later, after lunch and a nap, Nick pulled out a book and began reading. He saw her diamond wedding band sparkling against her finger as she held it open.

"What are you reading?"

"Poems. Wallace Stevens."

"Read me some."

"Didn't you bring your own book?" She looked at him with a moue of disapproval.

"I was too busy."

"Tough luck, darling."

"Be a sport."

She flipped the pages. "Do you remember this one? It's called 'Depression Before Spring'. 'The cock crows but no queen rises. The hair of my blond is dazzling as the spittle of cows threading the wind.' "

"Cows' spittle?"

"You think garden snake is better?"

"I don't know, but a snake is a . . . sexier creature, I think. A cow, well."

"You're not a poet, are you, darling? Think about all that translucent spit coming out of its pink mouth. Like a web, or something."

"OK, OK. Mercy."

"'Ho! Ho!'"

"Ho, ho, indeed."

Nick laughed. "All right, that's it. No more for you."

"I'll manage. Somehow."

"Pour more wine and shut up."

Hughes got up and retrieved the bottle, emptying what was left into Nick's glass. He looked at the horizon. "We should probably go soon."

"Yes, the children will be home. And Helena . . ." She trailed off. "Hughes, I keep forgetting to ask you: have you gone to see the sheriff, about Ed I mean?"

"No."

"Will you?"

"Yes."

"Today? When we get back?"

"All right, if that's what you want."

He watched Nick carefully replace the picnic items and her book in the hamper and he felt a need to protect her, from everything and everyone. He reached out and brushed a patch of sand sticking to the back of her knee. She smiled at him.

"Come on," she said, reaching her hand out.

He took it and together they left their beach.

*

Hughes made his way down Main Street to the sheriff's office, trying to figure out what he was going to say once he got there. It seemed a little silly, going to the sheriff about Ed, and it also made him nervous, although he wasn't exactly sure why.

He pushed open the heavy door and went up to the messy wooden desk in the entryway. A policeman who couldn't have been more than eighteen was doodling on the blotter in front of him, looking supremely bored.

"Hello," Hughes said.

"Hello, sir," the young man said, unperturbed that he'd been caught out drawing seashells on duty. "Can I help you?"

"Yes, I'm here to see Sheriff Mello, if he's around."

"Your name, sir?"

"Hughes Derringer."

"I'll go see if he's available."

Through the glass, Hughes could see Sheriff Mello sitting at his desk, flipping through some paperwork. "Fine," Hughes said. "Thanks."

The policeman trundled into the sheriff's office and closed the door behind him. He could see the young man's lips moving and Sheriff Mello looking up at Hughes. The sheriff raised his hand to Hughes and rose from his chair, following the policeman back through the door.

"Mr. Derringer," he said.

"Sheriff Mello."

"What can I do for you?"

Hughes looked at the young recruit. He had a small white piece of paper stuck to his chin where he had cut himself shaving that morning. "Could we talk in your office?"

"Of course," Sheriff Mello said. "After you."

The windows at the back of the office looked out onto a scorched, unkempt lawn.

"Have a seat, Mr. Derringer," the sheriff said, indicating a wooden chair in front of his desk.

The seat was slightly tight and Hughes had to adjust himself to find a comfortable position. "Look, I'm sorry to bother you about this. I was a little reticent about coming here, I'm sure you have more important things to do . . ."

The sheriff just looked at him, his blue eyes unblinking. He had sweat marks staining the underarms of his blue uniform, a fact that made Hughes feel vaguely disquieted.

"Well, it's about my cousin's son, Ed Lewis. His mother is a little concerned about the whole incident with that maid."

"I see," the sheriff said. "How are the kids holding up?"

"They're fine. Actually, it's almost like the whole thing never happened."

"Kids," the sheriff said. "Harder than coconuts."

"Yes," Hughes said, shifting again. "The thing is, I think what Mrs. Lewis would like to know about her son . . . well, it seems Ed said he helped you, and Mrs. Lewis is wondering, is worried, actually, about what he may have seen."

"Is she?"

Hughes felt like he was fourteen, sitting in front of the headmaster again. "Yes. So if, well, if you could set her at ease on that score, I suppose . . ."

"I understand Mrs. Lewis's concern for her son," Sheriff Mello said evenly. "But I am, how did you put it? Reticent? Yes, that was it. Reticent to discuss certain things, especially if it's unfounded gossip."

"Of course," Hughes said, wondering if that meant he was going to tell him or not.

"However, seeing as you're family." The sheriff leaned back. "It's funny, I've lived here all my life. But I've realized that expression seems to mean a whole lot of different things to different people."

Hughes had no idea what the sheriff was talking about, but he found himself gripping the arms of the chair. "Is that so?"

"That is so." The sheriff didn't move a muscle. "Anyway," he said finally, "the thing is, Mr. Derringer, when I asked Ed if he'd ever seen anyone else there, where the girl was found, he told me the two of you often took walks there."

"I see." Hughes felt his heart hammering in his chest.

"So, actually, I'm glad you came in. Saves me a trip to the house."

"Oh."

"Do you want to tell me about it?"

"The walks?" Hughes looked up at the ceiling, as if trying to remember. "I wouldn't say that's entirely true. We did walk through Sheriff's Meadow once, earlier this summer. Man-to-man kind of chat. The boy's father is . . . well, not all there. You know."

"Is that right? Something wrong with the boy's father?"

"He's just, I don't know, not very good at it, I suppose."

Sheriff Mello looked at him awhile, and evidently deciding something, nodded his head. "Right." He sat back in his chair. "Well, Ed also told us that maybe—he wasn't sure, mind you—that he might have seen Frank Wilcox there once. But he couldn't remember."

Hughes held his breath, waiting for the sheriff to elaborate. When he didn't say anything else, Hughes blurted out: "And?"

"And what?" The sheriff smiled.

"What did Frank say? I mean, if you can tell me. It's none of my business . . ."

"Well, Mr. Derringer, it seems that Mr. Wilcox was home

all night with Mrs. Wilcox. That is, of course, according to Mrs. Wilcox . . ." His last statement hung in the air like a question.

"Right."

"So, that's the long and short of it. Ed's information didn't really come to much, if you see what I mean." The sheriff tilted his head. "That is, unless you know anything that could help us?"

"Um, no. Wish I could I help. But no."

"For example, you might know something about Mr. Wilcox's private life that we don't. Something small, even. Or, perhaps, there's something you'd like to tell us about your nephew."

Hughes was silent. He sure as hell wasn't going to get any more involved in this mess than he had to.

"You see, Mr. Derringer, a community's like family. As I said before, everyone has their own definition of that. But my take on it is, when someone in your family does something really wrong, there's no point hiding it. Just makes it worse for everyone else."

"I really do wish I could help you."

"All righty, then."

Hughes made a motion, as if he would go, and then stopped. He knew he shouldn't say any more, but he couldn't help himself. "And I suppose, her friends or family, the maid I mean. Elena Nunes. They had nothing to say. About any of this."

"No. We didn't get anything out of them, no."

"Tight-lipped community, I suppose."

"Tight-lipped community." This time the sheriff laughed out loud. A dry noise. "Which one?"

❖

Hughes fled into the hot afternoon air. His nerves felt jangly. He should have gone to the sheriff with the information about Frank when the maid first turned up dead. He saw that now. But he'd been distracted. Anyway, it seemed Frank had an alibi. That's what the sheriff had said. Still, Hughes wasn't sure he believed it. Sheriff Mello sure as hell didn't.

He thought about the sheriff. He'd known him since he was a boy, when Rick Mello was still bagging orders at the local market. Yet the man had made him feel guilty. It wasn't his fault the sheriff's office hadn't done a damn thing about Frank Wilcox. Even if he had seen them go to the tennis courts, it didn't prove anything. And if Etta was willing to vouch for her husband, then . . . And Ed. He'd made it out like they'd been traipsing all over the country-side together. Could he have sincerely been trying to help and just exaggerated? But no, Hughes knew in his bones the boy was off. Way off. Even the sheriff seemed to have his doubts about him. Hughes thought about that mouse with the toothpick in its head. He needed a drink.

Hughes downed a couple of quick gin and tonics at the Reading Room, and then made his way home. The sun hadn't quite started its full descent. It was making hot pink streaks across the sky, like a child's finger paintings.

As he approached the house, he saw Nick on the front porch, still in her bathing suit and shorts, leaning over a boy and whispering something into his ear. The kid's hair was almost comical, sticking straight up like it had been stiffened with corn starch. Some friend of Daisy's, he guessed. Hughes smiled at the adoring expression on his upturned face. He knew how the kid felt.

Not yet ready for the question-and-answer session that he knew awaited him, Hughes went round to the back door and headed upstairs. After a shower and a shave, he steeled himself and went to find Nick and Helena, who were having cocktails.

"Hello, darling," Nick said. "How did it go with Sheriff Mello?"

Helena looked up too, her soft eyes expectant. And worried, he noticed.

"It went just fine," Hughes said, walking over to the bar.

"Well?" Nick said. "Don't be so coy. What did he say?"

"Nothing," Hughes said, dropping three ice cubes into a lowball.

"What do you mean, nothing? You've been gone for almost two hours."

"I mean Ed didn't see anything and doesn't know anything," Hughes said. "The sheriff was just humoring him. Letting him play detective, or something."

Helena leaned her head back against the wing chair, with something like relief.

"So, it's all right, then," Nick said, her voice calling him back to the sitting room.

"Yes," Hughes said. "Everything's just fine."

1959: August

As the party drew near, Nick seemed to get lost in the minutiae of Chinese lanterns and silver polish and white hydrangeas. Hughes would find his wife awake in the middle of the night, her little reading lamp on, revising the menu for the one-hundredth time.

His role was to stay calm and batten down the hatches. But the night before the party, he needed a little relief from the storm.

Nick was in the dining room, re-polishing the silver setting for the early supper. She had just finished scolding Daisy about the state of her room and Hughes took the opportunity to raid the kitchen and bar, before heading down to the boathouse to get drunk on whiskey sours. When he got there, he found Helena, also hiding out.

"What have you got there?" she whispered, gesturing to the bottle of whiskey and bowl of sugar he was carrying.

Hughes laughed. "You don't have to whisper, Helena. She can't hear us down here."

"I love Nick, but I can't stand all this . . . scurrying," Helena said. "Anyway, what is that?"

"Whiskey sours."

"I love whiskey sours," Helena said, almost wistfully.

"Me too," Hughes said, and pulled two lemons out of his back pocket. "Damn," he said, looking around, "I forgot the ice."

"And a shaker." Helena held her palms up, eyebrows lifted, the picture of disaster.

"No," Hughes said, winking at her. "I keep one here, behind the old anchor, for emergencies. But the ice is a problem."

"I could go on a mission." Helena smiled at him.

"Should we risk it?"

"You wait here." She rose and made a production of tiptoeing off, her patterned dress swirling behind her.

Hughes blew on the inside of the shaker to remove the dust and then put the sugar, whiskey, and lemon in and waited.

Helena finally returned with the small silver ice bucket that Nick had planned to use for the supper. Hughes had seen her polishing it earlier.

"I know, I know," she said. "But I had to; the other one was too big."

Hughes dropped a few ice cubes into the shaker and then joggled it briskly. He poured the sours off into the two plastic picnic cups.

"Madame," he said, handing one to Helena.

Helena took a sip. "Hughes, you really are a marvel with a shaker."

They sat quietly for a minute, enjoying the peace and the sharp cocktails.

"So, Helena," he said finally, "how's life?"

"What do you mean?"

"I don't know. Everything. Nothing."

"Everything and nothing," she repeated. "I suppose I'm happy everything turned out all right with the maid. With Ed, I mean. I know it didn't really turn out all right for her."

"I know what you meant."

"I worry about him sometimes." Helena drained her glass and Hughes refilled the shaker.

"Well, I'm sure the Scouts will do him some good." Hughes wanted to get away from this subject. "Straighten him out a little bit."

Helena looked up sharply. "I don't think he needs straightening out."

"No, well."

"He might not be like everyone else his age, but why should that matter? He's free."

"Free from what?" Jesus, she could be a kook sometimes.

"Free from . . . I don't know, what other people want him to be. Avery says . . ." but she tapered off. "Never mind." Helena held out her empty glass.

"Oh," Hughes said, studiously squeezing more lemon juice.

"Hughes," Helena's voice softened. "We really need money. Do you think you could talk to Nick for me?"

"I'll talk to her," Hughes said, patting her hand, an idea forming in his head. "Now, give me that empty glass."

The next morning was painful. Nick was up early ordering the children out of bed and Hughes went downstairs to help with breakfast. He had wanted to talk to her about his idea, but when she came into the kitchen, he realized she was in no mood.

Instead, he drove to Vineyard Haven to pick up the musicians. They were a ragtime band Dolly had recommended, the Top Liners or something. He waited at the curb and watched the *Islander* pull into dock, the dockhands rushing to the ferry slip to crank down the apron.

He watched several cars disembark, and then the foot

passengers. Hughes could easily pick out the musicians from the small crowd: they were wearing dungarees and lugging their instruments in beaten old cases. They looked as hungover as he was. Hughes walked over.

"Hello, boys."

They squinted at him, almost in unison. "You Mr. Derringer?" This from the one carrying the banjo case.

"That's right. The car's over here."

They put their instruments in the trunk and piled in, three in the back, two in the front with him, and he started the engine.

"Man . . . ." One of the boys in the back let the word slide into one long breath.

"Hot, hot, hot." The banjo player banged out a little rhythm on his knee.

They were all pretty young. Mid-twenties, Hughes guessed. One of the boys next him looked like he was asleep, his scruffy head laid all the way back against the seat. The other one, all dark hair and brooding eyes, ran his hand across the door upholstery.

"Where are you all from?" Hughes eyed the boys in the back through the rearview mirror.

"Around," the dark one said, still running his hand over the fabric on the door.

"Yeah," said the banjo player. "Here and there, and everywhere." Another tap, tap, tap on the knee.

The whole band laughed. Hughes kept his eyes on the road. Jesus, Nick was going to kill him if they turned up like this.

"You boys want to stop for some cokes?"

"Some cokes?" The dark one laughed. "No thanks."

✽

When he pulled into the back drive at Tiger House, Hughes saw Nick standing at the screen door, like she had been waiting for them.

The banjo player whistled. "Nice house."

"Hello," Nick said, crossing the lawn to greet them as they bundled out of the car.

The musicians stared at her, bug-eyed. Hughes covered his face with his hand.

"I'm Nick Derringer. Which one of you is Tom?"

"That's me," the banjo player said, not moving.

"Hello," the dark one said, rocking back on his heels, his trumpet case swaying in his hand.

Nick looked at them and then back at Hughes. "You all stay here," she ordered. "Darling, can I speak with you for a minute."

When they got inside the house, she turned on him and put her hands on her hips. "They're stoned," she said hotly, as if he was the one responsible.

"I wish I was stoned," Hughes said. "You didn't have to suffer through that car ride."

"Goddamn it, it's not funny."

"I'm not laughing," he said, trying to repress a smile.

"You can always find yourself a gin bottle and get to it, if you're so keen," Nick said tartly.

"Are those the musicians?" Daisy's little head appeared in the hallway.

"Daisy Derringer, go sweep the front walk, like I asked you to," Nick said. She walked into the kitchen, where the Portuguese girls were preparing the food. "Can you girls make sure the boys out there get some iced tea? And some sandwiches, I suppose. But not the tea sandwiches, there's some deviled ham in the pantry. They can have that. And for god's sakes, don't let them in the house."

Hughes stood in the hallway, pressing his fingers to his temples. His head was still pounding. "What can I do to help?" he asked, hoping it would include an ice pack and a dark room.

Nick turned in the kitchen doorway. "You could help the men with the bandstand. Make sure they don't put it in all crooked, like last year."

Hughes nodded. He found an ice chest of beer on the front porch; the delivery boy must have just left it there without bothering to alert anyone. He pushed his hand inside, lifted a bottle, and popped the cap with his Swiss Army knife. Then he sat down on the porch and started mulling over his plan for Ed. Something Helena had said the night before about being free had started him thinking.

Ed needed to go to boarding school and Hughes needed to pay for it, that was all there was to it. It was the only way he could gain some modicum of control over the boy. With Ed at school, Hughes could get reports and keep an eye on him. If the kid was just a snot-nosed jerk, he wouldn't get away with it for very long there. And if it was worse than that, if it was something more than just bad behavior, the truth would come out. The plan made him feel good. Life was always better when you had a plan.

He saw Daisy lollygagging along the fence. The fact that she obviously wasn't sweeping the walk made him smile.

"Hello there, sweetheart," he called out from the porch. "Where's your cousin?"

"I don't know," Daisy said, peering up at him. "He's disappeared. He said he was going to check the mousetraps."

Hughes blotted the image out of his head. Enough was enough: he would teach the boy a lesson about freedom. He hid his empty beer bottle in the rose bush and made his way down to check on the bandstand.

When the afternoon drew to a close, and the house had gone from hustle and bustle to total silence, Hughes headed upstairs to bathe and change for dinner. He was in the bedroom combing his damp hair when Nick returned from her own bath.

"Wait until you see my dress," she said, shimmying into her slip. "It's divine."

"Can you help me with these?" Hughes brought his cuff links over and dropped them into her hand.

She pulled his shirtsleeve straight, bringing the edges of his cuffs together.

"I've been thinking," Hughes said. "About Ed. About how you said he probably needed more structure."

"Did I? I think I meant he needed a father, a real one."

"Well, there's not much we can do about that. But I was thinking: Ed could go to boarding school. It would get him out of that house, away from Avery."

"Oh, Hughes, they can't afford it." Nick fixed the second cuff link in.

"No, but we can." He took her hand in his and Nick looked at him. "It would be something we could do for Helena, to make her life easier, without having to give Avery any money."

"Can we really afford it?"

"We can manage."

"I don't know," she said, shaking her head slightly. "I'm not sure how Helena would feel about it."

"She said herself that she's been worrying about him." Hughes let go of her hand and began adjusting his bow tie.

"She has been, that's true."

"She's family, Nicky. It's the least we can do. And with Ed gone, it might bring the situation with Avery into, I don't know, starker relief."

"Do you think so?"

"It's possible." Hughes watched her.

"It's very generous of you, darling. And very dear."

"I know how much you love her."

"Yes," Nick said. "Yes I do. Oh, Hughes, imagine if she had a real chance at being happy."

"First things first."

"Yes. You're right, it really is a very good plan. You're very clever sometimes."

"I try." He grinned at her.

"I'll talk to her this evening. Before the supper."

Hughes went to find the musicians and tell them they could change into their clothes in the boathouse. He wouldn't have been surprised to find them running around the back lawn in their skivvies. They would be leaving by the last ferry and he had arranged for a man in town to take them.

"When you're done you can bring your things back up here and he'll load them," Hughes instructed.

"Sure thing, Mr. Derringer," the dark one said, not looking up from his trumpet.

Hughes would have liked to give the kid a good backhand, but he set his expression to neutral and waited until they'd cleared out. Then he picked up the scattered beer bottles and cigarette ends and brought them into the kitchen to dispose of them.

One of the Portuguese girls watched him, shaking her head.

"I agree," Hughes said. "Not a good bunch."

The girl just smiled at him.

They had a few minutes before their dinner guests would start arriving and Hughes made his way toward the blue sitting room to fix himself a drink.

"Hello." He strode over to where his wife and cousin were seated, bending down to kiss their cheeks. "Don't you both look lovely."

Nick was wearing a dress the color of the evening sky, with gold stitching running through it. She glowed.

"Hello, darling."

"You were right," Hughes said, "that dress is something."

Helena got up and went over to the bar.

"I'll do that," Hughes said, but she waved him away, so he seated himself next to Nick, who smiled at him.

"You look . . ." he whispered into her ear.

"What?" she whispered back.

"I don't know . . . Heartbreaking."

She tilted her head back slightly and her red lips parted. He wanted Helena to go away and the party to go away and to just sit there with her and breathe in her sweetness until the clocks stopped.

When the Pritchards showed up, and then the Smith-Thompsons, Hughes could barely concentrate on the conversation. But after a while, he found his happiness wasn't exclusive; it began to expand to include Helena, and his friends and the hot summer evening and the antici-pation of the party. Nick had put on Count Basie and the ebb and flow of the jazz filled the sitting room, along with the cheerful sound of ice cubes hitting glass.

He watched his wife move around between their guests, her hand resting here on Dolly's arm, and there at Caro's waist, bending her head in to listen intently to something Arthur said and then laugh at Rory spilling his drink on the oriental rug. Everything felt good and right. Like it would last forever.

It lasted only until dinner, when the conversation turned to Frank Wilcox and the damn murder. Dolly had brought it up, and Caro had said something silly about the girl wanting to catch herself a big fish and Nick had gone off to some dark place, practically accusing their guests of being complicit in the crime.

Hughes had tried to set the tone right, pouring more wine and joking around, but he could tell they'd lost Nick for the evening. It made him angry. Caro was a nice woman, but she was a ninny and there was no reason for Nick to go spoiling everything over some foolish, offhand comment.

When they had finished eating, and their guests had moved out to the lawn to join the gathering crowd and listen to the first tune from the band, Hughes cornered Nick on the porch.

"Nicky, what's the matter?"

"What do you mean?" She wouldn't look at him.

"At dinner."

"I'm sorry," she said, twisting the fabric of the dress between her fingers. "I can't help it. Every time I think about that poor girl, I just can't . . . breathe."

Hughes could see she was close to tears. "All right, all right. Jesus. It's OK. Don't get upset."

"Well, I am upset, goddamn it." She turned on him. "Why can't you understand what's happened? Can't you feel it? Like everything good is . . . Like it means something else. Like everything is becoming infected. Why don't you see that?"

"Nick, you can't, I don't know, obsess about this. He's just a shit and what happened to the girl is a tragedy. But that's it. It's not any bigger or smaller than that."

Nick looked at him as he if were speaking a foreign language and then slowly nodded her head. "Of course, you're right, darling. I'm being silly."

He felt her slipping farther away from him, but there was nothing he could do about it.

"We should see to our guests," she said, crisply, smoothing out an invisible wrinkle in her dress. "It's not a very good party when the hostess has a crying jag on the porch, is it?"

"The hostess is perfect," he said. "Maybe she just needs a glass of champagne."

Hughes offered Nick his arm and guided her down to the front lawn. He went to the bar to get two glasses of champagne, but when he returned to the spot he had left her, Nick had disappeared.

Searching for her in the crowd of people, Hughes spotted Arthur Smith-Thompson heading straight for him.

"Hello, hello."

"Found the bar, did you?" Hughes clapped him on the back.

"Sure did." They both surveyed the party for a moment, and then Arthur said: "I knew that girl. The maid."

Hughes turned toward him and Arthur looked away.

"She worked for us last summer."

"Did she?" Hughes said. "I didn't know that."

Arthur was nodding his head. "Yes. Elena. She was . . ." Arthur stopped, and then said softly, "the kind of girl you couldn't help but look at."

Music drifted over them.

"I wouldn't be surprised if it was Frank. Who did it, I mean." Arthur swallowed the rest of his drink.

Hughes stared at him.

"She was like that. Seductive, I guess you could call it. Pull you in and then push you away."

There was a bitterness in his tone that made Hughes feel slightly sick.

"You know?" Arthur said.

"I'm not sure I do."

"I just hope Frank didn't fall for it. Would be a damn shame for him. I mean, Caro's got a point. It was only a matter of time before there was some kind of trouble, with that girl chasing after married men. That's what burns me. People running around, making a mess out of everything. First wanting this and then wanting that. Never stopping to realize there's somebody else in the room, if you see what I mean."

"Well, I hardly think we can blame the poor girl for getting murdered," Hughes said.

"But it *is* girls like that," Arthur said violently. "Never realizing what they have. Always wanting something else."

Hughes looked at his friend. Arthur's face had turned ugly. He thought about Eva, and then about Nick. And all at once he understood what his wife had meant. He had to find her.

"Excuse me, Arthur," Hughes said. "I should probably go see if Nick needs any help."

"Of course," Arthur said, but he wasn't listening.

The party was in full swing and it took Hughes ages to cross from one side of the lawn to other, stopping every few seconds to glad-hand their guests. The band was playing a Noël Coward song, and Hughes wondered, belatedly, how they planned to do ragtime without a piano. He laughed. They'd been had. It didn't seem to matter, though; their guests' voices were a dull roar, the line for the bar was long, but not too long, and couples had begun to dance happily to whatever the Top Liners saw fit to play.

He looked for Nick's dark hair and blue dress among the

white dinner jackets and pastel silks, to no avail. When he reached the bar, he found Daisy and her little friend with the dark bangs. They were mooning around, probably trying to figure a way to sneak some champagne.

"Hello, girls."

Daisy's friend had a funny way about her, dramatic and charming, answering all his questions like she was in a play. It made Hughes smile, but Daisy seemed embarrassed.

He took pity and asked the bartender to put a few drops of wine in some water for them, and then shooed them off to go listen to the band.

He continued to shake hands and kiss cheeks, but he was beginning to feel increasingly desperate to find Nick. At one point he saw her down by the bandstand, talking to his daughter and that boy, the one who had a crush on her. But by the time he got down there, they had all wandered off somewhere else. It was like being in a dream, where you try to run, but can only move in slow motion.

He was scanning the lawn for what seemed like the hundredth time when Dolly Pritchard found him.

"Hello," Hughes said. "I've been on a treasure hunt for my wife, but she keeps eluding me."

"Oh dear," Dolly said. "That doesn't sound satisfactory at all."

"No," Hughes said. "It isn't."

"You know, I think she said she was going down to the boathouse to cool off for a minute."

The band had gone on a break and now only laughter and the buzz of conversation filled the night. Hughes squinted toward the dock, and the small strip of beach, looking to see if Nick was dipping her toes in the water. She did that sometimes when she'd had too much to drink; she said it had a sobering effect.

"Toes are very sensitive, you know," she'd say. "Most people ignore them, but they're our first contact with the ground every day. Like antennae."

Hughes thought about all the little things, her small fancies, hundreds, thousands, enough to fill days. How had he missed all that? He thought again about what she'd said about the murder ruining everything. He did know what she meant, but she was wrong. Nothing had changed, not really; it was just with a thing like that, you had to choose sides. And when it came to your friends, you all had to smile while you did it, pretending you were in happy agreement. That's what made it hard, all the tension of pretense and false understanding. Hughes was beginning to realize that he was better at not choosing a side. He'd worn Eva like armor, against Nick, against the possibility he wasn't who he wanted to be. And the whole time, she'd been there, waiting, like something frozen in amber.

He felt an urgent tug at his sleeve and turned. Daisy was standing there, wild-eyed.

"Where's Mummy?" Her voice sounded squeaky, desperate.

"Daisy." He took her by the shoulder, a feeling of panic rising in him. "What's wrong?"

"Where's Mummy? I need Mummy."

"I don't know, sweetpea." Hughes looked down the lawn again. "I think she said she was going down to the boathouse to cool off."

His daughter wrenched out of his grasp and tore down toward the harbor. He called after her, but she didn't turn around. For some reason, his mind went back to the phone ringing in the house on Traill Street, the feel of the cold receiver pressed against his ear. He hesitated for a moment and then followed quickly, pushing past groups of guests who called out to him.

He made for the far side of the boathouse. From there, he could see the outdoor shower silhouetted against the sky. He heard water running through the pipes: Nick must be in the shower, which also meant she must be drunk.

As his eyes adjusted, he saw someone else, Ed, pressed up against the wooden slats, looking in. Hughes froze. He could feel the chemicals making their way through his bloodstream, cramping his limbs and constricting his lungs. Then, all at once, Daisy appeared from the dock end and Hughes watched her stop in her tracks. She started mumbling something that sounded like Sunday school lessons and Hughes saw Ed turn at the sound of her voice. He knew he should move, do something, but his legs were made of lead.

The two children were staring at each other, now, like they were communicating in some kind of secret, silent language. He could hear Nick start to sing in the shower, a sweet tune from earlier in the evening.

And then Daisy called out for her mother.

Hughes heard Ed say, "Curiosity killed the cat."

He felt his muscles tightening, coiling inside him.

"Satisfaction brought it back," Daisy said softly.

Hughes saw Ed cock his head, the same way he had after Hughes had hit him.

"What are you doing looking at my mother, Ed Lewis? Are you a sex maniac? Like Mr. Wilcox?"

"Don't talk about Mr. Wilcox." The boy's voice was hard and flat, but it lacked the mockery he had directed at Hughes. It was more . . . what? Defensive? Hurt? He couldn't put his finger on it, exactly.

326

"Those matches," Daisy said, "the ones from the Hide-away . . ."

The Hideaway, the matches, the sheriff. Like a latch being sprung, Hughes felt his muscles release and he was running.

"Daisy, get away from him. Now."

He watched his daughter step back quickly at the sound of his voice. Ed turned and faced him, almost like he was glad, like he'd been waiting for him. Hughes grabbed the boy's arm, his own momentum pulling Ed along with him toward the beach. He twisted the arm in his hand, hard, feeling the young muscle and sinew and bone resisting the pressure, and thought momentarily about breaking it. He imagined the satisfying snap, the surprise on Ed's face. He could feel the sense of triumph. But Hughes could hear his guests in the distance, so he released his grip slightly and put his face as close to Ed's as he could. He could smell his own breath, boozy, in the small space between them.

"Now, you listen to me." Hughes was panting. His scalp itched with sweat. "I know you. I know what you are." He tried to control his breathing. "Yes, I do." He wrenched the boy's arm again, cruelly. "So here's what's going to happen. If you ever come near my wife again, if you ever look at my daughter the way you did tonight, if you so much as breathe in their direction in a way I don't like, I will wait until you are asleep one night and I will come into your room and I will break your neck. I will break it, and then I will tell them you fell down the stairs sleepwalking." Hughes thought he saw a flicker of doubt in the boy's eyes, a sliding to the side as if he was considering the threat. "Do we understand each other?"

He watched the boy wince slightly, just a small movement between the corner of his lip and the crook of his eye.

He must be hurting him. Hughes began to straighten up, prepared to let him go, his message delivered, but Ed leaned in closer, putting his lips to Hughes's ear.

"It was research," the boy whispered. "Frank Wilcox and the girl. My mother and Mr. Fox. Aunt Nick and that trumpet player. I saw them."

Hughes felt all the energy drain from him, and his skin prickled. He could hear the boy's breathing while he paused.

"I told you," he continued, "no one says anything they really mean. None of it's real." Ed pulled back and looked at Hughes, as if he really wanted him to understand something. "I think—I don't know yet—but I think they're going about it all the wrong way."

Hughes could feel his brain shutting down; he let go of the boy's arm. Ed straightened up, rubbing the place where Hughes had held him. He searched his face for something, then nodded slightly, and walked slowly off, back toward the party. Hughes stood rooted to the spot. He could hear people laughing. He saw the lights of the boats in the harbor winking at him, and heard the masts pinging in the distance. The trumpet wailed out into the night. He closed his eyes.

He didn't know how long he stood like that, thinking of nothing, his mind smooth and empty. Finally, he turned away from the water. A lantern was lit in the boathouse, and he walked toward it. He saw Daisy sitting on the floor, her head on Nick's lap. His wife's hair was still damp from the shower, but she was wearing her evening dress, the gold thread leaping in the lamplight.

Out of sight, he leaned against the wall and listened.

"I don't care," Daisy was saying. "I hate all of them."

"Darling." Nick's voice was kinder, gentler than it usually

was when she was speaking to their daughter. "I want you to listen to me. I'm going to tell you this because someday it may be very important for you to remember. If there's one thing you can be sure about in this life, it's that you won't always be kissing the right person."

Hughes looked up at the sky and a noise escaped him, a strange, sorrowful sound he didn't know he was capable of making. He ran his hands over his eyes and then, stiffening his spine, he levered himself away from the boathouse, the rough surface of the clapboard pushing back against his palms.

He walked toward the door, and entered the lit interior, feeling the glow of the lantern on his clammy skin. Daisy's little tear-stained face looked up at him from her mother's lap, and Nick smiled at him, softly, conspiratorially.

"Here you are," Hughes said. "Just where I thought you'd be. My two best girls. I'm so glad."

ED

1964: June

I have this image of Daisy. It is early summer and we're standing on the porch of Tiger House. It's dusk and I've just come back from visiting my mother in the hospital in the city. She has stayed there longer than anyone expected and longer, I'm sure, than Aunt Nick and Uncle Hughes can afford. The hospital is a strange place and I'm having one of those moments in which where I've been and where I am don't connect. Where I'm wondering: how was I just in that place and now I'm in this other place, and none of it makes any sense. And then I look at Daisy and I have the sensation that, just at that moment, while I'm looking at her, she is unfurling. Right there and then, before my eyes. Becoming, as my father would have called it. She doesn't mention my mother or the hospital. She looks at me and says: "The Reading Room? I'm dying for a drink." And I say, "OK," or something. And then she slips her arm through mine and I can feel her bracelet through my shirtsleeve and it sends shivers up my spine. We step off the porch into the evening. And that's how it begins.

"I always have this strange feeling," the woman with the violet eyes was saying, "that everyone here is the same person."

We were standing at the Reading Room bar and Thomas

was waiting to take our order. Daisy just laughed, but I thought it was an interesting thing to say, and I moved closer to the woman.

"Gin and tonic for me," Daisy said. "Ed?"

I couldn't really concentrate on the drink order, because I was still thinking about everyone being the same. The room was full of men and women who looked like they could have all been born in the same second of the same year, even though, of course, they hadn't. Navy blazers; yellow blazers; green trousers; pink skirts with yellow whales; yellow belts with pink lobsters; Nantucket reds; Nantucket baskets; blue-and-white rep ties; yellow-and-purple rep ties; pink-and-navy rep ties. It made my head hurt.

"Ed?"

I looked up and saw Thomas drumming his fingers on the polished wood.

"Oh, hell's bells," Daisy said, turning away. "He'll have a gin and tonic, too."

I smiled. "Hell's bells," I said.

Daisy smiled back and poked me with her elbow. Only Daisy did things like that.

"Olivia, you know my cousin, Ed," Daisy said, turning back to the woman with violet eyes.

"I'm not sure."

I, for one, couldn't ever remember having seen this Olivia before. She was pretty, but a little too old to be that pretty. I put her somewhere between thirty-eight and forty, but she had the kind of looks that would have made a debutante popular.

"Ed's going to Princeton in the fall," Daisy said.

I always found this sort of conversation a bit odd, but one of the things I'd learned in boarding school was that alma

334

maters were some kind of character reference. It was just one of those things. Boarding school had been extremely educational in this way, teaching me how to decode these small intricacies that everyone else seemed to understand naturally, and I was grateful to Uncle Hughes for having sent me there, although I suspected he wouldn't have thanked them for it.

"Are you? Princeton? Well, that's nice." Olivia seemed distracted, but she pulled herself together, adding: "Go Tigers!"

I liked her. I could see the hem of her slip a little, and I liked that, too. She was exposed, and slightly uncomfortable. I was standing so close to her now, I could smell her perfume. She smelled like candied roses. I wanted to reach out and touch her hair, which was an unusual shade of red, feel its texture between my fingers.

Daisy was signing the chit, in that hasty way of hers. Scribble, scribble, and then shoving it away like she couldn't bear to look at it one minute longer. I'd watched her do it for years. At the Yacht Club, the Tennis Club, and here, where women were admitted into the inner sanctum every other Sunday.

I would have liked to stay and chat a little more with Olivia of the Violet Eyes, but Daisy handed me my drink, and said: "We have to go find my mother and father. Pay our dues. They are footing the bar tab, after all."

"Goodbye," I said to Olivia. "It was nice talking to you."

She smiled, but she was already looking for someone else to cling onto, in that sea of sameness.

Daisy grabbed my hand and said: "Stop dawdling, Ed Lewis," and we pushed through the small crowd out onto the dock, where women were trying not to get their heels stuck in between the planks. Outside, Daisy hesitated for a minute, her hand loosening its grip on mine, before she spotted Aunt Nick standing on the far edge, with Uncle Hughes close by.

Aunt Nick was not in the sea of sameness. She held a certain fascination for me, it was something about the way she moved, but I didn't particularly like her. And in many ways, underneath her unusual appearance, she was just like everyone else. It seemed to me that the world was made up of two camps: there were people like me and Daisy, who lived as honestly as we knew how, and then there was the rest of the world, who for various reasons couldn't help lying to themselves.

As we approached them, I could see Uncle Hughes recoil, but only with his eyes. It was a neat trick and I admired him for it, the way he could make his body say one thing while his mind said another. And although I knew he couldn't stand me, ever since the summer with Frank Wilcox, the funny thing was, I didn't dislike him. I was even a little sorry about all that. I hadn't meant to make him take against me, but I hadn't learned yet to keep certain things to myself. How to talk to people. Another thing boarding school had been good for.

"Hello, darling," Aunt Nick said, leaning in to kiss Daisy. I could smell the perfume she always wore, floral but with some hint of alcohol. "Hello, Ed."

"Hello," I said. I shook hands with Uncle Hughes.

"How is your mother?" Aunt Nick asked. She looked as if she really wanted to know.

"She's in the hospital."

"Yes," Aunt Nick said. "The doctor thinks she will be ready to come back home this summer. Did she seem . . . well?"

"I suppose." I never really knew what people meant by

that, only that you were expected to answer in the affirmative. By Aunt Nick's standards, my mother was not well. She was very angry and not all that good at hiding it, despite what seemed to be a considerable effort.

I could tell, during my latest visit, that she had been trying to communicate something to me, about Aunt Nick, I think. But, honestly, I wasn't sure why she was so angry. It wasn't as if she had been doing much before she went to the hospital, except sleeping in that dark room and fighting with my father.

"I hope so . . ." Here Aunt Nick trailed off.

Uncle Hughes put his hand on her arm.

"Mummy," Daisy said, "Ed just got here. He doesn't want to talk about the hospital."

"No, I'm sorry," Aunt Nick said, and looked around, probably to see if anyone had been listening.

"So, Ed," Uncle Hughes said, smiling. "What are your plans for the summer?"

"He's going to be my date," Daisy said, squeezing my hand, which was actually getting quite damp from her grip. "That is if he can stop mooning about after older women. You should have seen him," she smiled at her parents. "He could barely tear himself away from Olivia Winston long enough to order a drink."

"I wasn't mooning."

"Liar," Daisy said.

Uncle Hughes gave me one of his keen looks and I just made my face go blank.

"Oh," Aunt Nick said, looking over our heads toward the door. "Isn't that Tyler Pierce?"

Of course it was Tyler Pierce, which Aunt Nick knew because she was looking right at him. But Daisy turned anyway, and then turned back quickly.

"Who's Tyler Pierce?" Uncle Hughes asked.

"One of Daisy's beaux," Aunt Nick said, smiling that big, crazy salad smile she had.

"He's not a beau," Daisy said, but I could tell she wasn't being entirely truthful. I could always tell when Daisy was doing that, because it didn't fit well on her.

"Well, here he comes," Uncle Hughes said. He was also smiling now, not like Aunt Nick, but as if what Daisy had said amused him.

"Hello, Tyler," Aunt Nick said.

"Hello, Mrs. Derringer, Mr. Derringer."

He was standing right next to Daisy, but she didn't look at him, which was probably a good idea since he was staring at Aunt Nick.

Then he did say: "Hello, Daisy," so she had to turn to face him.

"Hello." She said it in a cool voice, but I could tell from her eyes that she wanted him to keep talking to her. "You remember my cousin, Ed."

"Of course."

We shook hands, but I got the distinct impression that he had no idea who I was.

"I was just on my way to the bar," Tyler said. "Can I get anyone a drink?"

"I'll go with you," Aunt Nick said. "Darling? Do you want anything?"

"No," Uncle Hughes said. "I'm going to try to get an oyster before they're all gone. Shall I get one for you?"

"Oh, yes, please," Aunt Nick said, and she looked at Uncle Hughes in a kind of soft, pretty way that made my hands twitch.

Daisy leaned back against the wooden rail and looked up at the sky.

"You still like him," I said.

"Yes, Ed, I still like him," she said quietly. I could see the muscles in her forearms flexing beneath her skin. She looked back at me suddenly, with heat in her voice and said: "But I don't like that way he has. It's too perfect and fake."

"Yes," I said. "It is fake."

"I know, and I sort of hate him for it sometimes." She scuffed the bottom of her shoe against the boards. Her shoes were yellow, I noticed, and flat.

"He stares at your mother," I said.

"What?" She looked at me like she hadn't heard me.

"Your mother," I said, "he looks at her."

"Who doesn't?" Daisy said. "Anyway, it has nothing to do with my mother. It's about what happened with us. We've slept together."

I didn't know what to say to that, so I didn't say anything. But it certainly was an interesting development.

"Last summer, if you were wondering. And don't stand there looking at me funny."

"I'm not," I said.

"Sometimes I hate everyone."

When she said things like that, I thought about touching her, on the shoulder, or her wrist. Just to see if her skin felt different at that moment. I hardly ever touched her, only when she touched me, really. And I had no desire to. Except at times like this, when she was in this kind of mood. Then I wondered if I touched her, if I would be able to feel it, like a change in temperature. But I knew I couldn't, I must not ever touch her when I was wondering about something.

"I want a drink," she declared.

"All right."

"Will you get me another gin and tonic?"

I walked back inside to the bar, where Thomas glared at me, but got me the drink anyway. I took a pistachio out of one of the bowls and snapped off the shell. I like the way, with a pistachio or a peanut, how it has this very hard shell and then another skin on the inside over the nut, like the shell isn't enough.

I looked around at the room.

The woman with the violet eyes was gone, but outside, on the front porch, I saw Aunt Nick talking to Tyler. She gave the impression of being half in, half out of the Reading Room, like she'd wandered out there without realizing and then had tried to correct the situation. Tyler was taller than she was and he had to bend his neck slightly to speak with her. I picked up the drink and made my way over to one of the windows that looked out onto the porch. If I leaned against the wall next to it, I'd be able to hear what they were saying without being seen. Oldest trick in the book.

I eyed the gin and tonic in my hand and then took a sip. I'd get Daisy another one. I bit down on an ice cube and felt it shatter between my teeth.

"I was really glad to see you here tonight," Tyler was saying, "because I made your lemonade today. Do you remember the secret recipe you told me?"

Aunt Nick laughed, like she didn't care what he was saying at all. "Did you? My goodness. When did I give away my secret recipe?"

"Ages ago, I guess. But I've never forgotten it."

"Oh, well, I'm glad."

There was a silence and I imagined him looking at her. And then he said: "Are you having a good time?"

"Yes, I suppose so." She laughed again. "What a funny thing to say. Of course."

"Good. I can never tell what you're thinking. You're one of those people."

"One of what people?"

"I don't know, the kind that's hard to read. You always look like you're having a good time, but I get the feeling that sometimes it's . . . I don't know, a show."

"This is a very deep conversation, Tyler. One I'm not sure I'm capable of carrying on after only two cocktails." Aunt Nick had her "don't be a fool" voice on.

"That's what I mean."

"What do you mean?"

"I think you're pretending. Right now. I can see it."

"Goodness, this is turning very strange."

"I can see you." He sounded very sure of himself and then he added, "Nick."

There was another silence, and I had to will myself not to look. Then Aunt Nick said: "Let go of my wrist, Tyler, darling. You'll make a scene."

She strode through the door, her back very straight, and saw me standing there off to the side.

"Oh, Ed," she said. "Where's Daisy?"

"Out on the dock." I looked at her to see how she would react. She must have known I could have heard, but she didn't say anything else. She just walked off in the other direction.

I thought about this, and what it meant. There were a million things she could have said, like "Tyler Pierce is very drunk," or "Goodness, that Tyler Pierce is a piece of work," or "I just had the strangest conversation with Tyler Pierce." But she didn't say any of these things. So, I thought about that. Then I followed her out to the dock, back to Daisy.

341

"Ed Lewis, you have got to be the slowest person alive," Daisy said when she saw me. "And what happened to my drink?"

I looked down at the gin and tonic and realized I'd drunk most of it. "I got waylaid," I said.

Aunt Nick was fiddling with the handkerchief in her pocketbook.

"Oh, fine," Daisy said. "I'll go get my own."

I watched her go back inside and head for the bar. From where I was standing, I could see her order her drink from Thomas, and then Tyler come up next to her and put his hand on the small of her back. I was going to go back in, but Aunt Nick stopped me.

"Ed, Uncle Hughes and I are going to go home for supper now. Will you make sure Daisy gets back all right? Don't go running around after the ladies. And don't let her drink too much. It's unbecoming."

"I don't run around after ladies," I said.

"Well, fine," Aunt Nick said, but she wasn't really listening. "I'll leave something out in the kitchen for you two. Sandwiches? I don't know. Remember to eat when you get home." She leaned in and kissed my cheek, and there was her perfume again, burning my nostrils slightly.

She walked over to Uncle Hughes, who was talking to some man in bright red trousers and an equally bright green belt by the oyster bar. She put her hand on his arm, and he turned and looked at her like he'd been waiting all night for that moment. Then they were gone.

I walked back inside and headed to where Tyler and Daisy were standing. He was grinning at her. I was very close to them, but they didn't notice. Sometimes I could do that, be surprisingly near to someone, and they didn't even sense I was there. I hadn't quite figured out the trick to it, but I knew it had something to do with being very still, not just on the outside, but inside my head, too. Everything had to go blank and quiet, and then it was almost as if I didn't exist.

"I do owe you an apology. I wouldn't blame you if you hated me. I behaved abominably last summer." He was saying this, but he was still grinning like it was a joke.

Daisy just looked at him.

"I felt terrible about it. I shouldn't have let you go the way I did."

"Yes," she said finally. "You were disgusting."

"I'm sorry. Can you forgive me?"

"I don't know."

"Let me make it up to you."

She looked like she was about to answer, but something made her turn and see me. She seemed startled. "Ed. For God's sakes, stop sneaking up on people like that."

"I wasn't sneaking," I said. It was true, I had been standing right there in plain sight.

"Well, you know what I mean." She stamped her foot a little.

"Your mother said I shouldn't let you drink too much."

"I don't need a babysitter," Daisy said.

"He's just looking out for you. Aren't you, Ed?" Tyler smiled at me. I got the feeling he thought I was slightly retarded, or something.

"I *am* looking out for Daisy," I said.

Tyler narrowed his eyes like I said something disagreeable. His stance altered ever so slightly, his head leaning back a bit to take me in. "Well, there's no reason to worry, sport," he said. "I'll take care of her."

I just watched him.

"Oh, Ed, really," Daisy said. "Don't get all weird."

Sometimes, I got the impression that Daisy really understood me, that she knew all about my work and that she approved, or at least tolerated it. But maybe I was fooling myself.

"We're going to go for a walk," she said. "What are you going to do?"

"I don't know," I said.

"Well," she hesitated. "I guess I'll see you back at the house."

She put her arm through Tyler's. He looked at me, his grin firmly back in place.

"Nice seeing you again, Ed." But he didn't try to shake my hand this time.

"Goodbye," I said.

I took a walk, too, down by the harbor as far as I could, and then up round the Old Sculpin Gallery. A few people on bicycles were waiting for the last ferry to Chappaquiddick. One, a young woman, wearing a kerchief over her hair, was alone. She was playing with the strap on her shoe, which was evidently broken, and hung limply to the side, resisting her efforts to make it buckle. I could feel myself starting to breathe a little harder. I thought briefly about getting on with them, but Chappy was so wild, I would probably get lost in the darkness and end up with poison ivy.

I walked up North Water Street and then took a left on Morse Street. I could feel the tennis courts calling, but I ignored the urge. I had learned that going over something again and again made it lose its magic. So instead, I went down Fuller Street, with its perfect little white houses and wrap-around porches. I saw someone, a woman, turn out ahead of me. I was quiet, walking on the balls of my feet, like Mr. Reading had taught me in Scouts all those years

344

ago. As I got closer, I could see by the shade of her red hair and the way she walked, with her shoulders a little hunched in, that it was Olivia of the Violet Eyes.

She opened the front gate to one of the houses and went in. I hung back a little, until I saw a light go on in one of the upstairs rooms. Then I let myself in the front gate, and moved through the shadow at the side of the house, where I could see clearly up into the window.

She passed in front of it and lifted the sash a bit higher, running her hand around her neck, as if she were hot. She pulled off her dress and her slip was pink, the color of a seashell. She disappeared for a bit then, and I thought perhaps she might not come back. But just as I was thinking of leaving, she returned. She stood very still in front of the window, then put a hand over her eyes. I could hear the sobbing, not because it was loud, which it wasn't, but because we were actually so close to each other, even if she was a good ten feet above me.

I wanted to go in very badly. I wanted to touch her, and find out what was underneath her skin. She was an interesting person, but she had cracks. And it was the cracks I was drawn to because they were the inside peeking out, a glimpse of what was hiding below the surface. The back fat spilling over the dress; the chewed cuticle; the smudged lipstick; the run in the stocking.

I knew I couldn't go in. If Frank Wilcox had taught me anything, it was that the Island was too small. He'd been lucky; Elena Nunes had only been someone's maid. But Olivia was one of us. She was off limits.

Still, as I walked away, out of her yard, leaving her sobbing softly to herself in her upstairs bedroom, I had a sense of satisfaction. I felt light, like anything was possible, like the world was my oyster. It wasn't always about doing, sometimes it was just thinking about doing it, standing by yourself in the dark and being honest about what you wanted.

I could hear the hush of the night around me as I made my way down North Water Street toward Tiger House. The sidewalks were empty, and I was greeted only with the sound of my own shoes hitting the pavement. I was thinking that the evening had been a good one. Then I saw them.

The dim porch light scattered shadows around them and gave Daisy's hair a glow like bright fire. They were standing so close together, yet their bodies weren't quite touching. Gray, dusty-winged night moths were skittering overhead, and I had the fanciful notion that they were attracted by the glow coming off Daisy, rather than the light above. His hand was in her hair, pulling her head back slightly. She was on the brink, not entirely in control, and it was as if what had begun earlier in the evening on that same porch, was about to be completed. Like a full bloom. And then he kissed her, and I knew there was going to be trouble.

1967: August

Tyler picked me up from the airport. I had just flown in from Cedar Rapids, and he was tapping the wheel of his olive-green car impatiently by the time I walked outside into the muggy Eastern air. My mind was still full of Iowa and its rolling plains and the small farmhouse near Elvira, and Tyler's clean, city looks and crisp shirt, not to mention those vinyl bucket seats, were like a shock to the system.

"Trunk's open," he said, so I put my suitcase and brief-case in the back.

"We'll have to make time if we're going to catch the last ferry," he told me angrily, when I got into the car. "I don't want to be stuck in Woods Hole."

I just looked at him and watched as his eyes slid uneasily off of me.

When we hit the Mass. Turnpike, he tried again. "So, your mother's birthday."

"Yes," I said.

"I know Daisy's excited you're coming. How long's it been since the two of you saw each other?"

"Nine months," I said. A Mexican restaurant in the city before Christmas. She'd spent the holidays in Florida with Aunt Nick and Uncle Hughes. I'd spent it at Tiger House with my mother, who'd talked a lot about some sewing business she wanted to start so she could buy back our old cottage. I didn't really listen; I preferred Tiger House, anyway.

"Well, there's been a lot going on. The wedding and all that."

Daisy had called a month earlier to tell me she was going to marry him. I suppose I hadn't been altogether surprised, but I found my mind had gone empty when she actually said it. For a while, all I heard was the scratch of the telephone line. Then I said: "What about college?"

"Oh, I don't know, I can take a semester off and then see. I'm not like you. If I could speed through college in three years, I would. But I can't and I don't want to wait. I love him, Ed, and I want to marry him. As soon as possible."

"Yes," I said, although that's not what I really meant.

Next to me, Tyler turned the radio on.

I leaned my head back and smelled the vinyl. It was new and had that hard, shiny smell that made me want to grit my teeth.

"Is your car new?" I asked.

"Yes. Nice, isn't she? Buick Riviera. Probably a waste of money, though." He smiled. "Nick says it reminds her of a lily pad."

"What does Daisy say about it?"

His smile faded slightly. "She says it's a car for a lounge-lizard." He laughed a little. "I guess she's right. It is a little too much, but I just really liked it."

"What color is it?"

"Gold."

"It looks green," I said.

His smile faded entirely. "I know," he said, and turned the radio up louder.

I didn't really listen to the radio much. But the woman at the farm in Iowa, Anna, had had one, and we'd danced to it, even though she had to keep fiddling with the knob to get it to come in clearly. Tyler's was pretty clear, but for some reason everything it played sounded jangly and ugly.

As we neared Wood's Hole, Tyler said: "I love this song." Then he glanced at me, as if for some kind of affirmation. "The Doors." He started singing along with the music. *C'mon, baby, light my fire.* I began to wonder what the inside of his skull looked like. Luckily for both of us, halfway through the song we arrived at the ferry and had to rush to buy tickets and get the car on.

It was almost dark when we reached Tiger House and the headlights made an arch against the cedar shingles as we pulled into the back drive. I thought about the blown-out barns I'd seen from the Lincoln Highway. Tornadoes. They'd had an outbreak in the winter and early spring, the worst on record. They'd pulled out stores and houses and killed a little girl near Elvira.

The back door opened and Daisy appeared.

"You made it," she said, running down the stairs toward us. She wasn't wearing any shoes. "Thank God. I was worried. I've given your mother nothing but awful presents today. You're going to restore my reputation, Ed Lewis."

She kissed my cheek. I liked the way she never wore perfume; she smelled like Ivory soap and the baby shampoo from the upstairs bathroom.

She turned to Tyler. Her face was alive and flushed. "Hello."

"Hello," he said. He smiled down at her.

I waited while she kissed him. I watched their mouths moving. A muscle flickered faintly at the curve of Daisy's jawline and I wondered what it felt like to be her, what she was searching for in all that human contact. Then again, she was a very physical person, always pushing forward, and

ED

it occurred to me that perhaps she wasn't looking for anything. Maybe she was just burning along her path.

I thought about Anna, in the living room of the small farmhouse.

"I've been so lonely," she had said when she asked me to dance, the remnants of dinner still cluttering the table.

I could feel the small muscles in her back moving under my hand as I held her, but there was no fire in her, just sadness. At least not until later, when I put the plastic bag over her head, and then all that life came to the surface and her face lit up like the Fourth of July.

I was wondering if what I was always looking for had to do with finding the true reduction of the physical spirit, when Daisy turned to me and said: "Crikey, Ed. Are you still here? Come on, we have to get you up to your mother."

I let her lead me toward the house, her arm hooked through mine.

"Did you enjoy your trip in Ty's loooxury car?" She was laughing as she drew out the word.

I didn't know why this was supposed to be funny, so I said: "He says it's gold, but it looks green."

"I know." She turned to me. "Oh, I hope you didn't say that to him. It drives him nuts. Even Mummy thinks it looks green, and she thinks it's the bees' knees."

"He said your mother told him it looked like a lily pad."

"Did she? So poetic." Daisy stopped at the back door. "By the way, Mummy's a little frantic. The angel food cake has gone missing." She leaned in and lowered her voice, cupping her hand around her mouth. "Mummy thinks some of the neighborhood boys got to it, but actually I saw your mother feed it to the dog next door." She laughed. Tinkle, tinkle like glass. "Come on."

The minute I walked into the house, I could feel it. Like

an earthquake building up. I looked at Daisy to see if she noticed it, too, but she seemed her usual self.

I've noticed that all houses have a feeling, like a particular perfume that you can smell when you walk in. Anna's farm had the odor of something erased and tired. Blown out. Tiger House, on the other hand, normally smelled of things well cared for, wood polish, starch, chiming clocks. Ding ding, every hour. That night, there was something else in the air. I felt my hands begin to tingle, like they did when something interesting was about to happen.

When I got to my mother's room, I was certain of it. It's true, her hair looked crazy, like some kind of bird's nest. But it was her face that was really altered, jerky and strained.

When Daisy left us alone, my mother pretended to be busy putting on her makeup. I could tell she had something on her mind. Ever since she'd gone to the hospital, she'd had this way of saying one thing and meaning another. I guess that's what they taught her to do, although I wasn't convinced this was a sign of mental health.

"How are you feeling, Mother?"

"Just fine, dearest," she said.

I waited and when she said nothing else, I said: "What happened to your hair?"

"I'm afraid I had a little run-in with the hairdresser. Daisy's treat. I suppose I was feeling a little blue this morning."

I noticed that she was wearing a blue dress, but it was the tigers that caught my eye. They sort of glittered in the light. She patted her big hair down and eyed me through the mirror.

I looked back at her and forced my hands to be still. I was beginning to feel a little light-headed.

"Did you say hello to your Aunt Nick?"

"I haven't seen her yet," I said. I thought about the cake my mother had fed to the dog.

"It's nice that Tyler could make it for the dinner." She started fooling around with some gold tube she'd pulled off the dresser. "I know how well he gets along with the family, especially your aunt. Although . . ."

There was something in her voice, the watchful eye, the electricity in the house.

"I must admit, I do wonder sometimes if it makes Daisy uncomfortable. He does dote so on Aunt Nick."

"Yes." I said. "He's watching her."

"Then again, Daisy's so lovely, she'd never say if it hurt her."

"What are you trying to say, Mother?"

She paused and turned to face me and I thought: *Here it comes*.

"I just wouldn't want to see Daisy get hurt, that's all. Nor would you, I imagine."

So that was it. She had picked Aunt Nick for the villain. That's what the cake had been about. Still, it was nice to see my mother trying to take some kind of control over her life. And maybe she was right. Maybe Aunt Nick was a villain. She wasn't an honest person, that was for sure. And as long as I'd known her, she'd been trying to control Daisy. Daisy just couldn't see it, through no fault of her own. I thought about Aunt Nick hurting Daisy and it made me go all still inside.

"No," I said. "I wouldn't let that happen."

"Of course you wouldn't," my mother said, picking at her dress. "It's just that your Aunt Nick, well, she can be stubborn when she thinks she's right. Sometimes, people like that need to be forced to see how dangerous their behavior can be. Do you know what I mean?"

I knew what my mother was up to. She wasn't very good at this game. My father had been a much better player, and I'd watched him do it to her over and over again when I was a child. A sort of master of the long con. But when I realized he'd been playing for peanuts, I have to say, I lost respect for him. Finding the essence of one dead actress isn't exactly a life's work.

I made up my mind to get a better lay of the land before I decided what to do about the Aunt Nick problem. I realized I'd been distracted, that I hadn't really been watching my family closely enough. For one thing, my mother seemed to be going off the rails again. That wasn't really a problem for me, but it might become one if she needed someone to take care of her. And if Aunt Nick was causing that trouble, well, something might have to be done to fix it. She was my mother, after all.

Then, of course, there was Daisy. That was another difficulty.

I began my research during cocktail hour. The first thing I noticed was that my mother was drinking and that Tyler was being his usual self.

"I want to thank you, Tyler," my mother said. "It really was so lovely of you to bring Ed with you for my little celebration."

"It was my pleasure," he said, which it obviously had not been. "Nick knew how much it would please you. Where was it? Iowa? Housewives and Hoovers?" He turned to me.

I had to keep from smiling at this point. If he only knew. "Yes," I said. "Exactly. Housewives and Hoovers." I wondered what he'd look like with a plastic bag over his face. If there was anything that would come to the surface, or if he would just let out one stupid breath, and be done.

353

When Aunt Nick came into the room, I saw his eyes move like magnets toward her. He watched the movement of her legs, first. And then her breasts. But mostly he watched her face.

She said something about hating dinner parties, which wasn't true, and Tyler's whole body moved in time with her words. Hands in hair, smile creeping across his face, his hips turning toward her.

"I, for one, am with Nick," Tyler said.

Daisy narrowed her eyes at him. It would be better if Daisy could be made to just hate him. But I knew it was too late for that.

When it was time to go to the table for dinner, Aunt Nick went to the kitchen and Tyler followed, offering to help with the plates. I hung back, pretending to see something interesting on the porch. Instead, I crept down the hall toward the summer kitchen, careful not to be seen from the dining room.

"I've found a good band for the reception," Aunt Nick was saying.

"Good," Tyler said, "because I want to dance with you."

"Tyler . . ."

"Nick."

"This has to stop. I mean it." To be fair, she did sound like she meant it.

"I've tried." Not as much conviction from him.

"It's cruel, Tyler, and I won't be a part of it." Her voice had dropped to a harsh whisper.

There was a silence and then Aunt Nick said in her normal tone, "Here you go, darling, take these out."

I didn't move and Tyler jumped a little when he saw me leaning against the wall outside the kitchen door.

"Jesus," he hissed, but he hurried into the dining room without saying anything more.

I followed behind him. The table was covered with pink flowers and my mother was sitting at the head of it, wearing some bizarre paper crown, which made her look foolish and, honestly, a little creepy.

I seated myself next to Daisy. I looked at her face, her bright eyes, small bare feet under the table. I felt a strange pain in my stomach. I was reminded of the Wampanoag arrowhead I had found the summer Frank Wilcox killed Elena Nunes. I had just joined the Scouts and we had spent the morning skinning rabbits up on Gay Head, and then digging over some of the cliffs. That's where I had found the arrowhead. I had given it to Daisy and watched her turn it over in her hand, her thumb brushing the rough surface. I had experienced that same pain then, just above my stomach, and it had made me uneasy. So, I had told her about the rabbits and then she threw up in the toilet.

"You'll never believe who I saw at Morning Glory Farm," Aunt Nick said. "That disgusting toad of a man, Frank Wilcox."

I had one of those moments when my brain waves felt like they were misfiring. Had Aunt Nick read my mind, or had my mind conjured the conversation? Hearing someone else speak his name took my breath away slightly. I couldn't believe he was real to anyone else.

"I didn't know he was still around," I said, wanting to ask a thousand questions. I felt, rather than saw, Uncle Hughes's eyes flicker over me.

"Neither did I," Aunt Nick said. "But there he was, large as life. You know, it was odd, but seeing him made me furious, for some reason."

"I hadn't thought about all that in forever," Daisy said.

I thought about it all the time. That night, eight years ago. The night that everything began to come into focus for me. At that point, I already had some inkling of what my work was going to be, but when he killed her, I couldn't believe it. It was like a kind of joy was released in me and it was the closest thing to love that I had ever felt.

I had been watching them all summer and I'd been going to their secret place during the day, when Daisy was at tennis, just to be there, to be around it and think. I had collected a few items, a bracelet she had apparently lost during one of their sessions, and a pack of cigarettes that had dropped out of his pocket. I was mesmerized by the two of them. They were like animals, but animals with no skins on, changing shapes and grunting and moaning. Sometimes, she almost sounded like she was singing. Mostly, I was fascinated by the violence with which he handled her. I had seen something similar, not long before, with Bill Fox and my mother, but my mother had seemed so passive, as if his words just slid right off of her. *You really are a slut*. But not Elena. It was like that was exactly what she wanted, like it set her free or something. I was enchanted. Of course, I was somewhat less enchanted when Uncle Hughes caught me there. But then he went back to the city to be by himself, which is what he really liked anyway, so it was fine.

That night, I followed them to the tennis courts, again. They were arguing on the path, an argument I had heard before. She wanted him to leave his wife, he said he needed time. Even I knew it was a lie. She must have known. She got very angry and slapped him. He pushed her roughly down the path until they reached the shelter.

Then she started begging. A mistake. This time, he hit her and she began to cry and he started tearing her clothes off. At that point, I thought it would end like it always did.

But she fought back. I wasn't more than fifteen feet away, but it was dark and, oddly, their fight didn't look all that different from their sex. He was on the ground, groaning. She had kicked him in the balls. He started cursing and crawling and that's when he must have picked up the rock, because he lunged at her, pulling at her hair with his free hand, pulling her down, and hitting her in the head with the other.

She only cried out once.

But he kept saying: "Fucking bitch, fucking spic bitch." All the while hitting her, thud, thud.

Then he just stopped. He looked at the rock in his hand like he didn't know where it had come from. He looked at her. I could hear him panting. He shook her, a small jerk, like you do when someone's having a nightmare. She let out a little half-gurgle, half-groan. Without hesitating, he straddled her, put his hands around her throat and throt-tled the life out of her.

Before he was finished, I saw her torso lurch up for a second and I could have sworn she was about to tell him something. Then she was just dead.

I wanted to stay around, to see what he did next, but my head was light and I was afraid I would cry out, or give myself away, so I staggered as quietly as I could in the direction of the old Ice Pond. I didn't get very far before I fainted.

I remember waking up, the tall marsh grass around me. The ground was damp and I could see the moon. The first thing I thought was: *Daisy*.

After dinner, we had more cocktails, and my mother was getting quite drunk by this point. Then we were all dancing to a record Daisy had bought, my mother pressed against Nick and the saddest look in her eyes.

One by one, everyone went off to bed, including me. But after lying there for a while, I got up again. My mind was full with the idea that Frank Wilcox was back on the Island. He had a new wife. I wondered what she looked like. I dressed and sat by the window in my bedroom and thought about what Aunt Nick had said earlier. How she could smell fall in the air, how it smelled like death and change.

I decided I had to find Frank. I couldn't sleep, anyway. I made my way quietly down the stairs, thinking about Uncle Hughes patrolling the house all those years ago. It made me smile. I planned on looking Frank up in the phone book, and was heading toward Uncle Hughes's office when I heard them whispering.

They were in the blue sitting room, which was the only way to the study, so I was forced to stop outside the door.

"I've told you," Aunt Nick was saying.

"I've heard what you've said, but it's not what you mean. It's not what you want. We're two of a kind. You have to stop pretending we're not."

All the lights were off downstairs and I inched forward so I could see them, making all my thoughts go still. Aunt Nick had her back against the wing chair and Tyler was standing close to her, gripping her upper arm.

"No," Aunt Nick said, not looking at him.

"Don't tell me that all this is enough. That it's ever been enough for you. I'm not blind, Nick."

"You have to stop this, Tyler. I'm sorry if I've given you the wrong impression . . ."

"God, I want to kiss you."

"Don't force me to hurt Daisy." Aunt Nick's voice had a sort of pleading tone. "If you care about either one of us . . ."

"You think I want to hurt her? But she's just not like us. It's nobody's fault, it's just the way it is."

"It is somebody's fault," Aunt Nick said, wildly. "It's my fault. Oh god, this all my fault."

Tyler moved in to kiss her, but I didn't wait around to watch; I had already seen enough to know what was going on. It was what was always going on with Aunt Nick.

I had to wait until the following night, but I did go see Frank Wilcox. I found his address in the telephone book. He was living in Katama, and I had to bike out there. It was around midnight and there was no moon, so the road was very dark, but I managed to find his drive.

It was a modest house, set a ways back from the road, a new-build from the looks of it. He'd obviously come down in the world. I did a little reconnaissance and found the downstairs was one big room, with a small kitchen off to the back. The nights were getting cooler, but their windows were still open. I pulled out my old Swiss Army knife, the one Uncle Hughes had given me, and cut the screen out of its frame. After taking off my Docksiders, I stepped inside.

The wooden floor was cool beneath my feet and I felt calm and well. The furniture looked rented, but there were some framed pictures on the mantel. A wedding and a vacation, Mexico maybe. It was hard to tell in the dark, but the wife looked young; Daisy's age.

There wasn't much to see, but I made a quick stop in the kitchen to grab a garbage bag, just in case.

The stairs were carpeted, so there was no problem keeping quiet as I headed up to the bedrooms. At the top, I looked around. There were three doors, two of which were closed. One would be a bathroom and the other, their bed-room. It was a bit of a conundrum. I pressed my ear to one and didn't hear anything. Ditto with the other. I decided the door in the middle was most likely the bathroom, so I chose the one on the end.

Turning the glass knob until I felt it hit the latch, I care-fully opened the door. It was a lucky thing the house was new; no squeaky hinges or swollen wood. But I realized what a stupid thing it had been to come on impulse, without checking anything out first.

The bed was only a few feet away from me. The woman was closest, her dark hair spread out like a fan on the pillow. She had her hands tucked under her head, and a bare shoulder peeked out from the quilt. She was young, and not particularly pretty. I put my hand out, very slowly, and touched a stray lock of her hair. It was soft, like a mouse.

I moved around to the other side of the bed, lightly fingering the trash bag. Frank was turned away from his wife, his face toward the window in the far wall.

As I stood over him, I could see, even in the dim light, how much he'd aged. He looked frail, old even. Thin gray hair fell sparsely over his forehead. His mouth was open and he was snoring lightly. There was a shadow on his pillow where his drool had collected.

I had a strange feeling, standing there. Disappointment, and a little anger. He was more my father than anyone, and I'd always imagined him forever strong and unwavering; his hands around Elena's throat in an instant, not a moment's hesitation. And yet, here was this old man, snoring away in his house full of rented furniture, totally unaware that a stranger had broken in and was watching him sleep.

I looked at the trash bag. It wasn't even worth it. I wanted to talk to him, to ask him what had happened, to

find out how he'd turned into this innocuous, broken nothingness. But I knew I couldn't. So instead, I pulled my
wallet out of my back pocket and removed the worn pack of
matches from the Hideaway that I always kept with me.
Carefully, I laid them on the bedside table, and then, taking
one last look at the man who had made me, I left the room.

1969: October

I remember asking Daisy about love once, what it felt like, and she said it was like tennis. I think she meant she had the same feeling when she was playing tennis, but for a long time I imagined two players squaring off, each trying to score points against the other. Over the last year or so, as I've lain in hospital after hospital, listening to doctors drone and nurses twitter while they try and fix me, I've had a lot of time to think and remember. And now, in this one, with its walls the color of mint ice cream, a different image has been coming to mind. In this one, there is a man and a woman and a dark staircase. And what happens there is love at its most honest because, just as I have long suspected, it is brutal and sudden, and the damage is permanent.

It was last summer, the summer after I made my visit to Frank Wilcox, and I returned to Tiger House in early June. Daisy and Tyler were still unmarried, a "long engagement" she called it. "Ty's just so busy," she had told me when I asked her about it the Christmas before, and I had allowed myself to be lulled into believing that it might not come off at all. But the wedding was set for August and, by June, there were no signs that a break-up was imminent. So, my mind started turning over the Aunt Nick–Tyler problem again.

On the ferry trip over to the Island, I tried to come up with a solution. I ordered a coffee and took it up on deck to think. It was early afternoon, a Saturday, and the *Island Queen* was full of day-trippers and hippies. I put on my Ray-Bans so I wouldn't have to squint, and put my mind to the task.

Obviously, getting rid of Tyler was the most appealing option. But it was risky. For one thing, he was a man, and pretty strong, which meant I would have to catch him by surprise and things would have a good chance of turning ugly. Secondly, Daisy wanted him. I didn't understand why, but I understood what it felt like to want something and I didn't want to take that away from her.

Aunt Nick would be easier to get alone. Some evening, in the dark, on the stringpiece of the Yacht Club, she might just go over into the harbor. Or perhaps a swimming accident off the dock. Everyone knew that when she drank too much she went for night swims.

But I didn't want to kill Aunt Nick. It wasn't because I liked her. Maybe it had something to do with her being such a strong force. Or perhaps it was that, despite all her duplicity, she made our lives more stimulating. I don't know. All I know is that I found my mind stalling at the thought of it.

I remembered watching her have sex with that musician all those years before. She had wrapped one of her legs around him as he lay on top of her and was stroking his neck softly. But the expression on her face. It was full of hatred, or disgust. Either way, it was so feral that, for a moment, I thought she might tear him apart.

I was thinking about this when a girl next to me leaned over and said: "Excuse me, do you have a light?"

I reached in my pocket. I always keep a lighter on hand for situations like these. I looked at her as I lit her cigarette.

She had pale hair and was wearing a big floppy straw hat that cast a shadow over her shoulders. She had freckles.

"Thank you," she said.

I found her immediately intriguing. She was carrying a map of the Island, the kind they gave out at the tourist office in Woods Hole.

"Is it your first trip to the Island?" I asked.

"Yes," she said. She looked at me from under her hat, a quick look and then away.

"Where are you staying?"

"At a bed and breakfast in Oak Bluffs."

She pretended to be busy with her map, so I didn't ask her any more questions. Instead, I waited. After a while, I took my trusty book of poems out of my bag and started flipping through the pages. I felt her look over at me again.

"Oh," she said after a while, "William Blake."

"Yes," I said, looking up.

"I love him. Ginsberg says he's a prophet."

I just looked at her.

"Well, that's what he says, anyway."

"Why a prophet?" I asked.

She laughed. "I don't actually know."

I smiled.

"I'm sorry. I'm bothering you."

"You're not bothering me."

"I'm Penny," she said.

"Ed."

"Listen, would you mind watching my bag while I go to the bathroom?" She adjusted her hat so she could see me better.

"I'll watch your bag," I said.

I watched her walk off toward the door that led down to the lower deck. Her feet pointed inward. Pigeon toes. I pulled her bag closer to me and, undoing the zipper an inch or so, slipped my hand inside. I felt something silky and pulled it out. It was a scarf with small roses on it, the kind a grandmother would wear. I put it in my blazer pocket for later.

I leaned back and felt the sun on my face. I thought about how many bed and breakfasts there might be in Oak Bluffs, and began making a list of the ones I knew offhand. Then I heard the ferry's horn, signaling our approach to the dock, and realized I still hadn't come up with any kind of plan for the problem awaiting me at home.

I hear the nurse's shoes against the linoleum before I actually see her. Swish, swish. Then her face is suddenly looming over me. She smiles when she sees my eyes are open.

"It's a big day today," she says, smoothing down my sheet and blanket. "Visiting day."

She checks my fluids.

"You're a lucky young man, you know," she says.

I would laugh if I could.

"Not everyone has a mother like yours. Some of them never have a visitor, not ever. Shame." She blows air out of her mouth and disappears from my sightline for a moment.

Then I hear her voice from somewhere near the door, disembodied. "But not you. Every Thursday like clockwork."

We have this conversation every Thursday, like clockwork. At this point, even if I could speak, I probably wouldn't need to say anything.

Suddenly her face is over mine again, like a balloon.

"Would you like to hear the radio?" She switches it on and leaves the room.

This is Ten-Ten-WINS. You give us twenty-two minutes, we'll give you the world.

Police investigating the murder of a San Francisco Yellow Cab driver several days ago now have evidence that the killer may be the same man responsible for four unsolved murders in the Bay Area over the past year.

The San Francisco Chronicle has received a letter from someone identifying themselves as the Zodiac, along with a piece of bloodstained cloth that appears to have been cut from the latest victim's shirt. Police are running laboratory tests on the material to see whether it matches the victim's blood type.

In a chilling message, the author of the letter taunts police, saying: "This is the Zodiac speaking. I am the murderer of the taxi driver over by Washington Street and Maple Street. The San Francisco police could have caught me last night if they had searched the park properly." The investigation is continuing.

What a grandstander. They've been running this story for months now and I'm kind of surprised they haven't caught him yet. He isn't very careful. And frankly, I find him a little tiresome. There doesn't appear to be any real integrity in his work.

Still, it's better than staring at the ceiling, I suppose. I wish they would open the window in here. I'd like to smell the air.

Tiger House was quiet when I arrived and I figured they must all be at the beach. I brought my bag upstairs to my bedroom and put my things away. I folded up Penny's scarf and placed it under my pillow. I was reading the timetable for the bus to Oak Bluffs when I thought I heard a noise coming from Daisy's room down the hall. I found Daisy pulling things out of her closet and laying them on her bed. All her treasures. The large stuffed animal she won at the West Tisbury Fair and some old makeup and comic books. On the floor was a brown cardboard box.

The air smelled fresh, full of the scent from the flowering tree outside her window.

She looked up and saw me, giving a small jump and laying her hand over her heart.

"Oh, Ed," she said. Then she crossed the room and kissed my cheek. "When did you get here? I would have picked you up at the ferry if I'd known."

"I took a taxi," I said. "Where is everyone?"

"I made Mummy take Tyler out on the boat to get him out of my hair, and Daddy's gone to the Reading Room for cards. And your mother . . ." She stopped. "Actually I have no idea where your mother is. So, it's just me and you."

"Yes," I said.

Daisy went back into the closet and reappeared with more trinkets.

"What are you doing?"

"Oh, just clearing things out. Making room for Tyler. We're going to haul out these old twin beds and get a nice new double bed for when we're married." She smiled. "Besides, it's probably time to get rid of this junk."

I walked over to the bed and looked down at the collection. I remembered how angry she was when I told her I'd found her hiding place. I picked up an old bottle of nail polish. Then I saw the arrowhead I'd given her, lying among the things destined for the cardboard box. My vision blurred a little.

ED

"Still, I do love this room just the way it is." She looked around. "The old wallpaper and the albizia tree. I'm being silly, but I'm a little sad about changing it."

"It's not silly," I said.

Daisy sighed.

"What are you going to do with your collection?"

"Oh, I don't know. Chuck it, I guess."

She went back into the closet, before popping her head out again. "Can you believe, in two months, I'll be an old married lady. Maybe I should invite Peaches to the wedding."

"So you're going to do it, then?"

"Do what?"

"Marry him."

"What on earth are you talking about? Of course I'm going to marry him."

I picked up the arrowhead and rubbed it between my fingers. "I don't think you should," I said.

She gave me a keen look and sat down on the bed. "Ed, I realize Ty's not your absolute favorite. But I love him."

"Yes," I said.

"Anyway," she said. "Nothing's going to change. Not really."

"I still don't think you should marry him."

"Besides the fact that you don't like him, give me one good reason." She sounded a little angry, now.

It was the moment to come clean. But I wasn't sure she was ready.

"Well?" she said.

"He loves your mother."

"Ed, honestly. Are you still banging that old drum?" She laughed.

I looked at her. "Have I ever lied to you?"

As she looked back, her expression changed. I'd seen that change before, when it dawns on someone that what is about to happen is very different from what they expected to happen. "Why would you say something like that to me?" She said it almost in a whisper.

"Because it's true," I said. "I've seen them."

"Ed Lewis, you shut your mouth," she said. But she got up from the bed and went over to the window, running her hand down the screen, and I knew she knew the truth in what I was saying. The thing was, she'd always known it.

After a minute, she turned back toward me. "I really don't understand," she said slowly. "I don't know why you'd want to hurt me like this."

When I didn't say anything, she pushed past me and walked out of the room. I looked down at the arrowhead in my hand. I went to drop it in the cardboard box, but the idea of doing that made my hand shake, so I put it in my pocket instead.

As I left the room, I found my mother outside the door. I knew she'd been listening. I could tell.

She was smiling. "Hello, Ed, dearest."

"Go have a cocktail, Mother," I said and left her standing there, gaping.

"Look who's here," the nurse says. "I told you."

Then I see my mother's face. Her eyes are soft. She looks older, older even than last week.

"Hello, dearest," she says, and brushes the hair off my forehead.

I don't like it when she touches me.

"How's he doing?" my mother asks the nurse.

"Oh, just fine," the nurse says. "The doctor will be in for a chat in a tick."

Then we're alone. My mother turns off the radio and pulls a chair up next to me.

"So," my mother says. "Let's see. It's been a busy week. I've been helping Carl set up his offices in the house in Oak Bluffs. I told you about that, didn't I, dearest? I know I've told you about Carl. Well, he found a place in Oak Bluffs, where he can set up an office, a sort of out-post, for his church. Carl says that ever since Teddy Kennedy killed that poor girl over in Chappy, the church has realized that there are so many people in need of help on the Island. And they picked him to set it up. We met at the hardware store, just like your father. I was going to buy a light bulb and he was there getting cleaning supplies. But I've told you that."

My mother sighs and gets up. She walks over to the window.

"He's so committed," she continues, "and he's been teaching me so many interesting things about myself, about self-actualizing and how so much of my past and even my past lives has been blocking me from moving on to the next level. I'm going to begin my auditing soon. Oh, Ed, dearest, he's so intelligent."

I've had to listen to a lot about this Carl fellow since my mother met him in August. Aunt Nick used to call my father a charlatan when she thought we weren't listening. I wonder what she'd say about my mother's new beau.

It seems all sorts of strange people have been drawn to the Island because of the Kennedy incident. Reporters, thrill-seekers, religious nuts. I heard his speech on the radio, Teddy Kennedy. He said he had wondered, after he left that girl to drown in the car, whether some awful curse actually did hang over all the Kennedys. It reminded me of Daisy, how she thought we had been cursed after we found Elena Nunes. Funnily enough, my mother told me that Teddy Kennedy had even gone to the Hideaway to hole up before realizing he had no choice but to go to the police. I wonder what Sheriff Mello made of that.

My mother is still talking about Carl when the doctor comes in.

"Good afternoon, Mrs. Lewis."

"Dr. Christiansen, hello." I hear the stiffness in my mother's voice. She doesn't like doctors.

"Hello, Ed." The doctor comes over to the bed. "How are we feeling today?"

I look at him.

He turns back to my mother. "I'm sorry we didn't get a chance to chat last week, but I was away at a conference."

"What I want to know, Dr. Christiansen, is why he's still not able to speak. You said that once he was here, it would take no time at all."

"Yes, that still is a bit of a mystery. As I told you when we first spoke, the damage to his T-one and T-two vertebrae should not permanently affect his vocal cords. Of course, the initial trauma coupled with the fact that he really made no improvements at the last hospital may mean that they're weak. Just like his fingers, if he wants to regain strength, he will have to work at it."

"Are you saying the physical therapy isn't going well?"

"To be honest, he's not as responsive as we'd like."

My mother comes over to me. "Dearest, you really must make an effort."

She's right, of course. But it seems pointless; there just hasn't been anyone I want to talk to.

✵

After Daisy ran out of her bedroom, I didn't see her until around supper time. I looked for her, I even went to the tennis courts, but she wasn't there.

Aunt Nick and Tyler returned first. Their hair was messy and their faces flushed from the sun.

"What a wind," Aunt Nick said. "It was really blowing out there."

Tyler was carrying her boat bag and he touched her bare shoulder lightly as he passed her on his way down to the basement. I saw her flinch. I suspected she didn't like him doing that in front of me.

"Hello, Ed," Tyler said.

Aunt Nick gave me a kiss and smoothed her hair down, but her eyes wouldn't meet mine. "I hope it wasn't too rough on the ferry," she said.

"No," I said. "It wasn't."

"Where's your mother?"

"In her room."

"And Uncle Hughes isn't back yet?"

"No," I said.

"All right. I'm going to shower and change. And then we'll have cocktails and you can tell me what you've been up to." She started up the stairs.

"Daisy's not here either," I said.

"What? Oh." She stopped and turned. She looked confused.

"She's upset," I said.

Aunt Nick's hand was gripping the banister and I could see her knuckles whiten slightly. "Did she say that?"

"No," I said. "I could just tell."

"Well, she is getting married in two months. Jitters, I suppose." Her voice was light, but her fingers never loosed as she climbed the stairs.

Uncle Hughes returned from the Reading Room a short time later and we were all gathered in the blue sitting room when Daisy came in.

"Hello," she said.

"Hey there, sweetpea," Uncle Hughes said. "Where have you been?"

"Just out walking," Daisy said.

"What'll it be?"

"Nothing, thanks, Daddy. I'm thirsty. I think I'll get a glass of water."

"There's some lemon water on the bar," my mother said. She wasn't drinking and she'd been eyeing me nervously for the past fifteen minutes.

"Thanks." Daisy walked over and picked up a tumbler.

I watched Aunt Nick watch her, her fingers curled around the stem of her martini glass.

"We saw the good reverend out sailing this afternoon," Tyler said, smiling. "Loaves and fishes and all that."

"Did you?" Daisy seemed distracted. "That's nice."

Tyler got up and walked over to Daisy. "Are you all right?" He started to put his arm around her but she shrugged it off.

"I'm fine. I just got hot and tired out walking."

"I went by the tennis courts," I said.

Daisy looked at me for the first time since she'd come in the room. But she didn't say anything.

Uncle Hughes also gave me a hard stare. "What were you doing by the tennis courts?"

"Looking for Daisy," I said.

"Daisy hasn't been playing tennis," my mother said. "Why is that, dearest?"

"She's been busy, planning her wedding, for Christ's sakes," Aunt Nick said.

"Will you all please stop talking about me like I'm not here?" Daisy set her glass down hard on the marble top of the bar.

"Daisy's right," Uncle Hughes said. "This is supposed to be cocktail hour, not the Spanish Inquisition."

No one said anything for a while. Then Uncle Hughes turned to Aunt Nick and said: "So what's for dinner?"

Nervous laughter rippled around the room.

Aunt Nick got up and put her hand in Uncle Hughes's. "I got some nice flounder from my little fish man."

Uncle Hughes looked at her and put his other hand on the crown of her head, like a cap. "That sounds perfect."

Tyler was staring at the two of them, his eyes like metal. Daisy saw his expression and I watched the muscles move in her face. Then she turned away.

"I'm going to change," she said.

"All right, darling," Aunt Nick said, but Daisy was already walking out of the room.

Aunt Nick was right; the flounder was delicious. I liked how she left the skin on, so that I could use my fork to peel it back and uncover the white flesh. I even ate part of the skin; it was crispy and salty, and had captured all the flavor of the seasoning.

Aunt Nick talked about the Fourth of July and how she thought a family picnic would be nice. Then Uncle Hughes told a story about hearing German planes bombing London on New Year's Eve and how he thought they were fireworks. My mother was unusually quiet, and Tyler seemed absorbed by the food.

After dinner, Daisy excused herself abruptly, the legs of her chair making a scraping noise against the wood floor.

"I'm going to see if she's all right," Aunt Nick said, after a moment.

Tyler made a move to stand, as well, but she turned on him. "You stay here," she said, her voice low and harsh.

My mother got up and began clearing the table.

"Let me help you," Uncle Hughes said, and patted my mother on the back.

Tyler and I sat facing each other. I looked at him and he looked at me. I could see it in his face, he knew I knew. My hands itched. I got up quickly from the table, before I did anything rash, and followed in the direction that Aunt Nick and Daisy had gone.

Out on the front porch, I could see Aunt Nick crossing the road and Daisy's smaller figure beyond, making her way down the front lawn in the darkness. I kept my distance, staying close to the fence on the far side. They were headed toward the boathouse. I went around the other side, past the outdoor shower.

The air on that side of the boathouse was humid from the run-off and I could hear the tap dripping and feel the slushy grass beneath my shoes. My soles made a sucking noise, which wasn't ideal. At the front of the boathouse I stopped and listened. I could see a light coming from around the corner and realized that Daisy must have lit one of the kerosene lanterns.

She was sitting on the small steps and Nick was sitting next to her, neither one saying anything.

I pulled my head back and leaned against the side, feeling the shingles digging into my shoulder blades.

After a while, I heard Aunt Nick's voice.

"Darling, what's the matter?"

Daisy didn't respond.

"Whatever it is, I think you should tell me. Is it about the wedding?"

"Do you remember," Daisy said, finally, "when you told

me that if there was one thing I could count on, it was that I wouldn't always be kissing the right person?"

"Yes, I remember."

"We were sitting in there. And you were stroking my head."

"Yes."

"But you were talking about yourself, weren't you? It wasn't about me at all."

"Daisy."

"No, no. Don't say anything, Mummy. I can see it, now. It's always been about you, hasn't it? Everything. I'm not even real to you. None of us are."

"You're real to me, Daisy. I know I haven't been the best mother. I'm probably not even a very good person. But you're real to me and I love you. What is this about?"

"God, Mummy. How can you even say that with a straight face?"

"What do you mean? Just say it, Daisy." Nick's voice was mineral.

"What do I mean? I mean everything. You don't care about anyone but yourself. You never have." Daisy's words were coming out in little pants, like a winded animal. "All my life, you've never been on my side. You've been jealous and hard and cold . . . any little bit of love from Daddy . . . And since you can't get that from him, you've . . ."

"I've what? I've what, Daisy?"

Daisy didn't respond.

After a while, Aunt Nick spoke, her voice softer this time. "I can't explain everything to you, darling. I can't tell you a whole lifetime of mistakes and missed chances and everything I've . . . I just never wanted to be ordinary. Maybe that's made me different, harder. But a family, well, it's complicated. I don't know what's brought this on, but I know I've hurt you, in so many ways. I know that. And I'm sorry."

Daisy was quiet, like she was thinking. "You really don't know what it is?" she said finally. "Are you being honest?"

"Yes," Aunt Nick said. "I don't know what I've done. Please just say it."

"I don't know," Daisy said, slowly. "I don't know what I thought."

"Darling," Aunt Nick started.

I inched closer again and looked around at them.

Aunt Nick's hand was on the steps between the two of them, as if she wanted to touch Daisy, but wasn't sure. Daisy had her head down and was looking at her feet.

"I don't know if I'm going crazy, or if you . . . Maybe it's the wedding and nerves, I don't know," Daisy said. "If it is, then I'm sorry. I'm sorry I said all those things." She stood up and started to walk away and then stopped. "But just in case, in case it's not me and he's right . . ." She trailed off again and looked out over the harbor. "I want it to stop, Mother. You have to stop."

Aunt Nick looked at her, shaking her head, a gesture somewhere between confusion and assent.

But I knew she wouldn't stop, even if she wanted to. She didn't know how.

Something in my chest felt heavy as I walked back to Tiger House. As I opened the latch on the front gate, I saw my mother standing on the porch. When I approached her, she grabbed my hand. It startled me; she rarely touched me.

"Ed," she said. "I've been waiting for you, I wanted to tell you something, about earlier, about Daisy and your Aunt Nick."

I looked at her. She seemed frightened.

"I heard what you told Daisy, about Tyler. I don't know if I've ever given you the wrong impression. I don't want you to put yourself in a situation . . ." She stopped.

I took my hand out of her grasp and patted her shoulder, the way Uncle Hughes had done earlier. "It's all right, Mother," I said. "Don't worry. It's going to be fine."

But it didn't feel fine. The house felt suffocating and I decided to take a walk to clear my head. I went along our stretch of beach for a while, thinking. I knew what had to be done, but for the first time in my life, I felt unprepared. Hesitant, I suppose, and I knew this was a dangerous thing. Like going to Frank Wilcox's house without casing it first.

I listened to the foghorns. They sounded plaintive. I thought about Daisy, saw her standing there with her hand over her heart, surprised to see me. I thought about how she always called me Ed Lewis, the way she stamped her foot when she was angry. How when we were growing up, she was the only one who really spoke to me, the only one who really noticed me.

I didn't know how long I'd been out, but when I reached the house I could see Aunt Nick and Uncle Hughes in the sitting room, drinking. They were very close to each other on the sofa, luminous from where I stood on the dark road. Their lamp was the only light left on, which meant everyone else must have already gone to bed.

I hopped the gate and quietly went up the front steps. I was going to go in and take the temperature, but their conversation stopped me.

"What did she say to you?" Uncle Hughes was asking.

"She . . ." Aunt Nick stopped. "She thinks I've done something."

"What?"

"Hughes. There's something I have to tell you."

"For Christ's sakes, what is it?"

"I've been going crazy with it. I don't want to hurt Daisy, or you, or anyone. I haven't been honest . . ."

Uncle Hughes looked at her, and then down at his hands. He was quiet for a while and then he said: "Nick, you don't have to explain anything to me."

"You don't know what it is," she said, her eyes searching his downcast face.

"Maybe I do; maybe I don't. But it doesn't matter. I know you. I know what you're capable of and what you're not capable of. And you're not capable of cruelty."

"Darling . . ."

"Nick, I love you," he said simply. "And I don't think there's a goddamn thing you could do or say now that would change that." He looked up at her. "So, you don't have to explain anything to me. I already know what I need to."

"Oh, Hughes." Aunt Nick put her hand to his face. "You have no idea. I've made such a mess of all of us."

"We've all made a mess of all of us," Uncle Hughes said. "But you're going to have to trust me at some point."

"Yes," she said. She shook her head. "I always thought our life was . . ." She stopped. "God, I was so wrong. I don't know if this will make any sense, but something has been happening . . . there's been someone, someone I can see myself in. And they've shown me just what a coward, what a goddamn little fool I've been all this time." She laughed softly, as if responding to some private, bitter joke. "I guess marriage," she said, "it's like cliff-jumping. You can't lose your nerve."

I didn't like this conversation. Something in Aunt Nick's manner, in her voice, was confusing me, like I was missing something important, and it bothered me. I had to stop thinking. I just needed to get all of this over with and be done with it. I took a breath, and went into the house, letting the door bang loudly behind me.

When I went into the sitting room, I saw a freshly made jug of vodka martinis on the bar. That was good. It would make things easier if she were drunk.

"Just out for a walk," I said. "I wanted to say goodnight."

"Goodnight, Ed," Uncle Hughes said. He was obviously wondering if I'd been spying on them.

"Goodnight," Aunt Nick said. She looked wound-up.

I walked over to her and leaned in to kiss her cheek. It was smooth and cool and I could smell her perfume and the vodka on her breath. "Goodnight, Aunt Nick," I said. Then I took myself up to my bedroom to wait.

I lay staring at the ceiling. An hour passed, maybe less, before I heard Uncle Hughes coming up. Enough time for the two of them to have finished off the pitcher of martinis. I hoped that Aunt Nick would go for a swim, that would be easiest. I knew that it might not come off tonight, that I might have to wait for the moment to be right. But when I didn't hear Aunt Nick's footsteps on the stairs, I got up and began to prepare myself.

I took my shoes out of the plastic bag helpfully provided by the shoe-shine man. I stretched it a little with my fingers to make sure it would be large enough. The details were important. This had to be carefully done. It had to look like an accident.

I went down to the second-floor landing and looked out the window. I couldn't see her, so I kept going. I looked in the sitting room, but it was dark and empty. Then I saw her out on the porch, finishing her drink. She placed her empty glass carefully on the railing and then covered her face with her hands and I could hear her start to cry. I had heard about people crying bitterly. Now I knew what it meant. It sounded like crunching gravel being pushed out of a pipe.

After a while, she wiped her eyes and straightened her back, pin-straight. I admired her in a way, just at that moment. But I thought about Daisy and the feeling passed. She picked up her glass and started toward the door. I stepped back into the shadow of the sitting room.

She passed me on the way to the kitchen and I moved quietly back up the stairs, taking them two at a time, to the second floor. The bedroom doors were all shut, like sleeping eyes. I moved to the corner of the landing, where I could stand next to the grandfather clock, unseen. I pulled out the plastic bag and waited.

I would put the bag over her head from behind as she rounded the corner toward her bedroom. When she stopped breathing I would slide her down the stairs. It would make noise, but not a lot, and I would have enough time to get at least to the middle of the next flight of stairs before Uncle Hughes or my mother came out of their bedrooms. It would look like I'd run down to see what was happening. Aunt Nick, too many vodka martinis in her, would have tripped and fallen.

It seemed like hours before she finally started up, a little unsteady on her feet. I could hear my own breathing and tried to make my mind go quiet, like I'd done so many times before. As she passed me in the hall, I came up behind her. But she turned. To this day, I don't know why she did. She couldn't have heard me. Still, there we were. Me: lifting the bag in both hands; her: brows furrowed, trying to make sense of it.

I was so close to her now.

"What are you doing, Ed?" For some reason, she whispered this, like we were sharing a secret.

I thought: *Now, now. She hasn't made any noise.* But instead, I said: "You. And Tyler."

Her eyes widened a little then, because she understood. She backed away from me. I started toward her. The situation wasn't going at all as planned; in fact, it was totally wrong. It was too risky. But I had no choice now but to go ahead with it.

I grabbed her, hooking my arm around her neck and twisting her against my body. She fought, harder than I expected, but then again, I hadn't counted on a direct confrontation.

Once I had her back to me, I put my hand over her mouth. She was scratching at my arm. With my other hand, I shook out the plastic bag. I could feel the blood pumping through my ears. I could hear her heels scraping on the floor as I dragged her toward the staircase. I felt panic. I had to do it quickly. I pushed her neck down with my elbow so that I would be able to get the bag over her head. She was making wet sucking noises beneath my hand.

Somehow, I managed to get the bag over her head and I tightened the opening around her neck. I could hear her inhaling the plastic. I was almost there.

Then, all at once, there was something around my own neck. A hand. Crushing my windpipe. I had no choice but to let go of her. And I knew it was over. I had failed.

I felt Aunt Nick fall from my grasp and could hear her coughing somewhere near my feet. The rustle of the bag.

"Nick." I could hear Uncle Hughes behind me.

I couldn't see her because my head was tilted back from the pressure, but after a moment I heard her say: "It's all right." It was more of a croak, actually.

Uncle Hughes pulled me around to face him. There was no point in fighting him or asking for mercy. I could see it in

382

his face. I thought about Daisy, about showing her where
the maid was killed and the arrowhead and the way Elena
Nunes tried to tell us her secrets before she died. It was my
turn, now.

"It's Tyler," I said.

Uncle Hughes looked at me, dead in the eye. And then
he pushed me down the stairs.

My mother has been reading to me. She does this every
week, reads me the current events from the newspaper, as
if I've gone blind, as well as being paralyzed and mute.

She reads to me for about an hour and then it's time for
her to go. Today, I hear about the antiwar demonstrations
in Chicago. They had to call in the National Guard and it
will apparently cost the city $150,000. The newspapers are
referring to it as the "Days of Rage." This bores me. In fact,
I don't think I've heard anything interesting for a year. Not
since that night.

Then my mother says, "Oh, I almost forgot to tell you,
we've had some drama at the house," and I think maybe my
luck is beginning to change.

She puts down her pile of newspaper clippings.

"Well, Daisy was down for the weekend. Did I tell you
that? I think I told you last week she was coming. Anyway,
guess who shows up? Tyler. He drove all the way from the
city, apparently. And, as you know, we haven't seen hide nor
hair of him since they broke it off."

My mother pulls her chair in a little closer. She doesn't
want the nurses to hear about our dirty linen.

"I have no idea how on earth he knew she was there, but
there he was, larger than life, sitting out in front of the
house in that ridiculous car of his. So, of course, I tell Daisy,

and dearest, you'll never believe what she does. She goes down to the basement and comes up with a bag full of tennis balls and her racket. I was just breathless with anticipation."

She's practically breathless now.

"So she goes out to the porch and calls his name. And when he looks like he's about to get out of his car, she reaches into the bag and takes out a ball, and then, oh, so carefully, she drops it and whacks it with all her might at his car. And Lord, she does have good aim, I'll say that for her."

I can see tears of laughter welling up in my mother's eyes.

"Well, then, of course, he starts yelling. But Daisy, she just keeps going, hitting one ball after the other until he finally has no choice but to drive away or have his windshield knocked out. Oh, Ed, I was nearly crying, I was laughing so hard.

"Then she comes into the house and sees me. And I felt a little sorry, because I didn't want her to think I found her heartbreak funny. I've told you how unhappy she was for a long time after he left her, poor little thing. But she just looks at me and says: 'Well, Aunt Helena. I think that fixed his bacon.' And then she laughs and says, 'Hell's bells,' in that old way of hers. I must say, dearest, I've never loved that girl more."

As my mother is telling me this, I can feel the muscles in my cheeks pulling and I realize I'm smiling. My mother is wiping her eyes, and she sees me. "Oh. A smile. Well, that's one for the books." Then she gathers up her things and kisses my cheek and then I think perhaps I don't mind hearing the news so much, after all.

✼

As I lay there at the bottom of the stairs in the darkness, I could hear them. I must have passed out, but at some point afterward, I was aware of what was going on around me.

"Oh, Hughes," Aunt Nick was saying, her voice rasping. I imagined that her throat had probably taken quite a beating from where I'd held her. "Oh, god."

I could hear her crying. I felt very cold.

"We have to call an ambulance," she said.

I could see her then. She was sitting next to me and I think she was touching me, but I couldn't feel her hand. "Ed? Ed, can you move? Hughes, get a blanket."

"I think . . ." But he didn't say anything else, so he must have gone.

Then, out of the shadow, I saw him lifting something over me and I had the strange thought that I was being buried.

"I don't think he can hear me," Aunt Nick said. "Did you call?"

"I called."

Then I could hear footsteps on the stairs.

Nick whispered: "Jesus, what are we going to tell Helena?"

"Listen to me." Uncle Hughes spoke very slowly. "He was sleepwalking and he fell down the stairs. We were both in bed and heard something and came out to check. Do you understand?"

"Yes," she said.

I didn't hear anything for a while but I saw small movements out of the corner of my eye. I blinked.

Finally, I heard Aunt Nick say: "Hughes. Listen to me, I tried to tell you." Her voice had some kind of urgency to it.

"I know . . ."

"No, you have to understand. Nothing happened. With

Tyler. It's not like . . . he just wouldn't stop. I think he thought that because . . ."

"Nick, I know."

I tried to move, but found I couldn't. There was some pain, but only in my skull. My skull felt like it might cave in. Aunt Nick leaned over me. She used her hand to cradle my head.

"Where's the goddamn ambulance?" she said.

"It's on its way."

Silence. Then: "Hughes?"

"Yes?"

"It's the strangest thing, but I have this feeling . . ." I had to strain to hear her now. "Like everything . . ." She stopped.

"Yes," Uncle Hughes said. "Everything is."

And with that, stars burst in my eyes and the whole world went dark.

"Well, it's a red-letter day for you," the nurse says. "You have another visitor."

"Hello, Ed."

It's Daisy. I can't see her, but I can hear her. I concentrate on my neck, but it doesn't move. I almost can't believe she's here. She's only come once before to see me, right at the beginning. I wondered if maybe she knew about the staircase and all the rest of it, and had decided she couldn't forgive me, as Aunt Nick had predicted.

But she's standing there over me with a smile on her face, so I guess she doesn't hate me, after all. She looks pale, but it's October and her tan will have faded by now. I look at her and try to make my eyes communicate what my mouth can't.

"My goodness," she says. "What are those wriggly eyes for?" She bends down and, placing her hand on the side of my face, kisses me on the mouth. It's light, like a butterfly wing.

"I'm sorry I haven't been to see you. I've been very sad. But I'm feeling better, now." Her blond hair is shorter, like a halo. She looks around. "It's so stuffy in here. Why don't they open a window?"

She sits down on the chair by my bed.

"So, Ed Lewis, they tell me you're not speaking to us anymore. What's the matter, cat got your tongue?"

I smile.

"Not good enough," Daisy says. "I'm not that easy anymore."

She opens a canvas bag she's brought with her, and I'm reminded of the story about tennis. "Since I'm sure you've already heard my whole sordid history from your mother, and since you don't plan on talking, I brought some poems along. I thought I might read to you, if you'd like. Unless you're bored with that?"

I just look at her.

"No? Good." As she pulls out the book, the nurse comes back in.

"I'm sorry, Miss Derringer, but we normally wash Ed's hair on Thursdays. After his mother leaves."

"Oh," Daisy says. "Well, sure. Maybe I can help."

"I'm sure he'd love that. Wouldn't you?"

"Oh, I'm sure he would." She winks at me.

There's a whole production while they get me out of bed and into a wheelchair. I'm a little annoyed because it's time I could be spending with Daisy. Then the nurse wheels me into the bathroom and Daisy follows behind. The nurse attaches a tray around my shoulders and neck, so the water can run off.

"So, I'm just going to get his hair damp and then we can shampoo him," the nurse says.

I don't know why I've never noticed the nurse's wrists before; they're so translucent they're almost blue. I realize I don't even know her name. I remind myself to pay more attention to her.

I feel the warm water running over my scalp. I look at Daisy. She smiles. She puts her hand out and the nurse squirts some of the pink soap into her palm. Then Daisy begins massaging my scalp. I can feel her hands, warm, against my head, the tips of her fingers making my skin tingle all the way to my shoulders. Some of the soapsuds slide down my forehead and into my eye. It stings and my right index finger twitches. The doctor is right. I need to make more of an effort.

"I'm sorry," Daisy says, laughing. "I'm not very good at this, am I? Maybe I'll let you do it and I'll read to him."

She leaves us in the bathroom and returns with the book. "Wallace Stevens," she says and shows me the cover. "All right, let's see." She flips through the book, smiling slightly at something on the page. "Oh, I love this one," she says. She leans against the wall and begins speaking: "The houses are haunted / By white night-gowns."

I listen to the sound of her voice and think it's the best thing I've ever heard. So clear and true and steady. I want to say the words with her. I try to force air up through my throat. Nothing happens.

"None are green / Or purple with green rings / Or green with yellow rings," she says. "None of them are strange."

I try again and this time I manage to make a small gurgle,

although no one can hear it because of the water running in the sink. But I can hear it.

"People are not going / To dream of baboons and periwinkles," Daisy says.

I look at her. I can hear her.

"Only, here and there, an old sailor, / Drunk and asleep in his boots, / Catches tigers / In red weather."

She looks at me. Her eyes are a little shiny, although it may be the steam from the water. I think about love and about all the nightgowns that are not white. I think about Aunt Nick, and Frank Wilcox, and even about Uncle Hughes. I think about Daisy and her book of poems. I think about tigers in red weather. I like that.

Acknowledgments

There are a number of people, some unwittingly, who have conspired with me on this novel. I am indebted to Wallace Stevens, whose poetry moved me to write this particular book, and to my grandfather, whose lovely memoir served as a starting point.

My editors: Kate Harvey at Picador, who has my eternal gratitude and troth of friendship for her immensely sensitive and ingenious editing; and the brilliant Judy Clain at Little, Brown, whose vision and commitment continues to blow me away. I owe them a lifetime of perfectly chilled martinis.

My publishers, Michael Pietsch at Little, Brown, and Paul Baggaley at Picador, and the whole band of talented people at both imprints, are to be thanked profusely.

Caroline Wood, my agent at Felicity Bryan, is – in a word – incredible. She has also taught me that, sometimes, there can be too many dinner parties.

I owe a huge debt of gratitude to Andrew Motion, who tutored me in the way of avocado pears, among countless other things.

In terms of longevity and loyalty, my biggest thanks go to the following writers:

Emma Chapman; Tom Feltham; Liz Gifford; Carolina Gonzalez-Carvajal; Kat Gordon; and Rebecca Lloyd James.

Finally, I owe a debt I cannot repay to my crazy, amazing family, who, frankly, have put up with a lot; my mother and father, Betsy Chapin and Eric Klaussmann; my brother, Eric Klaussmann; and my other dad, John Grummon.

Tigers in Red Weather:

questions and topics for discussion

1. Which of the five sections did you most enjoy?

2. Do you think the novel has a main character?

3. Is the murder important to the plot?

4. What do you think is at the heart of Nick and Helena's relationship?

5. Is Nick a heroine or a villain?

6. Why do you think Helena stays with Avery, despite her unhappiness?

7. Do you think that Nick is a good parent to Daisy?

8. What brings about Hughes's new-found feelings for Nick? Did you feel theirs was a moving portrait of a marriage?

9. With Ed's section, we shift into the first person. Did this change your experience of the book? Do you think Ed is rehabilitated at the end?

10. Did *Tigers in Red Weather* make you think of any favourite books or films?

Liza Klaussmann on how to make
a perfect vodka martini

The perfect vodka martini is an intensely personal thing. The best one that I've ever had was at the Hemingway Bar at the Ritz in Paris; they call it the Platinum Bullet, a purist's dream, a drink so dry it would make your toes curl. However, due to the extremely low temperature they keep the vodka at, recreating it at home is not very practical. Furthermore, an at-home martini is a more relaxed thing, and I like mine slightly "dirty." Proceed as follows:

> 3 oz of vodka (preferably Stolichnaya or
>   Grey Goose, chilled)
> 1 oz vermouth
> 1 tsp of olive brine
> 2–3 olives to garnish
> 1 trusty shaker
> Lots of ice
> 1 chilled martini glass

Fill the shaker with ice and pour in the vermouth. Shake consistently so that the ice breaks up a bit. Pour the vermouth into your martini glass, swirl it around so that it just coats the inside, then discard it. Next, refill the shaker with fresh ice, pour in the vodka and brine and shake for as long as your arm can stand it. Fill the glass. Garnish with olives and sip elegantly.